PENGUIN

THE PENGUIN BOOK OF SPANISH

MARGARET JULL COSTA has translated the works of many Spanish and Portuguese writers, among them novelists: Javier Marías, José Saramago and Eça de Queiroz, and poets: Sophia de Mello Breyner Andresen, Mário de Sá-Carneiro and Ana Luísa Amaral. Her work has brought her numerous prizes, most recently the 2018 Premio Valle-Inclán for *On the Edge* by Rafael Chirbes. In 2014 she was awarded an OBE for services to literature.

The Penguin Book of Spanish Short Stories

Introduced and edited by
MARGARET JULL COSTA

PENGUIN BOOKS

PENGUIN CLASSICS

UK | USA | Canada | Ireland | Australia
India | New Zealand | South Africa

Penguin Books is part of the Penguin Random House group of companies
whose addresses can be found at global.penguinrandomhouse.com

First published 2021
004

Introduction copyright © Margaret Jull Costa, 2021
Translation copyright © Margaret Jull Costa, Thomas Bunstead,
Peter Bush, Kit Maude, Kathryn Phillips-Miles, Simon Deefholts, 2021

The moral rights of the authors and translators have been asserted

Printed and bound in Great Britain by Clays Ltd, Elcograf S.p.A.

The authorized representative in the EEA is Penguin Random House Ireland,
Morrison Chambers, 32 Nassau Street, Dublin D02 YH68

A CIP catalogue record for this book is available from the British Library

ISBN: 978–0–241–39050–4

Contents

Introduction

An anthology, etymologically speaking, is a gathering or collection of flowers, and in this anthology my aim has been to gather together a collection of really fine flowers, stories dating from the nineteenth century to the present day, including writers across all of Spain's four languages – Basque (*euskara*), Castilian Spanish (*castellano*), Catalan (*català*) and Galician (*galego*). Choosing what to include was both a delight and a torment, a delight because it involved reading so many wonderful stories, most of which were entirely new to me, and a torment because choosing meant having to pick only some and not others. There are, inevitably, omissions (Juan Goytisolo, Dulce Chacón, Camilo José Cela, Antonio Muñoz Molina, Laura Freixas, to name but a few), but I also wanted, where possible, to choose and translate stories that hadn't previously been translated into English or which, in my entirely biased opinion, would benefit from a fresh translation. A confession: while I can read Spanish and Galician (which is very like Portuguese), I do not read Basque or Catalan. In the case of Basque, I have based my translations on the Castilian versions made by the authors themselves. In the case of Catalan, I turned to my colleague Peter Bush for his translations of Josep Pla, Quim Monzó and Teresa Solana. However, I could not resist doing my own translations of the stories by Catalan writers Carme Riera and Mercè Rodoreda, basing my translation of the former on the author's self-translation and of the latter on the excellent translation by Clara Janés. I learned later that in Riera's Spanish version of her own story she made radical changes, including cutting the first two pages of the original. She even changed the title: in the Catalan version it is *Retorn a casa* (Homecoming), in the Castilian version it is simply *Volver* (Return). A translation in more than one sense!

For me, the short story is not a truncated novel, but is more akin, perhaps, to poetry. The best stories create a world in just a few pages, just as the best poetry (in my view) encapsulates a moment in a few words or lines. It is never wise to read poem after poem, and it seems to me a mistake to read any collection of stories one after the other. Think of this rather as a box of chocolates; savour and ponder each story one or, at most, two at a time.

People have, it seems, always told stories, and, in Spain, the custom of the *cuento* can perhaps be traced back to the Arab tradition of story-telling, given that the Moors were a potent presence in Spain for more than seven hundred years. Those spoken stories from India, Persia and Arabia were, of course, later set down in such books as *The Arabian Nights*, but in Spain the story in its written form is usually deemed to have begun with the anonymous picaresque 'novel' *Lazarillo de Tormes* (1554), which wove together a series of stories all featuring a young lad and his many masters. This form was developed further by Cervantes in his *Exemplary Novels* (1613), which comprises twelve unconnected and very diverse stories. Cervantes was using the word 'novel' to distinguish his written fiction from the oral story, or *cuento*; over time, *novela* came to mean 'novel' and *cuento*, 'short story'. As in the rest of Europe, the written *cuento* really came into its own with the growth of literacy, the advent of the steam printing press, and the subsequent popularity of newspapers and magazines. In the early 1800s, Mariano José de Larra wrote what were called *cuadros de costumbres*, descriptions of contemporary life, often with a sharp, satirical edge. The short story as we know it really took off in Spain in the late nineteenth century, with novelists like Galdós, Pardo Bazán and Leopoldo Alas, and, as elsewhere in the world, it has to this day remained an essential genre for most writers.

In choosing the stories, I didn't think in thematic terms at all, but themes have emerged of their own accord. Perhaps inevitably, many of the stories deal directly or obliquely with the Spanish Civil War, which lasted from 1936 to 1939, and had a devastating effect on society both during and long afterwards. The stories included here cover both the brutality and the absurdity of war (Sender and Calders), the terrible divisions caused by any civil war (Rivas), the lingering grief and loss (Merino and Rodríguez), and the grim aftermath of poverty, repression and even mental illness (Delibes, Marsé and Laforet).

Realism and social comment are, of course, bound up in that first theme, but other stories reveal other lives from the various social classes:

the impoverished working class (Ignacio Aldecoa and Pombo), the wealthy middle class (Tusquets, Ayesta and Monzó), and the sunken middle class who don't quite fit in anywhere (Alas and Pla). Women also feature strongly (both as authors and characters), from put-upon, frightened or bored-rigid wives (Rodoreda, Matute and Baroja), to the woes or otherwise of the independent woman (Josefina Aldecoa and Millás), to the hormonal confusion of an adolescent girl (Puértolas).

As I read and re-read the collection, I was also very struck by how much fantasy there was in these stories. This may, of course, have to do with my own tastes, but while the fantastic and the ghostly have long been a strong thread in British and American fiction (thanks, perhaps, to Poe), I have always tended to think of Spanish literature as staunchly realist. Yet here, from the nineteenth century (Galdós and Pardo Bazán) up to the present day (Aixa de la Cruz), we have that same fascination with the inexplicable, and with the wilder side of our imaginations (Chacel, Rodoreda, Benet, Vila-Matas and Cubas).

There is also, thank heavens, a great deal of humour, sometimes black (Marías and Solana), sometimes absurd (Galdós and Cunqueiro), sometimes just very acutely observed (Molina Foix, Fraile and Cercas), and sometimes just joyfully playful (Azorín).

I have also included three pieces (Carrasco, Díaz-Mas and Cercas) which are, strictly speaking, memoir, but I was encouraged by biographer Claire Tomalin's comment that while the (auto)biographer cannot invent, he or she does still need imagination. And given our human tendency to lie or misremember or elaborate on the facts, any memoir is always tinged with fiction.

The stories are arranged chronologically according to the author's date of birth, but, as with any anthology, there is a delightful randomness about subject matter and style and tone, shifting from an absurd tram journey with a man who cannot tell fact from fiction to the jittery owner of what might be a magical talisman to two lonely hotel guests finding solace of sorts to a simpleton finding friendship for the first time, and those are just the first four stories. Feel free to read the stories in any order that takes your fancy, but, remember, only one or two at a time.

Margaret Jull Costa

BENITO PÉREZ GALDÓS

The Novel on the Tram

I

The tram was setting off from one end of the Salamanca neighbourhood and heading across Madrid in the direction of Pozas. Gripped by the selfish desire to get a seat before all the other passengers – who, naturally, had precisely the same intention – I grabbed the handrail of the stairs leading to the upper deck, placed one foot on the platform and climbed aboard, but at that very instant – I should have seen it coming! – I collided with another traveller entering from the other side. When I looked at him, I saw that he was my friend, Señor Dionisio Cascajares de la Vallina, a sensible, inoffensive fellow, who, on the occasion in question, was kind enough to greet me with an enthusiastic, heartfelt handshake.

Our unexpected collision had no major consequences, if you discount a slight dent inflicted on the straw hat perched on the head of an Englishwoman who was attempting to board the tram behind my friend and who, doubtless due to a lack of agility on her part, received a blow to her bonnet from his walking stick.

We sat down and, dismissing the incident as unimportant, started chatting.

Benito Pérez Galdós (1843–1920) is considered to be Spain's greatest nineteenth-century novelist, on a par with Dickens and Balzac. Born in the Canary Islands, he moved to Madrid when he was nineteen and spent most of his adult life there. He wrote novels, plays and stories, his masterpiece being *Fortunata y Jacinta*. Although his work is usually described as Realist, there is often an element of the fantastic in his writing (as in this story), and this was perhaps what attracted the film-maker Luis Buñuel, who based three of his films on Galdós novels: *Viridiana*, *Nazarín* and *Tristana*.

Señor Dionisio Cascajares de la Vallina is a celebrated doctor – although his fame does not rest on his deep knowledge of pathology – and a thoroughly decent man, of whom no one has ever said that he was likely to steal other people's property or kill a fellow human being other than in the pursuit of his dangerous and scientific profession. It is true that the trust he inspires in a multitude of families from all strata of society has much to do with his pleasant manner and his indulgent way of giving his patients only the treatment they want, but it is also a well-known fact that, in his bounty, he provides other services too, always of a rigorously honest nature, but which have nothing to do with science.

He knows more interesting things about people's private lives than anyone else, and is an obsessive asker of questions, although he makes up for the vice of over-inquisitiveness by his equal readiness to tell you everything he knows about other people without your even having to ask. You can imagine, then, how eagerly the curious and the loose-tongued seek out the company of this fine example of human indiscretion.

This gentleman and friend – well, he's a friend to everyone – was the person sitting next to me as the tram slid smoothly over the rails down Calle de Serrano, stopping now and then to fill up the few remaining empty seats. Indeed, we were soon so crammed together that I was hard put to know what to do with the parcel of books I had with me, and which I placed first on one knee and then on the other. In the end, fearing that I might be bothering the English lady sitting to my left, I decided to perch on top of it.

II

'And where are you off to?' Cascajares asked, peering at me over his blue spectacles, which made me feel as if I were being scrutinized by two pairs of eyes.

I gave a somewhat evasive response, and he, doubtless not wishing to miss the opportunity of gleaning some useful snippet of information, asked further questions, along the lines of 'And what's So-and-so up to these days? And where's So-and-so living?' and other similar enquiries, none of which received very fulsome replies.

Finding each attempt at conversation blocked, he finally set off along the path best suited to his expansive temperament and began to blab.

'Poor Countess!' he said, shaking his head and adopting an expression of selfless compassion. 'If she had followed my advice, she wouldn't be in the appalling situation in which she finds herself now.'

'No, of course,' I replied mechanically, thus paying the Countess my own brief tribute of compassion.

'You see,' he went on, 'she has allowed herself to become completely dominated by that man, and he'll be master of the house one day. The poor thing thinks she can solve everything by weeping and wailing, but it's not true. She should act now, because the man's an out-and-out bounder and, I believe, capable of the most heinous of crimes.'

'Oh, yes, awful,' I said, unthinkingly sharing in his imaginings.

'It's the same with all men of evil instincts and low social status when they rise a little in the world. They become utterly insufferable. One look at his face will tell you that no good will come of him.'

'Absolutely. It stands out a mile.'

'Let me explain the situation to you briefly. The Countess is an excellent woman, angelic, as discreet as she is beautiful, and she really does deserve better luck. However, she is married to a man who does not appreciate what a treasure he has and who devotes his life to gambling and all manner of other illicit pastimes. She, meanwhile, grows bored and weeps. Is it any surprise, then, that she should try to mask her sorrow by seeking honest entertainment elsewhere, wherever there's a piano? Indeed, I myself have told her as much. "Countess," I said, "life is too short, you need some diversion. In the end, the Count will repent of his folly, and your sorrows will be at an end." And I think I'm right.'

'Oh, I'm sure you are!' I said officiously, although I was as indifferent to the Countess's misfortunes then as I had been at the beginning.

'That's not the worst of it, though,' added Cascajares, striking the floor with his walking stick. 'Now the Count has got it into his head to be jealous, yes, of a certain young man who has undertaken to "amuse" the Countess.'

'It will be the envious husband's fault if he succeeds.'

'Now given that the Countess is virtue personified, none of this would

3

matter, no, none of this would matter if there were not a dastardly fellow involved, who, I suspect, will bring disaster down upon the household.'

'Really? And who is this fellow?' I asked, my curiosity piqued.

'A former butler, of whom the Count is very fond, and who has set out to make that poor unhappy, sensitive lady suffer. It seems he is in possession of a compromising secret and with that weapon intends to . . . well, I don't know quite what exactly. It's disgraceful!'

'It certainly is, and he deserves to be made an example of,' I said, joining him in unleashing my fury on the man.

'But *she* is innocent, *she* is an angel. Oh, but here we are at Cibeles already, yes, there's the Parque de Buenavista on the right. Stop the tram will you, my boy. I'm not one of those men who likes to jump off while the tram is moving and risk cracking my skull open on the paving stones. Goodbye, my friend, goodbye.'

The tram stopped and Señor Dionisio Cascajares de la Vallina got off, having once more shaken my hand and caused a second dent in the English lady's hat, had not yet recovered from the first assault.

III

I remained on the tram, and, the odd thing is, I continued to think about that unknown Countess, about her cruel, suspicious consort and, above all, about the sinister man who, to use the doctor's colourful turn of phrase, was about to bring disaster down upon the household. Consider, dear reader, the nature of the human mind: when Cascajares began telling me about those events, I found it irrelevant and boring, but it took scarcely a moment for my imagination to take up that same affair and turn it over and over in my mind, a psychological operation doubtless stimulated by the regular motion of the tram and the dull, monotonous sound of its wheels, grinding away at the iron rails.

In the end, though, I stopped thinking about what, in fact, held little real interest for me and, looking around the carriage, I began examining my fellow passengers carefully, one by one. Such different faces and such diverse expressions! Some seemed quite indifferent to those sitting next to them, while others reviewed the assembled crowd with impertinent curiosity; some were happy, others sad, one man was yawning, and another fellow further off was laughing; and, despite the brevity of the journey, not a few were impatient for it to end, for there is nothing more annoying than being in the company of a dozen or so people all gazing at each other in silence and counting each other's wrinkles and moles and any other imperfections on face or clothing.

It's strange, that brief meeting with people we have never seen before and whom we will probably never see again. When we get on the tram, there is usually someone else already there; others get on afterwards; some get off, leaving us alone and then, finally, we get off too. It's an image of human life, in which being born and dying are like those entrances and exits I've described, and which, as the generations of travellers come and go, are constantly renewing the small world of the tram. They enter and leave, they are born and die. How many have been here before us! How many will come afterwards!

And, to make the resemblance more complete, a tram contains a miniature world of passions. We judge many of those we see there to be excellent people, we like their looks and are even saddened when they leave. Then there are others who, on the contrary, we loathe on sight: we hate them for ten minutes, rather rancorously examine their phrenological character and feel real pleasure when they leave. And, meanwhile, the tram, that imitation of human life, keeps moving, constantly receiving and letting go, uniform, tireless, majestic, indifferent to what is going on inside, entirely unstirred by the barely repressed emotions of that dumb-show, always travelling along those two endless parallel lines, as long and slippery as the centuries.

IV

I remained immersed in this ocean of unsettling thoughts as the tram continued up Calle de Alcalá, until I was snatched from them by the sound of my parcel of books hitting the floor. I immediately picked the parcel up, and my eyes fell on the piece of newspaper that served as a wrapping for the books and so I idly read a line or two of print. My curiosity was immediately aroused. Certain names scattered over that scrap of newsprint caught both my eye and my memory. I searched for the beginning of the article, but could not find it. The paper was torn and, initially out of mere curiosity and subsequently with growing fascination, this is what I read:

The Countess was in a state of indescribable agitation. She was continually troubled by the presence of Mudarra, the insolent butler, who, forgetting his lowly origins, had dared to set his sights on her, a creature so far above him. The villain was constantly spying on her, watching her as one might watch one's prey. He was unconstrained by respect, and neither the sensibility nor the delicacy of that excellent lady proved an obstacle to his ignoble stalking of her.

Mudarra entered the Countess's bedroom late one night, and she, pale and agitated, and filled at once by shame and terror, lacked the courage to dismiss him.

'Do not be afraid, Countess,' he said with a forced, sinister smile that only increased the lady's anxiety. 'I have not come to harm you in any way.'

'Oh, dear God, when will this torment cease?' cried the Countess, letting one arm droop by her side in despair. 'Leave my room this instant, I cannot give in to your desires. How shameful to abuse both my weakness and the indifference of my husband, who is the sole author of my many misfortunes.'

'Why so upset, Countess?' asked the fearsome butler. 'If I did not hold the key to your perdition in my hand, if I could not divulge to the Count details regarding a certain young gentleman . . . but I will not make use of those terrible weapons. One day, you will understand when you see how selfless is the love I feel for you.'

When he said this, Mudarra took a few steps towards the Countess, who drew back from the monster in horror and repugnance.

Mudarra was a man of about fifty, dark, squat and bow-legged, with a bristling brush of wiry hair, a large mouth and prominent eye-teeth. His eyes, half-hidden beneath his beetling black brows, were filled at that moment by the most bestial and urgent feelings of concupiscence.

'Ah, such coldness!' he exclaimed angrily, when he saw the lady's understandable indifference. 'If only I were a certain impeccably turned-out young man! Why so fastidious when you know I could easily tell the Count . . . And he would believe me, you can be sure of that; the Count has such confidence in me that anything I tell him he takes to be the Gospel truth. And, given how jealous he is, if I were to give him that little piece of paper . . .'

'You villain!' cried the Countess in a fit of noble indignation. 'I am innocent, and my husband would never give ear to such vile calumnies. And, even if I were guilty, rather than buy my peace of mind at such a price, I would prefer a thousand times over to be despised by my husband and by everyone else. Get out of here this minute.'

'I have a temper too, Countess,' said the butler, swallowing his rage, 'yes, I, too, have a temper, and when thwarted . . . But since you're being so unpleasant, let's continue in that vein. I know what I have to do now. I have been far too indulgent for far too long. For the last time, I ask that we be friends. Don't force me to do something foolish, Countess . . .'

As he said this, Mudarra arranged his parchment-yellow skin and the stiff tendons of his face into something resembling a smile and advanced a few steps as if about to sit down on the sofa next to the Countess. She leapt to her feet, crying:

'Get out of here, you scoundrel! You know perfectly well I have no one to defend me! Get out of here!'

The butler was like a wild beast who has let slip the prey he had held for a moment in his claws. He snorted, made a threatening gesture and then, very slowly and quietly, left the room. The Countess, trembling and breathless, cowering in a corner, listened as his footsteps gradually moved off, the sound muffled by the rugs in the next room. When she thought he had gone, she could finally breathe more easily. She locked all the doors and tried to sleep, but sleep eluded her, her eyes still filled by the terrifying image of the monster.

CHAPTER XI. *The plot* – When Mudarra left the Countess, he went straight to his own room and, in the grip of a terrible nervous disquiet, began leafing through various papers and letters, muttering: 'I've had enough, she'll pay dearly for this . . .' Then he sat down, took up his pen, and set before him one of those letters, which he studied closely before beginning another, trying to copy the handwriting. He kept glancing feverishly from one to the other, and at last, after much labour, he wrote the following letter – in a hand identical to that of the original: *I promised to see you, and I hasten . . .*

The newspaper was torn at this point and I could read no more.

V

With my eyes still fixed on the parcel, I began thinking about the connection between what I had heard from Señor Cascajares de la Vallina and the scene I had just read about in that rag, a serial doubtless translated from some ridiculous novel by Ponson du Terrail or Montépin. I know it's nonsense, I said to myself, but the fact is she intrigues me, this Countess, this victim of the barbarous machinations of a ruthless butler, who only exists in the crazed mind of some novelist born to terrify simple folk. How will the wretch take his revenge? He would be capable of anything, of the kind of atrocity dreamed up by such authors to conclude a particularly sensational chapter. And what will the Count do? And what about the young man mentioned first by Cascajares and later by Mudarra in the newspaper serial. What will he do? Who is he? What exactly is the relationship between that unknown gentleman and the Countess? I would love to know . . .

VI

I looked about me on the tram and, O horror, my eyes alighted on someone who made me tremble with fear. While I had been absorbed in reading that interesting fragment of serial, the tram had stopped several times to let off or take on the occasional passenger. One such passenger was the man whose sudden presence had so shaken me. It was him, Mudarra, the butler himself, sitting opposite me, his knees touching mine. In a moment, I had examined him from head to toe and recognized him from the description I had read. It could be none other; even the most insignificant details of his clothes clearly indicated it was him. I recognized his greasy, swarthy skin; the untamable hair growing in all directions, like the snakes on Medusa's head; the eyes almost concealed by his wild, bushy eyebrows; the pigeon toes; in short, the same look, the same man in appearance, attire, in the way he breathed and coughed, even in the way he put his hand in his pocket to pay his fare.

Then I saw him take out a wallet and noticed that this object bore a large gilt M, the initial of his surname. He opened the wallet, removed a letter and studied the envelope with a demonic smile on his face. I could even imagine him muttering to himself:

'I've got her handwriting right off pat!'

It was, in fact, quite a short letter and the address on the envelope was written in a female hand. He looked at it hard, relishing his villainous handiwork, until he noticed that I, with indiscreet, discourteous curiosity, was peering over to read the address. He shot me a glance that struck me like a blow and immediately returned the letter to his wallet.

During the brief period of time it had taken me to read that fragment of a story, to ponder a little those strange events, and to find the unlikely, fantastical figure of Mudarra himself transformed into a living being and a fellow passenger on that journey, the tram had left behind it Calle de Alcalá, crossed Puerta del Sol and emerged triumphant into Calle Mayor, pushing its way past the other carriages, scattering the slower, loitering carts and frightening the pedestrians who, in the tumult of the street and dazed by the hubbub of noises, often failed to see the great hulk approaching until it was almost upon them.

I was still studying the man as one would an object of whose real existence one is not quite sure, and I did not take my eyes off his repellent features until I saw him stand up, call for the tram to stop and get off, only to disappear at once among the crowds filling the street.

VII

Several people got on and off, and the living décor of the tram changed completely.

I was feeling increasingly curious about an event that, at first sight, could be seen as having been shaped exclusively by my own mind out of the disparate sensations occasioned by that initial conversation and by what I had read subsequently, but which I now imagined to be true and undoubtedly real.

When the man I believed to be the evil butler got off, I sat thinking about the letter and explained it to myself in my own fashion, not wishing, in such a delicate matter, to prove any less fertile in imagination than the novelist and author of the fragment I had read moments before. Mudarra, I thought, eager to avenge himself on the Countess – that poor unlucky Countess! – copies her handwriting and pens a letter to the young gentleman, with whom something may or may not have occurred. In the letter, she invites him to her house; the young man arrives at the appointed hour and, shortly afterwards, so does the husband, duly informed of the meeting, so that he can catch his unfaithful wife in flagrante. Very clever! Now, while such a plan may have its pros and cons in real life, it works perfectly in a novel. The lady faints; the lover panics; the husband commits a terrible act; and behind the curtain lurks the fateful countenance of the butler, revelling in his devilish revenge.

I have read many novels, many of them very bad indeed, and it was I who gave that twist to a story that was silently evolving in my imagination on the flimsy basis of something a friend had told me, a few lines from a novel found on a scrap of newspaper and an encounter on the tram with a complete stranger.

VIII

On and on the tram went, and, whether because of the heat inside or because the slow, monotonous motion of the vehicle produces a kind of dizziness that can all too easily become sleep, the fact is, my eyelids began to droop, and, as I listed slightly to the left, I leaned my elbow on my parcel of books and closed my eyes. However, I continued to see before me the row of faces, male and female, some bearded, others hairless, some laughing, some stiff and solemn. Then, it seemed to me that, as if at the command of a shared muscle, all those faces began to wink and grimace, opening and closing eyes and mouths and revealing a series of teeth that went from the purest of whites to the yellowest of yellows, some sharp and others blunt or worn. The eight noses that protruded from beneath those sixteen eyes of diverse colours and expression kept growing then shrinking, and constantly changing shape; the mouths opened horizontally, emitting silent guffaws, or else extended outwards to form long snouts, similar to the interesting face of a certain estimable animal whose name is anathema.

Through the window beyond those eight faces, whose horrific visages I have just described, I could see the street, the houses and the passers-by, all moving very fast, as if the tram were travelling at vertiginous speed. To me, at least, it seemed to be going faster than any Spanish or French or English or American train; it was travelling as fast as you can possibly imagine a solid object moving through space.

As my lethargic state grew more pronounced, it seemed to me that the houses and streets and Madrid itself were disappearing. For a moment, I thought the tram was travelling through the depths of the sea; outside, I could see the bodies of vast whales and the sticky tendrils of a multitude of corals of various sizes. Small fish flicked their slippery tails against the glass, and some peered in with large, golden eyes. Unfamiliar crustaceans, large molluscs, madrepores, sponges and hordes of giant, misshapen bivalves, of a kind I had never seen, passed ceaselessly by. The tram was being drawn by some sort of swimming monster, whose oars, pushing against the water, sounded like the beatings of a propeller that made the watery mass churn with its endless turning. This vision gradually faded, and then it seemed to me that the tram was flying through the air, straight as a bullet, unbuffeted by the winds. There was nothing to be seen outside, only empty space; the clouds occasionally wrapped about us; a sudden, violent shower of rain drummed on the upper floor; then we emerged once more into pure, sun-flooded space, only to plunge back into the vaporous bosom of immense cloudscapes – now red, now yellow, now the colour of opals, now of amethysts – which we left behind as we journeyed. At other times, we passed through a place filled by glowing masses of the finest gold dust; at still others, the dust, which I fancied came from the movement of the wheels grinding down the light, was first silver, then green like powdered emeralds, and finally red like powdered rubies. The tram was being drawn now by some apocalyptic winged creature, stronger than a hippogryph and bolder than a dragon, and the sound of the wheels and the wings was reminiscent of the hum from the great sails of a windmill, or from a bumblebee the size of an elephant. We flew through endless space, never arriving anywhere, and many leagues beneath our feet lay the Earth, and on the Earth was Spain, Madrid, the *barrio* of Salamanca, Señor Cascajares, the Countess, the Count, Mudarra, and the unknown young man.

IX

I soon fell deeply asleep and then the tram stopped moving, stopped flying and I lost the feeling that I was travelling in a tram, and all that remained was the deep, monotonous rumble that never ceases during the nightmares that afflict one, be it in a train or in a cabin on board ship. I fell asleep. O unlucky Countess! I saw her as clearly as the piece of paper on which I am writing now; I saw her sitting at a table, resting her cheek on her hand, looking as sad and meditative as a statue representing melancholy. At her feet, a little dog lay curled, apparently as sad as his interesting mistress.

Then I was able to study at my leisure the woman I considered to be misfortune personified. She was tall and fair, with large, expressive eyes, a slender, almost large, but exquisitely shaped nose that stood out gracefully beneath the curve of her fine, blue-black eyebrows. She was simply coiffed, and, from that and the way she was dressed, it was clear that she did not intend going out that night, that terrible, terrible night! With growing anxiety I watched the lovely face I so longed to know, and it seemed to me that I could read her thoughts on her noble brow, where the habit of mental concentration had traced a few imperceptible lines that time would transform into deep wrinkles.

X

Suddenly the door opened and in walked a man. The Countess gave a cry of surprise and sprang to her feet in a state of great agitation.

'What do you mean by this, Rafael?' she said. 'What impudence! Who let you in?'

'Were you not expecting me, Señora?' said the handsome young man. 'I received a letter from you . . .'

'A letter from me!' the Countess exclaimed, in a state of still greater agitation. 'I wrote no such letter. Why would I?'

'But look, Señora,' said the young man, taking out the letter and showing it to her. 'It's in your own hand.'

'Dear God! What evil scheme is this?' she cried in despair. 'I did not write that letter. This is a trap that has been laid for me . . .'

'Calm down, Señora . . . And please forgive me.'

'Ah, I understand now. That vile man. I can guess what his idea was. You must leave at once. No, it's too late. I can hear my husband's voice.'

Indeed, a booming voice could be heard in the next room, and then the Count entered and, pretending to be surprised to find the young man there, he gave a rather affected laugh and said:

'Why, Rafael, fancy meeting you here. It's been such a long time. You came to keep Antonia company, I suppose. Well, do stay for tea.'

The Countess and her husband exchanged a dark look. In his confusion, the young man could barely manage to return the Count's greeting. I saw various servants come in and out; I saw them bring in the tea and then vanish, leaving the three main characters alone. Something terrible was about to happen.

They sat down. The Countess was as pale as death; the Count affected a wild hilarity, as if he were drunk; and the young man said nothing, answering only in monosyllables. Tea was poured, and the Count handed Rafael a cup, not any cup, but a particular one. The Countess stared at the cup with an expression of all-consuming horror on her face. They drank in silence, accompanying their tea with various tasty Huntley & Palmers biscuits and other titbits appropriate to the occasion. Then the Count gave another of those loud, crazy laughs peculiar to him that night and said:

'Well, this is dull! I can't get a word out of you, Rafael. Antonia, play something. It's been so long since we heard you. How about that piece by Gortzchach entitled 'Death'? You used to play it so well. Come now, take your place at the piano.'

The Countess tried to speak but could not utter a single word. Then her husband fixed her with his eyes, and she gave in, like a dove hypnotized by a boa constrictor. She got up and went over to the piano, and there the Count must have said something that terrified her still more, placing her in his infernal power. The piano spoke, a multitude of strings struck simultaneously; as the Countess's hands raced over the flats and sharps, they awoke in a second the hundreds of notes sleeping silently in the soundboard. At first, the music was a confusion of sounds that deafened rather than pleased, but then the storm abated, and a fearful, funereal song, like the 'Dies irae', emerged from the disorder. I felt I could hear the sad singing of a choir of Carthusian monks, accompanied by the low moans of a bassoon. Then we heard mournful cries, as one imagines the cries of condemned souls in Purgatory to be, pleading incessantly for a forgiveness that will be long in coming.

Then it was back to those drawn-out, raucous arpeggios, notes jostling with each other, as if quarrelling over who should arrive first. The chords rose and fell just as the foam of the waves builds and is lost. The tune ebbed and flowed in an endless swell, dwindling almost to nothing, then returning with more force, forming great, churning eddies.

I was swept away by that powerful, majestic music. The Countess had her back to me and so I could not see her face, but I imagined that, in her present state of bewilderment and fear, the piano must somehow be playing itself.

The young man was behind her, and the Count to her right, leaning on the piano. Occasionally, she glanced up at him, but she presumably found the expression in his eyes so terrifying that she immediately lowered her gaze and continued playing. Suddenly, the piano stopped, and the Countess screamed.

At that moment, I felt a hard blow on my shoulder that shook me violently awake.

XI

In the agitation of my dream, I had slid sideways and fallen on top of the venerable Englishwoman sitting next to me.

'You fell asleep on me!' she said, pulling a sour face and repelling the parcel of books that had fallen into her lap.

'Yes, Señora, you're quite right, I did fall asleep!' I answered, embarrassed to see how all the other passengers were laughing at me.

'I'm going to tell the conductor that you're bothering me. Shocking behaviour in a gentleman,' she added in her fractured Spanish. 'You seem to think that my body is a bed for you to sleep on. You are a stupid ass, sir!'

When she said these words, this daughter of Albion, who was already quite red in the face, turned bright scarlet. It looked as if the blood filling her cheeks and nose was about to burst forth from her glowing pores. She showed me four sharp, very white teeth, as if she were about to bite me. I begged her forgiveness for my discourteous behaviour while asleep, retrieved my parcel and reviewed the new faces in the tram. Imagine my surprise, dear, patient, kindly reader, when I saw before me the young man from my dream, Don Rafael in person. I rubbed my eyes to convince myself I was not still sleeping, but I was definitely awake, as awake as I am now.

It was him, it really was, and he was talking to the man sitting next to him. I pricked up my ears and listened as if my life depended on it.

'But didn't you suspect anything?' the other man was saying.

'Yes, but I said nothing. She seemed half-dead with fear. Her husband ordered her to play the piano and she didn't dare refuse. As usual, she played admirably, and, as I listened, I almost forgot about the dangerous situation we were in. Despite all her efforts to appear calm, there came a point when she could pretend no longer. Her arms grew limp, her fingers slipped from the keys, she threw back her head and cried out. Then her husband unsheathed a dagger and shouted furiously: "Play or I'll kill you!" When I saw this, my blood boiled. I went to throw myself on the wretch, but I had a feeling in my body I can't even describe. It was as if, suddenly, a bonfire had been lit in my stomach; fire was running through my veins; my temples were pounding, and I fell to the floor, unconscious.'

'Had you noticed no effects from the poison before?' asked the other man.

'I'd felt slightly unwell and had some vague suspicion that something was wrong, but that was all. The poison had been carefully prepared, because it took effect slowly and, while it didn't kill me, it left me with a condition that will stay with me for the rest of my life.'

'And after you lost consciousness, what happened then?'

Rafael was about to answer, and I was listening as if his words held a life-or-death secret, when the tram stopped.

'Here we are at the Palacio de los Consejos already. We'd better get off,' said Rafael.

Oh no! They were leaving before I could find out how the story ended.

'Sir, sir, a word!' I said when I saw them getting up.

The young man paused and looked at me.

'What about the Countess? What happened to the Countess?' I asked eagerly.

The only response I received was the laughter of the other passengers. The two young men, who were also laughing, left without a word. The only human creature who retained her sphinx-like serenity during this comical scene was the Englishwoman, who, indignant at my eccentric behaviour, turned to the other passengers and said:

'The man's a lunatic!'

XII

The tram set off again, and I was burning with curiosity to know what had become of the poor Countess. Did her husband kill her? I knew what the wretch's intentions were. Like all cruel souls, he was eager to have his revenge and wanted his wife to stand by helplessly and watch the death agony of that unwary youth, drawn there by the vile trap set by Mudarra.

But how could the lady continue desperately to maintain her calm, when she knew Rafael had drunk the poison? A truly tragic, blood-curdling scene, I thought, more and more convinced of the reality of the event. And people say these things only happen in novels!

As we passed the Palace, the tram stopped again, and a woman carrying a little dog got on. I immediately recognized the dog I had seen curled up at the Countess's feet; it was the same animal, with the same fine white hair and the same black spot on one of its ears. Fate decreed that this woman should then sit down next to me. Unable to contain my curiosity, I asked her:

'Is that pretty little dog yours?'

'Of course. Do you like him?'

I made to stroke one of the intelligent creature's ears, but the dog, misinterpreting this display of affection, barked and jumped onto the Englishwoman's lap, who again showed me her sharp teeth, as if she were about to bite me, exclaiming:

'You are *incorrigible*!'

'And where did you get the dog?' I asked, ignoring the Englishwoman's latest choleric outburst. 'If you don't mind my asking, that is.'

'It belonged to my mistress.'

'And what happened to your mistress?' I asked urgently.

'Oh, did you know her?' replied the woman. 'She was so very kind, wasn't she?'

'Oh, yes, a fine woman. But what exactly happened?'

'So you know about it? You've heard the news?'

'Indeed. I know precisely what happened up until that business with the tea . . . So the lady died, did she?'

'Yes, God rest her.'

'But how? Was she murdered or was it as a consequence of the shock?'

'What do you mean "murdered"? What "shock"?' she said, a mocking look on her face. 'You haven't heard the news, have you? She ate something that night which disagreed with her. She had a funny turn and had to take to her bed, where she remained until morning.'

Huh! I thought. She either knows nothing about the incident with the piano and the poison or else is pretending that she doesn't.

Then I said:

'So it was something she ate, was it?'

'Yes. I said to her that night: "Don't eat the seafood, Señora," but she took no notice.'

'Seafood?' I said incredulously. 'Don't give me that.'

'Don't you believe me?'

'Yes, yes, of course,' I said, pretending that I did. 'And what about the Count?'

'What Count?'

'Her husband, the Countess's husband, the one who took out his dagger while she was playing the piano.'

The woman looked at me for a moment, then laughed in my face.

'You may laugh, but don't think I don't know what really happened. You obviously don't want to give me the true version of events. Well, we'll see about that. This is a criminal case!'

'But you mentioned a Count and a Countess.'

'Wasn't the Countess the owner of the dog and her butler a man called Mudarra?'

The woman again roared with laughter, so loudly this time that I said to myself: 'She must be Mudarra's accomplice and is clearly trying to conceal the truth.'

'You're mad,' she said.

'Oh, yes, the man's a complete lunatic. He nearly suffocated me!' cried the Englishwoman.

'I know everything. Don't try to hide the truth from me. Tell me how the Countess really died.'

'What Countess are you talking about, man?' asked the woman, bursting out laughing again.

'Look, don't think you can fool me with your guffawing,' I replied. 'The Countess was either poisoned or murdered; I'm absolutely sure of it.'

XIII

The tram reached the *barrio* of Pozas, and I the end of my journey. We all got off. The Englishwoman shot me a glance indicating her delight at being free of me at last, and everyone went their separate ways. I followed the woman with the dog, bombarding her with questions, until she reached her house and went in, still laughing at my insistence on poking my nose into other people's lives. Finding myself alone in the street, I remembered the original object of my journey and made my way to the house where I was to deliver the books. I returned them to the person who had lent them to me and then strolled up and down near the church of Buen Suceso, waiting for the tram to return and take me back to the other side of Madrid.

I couldn't stop thinking about the unfortunate Countess and was becoming more and more convinced that the woman I had spoken to on the tram had wanted to deceive me by hiding the truth about the whole mysterious tragedy.

XIV

It was getting dark when the tram was ready to depart. I climbed on board, and who do you think I saw? The Englishwoman, sitting in the very same seat. When she spotted me and when I again sat down beside her, the expression on her face was indescribable. She once more turned bright scarlet and exclaimed:

'Not you again! I'll have to complain to the conductor.'

So immersed was I in my tangled thoughts that, ignoring what the Englishwoman was saying to me in her laborious, hybrid Spanish, I said:

'There is no doubt in my mind that the Countess was either poisoned or murdered. You have no idea how ruthless that man is.'

The tram moved off, stopping every now and then to pick up passengers. Near the Palacio Real, three people got on and sat down opposite me. One of them was a tall, thin, bony man with very hard eyes and a resonant voice that commanded respect.

They had not been seated ten minutes when the man turned to his companions and said:

'The poor thing! How she cried out in her last moments. The bullet entered above her right clavicle and then penetrated her heart.'

'What?' I exclaimed, addressing myself to them. 'You mean she was shot? Wasn't she stabbed to death?'

The three men stared at me in surprise.

'No, she was shot,' declared the tall, thin, bony man in a rather surly tone of voice.

'And yet that woman claimed she'd died of food poisoning,' I said, feeling more intrigued by the minute. 'Tell me, what happened?'

'What has it got to do with you?' asked the man sourly.

'I'm very keen to know how this terrible tragedy ended. It's like something out of a novel, isn't it?'

'What do you mean, a novel? You're either mad or you're making fun of us.'

'This is no joking matter, sir,' said the tall, thin man.

'Do you think I don't know? I know everything. I was a witness to various scenes from this horrible crime. But you say the Countess died from a bullet wound.'

'For heaven's sake, we weren't talking about a Countess, but about my dog who got shot accidentally while we were out hunting. If you want to joke, then we can meet elsewhere and I'll give you the answer you deserve.'

'I see. Now you want to cover up the truth,' I said, believing that they wanted to put me off the track by making the poor Countess into a dog.

The man was just preparing his riposte, doubtless a more violent one than the situation called for, when the Englishwoman tapped her forehead as if to tell them that I wasn't quite right in the head. They calmed down then and didn't say another word for the rest of the journey, which ended for them in Puerta del Sol. They were probably afraid of me.

XV

I was still totally consumed by this business and quite incapable of quietening my mind, however hard I tried to reason my way through the whole complex matter. Instead, I grew even more confused and was quite unable to get the image of the poor woman out of my head. I seemed to see in every one of the ever-changing faces on the tram some fact that might contribute to explaining the enigma. My brain was horribly overexcited, and that inner turmoil must have shown on my face, because everyone was staring at me as one might stare at some extraordinary sight.

XVI

Another thing occurred to trouble my poor head on that ill-fated journey. As we were travelling along Calle de Alcalá, a man and a woman got on, and the man sat down next to me. He seemed deeply affected by some recent shocking event, and I even thought I saw him raise his handkerchief to his eyes now and then to dry the invisible tears he was doubtless shedding behind the green lenses of his huge spectacles.

After a while, the man said softly to the woman who appeared to be his wife:

'There are suspicions that she may have been poisoned, you know. Don Mateo just told me. The poor woman!'

'How dreadful! I'd wondered about that myself,' replied his consort. 'But what can you expect from such villains?'

'I swear I'll leave no stone unturned to find out.'

Then I, all ears, said in an equally low voice:

'It's true, sir, there was a poisoning. I know that for a fact.'

'What? You know? You knew her too?' said the man in the green spectacles eagerly, turning to me.

'Yes, she suffered a violent death, of that I am quite sure, however much certain people would like us to believe it was food poisoning.'

'My feelings exactly. She was such an excellent woman too. But how do you know?'

'I just know,' I said, pleased that he didn't take me for a madman.

'Then you must testify in court. They're drawing up the indictment now.'

'I'd be glad to and to see those scoundrels punished. Oh, I'll testify all right.'

My obsession had reached such extremes that I had allowed that event, half-dreamed, half-read-about, to take me over entirely, and I believed it as surely as I believe this is a pen with which I'm writing.

'Indeed, sir, we must clear up this enigma so that the perpetrators of the crime can be punished. I will testify that she was poisoned with a cup of tea, just like the young man.'

'Did you hear that, Petronila?' said the man in the spectacles to his wife. 'A cup of tea!'

'I'm astonished,' answered the lady. 'The lengths these men will go to.'

'Yes, a cup of tea. The Countess was playing the piano . . .'

'What Countess?' asked the man, interrupting me.

'The Countess, the one who was poisoned.'

'We're not talking about a Countess, man!'

'So you're another one determined to cover the whole thing up.'

'No, no. There was no Countess or Duchess involved, but the laundress who lives in the same building as us, the pointsman's wife.'

'A laundress, eh?' I said mischievously. 'So you want me to believe that she was a laundress, do you?'

The man and his wife looked at me mockingly, then mumbled something to each other. From a gesture the woman made, I realized that they were convinced I was drunk. I stoically said nothing more, opting to treat that disrespectful supposition with the silent scorn proper to large souls. My anxiety was growing. The Countess did not leave my thoughts for a second, and I had become as deeply concerned about her sinister end as if the whole affair were not the result of the unhealthy lucubrations of my own imagination, under the influence of successive chance encounters and conversations. In order that you can see to what extremes my madness brought me, I will describe the final incident on that journey and the extravagant way in which I brought to a close that painful struggle with my reason, embroiled as it was in that battle of shadows.

XVII

The tram was just entering Calle de Serrano, when I looked out through the window ahead of me at the dimly lit street. I saw a man walking past and I cried out in surprise and shouted wildly:

'There he is, there is cruel Mudarra himself, the perpetrator of all those crimes!'

I told the tram to stop and scrambled to the door, stumbling over the feet and legs of the other passengers. Once in the street, I ran after the man, yelling:

'Stop that man! He's a murderer!'

You can imagine the effect of these cries in that peaceful area of Madrid.

Passers-by detained the man – the very man I had seen earlier in the tram – while I bawled:

'He's the one who prepared the poison for the Countess, the one who killed the Countess!'

There was a moment of indescribable confusion. He said I was mad, and, of course, we were both immediately marched off to the police station. I have no recollection of what happened after that. I cannot remember what I did that night in the place where they locked me up. My most vivid recollection after these strange events is of waking from the deep lethargy into which I fell, a drunkenness of the mind produced by what exactly I really don't know, by one of those passing episodes of mental derangement of such interest to scientists as the precursors of hopeless insanity.

As you can imagine, nothing came of the matter, for the unpleasant fellow I had named Mudarra was, in fact, an honest grocer who had never poisoned a single Countess in his life. And yet, for a long time afterwards, I persisted in my delusion and would cry out:

'Poor unfortunate Countess! Whatever the others may say, I still stick to my guns. No one will persuade me that you did not end your days at the hands of your enraged husband.'

XVIII

It has taken some months for these ghosts to return to the mysterious place whence they arose to drive me to the brink of insanity, and for reality to re-establish itself in my mind again. I laugh now when I think of that tram ride, and the concern I once felt for that imagined victim and which I now devote – would you believe it? – to my companion on that distressing journey, the irascible Englishwoman, whose foot I dislocated when I was rushing to get off the tram in pursuit of the supposed butler.

Madrid, November 1871

EMILIA PARDO BAZÁN

The Talisman

This story, although true, should not be read by the light of day. I'm telling you this now, dear reader, so don't say I didn't warn you: you will need some light, but avoid electricity or gas or even oil, and use instead one of those charming, elegant candelabra made to hold three candles, and which barely shed any light at all, leaving most of the room in darkness. Or, better still, go out into the garden and sit by the pond, where the magnolias give off their intoxicating perfume and the silvery moon shimmers and glows, and there listen to this tale of the mandrake and Baron de Helynagy.

I met this foreign gentleman in the simplest, least novelistic way possible: I was introduced to him at one of the many parties held by the Austrian ambassador. The Baron was first secretary at the embassy, but neither the post he occupied, nor his appearance, nor his conversation – which was much like that of most people one meets at such parties – justified the mysterious, insinuating tone of the person who introduced us, the tone one might use to announce some significant event.

My curiosity was aroused, and so I decided to observe the Baron more closely. He seemed a very refined fellow, in the rather starchy manner of the diplomat, and handsome too, with the somewhat impersonal good

Emilia Pardo Bazán (1851–1921) was born in A Coruña in Galicia, and many of her novels are set in that region. She married at sixteen and moved with her husband to Madrid, where she lived until her death. She was a prolific writer and is often credited with introducing Naturalism into Spanish literature. Her most famous work is *Los Pazos de Ulloa* (*The House of Ulloa*). She and Galdós became lovers for a time, and remained friends throughout their lives. She took a keen interest in politics and played an important role in the development of the feminist movement in Spain.

looks of all society men, groomed to perfection by his manservant, his tailor and his barber – and thanks above all to starch, for everything about him was starched. As for the Baron's moral and intellectual qualities, it was hard to make an assessment in such mundane circumstances. After half an hour of talk, I again thought to myself: I really can't see why they make such a fuss about the man.

As soon as my conversation with the Baron was over, I questioned various people about him, and what I learned only increased my initial curiosity. They told me that the Baron was in possession of a talisman. Yes, a real talisman, something which, like Balzac's *peau de chagrin*, allowed his every wish to be granted and guaranteed him success in all his enterprises. I was told of strokes of luck that could only be explained by the magical influence of that talisman. The Baron was Hungarian, and although he claimed to be descended from the glorious Magyar prince, Taksony, he was, in fact, the last remaining member of the Helynagy family and had been living in poverty, never leaving his ancient ancestral abode in the mountains. Suddenly, a series of strange coincidences placed in his hands a sizeable fortune: not only did various rich relatives die rather opportunely, with him as their sole heir, but when undertaking restoration work on the ancient Helynagy castle, he also happened upon a hoard of money and jewellery. As befitted a man of his rank, the Baron then presented himself at the court of Vienna, and his extraordinary luck thereafter could only be explained by some mysterious protective power. If he gambled, you could be sure that he would win all bets. He was involved in three duels, and in all three he wounded his opponent; his last opponent's wound proved fatal, which seemed like a warning from fate to anyone tempted to take on the Baron in future. When the Baron fancied a career in politics, the doors of parliament opened wide, and his post at the embassy in Madrid was only a first step on the ladder to a higher position. It was already rumoured that next winter he would be appointed Minister plenipotentiary.

If this was not all just some tall tale, it would certainly be worth finding out precisely what kind of talisman could achieve such enviable results, and that is precisely what I decided to do, because I have always believed that one should, on principle, believe in the fantastic and the miraculous, and anyone who doesn't – at least between the hours of eleven at night and five in the morning – is clearly sixpence short of a shilling, which is to say, a downright fool.

In order to achieve my goal, I chose a very different tack to the one most people might take: I went out of my way to engage the Baron in conversation, but never said a word about the talisman. For a while, though, my strategy produced no results whatsoever; the Baron never once confided in me, and, far from the smug glee of someone certain of his luck, what I sensed in him was sadness and disquiet, a kind of dark pessimism. On the other hand, his repeated allusions to earlier days, to more modest, obscure times, and to his sudden rise to the top thanks to a dizzyingly fortunate stroke of luck, confirmed the version doing the rounds. The announcement that the Baron had been summoned to Vienna and that his departure was imminent made me lose all hope of learning more.

I was thinking precisely this on an afternoon when the Baron arrived unexpectedly at my house. He had presumably come to say goodbye and was carrying an object that he placed on the nearest table before sitting down and looking nervously around, as if to make sure we were quite alone. I felt a rush of excitement because I immediately guessed, with quick, feminine intuition, that he was about to tell me about the talisman.

'I have come here to ask you an enormous favour,' he said. 'As you know, I have been called home, and I suspect that the visit will be rather brief and rushed. I possess an object . . . a kind of relic . . . and I fear the vicissitudes of the journey. In fact, I'm afraid someone might steal it, because it is a widely coveted thing to which ordinary people attribute amazing powers. News of my journey has already spread, and it's highly likely that some plot is afoot to take the object from me. I am entrusting it to you, and, if you could keep it safe until my return, I will be forever in your debt.'

So that precious talisman, that rare amulet, was there on the table, just a few steps away, and it was going to be left in my hands!

'Rest assured,' I said earnestly, 'if I do keep it, it will be perfectly safe, but, before I agree to do so, I would like you to tell me exactly what the object is. I've never asked you any indiscreet questions, but I know what other people say, and I understand that, according to rumour, you possess an amazing talisman, which has brought you all kinds of good fortune. I will only take care of it for you if I know exactly what it is and if it really does merit such interest.'

The Baron hesitated. I could see that he was gripped by uncertainty, unable to decide whether or not to speak truthfully and frankly. In the end, honesty won out, and he said:

'You have touched the wound in my soul, Señora. I live in a state of constant grief and torment because I can never know whether I do possess a genuine treasure with magical qualities or am merely clinging superstitiously to a worthless fetish. For the children of our century, faith in the supernatural is always a tower that is easily toppled: the merest breath of wind will bring it crashing down. People think I am "happy", when, in fact, I am merely "fortunate". I would be happy if I could be absolutely sure that the object in that box really is a talisman that grants my every wish and parries the blows of adversity, but I really do not know. What can I say, except that, one afternoon, when I was very poor and a complete nobody, an Israelite from Palestine passed through Helynagy and insisted on selling me the thing, assuring me that it would bring me endless good fortune. I bought it just as one buys all kinds of useless knick-knacks, and then consigned it to a drawer. Shortly after that, things began to happen that changed my luck completely, although they could equally well be explained without recourse to miracles.' Here the Baron smiled, and his smile was infectious. Then his face assumed its usual melancholy expression, and he said: 'Every day, we see some man or other achieving something he does not deserve, and it's almost commonplace for inexperienced duellists to defeat celebrated swordsmen. If I were convinced that talismans really do exist, then I could enjoy my wealth with a quiet heart. What troubles and depresses me is the idea that I might be the plaything of a piece of mere fakery, and that, when I least expect it, the grim fate of my ancestors will once again fall upon me. You can see how wrong they are, those people who envy me, and how my tormenting fear of the future is a very poor reward indeed for my much-vaunted good fortune. Nevertheless, I have enough faith left to ask you to look after this little box for me . . .'

This frank confession explained the sad look I had often noted on the Baron's face. His state of mind seemed to me truly worthy of pity, because, in the midst of his great good fortune, his soul was constantly gnawed at by doubt, which kills and corrodes everything. The victorious arrogance of great men always stems from their absolute confidence in their own lucky star, and the Baron's lack of belief rendered him incapable of feeling that sense of triumph.

The Baron got to his feet and, picking up the object he had brought with him, he removed a black satin cloth to reveal a small box made of rock crystal edged with silver and with a silver lock. He lifted the lid, delicately removed a kind of linen shroud decorated with lace, and what I saw there was truly horrible: a grotesque, black figurine about a span high, like a man's body in miniature. The Baron was unsurprised when I drew back in disgust.

'What on earth is it?' I felt impelled to ask.

'This,' he replied, 'is one of nature's marvels, something that can be neither imitated nor faked. This is the root of the mandrake plant. The superstition that attributes rare virtues to the anthropomorphic mandrake is as old as time itself. They say the plant grows from the blood of people who were executed, which is why, in the night or in the small hours, you can hear it moaning as if it were inhabited by a captive soul filled with despair. But for heaven's sake be sure always to keep it wrapped in silk or linen, because only then will the mandrake offer its protection.'

'And do you believe all that?' I exclaimed, looking hard at the Baron.

'Ah, if only I did!' he responded in such an embittered voice that, at first, I didn't know quite how to respond. Shortly after this, the Baron left, repeating his plea for me to take every possible care with the small box and its contents. He would, he said, be back within a month to retrieve it.

And that is how the talisman came into my keeping, and you will understand when I say that, afterwards, I did take time to study it more closely, and I must confess that, although the whole business about the mandrake legend seemed to me like a ridiculous old wives' tale, a vile superstition from the East, I could not help but be troubled by the strangely perfect way in which that root imitated the human body. I thought it probably was a counterfeit, but my eyes soon undeceived me, convincing me that the hand of man had played no part in the making of that phenomenon, and that the homunculus was, indeed, the root of the plant just as it had been torn from the earth. I asked various trustworthy people who had lived for a long time in Palestine, and they assured me that it is impossible to fake a mandrake, and that the shepherds in the hills of Gilead and on the plains of Jericho dig up the roots and sell them.

It was, alas, doubtless the very strangeness of the matter – which was entirely new to me – that pricked my imagination. The fact is I began to feel afraid, or, rather, what I felt was an irrepressible feeling of repulsion for the wretched talisman. I had put it with my jewellery in the safe in my bedroom, and I immediately began to have difficulty sleeping, tossing and turning in bed, terrified that, when all was quiet, the mandrake would utter one of those lugubrious moans, turning the blood in my veins to ice. I would wake, trembling, at the slightest noise, and sometimes the wind rattling the windows and buffeting the curtains would be enough to make me think it was the mandrake speaking in voices from the next world . . . In short, the stupid thing was ruining my life, and so I decided to remove it from my room and place it in the glass cabinet in the living room, where I kept a few coins and medals and other old trinkets. Therein lies the origin of my eternal feeling of remorse, the sorrow that will never leave me, because, as fate would have it, a new servant, tempted by the coins in the cabinet, broke the glass in order to steal the coins and trinkets, as well as the little box containing the talisman. This was a terrible blow. I informed the police, and the police searched everywhere, and they did indeed find the thief and recover the coins, the box and the shroud; but the servant admitted that he had thrown the talisman down a drain somewhere, and not even the most painstaking and richly rewarded of searches would ever find it.

'And what happened to the Baron de Helynagy?' I asked the woman who told me this strange story.

'He died in a train crash on his way back to Spain,' she replied, looking paler than usual and turning away.

'So the talisman was real, then?'

'Good heavens,' she retorted, 'there is such a thing as coincidence, you know.'

LEOPOLDO ALAS, 'CLARÍN'

Duet for Two Coughs

The Aguila Hotel casts its enormous shadow over the sleeping waters of the harbour. It is a huge, square edifice, a rambling, rather graceless five-storey building, an accidental utopia, a shelter for travellers, a joint-stock company of indifference, a joint-stock company with an ever-changing team of managers and a staff of twenty who are different every week, along with dozens and dozens of guests who don't know each other, who look straight through each other, who are always 'other' and yet whom every guest assumes to be whoever was there the night before.

'You're more alone here than you would be in the street, or in the desert,' thinks a 'shape', a man wrapped in a loose summer overcoat, as he smokes a cigar, elbows resting on the cold metal balustrade of his third-floor balcony. At that height, and in the darkness of that cloudy night, the light from his cigar looks like a glow-worm. That sad spark sometimes moves, dims, disappears, then blazes forth again.

'A traveller smoking,' thinks another shape two balconies along to the right, on the same floor. And a weak chest, a woman's chest, breathes out

---

Leopoldo Alas, 'Clarín' (1852–1901). After studying Law at the University of Oviedo, he moved to Madrid in 1871, where he immediately became caught up in the political and literary debates of the age and began a career as a literary critic and journalist, writing under the pen name 'Clarín' ('Bugle'), making as many friends as he made enemies. In 1883, he returned to Oviedo, where he took up a teaching post and began writing his first novel, *La Regenta*, which was published in two volumes in 1884 and 1885. *La Regenta* is both a tale of adultery and a scathing satire on the Church and on provincial life in Spain. The novel caused an enormous scandal at the time and, for a long time, was banned under Franco, with the government censor only giving permission for it to be reprinted in 1962. He wrote one other novel, *Su único hijo* (*His Only Son*), and two collections of short stories.

as if sighing, taking some small consolation in the uncertain pleasure of finding unexpected company in her solitude and sadness.

'If I were suddenly to feel very ill, if I were to cry out so as not to die alone, that smoker would hear me,' the woman thinks, clutching a thick, perfumed winter shawl to her delicate, fragile breast.

'There's a balcony between us, so that must be room 36. This morning, when I had to get up to call the maid because she didn't hear the bell, I saw an elegant pair of boots in the corridor outside that door.'

A distant light suddenly vanished, with an effect like lightning, which you only notice when it's gone.

'That's the beacon at the end of El Puntal beach going out,' thinks the shape in room 36 rather glumly, feeling even lonelier in the night. 'One less person to keep watch, another one falling asleep.'

The steamships in the harbour, the big-bellied barges at the dock, just near the hotel, now resemble shadows among the shadows. In the darkness, the water takes centre stage and glitters faintly, like an optical illusion, like the glow of an extinguished light retained by the retina, an illusory phosphorescence. In the gloom, all the more painful for being incomplete, it seems that both the idea of light, and the imagination struggling to make sense of the vague shapes, need help in making out what little can be seen below. The barges move only slightly more perceptibly than the minute hand on a big clock, but now and then they bump against each other with a soft, sad, monotonous thwock, accompanied by the sea in the distance, like the clicking cry of a barn owl trying to impose silence.

The town, a town of businessmen and bathers, is sleeping; the whole house is sleeping.

The shape in room 36 senses an anguish in that silent, shadowy solitude.

Suddenly, as if he had heard a great explosion, he's shaken by the sound of a dry cough, repeated three times like the gentle call of an early-rising quail; it comes from his right, two balconies along. Room 36 looks over and notices a shape that is only slightly darker than the surrounding darkness, the same shade of black as the barges down below. 'The cough of someone ill, the cough of a woman.' And room 36 shudders and thinks of his own situation; he had forgotten that he was engaged in a rakish act of folly, namely, smoking a cigar and standing in the cool air gazing sadly out at the night. A rather funereal orgy! He had been forbidden to smoke or to open his balcony door at that hour, even though it was August and there wasn't so much as the breath of a breeze. 'Inside! Inside! To your tomb, to your horrible prison cell, to room 36, to bed, to your niche in the cemetery wall!'

And without another thought for room 32, room 36 disappeared, closed the balcony door with a sad, metallic squeak, a sound that had a melancholy effect on the shape to the right, much as the disappearance of the light near the beach had had on the shape smoking the cigar.

'Entirely alone,' thought the woman, who, still coughing, had remained where she was while she had company, a 'company' that was rather like that of two stars, which, seen from below, appear to be close together, like twins, but which, out there in the infinite, can neither see each other nor know of each other's existence.

After a few minutes, having lost all hope that room 36 would come back out onto his balcony, the woman who coughed also went inside, like a corpse in the form of a will-o'-the-wisp breathing in the fragrance of the night and returning to earth.

One hour, then two hours passed. On the stairs, in the corridors, the footsteps of a late-returning guest could occasionally be heard; rays of light came and went, slipping in through the cracks in the doors of those luxurious cells, horrible in their vulgar uniformity.

A few clocks in the town sang out the hour; solemn tollings preceded by the light infantry, less lugubrious and less significant, of the quarter hours. In the hotel, too, there was a clock that repeated the same warning note.

Another half hour passed, again noted by all the clocks.

'I know, I know,' thought room 36, tucked up beneath his sheets now; and he imagined that the solemnly tolling hour was like the signature on the IOUs being presented to life by life's creditor, death. No more guests would arrive now. Soon everyone should be asleep. There were no more witnesses; the skulking beast would not come out now and would be alone with its prey.

And, as if beneath the vault of a crypt, room 36 began to echo to a rapid, energetic cough, which carried within itself a hoarse wail of protest.

'The clock of death,' thought the victim, that is, room 36, a man in his thirties, familiar with despair, alone in the world, with, as sole companion, the memories of his childhood home, lost in a distant past of misfortunes and mistakes, and with a death sentence pinned to his chest like an address label on a parcel on a train.

And, like a lost parcel, he travelled around, from town to town, in search of healthy air for his ailing chest; from inn to inn, like a pilgrim of the grave, and every hotel he chanced upon now looked to him more and more like a hospital. His was a terribly sad life, and yet no one pitied him. He did not even find sympathy in the serialized stories in the newspapers. The Romanticism that had shown some compassion for the consumptive was long gone. The world had no time now for mawkish sentimentality, or perhaps those feelings had moved elsewhere. The people that room 36 envied and rather resented were the proletariat, who were now the object of everyone's pity. 'The poor worker, the poor worker!' everyone said, and no one gave a thought for the 'poor' consumptive, the poor condemned man ignored now by the newspapers. If someone's death was of no importance to the news agencies, then why should the world care?

And he coughed and coughed in the grim silence of the sleeping hotel, as indifferent as the desert. Suddenly, he thought he heard a kind of distant, tenuous echo of his cough . . . An echo . . . in a minor key. It was coming from room 32. There was no one staying in room 34 that night. It was an empty grave.

Yes, the woman in room 32 was coughing, but her cough was, how can I put it, gentler, more poetic, more resigned. Room 36's cough protested and sometimes roared. Room 32's cough was almost like the response in a prayer, a miserere; it was a shy, discreet complaint, a cough that hoped not to disturb anyone. To be honest, room 36 had not yet learned how to cough, just as most men suffer and die without ever learning how to suffer and die. Room 32 coughed with a degree of skill, with a wise, ancient, long-suffering pain usually to be found in women.

Room 36 began to notice that her cough accompanied him like a sister watching over him; she seemed to cough in order to keep him company.

Gradually, half-asleep, half-awake and slightly feverish, room 36 began to transform room 32's cough into a voice, into music, and he seemed to understand what she was saying, just as one can vaguely understand what music is saying.

The woman in room 32 was twenty-five and a foreigner; she had come to Spain out of hunger, to work as a governess to the nobility. Illness had driven her from that particular haven; they had given her enough money to be able to wander alone through the world, from hotel to hotel, but they had taken her pupils from her. *Of course.* They feared contagion. She didn't complain. Initially, she thought of returning to her own country. But what was the point? No one was waiting for her there; besides, the climate in Spain was – quite unwittingly – more benign. This place seemed very cold to her, though, the blue sky sad, a desert. She had travelled north, where the landscape was more like home. All she did now was move from town to town and cough. She was still clinging to the mad hope that she might find some town or village whose inhabitants had a fondness for dying strangers.

Room 36's cough filled her with pity and aroused her sympathy. She realized at once that he, too, was a tragic case. 'We're singing a duet,' she thought, and even felt slightly ashamed, as if this thought were indiscreet on her part, like a night-time assignation. She coughed because she couldn't help it, but she had tried to suppress that first bout of coughing.

Room 32 was also drifting off into a slightly feverish half-sleep, verging on delirium. She, too, 'transported' room 36's cough into the land of dreams, where all noises have words. Her own cough seemed less painful if she 'leaned' on that manly cough, which protected her from the darkness, the loneliness and the silence. 'This must be what it's like for souls in purgatory.' By an association of ideas, natural in a governess, she went from purgatory to the inferno, Dante's inferno, and saw Paolo and Francesca embracing in the air, borne along by the infernal hurricane.

The idea of the couple, of love, of the duet arose not in room 36, but in room 32.

Fever prompted in the governess a certain erotic mysticism. Erotic? No, that's not the right word. Eros represented healthy, pagan love, and there was nothing like that here. Nevertheless, it was still love, the tranquil love of an old married couple, finding companionship in grief and in the solitude of the world. So what room 32's cough was saying to room 36 was not so very far from what room 36, in his delirium, had sensed:

'Are you young? So am I. Are you alone in the world? So am I. Are you horrified by the idea of dying alone? So am I. If only we could meet! If only we could love each other! I could be your shelter, your consolation. Can't you sense in the way I cough that I am kind, delicate, discreet, home-loving, that I would make of our precarious lives a soft, warm, feathered nest, so that we could approach death together while thinking of something else – affection. How alone you are! What good care I would take of you! How you would protect me! We are two stones dropping into the abyss and which, knocking together as they fall, say nothing, see nothing, don't even pity each other . . . Why must it be like that? Why shouldn't we get up now and unite our twin griefs and weep together? Perhaps out of the union of two griefs there might spring a smile. My soul is crying out for that, yours too. And yet, as you see, you don't move, nor do I.'

And the ailing woman in room 32 could hear in room 36's cough something very similar to what room 36 was wanting and thinking:

'Yes, I'll go over there. It falls to me, after all. I may be ill, but I'm a young man, a gentleman. I know my duty. I'm going over there. You'll see, despite our tears and the prospect of death, how delightful it will be, the love you know only from books and your imagination. I'm going, yes, I'm going . . . if only my cough will let me, oh, this wretched cough! Help me, protect me, console me! Your hand on my breast, your voice in my ear, your eyes gazing into mine . . .'

Daybreak. These days, not even consumptives are consistent in their romantic longings. Room 36 woke up, having forgotten all about his dream and about the duet.

Room 32 had not perhaps forgotten, but what could she do? She might be sentimental, but she was neither mad nor a fool. She did not for one moment think of making her night-time illusion – the vague consolation of that accompanying cough – a reality. She had offered herself up in good faith, and even when awake, in the harsh light of day, she still approved of her intention; she would have devoted the rest, the miserable rest of her life to tend to that man's cough. Who could he be? What would he be like? Bah! Probably the same as all those other Russian princes from the land of daydreams! What would be the point of trying to meet him?

Night fell again. Room 32 heard no one cough. She could tell from various sad signs that no one was staying in room 36. It was as empty as room 34.

And so it was: forgetting that to change position is merely to change discomforts, the consumptive in room 36 had fled that particular hotel, where he had suffered so gravely, just as he had in all the others. A few days later, he left the town too. He didn't stop travelling until Panticosa, where he encountered his final hotel. It's not known if he ever recalled that duet for two coughs.

The woman lived on a little longer, two or three years. She died in a hospital, which she preferred to the hotel; she died among the Sisters of Charity, who were of some consolation when the fateful hour came. Psychology makes us wonder if, one night, unable to sleep, she ever thought wistfully of that duet for two coughs, but she wouldn't have done so in those final solemn moments. Or perhaps she would.

MIGUEL DE UNAMUNO

The Likeness

Everyone either avoided all contact with Celestino the Fool or else treated him, at most, as a plaything with which to amuse themselves, and for those reasons the poor fellow tended to avoid other people and to go for solitary walks in the empty countryside, immersed in his surroundings, innocently observing nature's pageant. Celestino the Fool lived very much *inside* the world as if inside a womb, interweaving reality with fresh, child-like dreams, which were quite as real to him as reality, in a kind of permanent state of childhood, as attached to that living kaleidoscope as the foetus is to the placenta, and, like the foetus, utterly unaware of his own existence. His soul simply absorbed everything; everything was merely a part of his consciousness. He would walk through the empty poplar groves by the river, chuckling at the ducks splashing about in the water, at the brief flights of birds and the spiralling flutterings of pairs of butterflies. One of his favourite tricks was to turn a beetle over onto its back on the ground and watch its legs waggling in the air.

Miguel de Unamuno (1864–1936) was essentially a philosopher, but he also wrote novels, short stories, poetry and plays. He wrestled with the need to reconcile Reason and Faith, most notably in *The Tragic Sense of Life*, a concern that is present in everything he wrote, for example in the novels (for which he invented the term *nivola*) *Abel Sánchez*, *Niebla* and *San Manuel Bueno, Mártir*. He was a very complicated man. Although himself a Basque, he spoke out against the preservation of the Basque language; although an outspoken critic of the monarchy and, subsequently, of the dictatorship of Primo de Rivera, and although he celebrated the Second Republic that followed the overthrow of Primo de Rivera, he later supported the Nationalist uprising led by Franco, which he felt would protect Spanish values. However, repelled by the brutality of the Nationalist troops, he quickly turned against them and, after a very public dispute with General Millán-Astray, in which Unamuno denounced the Nationalists' policies, he was put under house arrest and died soon afterwards.

The only thing that troubled him was the presence of the enemy – mankind. Whenever a grown man approached him, Celestino would eye him warily and smile at him with a smile that meant: 'Don't hurt me, I'm harmless.' And if that man came closer, Celestino would immediately look away from those indifferent, loveless eyes, wishing he could shrink to the size of an ant. If an acquaintance greeted him with a 'Hi there, Celestino', he would meekly bow his head, expecting the inevitable clip round the ear. And if he caught sight of some boys in the distance, he would immediately quicken his step, for he had an absolute horror of boys and with good reason. They were the worst of the worst.

One morning, though, Celestino encountered another solitary walker, and when they passed, and Celestino proffered his usual wary smile, he saw in the other fellow's face a reflection of his own smile, a look of recognition. And, when he turned round, he saw that the other fellow had turned round too, and they again smiled at each other, at the likeness. All that day, Celestino felt happier than usual, his soul full of an unaccustomed warmth, a warmth created by the mere fact that the world had reflected his own simple self back at him in the form of a human face.

The following morning, they met again just as a noisy sparrow alighted, chattering, in a nearby willow tree. Celestino pointed this out to the other man and said, laughing:

'Look at that bird! It's a sparrow!'

'Yes, you're right, it's a sparrow,' said the other, laughing out loud.

Excited, they both laughed long and hard, first at the bird, which joined in with its chirruping, and then simply because they were laughing. And so it was that those two simpletons became friends, in the open air and beneath God's sky.

'What's your name?'

'Pepe.'

'I'm Celestino.'

'Celestino . . . Celestino . . .' cried Pepe, again bursting out laughing. 'Celestino the Fool . . . Celestino the Fool . . .'

'And you're Pepe the Fool,' retorted Celestino rather huffily.

'That's right, Pepe the Fool and Celestino the Fool!'

And the two fools roared with laughter at their own foolishness, gulping down great mouthfuls of air as they did so, and their laughter was lost in the wood, becoming one with the countryside's many other voices.

From that first hilarious encounter onwards, they would meet each day to go for a walk together, to exchange impressions, pointing out to each other whatever God set before them, living *inside* the world, lending each other warmth and encouragement like twins sharing the same womb.

'It's hot today.'

'Yes, you're right, it is hot today.'

'It's usually hot at this time of year.'

'That's true, it is usually hot at this time of year . . . and in winter, it's cold.'

And so they went on, feeling how very alike they were and enjoying their constant discoveries of things that we think we have already discovered because we've crystallized them into abstract concepts and placed them in logical pigeonholes. For them there was always something new under the sun, every impression was new, and the world was a thing in a state of perpetual creation and devoid of even a hint of deceit. Pepe nearly exploded with joy when he first saw a beetle with its legs in the air! Indeed, so excited was he that he picked up a pebble to express his excitement by squashing the poor creature, but Celestino stopped him, saying:

'No, no, it's not a bad beetle . . .'

Pepe's simplicity was not like that of his new friend, congenital and unchanging, but, rather, extraneous and progressive, owing to a softening of the brain tissue. Celestino realized this, although without quite knowing that he did; he vaguely grasped what it was that set them apart despite their similarities, and out of that unconscious realization, buried in the dark depths of his virgin soul, sprang a feeling of love for poor Pepe, a love that was, at once, that of a brother, a father and a mother. When his friend occasionally fell asleep on the river bank, Celestino would sit beside him, shooing away the flies and the bumblebees, throwing stones into the pools to silence the frogs, making sure that the ants didn't run across his sleeping friend's face, and keeping a look-out for any approaching men. And, if he ever caught sight of any boys, his heart would start to race and he would move closer to his friend and stuff his own pockets with stones, just in case. When a smile flickered over the sleeper's face, Celestino would smile too, imagining the world in which his friend lay immersed.

In the streets, the boys would run after them shouting:

> *One fool plus another fool*
> *Make two fools twice over!*

When, one day, a young scamp actually hit Pepe, a hitherto dormant instinct awoke in Celestino and he ran after the boy, raining down on him slaps and smacks. Simultaneously angered and elated by the fool's unexpected rebellion, the gang of hoodlums then set upon the pair, and, while shielding his friend, Celestino heroically fended them off with kicks and shoves until the constable arrived, putting the gang of boys to flight. And yet it was Celestino who was given a telling-off . . . so, the constable, too, was just like other men!

As Pepe's imbecile condition progressed, his senses became so dulled that all he could do was repeat drowsily whatever his friend showed him, as if he were the interpreter of the passing cosmorama of the world.

Then, one day, Pepe did not appear, and Celestino searched for him everywhere, eyeing with loathing any gangs of boys and smiling even more broadly at any men he encountered. Eventually, he learned that Pepe had died, just like a little bird, and, although Celestino didn't quite understand what death meant, he felt something like a spiritual hunger. Picking up a stone and putting it in his pocket, he went to the church where he used to be taken to attend mass; there he kneeled down before one of the Christ figures, then sat back on his heels and, after quickly crossing himself several times, he repeated over and over:

'Who killed him? Tell me who killed him . . .'

And, with his gaze still fixed on the Christ figure, he remembered hearing in a sermon once that the crucified Christ used to bring the dead back to life. He cried out:

'Bring him back! Bring him back!'

When he left the church, a gang of boys surrounded him: one of them tugged at his jacket, another knocked off his hat, another boy spat at him and they all kept chanting: 'Where's the other fool? Where's the other fool?' Celestino withdrew into himself, and his courage – the child of his love for Pepe – vanished completely. Murmuring 'Wretches, devils, swine, you're the ones who killed him . . . you swine', he dropped the stone he'd been carrying and hurried off to the safety of his own house.

When he resumed his solitary walks in the woods by the river, the waves of new impressions – which he received like spiritual blood from the placenta of the open countryside – clustered around the vague, shadowy image of his sleeping friend's smiling face and took on new life. Thus he humanized nature, anthropomorphizing it in his own fashion, simply and unconsciously; he poured into those new impressions, like the very substance of life itself, all the paternal–maternal tenderness that had sprung up in him through his contact with Pepe, his fellow fool, and, without fully understanding quite what was happening, he caught a vague glimpse of God smiling down from heaven with a smile made in the likeness of a human smile.

RAMÓN DEL VALLE-INCLÁN

The Poor Wee Child

'Thus was my ill-fated adventure . . .'
Macías*

The oldest old lady in the village is walking hand-in-hand with her grandson along a bleak, deserted path flanked by green verges that seem to stand frozen in the dawn light. She is bent and breathless, giving advice to the boy, who is silently weeping.

'Now that you'll be earning your living, you must be humble, that's God's law.'

'Yes, Señora.'

'You must pray for those who help you and for the souls of those you have lost.'

'Yes, Señora.'

'If you ever go to the fiesta of San Gundián and have enough money, you must buy yourself a reed cape, because it's always raining.'

'Yes, Señora.'

And on they trudge, grandmother and grandson, on and on and on . . .

The very emptiness of the path makes those monotonous childish responses even sadder, as if he were taking a vow of humility, resignation and poverty when his life is only just beginning. The old lady plods

---

Ramón del Valle-Inclán (1866–1936) was born in Galicia, studied in Madrid, where he also worked as a journalist, and travelled widely in Latin America, particularly Mexico. He was a novelist, playwright and poet and one of the great literary figures of his day. During the First World War, he worked as a war correspondent, visiting the front on several occasions. He wrote novels on a variety of subjects – the Carlist wars, an imaginary Latin American dictator, the corrupt court of Isabel II – but is perhaps best known for his remarkable plays, particularly *Divinas Palabras* and *Luces de Bohemia*, which revolutionized Spanish theatre and have been staged several times in English. This story reflects both the dire poverty and the fatalism of many people in Galicia.

* A Galician troubadour and one of the last of Galicia's medieval poets.

painfully along in her wooden clogs, which clack-clack on the stones in the road, and she sighs beneath the apron that she's wearing tied not about her waist but about her head. Her grandson is crying and shivering with cold in his ragged clothes. He's a fair-skinned child, his cheeks scorched by the sun; his lank, pale hair, like corn silk, has been brutally shorn, like that of a serf from another age.

In the pallid dawn sky a few faint stars still shine. A fox fleeing the village runs across the path. The sound of dogs barking and cockerels crowing can be heard in the distance. Slowly the sun is beginning to gild the tops of the hills; the grass glitters with dew, new fledglings flutter timidly about in the branches, having left the nest for the first time; the streams laugh, the groves of trees murmur, and that sad, deserted path flanked by green verges stirs into rustic life. Flocks of sheep go clambering up the sides of the hills, women sing on their way back from the fountain. An old villager with a shock of white hair urges on his pair of oxen when they stop to nibble at the hedges; he's an old patriarch with a very carrying voice.

'Are you going to the Barbanzón market?'

'No, we're going to San Amedio, looking for a master for the boy.'

'How old is he?'

'Old enough to earn his own living. He turned nine in July.'

And on they trudge, grandmother and grandson, on and on and on . . .

Beneath the pleasant sun shining down on the hills, other villagers come and go. A lively, weather-beaten horse-dealer comes trotting past accompanied by the cheerful clinking of spurs and horseshoes; old peasant women from Cela and Lestrove are heading for the market carrying chickens, flax and rye. Down below, in the hollow, a boy is energetically shooing away the goats cavorting about on the rocks. Grandmother and grandson stand aside to let the archdeacon from Lestrove pass on his way to preach at a village feast day.

'May God grant us all a good day, sir!'

The archdeacon reins in his mare, which had been trotting along at a gentle, pedantic pace.

'Are you going to the market?'

'What would poor people like us do at the market? No, we're going to San Amedio to find a master for the boy.'

'Does he already know his catechism?'

'He does, sir. Being poor doesn't mean you can't be a Christian.'

And on they trudge, grandmother and grandson, on and on and on . . .

In the misty blue distance they can make out the cypresses growing around the chapel in San Amedio, dark and pensive, their shrivelled tops anointed by the golden morning light. In the village, all the doors stand wide open, and the hesitant white smoke rising up from the chimneys vanishes in the light, like a peace greeting. Grandmother and grandson reach the entrance to the chapel. A blind man is sitting by the door begging for alms and gazing up at the sky with eyes that resemble two pieces of whitish agate.

'May the blessèd St Lucía preserve your dear eyes and give you health enough to earn your daily bread! May God bring you money both to give and to keep! Good health and good luck in the world! Such generous souls can't possibly pass by without giving a poor man some charity!'

And the blind man holds out a dry, withered palm. Still holding her grandson by the hand, the old woman goes over to the man and murmurs sadly:

'We are poor too, brother. I was told you were looking for a servant.'

'They were quite right. The one I had before got his head cracked open at the fiesta in Santa Baya de Cela. He's not been right since.'

'I've brought you my grandson.'

'Good.'

The blind man reaches out, feeling the air with his hands.

'Come here, boy.'

The old woman gives the boy a gentle shove, and the boy trembles like a meek, cowardly sheep before that surly old man wrapped in a tattered soldier's cape. The withered, importunate hand rests on the boy's shoulders, then feels down his back and up and down his legs.

'Are you sure you won't get tired having to carry bags on your back?'

'No, sir, I'm used to it.'

'To fill them up you'll have to knock on many doors. Do you know the streets of the villages well?'

'When I don't know, I'll ask.'

'And at fiestas, when I sing a song, you have to join in with the chorus. Can you do that?'

'I can learn, sir.'

'Being servant to a blind man is a very desirable job.'

'Yes, sir.'

'Well, now that you're here, let's go up to the manor house in Cela. The folk are more charitable up there. We won't get anything in this wretched place.'

The blind man struggles awkwardly to his feet and rests his hand on the boy's shoulder, while the boy gazes sadly out at the long road ahead, at the lush, green fields smiling in the morning peace, the scattered village houses, the distant mills, the vine trellises obscuring the front doors, and the blue mountains with their snow-capped peaks. By the roadside, a boy is bent over scything grass, while a cow with quivering pink udders grazes quietly nearby, dragging its halter behind it.

The blind man and the boy move slowly off, and the grandmother dabs at her tears and murmurs to herself:

'Poor wee child! Nine years old and already earning his daily bread, thank God!'

PÍO BAROJA

The Unknown

Husband and wife settled into the carriage. After stowing away their luggage, he donned a light grey overcoat, pulled on a cap, lit a cigarette and sat staring indifferently up at the ceiling, while she stood gazing out of the window at the autumn dusk.

From the carriage she could see the small coastal town, with its dark houses huddled together against the wind from the sea. The sun was gradually withdrawing its light, which glinted metallically on windows, scaled rooftops blackened by the damp air, then rose up the dark church tower until it lit only the metal cross on the belfry, which stood out triumphant and red against the grey of twilight.

'Well, we certainly had quite a wait,' he said, blowing out a cloud of smoke. He spoke in the mannered tones of a Madrid dandy.

She spun round to look at her husband, briefly studied him and his pale, beringed, manicured hands, then turned back to the window.

The station bell rang, giving the signal to depart, and slowly the train began to move with the sigh made by chains and iron forced out of their inertia; the wheels made an infernal racket, clattering clumsily over the turntables outside the station; the engine gave a wild, energetic whistle;

Pío Baroja (1872–1956) was born in San Sebastián, but his family moved to Madrid when he was only seven. Although he went on to study medicine, he practised only briefly in a small town in the Basque Country, instead, for a time, taking over the running of a bakery in Madrid inherited from an aunt. It was in Madrid that he began to write for newspapers and journals, and, in 1900, he published his first book, *Vidas sombrías*, a collection of short stories, whose protagonists were fishermen, bakers, vagabonds, prostitutes and, as in the story included here, the bourgeoisie. He read voluminously and was particularly taken with Nietzsche and Schopenhauer, whose pessimism chimed with his own. He was greatly admired by John Dos Passos and by Hemingway.

then the motion of the train grew more regular, and there began the parade of villages, orchards, cement factories, windmills and then, with vertiginous speed, hills and trees, linesman's huts, empty roads and hamlets barely visible in the gloom of dusk.

As night came on, the landscape changed; the train stopped occasionally at isolated wayside stations surrounded by threshing floors on which stood piles of burning stubble.

Inside the carriage, husband and wife were still alone; no other traveller had joined them; he had closed his eyes and was dozing. She would have liked to do the same, but her brain seemed to insist on summoning up troubling memories that would not let her sleep.

And what memories they were! All of them so cold and charmless.

Of the three months spent in that seaside town, all that remained were stark visual images, but nothing intense, nothing heartfelt.

She could see the town on a summer's night, beside the broad river estuary, its waters flowing indolently along through green maize fields; she saw the empty beach, washed by the sea's languid waves; she recalled August sunsets, with the sky full of red clouds and the sea stained scarlet; she recalled the steep hills thick with yellow-leaved trees, and, in her imagination, she saw joyful dawns, blue skies, mists rising up from the salt marshes before dispersing, towns with elegant towers, bridges reflected in rivers, huts, abandoned houses, cemeteries hidden in the folds of hills.

And in her head she could hear the sound of drumming, the sad voices of the peasants driving their cattle, the solemn lowing of oxen, the creaking of carts, and the slow, sad tolling of the bells for the Angelus.

And along with those memories came other images from the land of dreams, echoes from childhood, thoughts that rose up from her unconscious, the shadows formed in her mind by lost illusions and dead enthusiasms.

Her memories glowed inside her, like the stars illuminating the fields with their pale light, cold images imprinted on her retina, but leaving no trace on her soul.

Only one truly touching memory stepped down from her brain to her heart. It was the night she had crossed from one side of the river to the other in a boat, without her husband. Two tall, strong young sailors, with the typically stony faces of Basque men, were rowing. To keep time, they sang a strange, monotonous but terribly poignant song. When she heard it, her heart was filled with a strange, unwonted languor, and she asked them to sing more loudly and to head further out to sea.

The two men rowed hard away from the land and continued to sing those serene Basque folk songs that cast their mournful notes upon the splendid evening light. The water trembled and shimmered blood-red, tinged by the dying sun, while the restful sounds dropped into the silence of the tranquil sea and the rise and fall of the waves.

And when she compared that memory with others from her life full of otherwise all too predictable sensations, when she thought of the dull future awaiting her, she felt an intense desire to flee the monotony of her existence, to leave the train at one of those country stations and set off in search of the unknown.

She made a spur-of-the-moment decision and waited for the train to stop. She saw a station approaching as if emerging new-born out of the darkness, then, stopping before her, its empty platform lit by a lantern.

She lowered the window and reached for the handle.

As she leaned out to open the door, a shiver ran down her spine. There was the darkness, watching and waiting. She drew back. And suddenly, seamlessly, the night air restored her to reality, and all her dreams, memories, longings vanished.

She heard the signal to leave, and the train resumed its mad race through the dark countryside full of shadows, and great sparks from the engine flew past the windows like brilliant eyes suspended in mid-air . . .

AZORÍN

The Reverse Side of the Tapestry

Where will the poet Félix Vargas begin his story? Félix needs to write a story; he's lying on his bed having just returned from a long morning walk; from his supine position, he can see the overcast sky, a pale ash grey. If he sits up a little, he can make out the sea on the far horizon: more grey, a vast sheet the colour of tarnished silver. Félix Vargas isn't thinking about anything; well, he does occasionally think about something, but everything seems distant, remote, as if in a dream. He is actively trying not to think, and gradually images begin to surface in his brain. Now he can see a small room in Paris, a young man dressed in black: himself. What is Félix Vargas doing there? Where has he been? Where will he go? The poet doesn't know. But is that man the same Félix Vargas who is lying here now, on a bed in the little house in the Errondo-Aundi district of San Sebastián? Can he be both one and many? And when he sheds his fleshly shell, what will become of him? What will happen to his mind, his unique, pure, pristine mind? On this grey day of leaden skies, surrounded as he is by intensely dark green scenery, Félix Vargas feels simultaneously immersed and dispersed in all that matter. Where has he come from, the Félix Vargas living in that small hotel room in Paris?

Azorín (1873–1967) was the pseudonym of José Martínez Ruiz. Born in Alicante, he studied law, but abandoned his studies to become a writer and politician. He was a consummate stylist and published novels and several collections of short stories, as well as literary criticism and essays. The protagonist of this story, Félix Vargas, a character who also turns up in the eponymous 1928 novel, is Martínez Ruiz's alter ego. At the outset of the Spanish Civil War, Azorín fled to Paris, returning to Spain in 1939, where he found himself in 'inner exile', along with other intellectuals who had not overtly supported the Nationalists. Accepting Franco's regime was the price he had to pay in order to be allowed back, and his attitude to that regime remained ambivalent.

What will happen to him the next moment, the next day, the next month? Will his fate be different from that of this real, authentic Félix Vargas currently imagining the future of that other Félix Vargas? Suddenly, in the small room in Paris, a mysterious, enigmatic character appears beside the poet – the poet Félix Vargas is imagining and who has not yet noticed this new arrival. Equally suddenly, this unreal character places one hand on Félix's shoulder and says with a smile: 'At this very moment, a clown in Albacete in Spain, a long, long way from here, has decided to go to work in the circus next Sunday; his fever has gone and he can return to his chosen profession. His reappearance next Sunday will cost you your life.' The imaginary Félix Vargas shudders. Does he shudder or does he smile incredulously? Yes, perhaps he smiles, but then he pauses to think. His life depends on that clown in Albacete going to work; if the clown goes to work on Sunday, he, Félix, will die. How strange. How odd. No, not odd at all. Does anyone know what fate has in store for them? Do we know what is being woven for us – as Saavedra Fajardo put it – 'on eternity's looms'? If only we could see the reverse side of the tapestry, the tapestry of things, *our* tapestry! And here, in San Sebastián, in the little white house with green shutters high up on a hill in Errondo-Aundi, the real Félix Vargas, the one imagining the other Félix's fate, really does shudder. The sky is grey and the silence profound. An illustrated magazine lies open on the table, and, were the poet to sit up, he would see again, for the hundredth time, two photographs: one shows a collision between a racing car and a heavy truck on the Alcázar de San Juan–Albacete road; the other shows a pretty young woman, and the caption below reads: 'La Mancheguita – The Girl from La Mancha – fresh from her triumph in Paris.' Over the last two days, in the café, in the house, in the street, Félix Vargas has seen those same two photographs over and over, both in that magazine and in others too. In Paris, in that small hotel room, the mysterious character has placed one hand on the imaginary Félix's shoulder, has spoken and disappeared. And far off in southern Spain, in Albacete, we suddenly see a car repair shop. Everything is still a little vague, blurred and confused; the poet, the real one doing the imagining, doesn't yet know what order these new images should be in. Yes, a car repair shop. And a man needing one of the headlights on his truck fixed. Will that work? Will that be a way of reaching a conclusion? Yes, yes, onwards: the owner of the truck needs a headlight mending; he's about to go on a journey; he's about to leave Albacete to drive to Alcázar de San Juan . . . And meanwhile, what is happening in that small hotel room in Paris? What is the poet doing? The character that Félix Vargas has dreamed up is definitely a poet, that much is certain; he will thus be surrounded by an air of delicacy and refinement, in marked contrast to the terrible fate awaiting him. The real Félix Vargas half sits up in bed; he scrutinizes the grey sky, then the sea, then the whole city; for a moment he notices how the sea – which serves as a backdrop – can be seen through the ironwork on the bell tower of the Church of the Good Shepherd. He's not thinking anything now; he's left the story for another day. He tries to imagine other things, but his mind – his subconscious – continues to work away; the poet knows how fruitful idleness can be; his best work, his most beautiful verses, his most original stories all depend on such periods of idleness; if Félix didn't have such moments, he wouldn't be able to write, he would never have any ideas; were he in a perpetual state of agitation and busyness, his mind would be utterly sterile.

Into his head comes the image of a young mechanic who works in the repair shop; the owner of the truck and the young man agree that the headlight will be repaired in the next few days. Meanwhile, the poet in Paris has left the big city. All of this – Félix's life and what happens in the repair shop in Albacete – should happen simultaneously. Slowly, painstakingly, a tapestry is taking shape on eternity's looms: the tapestry of Félix Vargas's life. We don't know what figures or designs will appear there; if we were to look at it from behind, we would be able to make out something, but we can't do that. Sometimes in life, it seems that a presentiment, a brilliant flash of intuition, allows us a glimpse of the reverse side of the tapestry; the door to the mystery opens just a crack and, if we peer through that crack, we can vaguely see what is being woven in the workshop; but such visions are the exception; we walk through the world, past all kinds of things, with no inkling of how those things might decide, or already are deciding, our future, our life.

Félix Vargas again scrutinizes the sky; the sky of Vitoria, of Álava, is also grey like this, Álava being a transitional land between the bare, flat landscape of Castile and the lush, romantic Basque Country. During the days before the headlight is mended, the imagined character, the other poet, could go to Vitoria; yes, before arriving in Madrid, the fictitious poet stops in Vitoria. In Albacete, the young man charged with repairing the headlight forgets to do it, and the owner of the truck has to call in at the workshop again. On the very day he does so, the imaginary Félix leaves Vitoria and travels to Burgos; as the poet enters his hotel room in Burgos, the repair man is promising the owner of the truck that he'll have the headlight repaired and ready for next Monday; in order to do this – it shouldn't take long – he'll have to work on Sunday. There are three stories going on at this point, at least for anyone with the necessary sorcerer's eyes to see them. On the one hand, the real poet, lying on his bed, is contemplating the sky and thinking about his literary creation; on the other, the two fictitious characters, the other Félix and the workman in Albacete, are each going about their business synchronically, like the mechanism of a watch; and finally, in the realms of eternity, the finest, slenderest and most ethereal of hands are silently weaving a tapestry. The tapestry the real Félix is currently imagining? No, not just that one. The real one too, the tapestry of the poet imagining a fictitious tapestry and not giving a thought to his own.

On Sunday morning, Mr Brown the clown – the clown who is part of the circus performing in Albacete – wakes up free of fever; he rises from his bed and calls out to his landlady, Doña María. At the very moment Mr Brown is telling Doña María that he intends returning to work that evening, the poet arrives by car in Madrid. His fate has been decided: because Mr Brown is going to work that evening, the poet is going to die. The mechanic will not finish mending the headlight, instead he'll leave the workshop early to go to the circus and see that very popular clown, Mr Brown. However, the owner of the truck must, without fail, set off that same night. The truck, laden with large casks of wine, will leave Albacete in the dark, heading for Alcázar de San Juan. The poet Félix Vargas, the fictitious one, has already arrived in Madrid; when the truck is leaving Albacete, he is in a café with his friends. One of them suggests they drive to Albacete together, and, moments later, they race off in a magnificent car, while the truck sets off with only one working headlight . . .

The poet pauses; yes, this string of images is just what he needs; now all the settings and circumstances are there, perfectly aligned so that disaster can strike. A stream of light, the light from the car's powerful headlights, speeds down the road in the darkness. Suddenly, the driver sees a single headlight up ahead, that of the truck; the car is driving on the right; the driver imagines that the one headlight on the truck is also on the right-hand side of the vehicle. Then, suddenly, there is a terrible, formidable crash. A pile of tangled metal, shards of glass, blood, faint groans, a death rattle.

The poet, the real one, turns his thoughts to other things. The story is basically there, the details will come later. Let's give the imagination a rest and do something else. Félix Vargas walks down from Errondo-Aundi into San Sebastián, in search of his friend Pedro Magán; they're supposed to be going for a drive in Pedro's brand-new car. The poet strolls along, feeling rather pleased with himself. The morning has definitely not been wasted; in leisurely fashion, almost unconsciously, he's polishing the imagined story; he adds a detail here, makes a change there. He has reached the town. He walks past a café. He stops for a moment on the Paseo de los Fueros, and there looks back at his little white house with the green shutters. But who is in that café?

'Félix! Félix!'

Who's calling him? Who do you think? La Mancheguita, Nati Durán herself; there she is with her warm smile, her green eyes, her cool, moist, red lips.

'Nati! What are you doing here?'

'I've just got back from Paris.'

'What a delightful coincidence!'

'Come in and sit down.'

'I can't. I'm meeting a friend.'

'What do you mean, you can't? Oh, you, always so immersed in your thoughts! Come on. Don't you love me any more?'

'Of course I love you. And how pretty you're looking, Nati!'

'As I always do, you mean.'

(In eternity, the slender, delicate, mysterious hands are weaving Félix Vargas's tapestry. And they are weaving now with great excitement! Since the angels are the friends of poets, one can understand the excitement of those angelic weavers.)

'Come on, Félix, come and have lunch with me. We haven't seen each other for ages . . .'

'You're right, Nati, but I certainly hadn't forgotten you.'

'Why don't we have lunch together today? I'm leaving tonight . . .'

'Tonight?'

'Yes, I'm off to Buenos Aires.'

'Buenos Aires? Well, in that case, yes, let's have lunch together. Who knows when we'll meet again!'

'That's my poet! I'll draw up a menu. Can you wait?'

'What better menu can there be than seeing you, Nati! I've often thought of you in the last few days.'

'Really? Tell me about it . . .'

Two hours later, news of Pedro Magán's death reaches San Sebastián; the car he was driving plunged off a precipice and was smashed to smithereens.

(In eternity, the angelic weavers – such slender, delicate hands! – smiled sweetly as they wove those last few threads into the poet's tapestry.)

EDUARDO BLANCO AMOR

The Biobardos

We went back to Auria when I was eleven, after my father had passed away, although I was just a baby when we left there in the first place, because I wasn't actually born in Auria, but in Ponte Barxa, right on the frontier with Portugal, where my dad was working as a border guard and did right up until he died; my sister Alexandrina and my brother Alixio, who was the eldest, they were both born in Auria, but she died of small-pox in Calahonda when she was only seven and he ran away with the gypsies – well, we never found out really whether they took him or whether he ran away, but he didn't come back.

Anyway, my mother was left with a widow's pension of about thirty pesetas, barely enough to buy a crust of bread, and she got it into her head that we ought to go back to Auria where her parents had left her a little house with a bit of a garden near Ponte dos Pelamios, and where she could keep chickens and a pig to fatten up and sell, because my mum, you see, never really settled in Madrid or Algeciras or Alcántara (and certainly not in Ceuta, where she cried solidly for a year and a half), as if those

Eduardo Blanco Amor (1897–1979) was born in Ourense. He was a writer and journalist who wrote in both *galego* and Spanish. He began working at *El Diario de Orense* when he was just seventeen and quickly became part of the literary scene, promoting *galego* culture generally. In 1919, he emigrated to Buenos Aires, Argentina, where he worked with other Galician émigrés to foster his mother tongue. He published his first novel, *Os Nonnatos*, in 1927, and continued to publish novels, poems and plays throughout his lifetime. He returned briefly to Spain in 1933, where he became great friends with Federico García Lorca, but left again at the outbreak of the Civil War in 1936. He continued to defend the Republican cause from Buenos Aires, and for the next twenty years wrote exclusively in Spanish, only returning to *galego* in 1956. He went back to Spain in 1965, and, despite government constraints, continued to publish – one long novel and two plays.

other places didn't have chickens and pigs as well, but, as soon as she got some, she stopped grieving for my father and talking about Alixio as if he were still a little baby and she gave all the chickens Christian names and called the pig Algabeño after the matador and the cockerel Canalejas after the prime minister.

According to the other boys in Auria, I talked like someone from Andalusia because I spoke differently from them, and they used to try and get me to talk just so as to make fun of me, well, they pretended they weren't, but I could tell, besides, I didn't talk like an Andalusian, but like someone from Madrid, a way of speaking I picked up later – it wasn't my fault I said things like *'anda la osa, nos ha jodío, vaya leche, oye Ninchi'* ('cor, bloody hell, good grief, oy, mate') – and they nicknamed me 'Ninchi' and started playing tricks on me, teaching me rude words in Galician, and my mum would slap me hard whenever I innocently came home and repeated the words the local lads had taught me, 'Tell your mother to give you some money so that you can buy a nice bit of c*** for your tea.' And they pulled my hair and dug their fists into the small of my back whenever we played leapfrog, and, when we went swimming in the river, they would tie knots in my shirt, then dunk the shirt in the water, and then the only way you could untie the knots was with your teeth.

I knew this would stop eventually, as it had in the other places I'd lived, and I just had to put up with it until I got the hang of things and talked like the boys in Auria did. When I'd been there about four months, one of the boys said:

'Hey, Ninchi, we're beginning to think you're not so bad after all and so we're going to take you fishing for *biobardos*.'

'I don't know how to fish,' I said, even though I did, because my dad used to take me with him to the harbour in Algeciras, but I sensed they were up to something.

'Exactly. Only someone new to the town can catch a *biobardo*.'

'There are other, newer boys.'

'Who?'

'There's Bósimo, the son of the man who sells cheese from Villalón, he arrived after me.'

'It can't be just anyone, even if they're new. If just anyone would do, we'd be rolling in it, because you may not realize it, but people are even madder about *biobardos* than they are about trout or lamprey. With rich people you just have to name your price,' said Pepe O Melondro, who was the leader of the gang, not because he was older but because he had a deep voice, like a man, which is why people also called him The Growler. 'The *biobardos* won't come if you're not new to the town, plus, they only pass twice a year, otherwise we'd all be earning money hand over fist just by calling them. Because you don't catch them with a net or a hook, you see, you have to call them by name and then they come and hop into your bag. If you like, we can take you there, to the special place, because you can't catch them just anywhere on the river, not the really good ones, because the bad ones are no better than ordinary fish.'

'What *are* you talking about?'

'We leave you in the right place, see, and because we can't stand there beside you, us not being newcomers, we keep watch from a distance just so's you won't feel afraid, because some boys get really scared alone there at night.'

'No, I don't want to. Find someone else.'

'There isn't anyone else. Because as well as being new, the name of the boy doing the fishing has to rhyme with the fish. Your name's Leonardo, isn't it?'

'Yes.'

'You see, Leonardo *biobardo*, perfect. How lucky, eh, you being new here *and* being called Leonardo. Now the sack or bag you catch them in has to be made of very clean, white linen burlap, well, if you don't happen to have a linen burlap bag, it still has to be white and very clean.' Melondro was extremely clever, he seemed to know all the words in the world and to have them lined up behind his teeth ready to unleash them at the right moment, almost without taking a breath.

'And it has to be tomorrow without fail while the moon's in our favour, because right now it's the moon of Santiago and the river will be seething with *biobardos*. We'll fill the bag full, you might even need two.'

That night when I went to bed and saw the old moon just brushing the top of Santa Ladaíña hill, it took me a while to get to sleep.

My mother burst out laughing and called me a fool and told me it was just a story made up by the boys in Auria, who were terrible practical jokers the lot of them, and the only reason I didn't realize this was because

I hadn't been brought up there. They'd played the same trick on many boys before and some of them had gone a bit funny afterwards and wouldn't talk to people, as if they weren't quite all there, which is why whenever someone seemed to be in a daze, for whatever reason, people used to say that he was 'thinking about the *biobardos*'. Still, she let me have the bag where she'd kept the beans given to us by our relatives from Vilar das Tres. It was high summer then and my mother used to sit up all night, sewing cotton trousers for Demetrio, who kept a clothes shop in the Ferrería, and, since the attic room where we slept was crawling with bedbugs, in the hot weather, my mother didn't mind whether I came back early or late.

They were waiting for me by the tollbooth on Ponte Vella just before midnight, and we walked down to the river in silence. The river was still gathering up slivers of the old moon, the weary moon, like a slice of over-ripe pumpkin dissolving, or like yellow butter, a sticky light slipping over the stubble and melting beneath the pinewoods on the slopes of Santa Ladaíña, glinting ever redder, like the red-hot metal at the Malingre foundry or the metal in Catapiro's forge when it's plunged in the water, not hissing any more, but glowing lazily, quietly, softly; everything was warm and quiet, smelling of summer river, the heavy smell of summer, warm summer pools, over-ripe pumpkin, the dead fermenting summer moon, sliding down to meet the damp clumps of moss, the scraps of dying yellow in the water and the silent summer bubbles, and the frogs, so many that the air was thick with their singing and with the summer smell of mud, the red light in the pools, the gluey slime, the larger stones grey among the smaller, white pebbles, and the great dark hollows of thick summer air and the shadows growing, growing, deepening, spreading so fast you couldn't see the other side of the river any more, as if all the lights had suddenly been turned out – frightening.

They left me alone on top of the Pena dos Afogados, and some crouched down not too far away, behind the pillars of the bridge, while others perched in the big alder trees. Melondro's voice came to me, and it sounded different, scary, as if it were rising up from the depths, even deeper than a grown man's voice, and it reached me on the air above the croaking of the frogs, and I held the bag open with both hands, my hands lit by the ripe yellow light that cut everything in two, and I started repeating what Melondro was telling me to say, while I stared straight ahead, all the while holding the bag.

'It's me, Leonardo.'

'It's me, Leonardo.'

'*Biobardo*.'

'*Biobardo*.'

'Jump into my bag, *biobardo*, it's me Leonardo.'

'Jump into my bag . . .'

A breeze suddenly touched my forehead, nose, lips, and entered my eyes like a crack of light, and something dropped into the bag like a stone.

'It's me, Leonardo.'

'It's me, Leonardo.'

Again that light from the water, trembling and glittering in the air, and immediately the bag grew heavier, and beads of sweat appeared on my brow.

'Jump into the bag.'

'. . . into the bag.' And another, and another, even though Melondro kept moving around behind me and shouting out and I kept repeating what he said.

'*Biobardo*.'

'*Biobardo* . . .'

And the bright light leaping, curving up from the circle of the water, trembling in the air for a moment, like a dart, glittering briefly in the darkness, brushing my forehead, nose and mouth with its breeze as it passed.

'How many have you got?' yelled Melondro, nearer now, his sarcastic voice slightly uncertain. I could hear muffled laughter coming from the trees and someone imitating the hooting of a little owl or the screech of a barn owl.

'I don't know. About a dozen or more . . .' I was still standing beside the rock, in a patch of fading moonlight, holding out the now weighty bag.

'. . . possibly two dozen. It's almost too heavy for me to hold.'

The other boys came out from where they'd been hiding and drew closer, in silence; then they all burst out laughing. Melondro drew a little closer too, but still kept his distance.

'What did you put in the bag?' he asked. 'Because the bag's full,' he said to the others, who immediately stopped laughing and stepped back.

'I didn't put anything in, it filled up on its own, every time we shouted out. They came from the river, leaped through the air and into the bag.'

'I don't believe it! Turn this way. Crikey, the bag's full and sort of glowing.'

I turned to where the voices were coming from, struggling to hold the bag. Melondro took another step forward.

'Bloody hell, it's really full! And he hasn't budged from the spot either. Empty it out onto that stone!' His voice shook and grew still hoarser.

I emptied out the bag and, as soon as I did, all the weight went. Out of it dribbled only a dusty, blue, flickering light like the flame of a damp match.

JOSEP PLA

Counterpoint

Translated from the Catalan by Peter Bush

My eyes suddenly opened and I was shocked to find myself under that
low ceiling in a strange, purple light. It lasted a second: an abrupt jolt of
the train cleared my head and woke me up. The first movement I make
every day when I come back to life is to reach out, grab a cigarette and
smoke it, stretched out on my bed. My arm mechanically dropped out of
the couchette and fell into the void . . . While I retrieved my hand and
put it in the pocket of the jacket hanging over my feet, I thought what a
highly uncomfortable place a sleeper is for a man of sedentary ways.
Reclining in my bunk, taking my first puff, I looked through the crack
between the window and the curtain. Two lights shone outside illumin-
ated by a distant, hazy glow I took to be the moon.

I was trying to find a position for a relaxed smoke when I remembered
that a travelling companion was sleeping in the couchette below. I was
tempted to put out my cigarette. Then I thought it was more than likely
he was sleeping like a log. I peered down. The hazy, purple light in the
compartment was bathing my companion's face in a mauve sheen. He was

Josep Pla (1897–1981) was born in Palafrugell, Girona. He went to Barcelona University, where he
began studying medicine before changing to law. He read voluminously and began working as a
journalist in 1919 and was a correspondent in various European cities. In 1924, he was forced to
leave Spain because of an article he wrote critical of the then dictatorship. He continued to travel
widely and, in 1925, published his first book, *Coses vistes*, a combination of travel book, stories,
literary portraits and personal memories. It was a huge success. After working in Madrid as a
parliamentary correspondent, he left when the Civil War threatened, living in Marseilles, Rome
and Biarritz, before returning to Francoist Spain in 1938. Disillusioned with the post-War situation, he went into a kind of self-exile in Palafrugell, but continued to travel and to write. His
collected works fill forty-seven volumes.

flat out with his two hands behind his neck, and deep in the dark I could see two open, motionless eyes.

'I really must apologize . . .' I said, showing him the match apologetically.

'Please go ahead . . .' he replied, without stirring. And a moment later: 'If you aren't sleepy and don't mind, switch the light off and open the window. Let a little fresh air in. The air gets foul in these sleeping cars . . .'

I drew the curtain. A thick, grey light filled the compartment. I glanced outside: a large, pale moon hung languidly in the sky. The train was travelling over open, level land fronted by an endless expanse of tall, slender poplar trees that had been planted in symmetrical rows. The land seemed as if it were flooded, because you could see the moon spiralling across the water. When the train passed, the poplars turned dizzily around on themselves. The moon's silvery light splashed the trees, and a soft, gauzy, blue mist hovered above the soil deep within the blurred, tremulous avenues. Behind the glass, the front line of trees hopped about in a grotesque syncopated rhythm as the sleeping car jolted and jarred.

Smoking and gazing through the window, I managed to amuse myself until we reached the first station. In the early morning, when a train comes to a halt, a deep silence descends at these small stations. Sleeping passengers snore more loudly; rain clatters on the tin roofs over the platform; if it's not raining, you hear the wind rustling the leaves of the acacias in the station garden. These gardens that you see only briefly are quite pretty in a modest, impish way and are such a consummate resolution of the tiny, spare space that their presence seems ineffable. In the dim light, you sometimes hear a solitary frog croak or a cockerel cry. The footsteps of a man carrying a lantern drown the mournful echoes. A sleepy passenger walks by, out-of-sorts in his crumpled Sunday best. People who travel in their smartest clothes put me on edge and make me feel ill at ease . . .

I was daydreaming about all these trivial things when I heard my travelling companion start to hum a song that was in vogue. Astonished to hear such a thing at that time of day, I turned round; I wasn't quick enough, the song was over. I then heard the sound of words, but the train had set off again and prevented me from catching them.

'What was that?' I asked, looking at him.

'If my memory's not playing tricks on me, last night you said your name was, I'm sorry . . .'

'Joncadella, Joan Joncadella . . .'

'Joncadella . . .' he repeated with a voice I thought betrayed real curiosity, even a touch of emotion. 'Years ago I knew a Joncadella family; he was an architect and, if I remember correctly, he married Maria Camps . . .'

'Maria Camps? That's my mother's name . . .'

'Maria Camps, from Valls. Are you from Valls?'

'That's right, I am . . .'

'How strange!' he exclaimed, sounding even more interested, as he sat on his bunk and peered out, smiling up at me. 'Maria Camps' son! That's a real twist! I knew your mother very well. You must think that's rather odd.'

'I think you must be her age . . .'

'Excuse me, she's quite a lot younger. She must be nearly forty.'

'Right: she's forty.'

'What a surprise! You and I meeting up in this compartment, so far from home . . .'

'Well, you know now – it's a small world.'

'So then, is your mother well?'

'In fine health, thank you.'

Day began to break, the sparks from the engine still flew past the window. The lights on the outskirts of the town flickered deep in a valley surrounded by a mass of trees. The autumnal night had left the earth white and damp. A flock of birds glided over the town. The trees dripped.

When I was most absorbed by that landscape, I suddenly saw my travelling companion peer out from his couchette and stare at me, as if there were something he couldn't understand. I was taken aback and didn't know what to say. After a while, he forced a smile that was far too sweet and said: 'Maria Camps' son! I was on very, very good terms with your mother!'

'On such very good terms?' I asked, surprised he'd been so close.

'Did she never mention me? Allow me to repeat my name: Salvat, engineer, from Barcelona.'

'Salvat . . . Salvat . . . That's right, I *have* heard of you.'

'Often?'

He said this, straightening up, putting one foot on the floor and resting the other on the bed.

'In fact, I remember just one occasion. When I was sifting through some old papers not very long ago, I came across the photo of a young man from the year . . . perhaps it was 1900. I immediately assumed it was a family photo and was delighted by my find. The way people dressed in those days! I'll be frank: I felt that the person in the photo had overdone it. It seemed like the photo of a vain, bumptious fellow. I remember how my mother, who was by my side, took it from my hands. She gazed at it for ages; I couldn't tell you whether she was actually looking at it or day-dreaming. Then she put it in a book and said, "It's Salvat, Salvat the engineer . . ."'

Listening to me with his mouth half open, Senyor Salvat had stood up in the middle of the compartment, in his pyjamas. When I'd finished, he glanced at me with a mocking glint in his eyes, clearly disappointed: 'Is that all? Not much . . .'

'Senyor Salvat, you'll catch cold, believe me! Get back into bed. It's very early.'

'By the way, excuse me, did you say you thought it was the photo of a bumptious man . . . You're young. Aren't *you* a bit on the bumptious side?'

'I couldn't really say . . . Very likely.'

'Of course . . . If you weren't, you'd be a rather strange young man.'

'Senyor Salvat, you're being rather foolish. Get back into bed, you'll catch cold . . .'

He didn't budge and merely responded: 'It's only natural that you wouldn't know . . . But isn't a chance a wonderful thing? I've been turning this nonsense over in my head all night, and in the morning I wake up to this surprise . . .'

'What *do* you mean?'

He hesitated for a moment, then smiled rather perfunctorily.

'I don't know how to put this,' he retorted. 'It's possibly rather delicate. On the other hand, it really couldn't be much simpler . . . I was in a relationship with your mother . . .'

'A relationship . . . what on earth . . . ?'

'I almost married her . . .'

'You did?' I said, my eyes bulging. I struggled to control the feeling of disgust his words provoked. It was precisely that: a surge of revulsion. After that unpleasant remark, I felt as if I were suspended in mid-air, sweating, distraught to find myself face to face with that strange piece of news. Who was this man? Why was he talking to me like that? The matter-of-fact, familiar tone of voice seemed incredibly fake and intolerably hypocritical. I looked hard at him. I thought he was appallingly vulgar, standing in the middle of the compartment, eyes lowered, posing thoughtfully, hands inside his dark pyjama pockets, his thin frame, his messy wisps of grey hair and ravaged yellow features. Nevertheless, I felt that this man might be concealing – as any man foreign to your habits and your usual field of vision might – a mysteriously elusive element, something that could rock images essential to your well-being, the ones you have cherished so dearly – an intolerable shock to your system. As I stared at him, I remembered my mother's face . . . And her face seemed more idealized than ever. I couldn't think why. Stunned by that image, I felt as if my blood and inner humours had been sucked dry, and my body felt as stiff as a board. From then on, outwardly, I acted normally in every way, but I wasn't completely there. I made no effort to behave in that man's presence as anyone else would have done.

'Indeed,' I heard him say quite casually, 'I almost married her. We were in a relationship for three years. We were never engaged but what difference does that make? It was a deep friendship. I even reached the point,' he said smiling bitterly, 'of choosing the witnesses. Forgive me for saying this, but I think it very odd that . . .'

'Perhaps I did hear something once . . . many years ago . . .'

'Who mentioned it?' he rasped.

'Perhaps it was my mother . . . or perhaps it was someone else, I'm not sure.'

'And what did she say?'

'I don't know, I really don't . . . It was so long ago! Besides, Senyor Salvat, you should realize that I'm not really interested, not at all, to be blunt.'

I now struggle to remember how I could have said that courteously, even shyly. He probably noticed and laughed nervously, in a mocking, self-satisfied tone that depressed me even more.

'In any case, it wasn't that long ago!' he exclaimed, clearly appalled.

'Why do you want to make me any older than I am? You youngsters are sometimes far too cocky. Your time will come too ... Time forgives nobody, Senyor Joncadella. Well, as I was saying a moment ago, I knew your mother intimately. She was a splendid young creature; a charming woman. And very pretty ...'

'And still is!' I interrupted him, with a chuckle.

'I don't doubt it. She was very pretty and extremely nice. She was so fond of music. I whiled away many a delightful hour listening to her sing as she played the piano. If I remember correctly, I gave her several albums of songs by the Romantics ... What else could one do in Valls? I expect you'll agree that Valls is a very sleepy little town. At the time, I was assigned to the railways division. My position was hardly onerous. I was acquainted with very few families in the town, three or four at most. We used to meet at the Ricards', a young married couple who were childless. We enjoyed their company. Whatever happened to the Ricards? We met, went for walks, went on excursions, and made music. Everyone admired Maria Camps, and I think all the men were in love with her. She must have been fifteen or sixteen and was always laughing. I shouldn't say this, but she did have a soft spot for me. She made a great impression on me. I think we came to love each other. It was a long-drawn-out process, because we were going out for three or four years. By the end, I think we really were in love ...'

He paused briefly, and began again:

'She and I ...'

'Hey!' I shouted, cutting him dead.

'Go on ...'

'Are you mad or simply acting as if you were? Do you know what you're saying? It's quite intolerable ...'

'Quite intolerable,' he repeated modestly, crestfallen, leaning his head on his shoulder. 'Why do you attribute to my words a meaning they don't have? I think it's what one does: people in love kiss and that's that. What's wrong if they do? Don't you agree? You, too, must have been in love. Would you think it right if I spoke slightingly of *your* loves? So many things happen, so many small, indescribable things when one is in love! Trifles, really. Kisses ... Who would ask for anything more? They're so harmless and diverse! However, there's something else that you will never understand, and that is the way people in love behaved twenty-five years ago. It was – how should I phrase it? – warmer, more tender, more musical . . . Naturally, material matters were as important as they are now. Enough said: I was poor, I had a wage, and was a young engineer just out of college. I had nothing to show that I might be a man of brilliant prospects. There's the rub. She very likely wanted to marry me, but I was so paltry! She married your father, laughing with the same smile on her face as if she'd been marrying me. Odd, isn't it?'

I couldn't think what to say. Then he rattled on: 'I'll never say what I was thinking about last night . . . No, I *will* tell you, because you've been such a surprise. Listen: the Camps family, in Valls, lived in a house on the outskirts with a huge garden fenced off at the rear by a line of cypresses that concealed a low wall with a gate. Beyond that were fields and open country. In the evening, I used to go for a stroll there and watch Maria's lighted window: I could sometimes see the moon behind the cypresses. At that hour of the day, they seemed to be tickling the Earth. A moist glow above a thousand small sounds and movements, the fresh green grass glistened, water splashed into the trough, crickets and toads sang and croaked endlessly in the distance. I would sit on a rock near the cypresses and spend ages gazing at the window, and I sometimes saw a shadow pass behind the light curtain. One day . . . Perhaps you'd rather not know? If not, just tell me . . .'

'Go on, go on . . .' I replied, more dead than alive.

'One moonlit night . . . I'm sure you'll find this so very trite . . . I saw her walking down the garden towards the cypresses. Where was she going? I thought about that for a second, and then thought of other things. Youth is a time for feelings in turmoil. Hazy, troubling images hurtled through my mind, so numerous I felt I was losing consciousness. It was too lovely. I'd been visiting that spot for months hoping to encounter her there one day. Well, it had happened. She had crossed the garden and I heard her turning the key in the garden gate. I saw her come out into the open country. I saw her look up at the stars. How long? I couldn't say. The fact is I suddenly found myself opposite her, I don't know how. When she saw me, she made a strange face, but said nothing. She put a finger to her lips, signalling me to be quiet, and then I saw her look up at the lighted window, nervously chewing the corner of the handkerchief she was gripping tightly. She was wearing the dress I liked: white, with blue polka dots. I'm speaking about something that happened over twenty years ago. When the weather was fine, girls her age used to wear socks and show off their delightfully fresh, pink legs. We walked slowly along looking for the rock where I sat every night. What should I do? She kept her eyes on the lighted window. In fact, I kissed her on the cheek, and said nothing. She looked at me, laughed, and made me blush. She turned around and rested her head on my shoulder. My heart thudded, and I remember taking my hat off and looking up at the stars. I don't know if we held hands . . . A long time later I kissed her again. I was dazzled, and her skin felt so cold . . .'

At that point, I must have made a really strange face, because he stopped dead with an ingenuous look on his face. I found that man so repugnant I could stand it no more. I was tempted to pull the emergency cord. I lost my presence of mind. Perhaps I simply grabbed him.

'What's wrong?' he asked sheepishly, slightly surprised and disconcerted.

That heated moment passed, and I restrained myself. What could I do? He clearly wanted to annoy me. I found his affable, polite manner and sardonic tone bewildering. I felt deeply distressed. What kind of man was he? I'd used every means possible to suggest that his words were hurtful. I'd insulted him. He'd ignored me. I opted for the only solution: to get dressed and go out into the corridor.

'I don't think it's such a big deal!' he exclaimed knowingly. 'Does it upset you to think that I went out with your mother? What's wrong with that? How can I ever think it was unnatural, if I was there? Because I was there, believe me! Don't doubt it for one moment. You'd rather not believe I was in a relationship with her? Well, you're wrong. The Ricards will tell you. You must know them, of course. Ask them. I almost married her. I repeat that. It's true . . . And, to return to what we were saying: she kissed me too that evening. What were we expected to do? It was a noisy kiss. It was all quite innocent. Then she laughed and said she thought she had sinned and that she'd have to confess. You see what young things we were. I became very serious, and she again placed one finger on her lips. Perhaps it was her first kiss. Some people don't think these things are important: I'm the more emotional, sentimental kind. It's a matter of character. I've always remembered those moments. Do you know how it all ended? I saw her keep looking up at the lighted window, and suddenly her eyes bulged and she seemed to freeze. A shadow was moving behind her bedroom curtain. The curtain seemed to rip open and a bright light shone out from the room. Someone shouted out and a silhouette appeared in the square of light. "Maria!" cried a voice that slowly faded into the night.

'She stared at me for a moment, then jumped up and ran off. I watched the white wraith wandering beneath the moon. She opened the garden gate among the cypresses and disappeared. I sat on the rock for a few seconds. Then someone closed the bedroom window and lowered the shutter. We all met the day after that at the Ricards'. As ever, she was at the piano. I'm fond of music and turned the pages for her. As she was playing, she told me – without looking at me – that it was her first kiss. I blushed when I heard that, like a young child, and someone asked if I was feeling unwell.'

I left him in mid-flow. I hurriedly opened our compartment door. I finished dressing in the corridor. I knotted my tie while gazing through the window at a village. Then I went back inside to retrieve my luggage. I saw him lying there on his couchette, his hands behind his neck, staring up at the ceiling.

I don't know how long I stayed in the corridor. Maybe three or four hours. The train seemed as if it would never reach Paris. In the state I was in, the hours seemed endless. At one point I even almost alighted at the first stop and continued on the next train. I think that from the corridor I once heard snoring in the compartment . . .

I even bumped into him again at the exit from the Gare d'Orsay. When he saw me, he pleasantly doffed his hat in my direction.

ROSA CHACEL

The Genie of the Night and the Genie of the Day

As I walked across the square on my way home – by which time night had fallen – I thought I spotted among the trees the Genie of the Night. Something resembling a black dove flew past, brushing my face, a black dove that kept fluttering around me, sometimes vanishing into the trees where the shadows were dense enough to mimic its black underbelly.

I barely felt that touch, yet it lingered on my cheek and made the muscles in my face contract. I probably looked as if I were smiling, and that's certainly how it seemed to me: my smile had the introspective look of someone making a long-drawn-out confession.

The shadow cast by its presence was as warm and soft and elusive as the secret places among the folds of a piece of velvet, impenetrable to the eye.

I thought all this in the time it took me to cross the square, then I abandoned the idea, although the sensation did not abandon me.

Later, at home, I began hearing a voice coming in through the open window: a Gluck opera being broadcast on the radio. And again that soft something brushed my cheek, a breeze perhaps. I had left the door open.

Rosa Chacel (1898–1994) was born in Valladolid, but moved to Madrid when she was ten. Home-schooled by her mother, she later went to art school, but decided that she was more interested in literature, becoming a regular at the Café Granja El Henar and the Ateneo, frequented by other aspiring writers. A feminist at a time when this was something of a novelty in Spain, she eventually married the artist Timoteo Pérez Rubio, and they went to live in Rome for five years. She wrote her first novel, *Estación, Ida y Vuelta*, in 1930, then devoted herself to bringing up her son until the Civil War. Her husband joined the Republican army and she worked as a nurse. At the end of the war, the family moved to Brazil, where they lived for three decades. When her husband died, Chacel returned to Spain and resumed her writing, most notably *Memorias de Leticia Valle* and the poignantly nostalgic *Barrio de Maravillas*.

I was standing in front of the mirror, shaving foam on my face, when I again felt that something passing close by and carrying me off towards a memory. I felt as if I were back in the square; I relived the moment when I had followed with my eyes that shadow within the shadows; again I felt myself wrapped in that pitch-black velvet and saw a diamond necklace glittering around a black throat, or, rather, around the throat of a black dove. But this was no longer taking place in the square; my memory was following a new route, the voice of Armide* had reached a brightly lit foyer with a flowing marble staircase, and had entered a dark room, at the far end of which glowed a living picture, a spacious square compartment, where the voice was strolling about, dragging behind it a majestic cloak of grief, the notes falling away, dropping like leaves in the gusting melody. The dark part of the room was full of a sound like a vast intake of breath, as if an enormous bird had fluffed up its feathers and was emerging out of the gloom at the back of the boxes and making its way over the ringlets, the bare shoulders, and bosoms resting on the balustrades. There it stopped, filling the room with its dark, all-embracing dominion, against which only Armide's voice prevailed, shining out like a bright remembered light.

Suddenly, everything vanished: a bell was ringing insistently at the other end of the house. I picked up the phone and asked a question; a warm, cordial voice replied:

'Yes, I'll wait for you downstairs. Don't be long.'

I hung up. I dialled a number and asked again; an even gentler voice responded:

'Yes, I'm waiting. Don't be long.'

Reality once more filled my thoughts and once more I became aware of minor details, such as what you need to put in your pockets, and which windows you have to close when you leave the house.

I went downstairs, and we glided off down the avenues; we skirted the squares, leaving behind us the solitary glitter of brilliant, sloping lawns; we drove around the outer edges of large country estates until we reached the most densely wooded of them all, behind whose railings were confined the most silent of cedars, the most lethargic of magnolias, and where

* The main character, a sorceress, in the Gluck opera of the same name.

the gates opened as we arrived and the sandy path crunched beneath the wheels of our car as we proceeded down the drive, its headlights feeling their way along the meandering bends and curves like the antennae of a beetle.

As on other occasions, we did not have long to wait, but, when she leapt into the car ahead of me, I could not immediately follow, because between her and me *She* appeared. I stood for a moment frozen, holding the door open as if for someone needing to accommodate a dress with a very long train. Respectfully, courteously, solemnly, I waited for her to enter, and the car was filled with the most enormous shadow: the deity with the black, feminine breast of a dove.

To the right, in the open spaces between villas and houses, groves of willows stretched along the muddy banks of the river, where pools glinted in the moonlight, and in silence, leaning one against the other, we sat braced – as if for a sudden joy to strike our hearts – for the small leaps made by the car as it bumped over the potholes in the road.

Then there was the orchestra under the pergola, the frosted glasses on the tables, and the rhythm twining about the familiar melody which we knew from beginning to end. Like poems learned as children, the peculiar rhythm traced its ups and downs in our memory, and we repeated it, travelled it lightly, slowly, crazily, as if it were a rhythm we need not name, the one that snakes and flows beneath our state of abandon, rocking us the way the waves rock seabirds.

There was also a moment – the orchestra succumbed to a sudden irritable burst of anger – when a hand rested on my shoulder and carried me off to the bar; there we drank our drinks, holding the stem of the glass with the tips of our fingers, while we hatched a plan that resembled a tersely shining road rising before us, brilliantly prosperous and easy.

And then, once more, the dancing and the frosted glasses; again the car and the willows passing by on the left, the railings surrounding the estate, and the crunch of gravel beneath the wheels.

Later still, the avenues, the glitter of those brilliant, sloping lawns and, finally, from afar, sleep. I wanted to hear the lulling silence in the room, but the buzzing in my ears got in the way; the presence in my blood of the alcohol of reality could not be quelled. The memory of words and of concrete ideas kept bubbling up their turbid gases like a storm refusing to move off. And, at the same time, a gentle breeze was wafting in through the window, its velvet tail brushing my brow as if the peace and deep blackness of the night, the body of that happy deity, were preparing me to rest beneath its dark, watchful eye.

I heard something pecking at the windowpane. A few brief, sharp, intermittent taps, as if the wind were banging some hard object against the glass. I half-opened my eyes and saw a yellow light, full and ripe. Then I realized what it was that was pecking at the window.

The Genie of the Day was perched on the balustrade of the roof terrace, impatient and 'as bald as an eagle'. Its talons scraped against the concrete, scratching the skull of the house.

The yellow light pushed its way pitilessly into the room, as violently as the water emerging snorting from the two taps. It, too, seemed to splash out when it collided with other shining objects, not illuminating but, rather, obfuscating them. Things remained hidden and as if numbed by the rapidly accelerating brightness.

The day, as predictable as an unchanging alphabet, was revealing itself to be strangely and elusively impregnable, and, rising up from the street, came the sound of a remnant of anxiety, the clatter of iron wheels, approaching and growing louder as it approached, then slowly moving off, only to approach again and again move off.

The horror of plunging into that rushing current of jarring activity prevented me from remembering logically and in an orderly fashion the series of duties awaiting me. I didn't want to have to face any real difficulties because I knew they were not entirely insoluble: I preferred to believe I was under threat by that power beating its yellow wings, against which the only possible defence was invincible apathy and denial. In vain, I tried to take refuge in sleep; in the house, though, activity had awoken like a creature with metallic wings furiously issuing its morning call. I picked up the phone and asked a question: it was that same impersonal voice waiting for me, the one that was supposed to give me an answer. It said:

'No, not today. Today is impossible.'

I hung up and went over to the door. I had to begin, I had to remember that the first duty of the day would have to be something as painful as writing a letter or filling in an accounts ledger. Before I could make a decision, though, the phone rang again. I picked it up: the voice was personal, unmistakable, and it poured into my ear like an endless flood into which flowed all the waters from every mountain stream. I listened. The clear flow of that voice was filling me with clarity about everything; the kind of blinding clarity that provokes mirages, that dazzles and sets the outlines of objects trembling. I tried in vain to change the course of that flood, to deny or rectify something. In vain. Inhuman and deaf to my pleas, the cataract continued to flow until it had reached its full height. And so it was: it had arrived.

I don't know how I made it from my house to the office, but, once there, I opened drawers and filing cabinets with their respective keys; I sorted out files, I corrected the work of draughtsmen and typists. Meanwhile, the flood had reached my throat, with, bobbing about in it, fragments of what I had said which writhed about like bits of dissected snake.

In the midst of my transactions and calculations, in the midst of my columns, always keeping a rigorous eye out for any dastardly errors, I continued to converse with my colleagues, insisting on certain futile details, repeating statements that had gone unheard, and I could not erase the resentment planted in me by that story which hinted at a betrayal by a woman who was not my lover. No, she wasn't. I swore to myself that she wasn't, at the same time asking myself: is anyone else? Beneath the light falling on that piece of paper, how could I possibly remember what I might have experienced in other, at the time, unimaginable regions? I could not help feeling somewhat embittered, but I continued to converse, I continued drafting or adding up numbers, I continued answering the questions put to me by my assistants: a brusque 'No', a violent 'No', filled by a blind, desperate desire always to say 'No'.

Until the time came to return the papers to their files, to close drawers and filing cabinets, go out into the street and stand stock-still on the pavement.

After a few minutes of immobility, I tried to consign these thoughts to oblivion, but my feet were caught fast in shifting sand dunes. The avenue, as searingly hot as a desert, could devour anyone who tried to cross. Standing there, petrified with indecision, stood many men prepared to sell their souls to the devil, to commit any crime they were asked to commit. Others had reached the café terraces, where they were sitting before a drink that might wash a little kindness into their veins. I, though, was incapable of joining them: the floodwaters rising up in my throat were about to overflow, they were growing with the light, and the light had reached its highest point.

Over the summit hovered a voracious power, and above those other men wings were unfurled that cast no shadows.

RAFAEL DIESTE

Light and Silence

I know perfectly well that what happened to me won't result in a new system of metaphysics, but will require, rather, analysis by some insightful doctor. However, were I fond of clever phrases, I would say this: I had never before felt in such close proximity to the terrible, empty presence of Señor Nobody as I did on that night. Not that I wish to frighten you, of course, and, besides, it was of no real significance, but let me tell you what happened anyway.

I had been living in the city for some years. All that remained of the family inheritance in the small village where I was born and where my parents both died were a few pieces of land and a house, and in the house some old bits of furniture . . .

Land and house had been left in the charge of a loyal farmhand who had worked for the family all his life, and he it was who, in a letter written in a clumsy scrawl, urged me to go back. He needed me to sift through the ancient piles of documents in order to help resolve a boundary dispute.

It was almost dark when I arrived at the house in the rickety old carriage that made the daily journey between my village and the nearest train station, and which involved spending two hours listening to the driver

Rafael Dieste (1899–1981) was born in Rianxo in Galicia. He was a writer and philosopher who, as well as poetry, short stories, plays and novels, also published newspaper articles and books on mathematics and philosophy. A staunch supporter of the Galician language, he himself wrote both in *galego* and Spanish. In 1939, following the Spanish Civil War, he moved first to Paris and eventually to Buenos Aires, where he lived in exile until 1961. On his return to Galicia, he began publishing with Editorial Galaxia, a publishing house devoted exclusively to writers writing in *galego*.

shouting and stamping his feet as he tried to whip some life into his poor, woebegone horses. Once there, I had a brief conversation with the farm-hand while I devoured the supper served up to me by his wife.

Then I was left alone to leaf through a pile of papers in what, in better days, had been a spacious salon, separated from my bedroom by a long corridor . . .

I've always been easily startled, and I still find solitude, darkness and silence strangely troubling.

That night, when I was alone – yes, why not say it? – anxiety began to scratch away at my imagination.

With its damp-stained walls and wooden beams, the house – which had made such an impression on me as a child – seemed even darker and more labyrinthine, filled as it now was with sudden bursts of memory.

The low ceilings, the roof-beams disappearing off into the gloom, gave an illusory sense of space, and the dim light from my one stump of candle only made its edges more elusive, the hidden corners more suspect.

The shadows from the corridor entered the room in cold gusts and clustered together along the walls, pressing ever closer in, hoping, like stealthy, subtle criminals, to extinguish that somnolent light.

The flickering flame succeeded intermittently in shooing away those besieging shadows, but they soon filled the corners again with their dense, dark troops.

In going through the documents, I realized, at one point, that I needed to check some papers I had left in the bedroom. I got up and left the room with that one candle still burning.

Along the corridor, the shadows' thousand talons caught at my clothes like brambles, but I ignored them, as would any sensible man, even though my heart was going at it hammer and tongs. I walked past many open doors without so much as a tremor.

Only when I reached my bedroom did I take out the box of matches and strike one. In fact, I blithely struck three, for only the third one took. To protect the flame, which a treacherous draught was about to extinguish, I cupped my hand around it. Then I looked defiantly about me . . . Nobody.

I picked up my papers, threw down the match and headed back along the corridor.

But who was in the room now?

I saw nobody. I saw only the glow of the candle filling the doorway, but that glow could not possibly be alone. Do you know what I mean? For some reason, that restless red glow framed in the doorway gave me a strange feeling, the strange certainty that there was someone in there, someone absorbed in thoughts couched in some impenetrable logic. Perhaps when I went in, he would raise his head and look at me, perplexed, as do all intruders when caught in the act. Because that glow was no longer mine. It was *his*.

That red glow could neither be there alone nor could it be mine.

I don't know if I said all this to myself at the time, but, as I prepared to enter the room, I resolved to face that look of perplexity with some remnant of dignity . . .

I went in, and a wave of horror made me freeze . . . For there in the sad, silent room was nobody.

RAMÓN J. SENDER

The Boy

On a trip to Asturias we gathered together a vast number of anecdotes and incidents, enough to fill several volumes. Near Villafría – on the outskirts of Oviedo – many groups of workers suspected of firing on soldiers were shot. The officer overseeing the removal from their homes of one such group saw that, among the men, young and old, was a boy of about fifteen. Someone doubtless still knows his name and may even have a photo of him. He was a skinny lad, with a child-like face and a sharp profile. He might well have been a *guaje*, the kind of boy who works down the mine, getting used to life underground by carrying the picks and lantern of his master, the real miner. Like the others, the boy had his hands bound, and was dragged to the place of execution, one of those roads that run alongside green fields. When the officer saw him, he could not help but notice the boy's childish features, and the voice which, in all circumstances, even the very worst, insists on gauging the degree of baseness of every act, that voice spoke to his innermost feelings.

When the hands of the soldiers slid down the barrel to the bolt, and the rifles were taking aim, the officer held up one hand to stop them and asked the boy:

Ramón J. Sender (1901–1982) was born in Chalamera in Huesca province. He left home when he was seventeen and went to live in Madrid, where he worked as a journalist until he was sent to Morocco for his military service. In 1927, he was imprisoned for his anarchist views and fought for the Republicans in the Civil War. When his wife was killed by the Nationalists, he went into exile with his two children, finally settling in the United States, where he taught Spanish literature at the University of Southern California. He wrote over forty novels, as well as essays, newspaper articles, biographies and eight collections of short stories.

'What were you doing when you were taken prisoner?' and he pointed up at the house.

The boy said he'd been taking care of his two-year-old brother.

'Where's your mother?' asked the officer.

'She's dead.'

The boy answered with the serenity of any fifteen-year-old in the face of tragedy. The officer wanted to know more:

'And your father?'

'He was killed too.'

After a brief silence, the boy added, looking back at the house.

'The little one's all on his own.'

The officer told him he had eight minutes to return home and find someone who could look after the child. A man standing near the officer saw that the surrounding hills and valleys provided a perfect opportunity for the boy to run away. Those eight minutes would be more than enough for him to make his escape, and so he offered to go with the boy and keep an eye on him. The officer – once again conscious of that moral gauge, with all its different gradations of baseness – declined. He had foreseen that possibility, and the idea did not displease him. Not that he said as much, but the thought occurred to him again as he watched the boy disappearing over the first hill.

Shortly afterwards, shots rang out. Half the men fell to the ground. In full view of the survivors, the soldiers gave the *coup de grâce* to the wounded and immediately cut the twine binding their wrists. Minutes later, the other men fell.

The bodies were dragged over to one spot and placed in a pile. As the soldiers dragged the bodies over there, they noticed that some were still alive, and again shots rang out, delivering the *coup de grâce*, more spaced out this time, more hesitant perhaps.

Then coming down the hill, walking calmly and confidently, came the boy. He had heard the shots; he could see the bodies being dragged aside and the wounded being finished off. And yet on he came, utterly impassive.

He stood in the place indicated. It took only three shots to kill him. No need for a *coup de grâce*.

MAX AUB

Ingratitude

She was already quite old when her daughter was born. And when her husband died just a few years later, she cherished the little girl as if she were the apple of her eye.

Her daughter proved to be a sickly child, with a rather absent look in her blue-grey eyes, a meek, indifferent smile, soft, rather lank hair, and a slow, almost grave way of speaking.

She liked to stay close to her mother, winding wool and helping her with the sewing.

They lived in a very humble house by the roadside that must once have been home to a navvy.

The mother embroidered for a living. Every two weeks or so a wagoner would deliver lengths of cloth and take away others that she had duly stitched and embellished. However, the wagoner died after being kicked by a donkey driven half-mad by a horsefly bite. His son, Manuel, took over and continued to come and go with the same regularity. When the old lady's daughter, Luisa, turned seventeen, Manuel took her away with him. The mother was too poor to put on a proper wedding, but she gave

Max Aub (1903–1972) was born in Paris, the son of a French-Jewish mother and a German father. At the outset of the First World War, his father was on business in Spain and unable to return to France. His wife and son joined him and later took Spanish citizenship. Like his father, Aub worked as a travelling salesman, travelling all over Spain. In 1939, following the Spanish Civil War, Aub crossed over into France, where he was denounced to the Vichy regime as a militant communist and a German Jew. He spent three years in work camps, first in France, then in Algeria. In 1942, he managed to escape to Casablanca. There he was able to get a boat to Mexico, where he was later joined by his wife and children, and where he spent the rest of his life. He published three novels on the Spanish Civil War: *Campo cerrado*, *Campo de sangre* and *Campo abierto*, as well as a large number of short stories and novels on other themes.

her daughter whatever she could: pots and pans, a black dress, and a pewter ring that her late husband had bought for her at the Santiago market.

Luisa was really all she had, and she felt herself shrinking in on herself as she watched her get into the wagon and disappear off into the distance. She watched until all she could see was the cloud of dust kicked up by the mule and the wheels of the wagon.

She was left alone. Since she didn't even own a dog, all she had for company were the few sparrows that flew over the fields flanking the road, alfalfa to the right and sparse wheat to the left.

Yes, she was left alone, completely alone, and found it hard to do her embroidery because her eyes kept filling with tears whenever she thought of Luisa. Initially, her daughter would send news via Manuel, saying that she was very happy, news that was occasionally accompanied by a jar of home-made jam. Six months on, Manuel announced that they would soon be expecting their first child. The old lady wept for a whole week, then took on more work so that she could buy enough fabric to make a few smocks and shawls for her grandson, gifts that were gratefully received by Manuel. The old lady was always convinced that the baby would be a boy, and she was right. Then, a few months after the child was born, Manuel told her he was going to take on another driver to help in his growing business. Two weeks later, a lad called Luis turned up, a strapping, ruddy-faced fellow, none too bright, who always sang the same song over and over:

Bom, bom, tiddely om pom pom!
Bom, bom, tiddely om pom pom!

Manuel and his wife moved further away, and rarely bothered to send news to the old lady, leaving her to assume that they were all fine. This silence gradually began to eat away at her. 'That's what kids are like,' she would say to console herself, but then she would remember how she had treated her own mother. She would spend hours and hours sitting by the roadside waiting for someone to bring news of her daughter and grandson, but no one came, and slowly the old lady began to wither away.

She'd never had many pleasures, but she no longer enjoyed even the few she'd had; she stopped eating or sleeping, and spent her time battling against the word 'ingratitude', which buzzed around her like a stubborn fly; she would swat it away, but it would always return. 'That's what kids are like,' she would say, but then she would always remember how she had treated her own mother. Withered and motionless, she gradually turned into a tree, but not a beautiful tree: its bark was rough, its sparse leaves full of dust; it resembled a bent old lady by the side of the road.

The hills round about were bare, the soil sometimes grey, sometimes reddish in colour; the road descended slowly down into the long, narrow valley, which was only green at the very bottom, where the road curved near the stream dotted with rocks.

There was nothing special about the tree, except that it was the only one. And it's still there today.

MERCÈ RODOREDA

Like Silk

I first entered that cemetery of weeds on a windy day towards the end of September in a year I cannot now recall. I did so not because I knew anyone who was buried there, but simply in order to breathe in the peaceful cemetery air, and, above all, to escape from the wind whose wings were lifting my skirts and filling my eyes with dust. I couldn't visit my own beloved dead person, although I saw his face on my bedroom wall every night. His brothers and sisters had wanted to bury him in their village because they had a plot there, and that village was far away; I would have to take a train to get there, and I couldn't afford the ticket, indeed, I was earning less and less with each day that passed because my sight was beginning to fail; I could only work in the afternoons, and a time would come when I would no longer be able to go to people's houses to do their sewing.

There was less dust in the cemetery than in the street, but the wind's wings still set everything trembling. A wreath of still-fresh flowers had fallen from some grave or other, along with a small bouquet, which, bowled along by the wind, came to a halt at my feet. I was walking past graves adorned with statues. One grave resembled a small, round house with an ivy-covered roof and was surrounded by some alarmingly ancient

Mercè Rodoreda (1908–1983) was born in Barcelona and wrote exclusively in Catalan. She is considered to be one of Spain's and Catalonia's finest writers. She lived in exile in Geneva for many years, and it was there that she wrote a number of her books, including her best-known novel *La plaça del Diamant*, which many believe to be the best post-Civil War novel written in any of Spain's languages. She also published three collections of short stories, which show her astonishing range as a writer, from realism to impressionism to fantasy, portraying the often narrow lives of women with rare sympathy.

prickly pears. As I was walking along one of the most sheltered paths, a thought made me pause. Then suddenly, completely without warning, a gust of wind, like a blow from a great wing, would have knocked me to the ground if I hadn't grabbed hold of a tree trunk. The gust whisked past, scooping up leaves and whistling as it did, as if it were laughing at me. What I was thinking as I stood there was that the earth, although it might be of various different colours, is the same the world over, and, if so, then the earth in the cemetery I had wandered into was the same earth as that in the cemetery where my poor beloved lay sleeping. This discovery consoled me. I let go of the tree, an extremely gnarled, old olive tree, bent and battered by the wings of every passing wind, growing beside a very simple grave, a grave to which I immediately took a liking because the elements had eaten away at the stone and it appeared to have been abandoned. I touched it in order to make it mine. In the crack between the grave and the headstone grew a weed that bore a few tiny yellow flowers, so glossy they might have been made of porcelain. My own poor beloved would have liked them. I couldn't get the image of them out of my head: I saw them in every patch of sunlight, in the yellow scarf worn by some girl I passed, in the golden stripes on flags . . . I explained this to the face on the wall, which appeared each night as soon as I turned out the light, emerging from a stain the colour of bile: first his eyes and then his mouth. His forehead and cheeks, the fleshy parts, took a little longer, then there he was, slightly blurred, but not bothering me in the least, and certainly not making me feel like screaming or running away. Sometimes, he would weep. His whole face would crumple, and a tear would well up in his right eye, where it would hang suspended for a moment, glinting and trembling, before slipping down his cheek. The following morning, though, there was nothing to see.

'I don't like visitors coming to this holy place to eat, so don't do it again!' I had never seen the sexton before and, for more than a week perhaps, ever since that first very windy day, I had got into the habit of making a daily visit to the cemetery; he, it would seem, had been watching me, because I had only ever eaten there on a couple of occasions, sitting on one of the graves, and then only a snack of bread and some chocolate, so as not to waste time going home for lunch. I looked at him as if I hadn't heard, and he shuffled off, grumbling as he went, a small, shrunken figure pushing a wheelbarrow full of leaves. I was not at all pleased. I arranged the weeds so that the little yellow flowers covered the letters on the headstone; if I could, I would have erased the names completely because they refused to let me believe what I wanted to believe: that this was the grave of the dead person I had loved, *my* dead person. I would occasionally take a flower there, sometimes large, sometimes small. The gardener who lived on the corner knew me by now and, without my even asking, he would wrap the stem in silver foil to make it look still prettier. I would crouch down, carefully place the flower on the grave, then go and stand next to the olive tree, my arm about its trunk, in order to admire my flower. I would pray then. I can't say exactly what I prayed because I've never known an entire prayer off by heart, and all it takes to distract me is a passing fly or anything really, even some motionless object. I would sometimes wonder what he would have been like, when he was walking the streets, fully clothed and breathing, the dead person inside the grave, I mean, and who I'd never known. Or else I would talk to Jesus, who I'd loved the moment I saw his picture. The thought of speaking to the Holy Spirit, though, had always made me laugh – I mean, what could you possibly ask of a dove? 'Jesus, please help me buy a flower and make sure the sexton doesn't tell me off . . .' And sometimes, instead of talking to the sweet, fair-haired boy who had gone barefoot in the world while his father made wardrobes and tables, I would burn with desire to know what kind of blue the sky would be far away, and, at night, looking at the face on the wall looking at me, I would take a piece of that sky and draw it up over me like a sheet.

All Saints' Day was approaching, and, a week before, I stopped going to the cemetery because the place was positively heaving with people. It was full of families cleaning the graves and niches and taking bunches of chrysanthemums and lilies to their poor loved ones. I so missed going that it was almost like being dead, as if I'd been thrown down a deep, dark well. I dreamed about the weeds, about the iron-grey spikes on the prickly pears, about the avenue of cypress trees. When I decided to go back, I almost flew there. At the top of the path, I stopped in my tracks, and the flower I was carrying fell from my hand. I didn't recognize my grave. Someone had touched up the lettering with some kind of gold paint, not black or grey, and the weed had been torn from its crack; a few yellow petals lay withering on the stone. I picked up three of them and, clutching them in my hand, not knowing quite what to do with them, I walked almost mechanically over to the olive tree and wept and wept until it grew dark. I didn't want to leave, thinking something dreadful would happen to me if I did, but my eyes were stinging and I was cold. Before setting off home, I looked around me. Everything seemed so soft and airy, and yet my legs felt like lead. And while I was wondering fearfully if the sexton would already have locked the gates, I heard the sound of beating wings above the olive tree, as if a huge bird had got its feet caught in the branches and was struggling to free itself. Then the wind got up.

I slept badly, troubled by the sheets, by my arms, by the face on the wall, by everything. When it was time to get up, I felt even more exhausted than when I'd gone to bed, but I was determined not to be frightened off. In the crack between grave and headstone I would plant another weed with yellow flowers. The many paths in the cemetery I had still not yet walked down must be full of the same weeds. And when they had grown tall enough, I would make sure they obscured the lettering and then leave the rain to do the rest. A surprise awaited me: on the grave lay a bouquet of flowers, as fresh as the morning and all of them pink. I put my arms about the olive tree, breathing fast, as if I couldn't get enough air into my lungs. And, gradually, the clear sky clouded over and, when it began to rain, I surreptitiously – making sure the sexton didn't see – picked up the bouquet as if it were a nest of vipers and flung it into the undergrowth.

I couldn't rest. I kept going to the cemetery at different times, hoping I might meet the person who had left that bouquet and uprooted my weed. And, just as I was beginning to believe that such a person had never existed and that it was all the sexton's fault, I found on the grave a dozen white chrysanthemums tied with a gleaming ribbon. The sight made me feel quite sick. Almost kneeling on the ground, but still clinging to the olive tree, I choked back my sobs and my tears, for I could only afford to take a single flower. I don't know how many hours passed, but I realized that it must be very late because the sky had grown as dark as a wolf's mouth, and in front of that wolf's mouth something flickered. What? A shadow? A huge, outstretched wing? But it was so intermingled with the darkness that, in the end, I decided that my senses must be deceiving me, and that what I was seeing wasn't real, because, ever since I'd been driven almost to despair by the thought that someone had stolen that grave from me, I had never again seen the face on the wall. In fact, it had never been there. The face wasn't on the wall, it was in my head. My poor departed one wasn't thinking about me, he couldn't. I was the one thinking about him. To cheer myself up a little, I said almost out loud: 'It's a dream.' So was the wing, and so was the me caught up in that dream, it was all false . . . Immediately above my head, the beating of a pair of real wings made me hunch down, and a gust of wind ruffled my hair. 'I'm locked inside the cemetery.' Unable to see where I was putting my feet, I started running down the almost invisible path, convinced that, at any moment, I would fall face-first and break my teeth. The gate was closed. Terrified that I would have to spend the night among the dead, surrounded by the rustle of wings and shadows, by the creaking of branches shaken by gusts of wind coming from who knows where, I raised my eyes to heaven, begging for mercy, and, even as I did so, the hinges of the gate creaked. Some invisible person had opened the gate. 'Thank you, Lord Jesus.'

All night I tormented myself with the question: should I go back to the cemetery? A solution of sorts came with the dawn, when the cart bearing souls away suddenly appeared before me. It was flying towards the moon, and the souls of the evildoers fell off the cart the moment they tried to clamber on board, while those who had been good instantly found themselves grazing in heaven's meadows and, with a wing on one side of their head, were rapidly gobbling up the grass of the fortunate. When I woke in the morning, I felt slightly feverish. I wandered about the house in a daze, not knowing what to do, not knowing what I was looking for or what I wanted, with the thread of my memory all tangled and lost. I didn't even have any soup for my lunch, because I'd left it on the stove and it had boiled dry. Unable to bear this battle with life, when the fateful hour arrived, I left the house. Everything in me was leading me where I didn't want to go. I strode briskly along the streets. Once, when I took an extra deep breath, my nostrils were filled with the stench of tar. Everything was utterly still, so much so that I suddenly became aware I was being followed. I couldn't hear any footsteps, but I was definitely being followed. That someone turned out to be seven children, all more or less the same size; their eyes were closed and their faces waxen. If I had reached behind me, I could have touched one of them. The nearest child was me when I was seven: I was wearing black woollen socks and a pinafore with little pockets. Standing outside the cemetery, surrounded by silence, I took two deep breaths and my heart and mind grew calmer.

There was a light on in the window of the sexton's house, and one half of the gate had already been closed. Making myself as small as possible, I slipped inside the cemetery, and instead of turning right, I turned left: I would have to make a long detour and go past the corner where the discarded funeral wreaths lay rotting, but at least I would avoid the avenue of cypresses, where the sexton might have seen me, and I dreaded to think what he would have said then. When I reached the grave, I stopped. The children had vanished and, for a moment, the solitude was almost painful. Not a blade of grass, not even one sad leaf moved. Everything felt so very delicate that I didn't have eyes enough to take it in. Finally, with my arms outstretched, I announced softly to no one in particular that this was all mine: this whole garden of the dead, from one wall to the other, and even deep inside, even down to the very deepest roots and up to the vault of the sky, which no one can tell where it begins, still less ends, with a sliver of moon staining with yellow the point where sky meets sea. There was no sign of the chrysanthemums, but on the ground, on the gravestone, lay something black, about the length of my arm; it gleamed slightly: it was a feather. However much I wanted to touch it, I didn't dare, because its sheer size both frightened and intrigued me. What bird's wing or tail could sustain a feather that size? Holding my breath, I crouched down and merely studied it for a while, until I could stand it no longer, and then I ran one finger over it several times: it felt like silk. 'You'd look lovely in a vase,' I said. And, just as I was about to pick it up and take it home, a great flapping of wings and a gust of wind hurled me against the olive tree. And everything changed. The angel was there, a tall, black figure standing on the gravestone. The branches, the leaves, the sky with its three stars already belonged to another world. The angel stood so still he didn't seem real; then he leaned to one side, as if about to topple over, and, very gently – perhaps to lull me to sleep? – began to rock from side to side, again and again . . . Just when I thought he would never stop, he flew upwards, like a kind of exhalation, piercing the air, then dropped down to the ground again like a vapour. When he was only a few feet away, I started to run. I ran like one possessed, skirting the graves, stumbling over the undergrowth, suppressing a desire to scream. Convinced that I had escaped the angel, I stopped, my hands pressed to my heart, so that it would not escape my chest. Oh, dear Lord, there he was before me, taller than the night, wrapped in cloud, his trembling wings as vast as sails. I looked at him and he looked at me, and we spent a long time, a very long time, looking at each other, as if bewitched. Still looking, I reached out an arm, but a blow from one wing made me draw back. 'Go away,' I heard a voice say, a voice I no longer recognized as mine. And I again reached out an arm. Another blow from that wing! I started shouting like a mad thing: 'Go away! Go away! Go away!' The third time I reached out my arm, I touched a prickly pear, and suddenly, how I don't know, I crouched down behind it, convinced that the angel wouldn't see me. The sliver of moon, now high in the sky, was spitting fire all around.

I crawled along the ground like a worm, on my elbows, on my belly, getting caught on things, tearing my clothes on invisible thorns, wishing I could fall asleep for ever on the crunching leaves, not knowing where I would end up or if I would ever get out of the cemetery. After many twists and turns, I reached the avenue of cypresses; a bitter smell of sun-warmed orange blossom – coming from where exactly? – made me feel dizzy, and with my eyes closed – as a way of killing the angel – and brushing aside the small twigs scratching me, I stood beside the nearest cypress tree. My arm ached from the blows the angel had dealt me, and the cut on my cheek made by the prickly pear was bleeding. On the other side of the path, as still as death and surrounded by a starry glow, the angel was watching me. I could no longer move. Tiredness prevailed over fear.

Was it midnight, or was I just dreaming that it was midnight? My poor beloved was somewhere far away, weeping because I had forgotten him, but a voice coming from behind a sun the colour of wet plaster and looking more like the moon was telling me that the angel was my dear departed one, that there was nothing in the grave at all: no bones, not even a remnant of the dead person. There was no need to buy another flower, whether small or large, nor to choke back my tears; I needed only to keep laughing until the moment when I, too, became an angel . . . And I felt like yelling – loud enough for the hidden voice to hear me – that I didn't like wings or feathers, that I didn't want to be an angel . . . but I couldn't. The voice ordered me to look. A low-hanging mist was spreading over the cemetery like a sheet for all those lying abed, hands clasped in prayer; that mist was filling me with a sense of well-being. Different smells reached me now, the smell of honey and the sort of grass that grows only by the light of the stars, and I was no longer standing near the cypress tree, but in a small square surrounded by graves. The angel, its wings resting on the ground, was sitting on a wooden bench as if he'd been waiting there for me since I was born, and I remember thinking: If he lets his wings drag on the ground like that, the feathers will fall out and end up being scattered about cemeteries everywhere. My legs were beginning to feel cold in that mist, which was growing ever whiter and thicker, but on I went. I slithered down a frost-covered slope. I was, against my will, approaching the angel, who continued to look at me, and, when I was very close, he drew himself up to his full height, his head touching the moon, and the smell of grass became the smell of the good, black earth that was burying me, the kind of rich soil you can plant absolutely anything in, knowing it will grow. Among the graves and the dead leaves I could hear the murmur of water and see a thread of something glinting, and the angel opened his wings wider and wider and, when I was really close, when I could feel his sweetness mingling with mine . . . I never will understand why I felt such a need for protection, but the angel must have sensed this, for he wrapped me gently in his wings, and I, more dead than alive, touched them so as to feel their silk and then I stayed inside for ever. As if I were nowhere at all. Imprisoned . . .

ÁLVARO CUNQUEIRO

Jacinto's Umbrella

Guerreiro de Noste was walking in the mountainous region known as Arneiro when he met a man carrying a slate-grey umbrella considerably taller than him. Guerreiro greeted the man and expressed his surprise at the size of the umbrella, which was far larger than any he had seen before.

'Oh, that's nothing!' said the man, a small, red-faced fellow with a grizzled moustache.

And he showed Guerreiro the handle of the umbrella, which was a human face with glass eyes and a beard made of fur, and a wide red mouth resembling that of a real live human being.

'That's some mouth,' said Guerreiro.

'Umbrella, stick out your tongue!' ordered the owner of the umbrella.

And the umbrella stuck out its tongue – a very long, red tongue, like a dog's tongue, which affectionately licked its owner's hand. The owner duly took off his beret and placed it on the ground before Guerreiro, who tossed a peseta into it.

'Is that a trick?' asked Guerreiro, his curiosity piqued.

The stranger laughed.

Álvaro Cunqueiro (1911–1981) was born in Mondoñedo, Galicia, and wrote in *galego* and Spanish. He abandoned his university course in Santiago de Compostela to become a journalist and got to know many of the foremost writers of his day. He was a member of the Falangist party in the Civil War and worked on the pro-Franco newspaper *ABC* until 1944, when he ended his collaboration with the regime. He returned to Galicia, where he joined *El Faro de Vigo* and subsequently became chief editor. During this time, he wrote many articles under various pseudonyms, as well as poetry, novels and short stories, showing a particular penchant for the fantastic. His best-known works are the novels *Merlín e familia e outras historias*, *As crónicas do sochantre* and the story collections *Xente de aquí e de acolá* and *Escola de menciñeiros*.

'No, there's no trick to it, it's my brother-in-law Jacinto.'

And he explained that his brother-in-law Jacinto had come across the umbrella in a field, in Friol, and thought it a very fine umbrella, albeit somewhat on the large side. Since the umbrella appeared to have been mislaid, and because, at that very moment, it began to rain really hard, he had picked it up, pleased as punch. When Jacinto unfurled the umbrella, it opened, then immediately closed, swallowing Jacinto whole. It then opened again and flew through the air before landing outside Jacinto's house, next to the barn. Lost somewhere inside the umbrella, Jacinto shouted through the handle, which had not yet sprouted a beard. His wife, his in-laws and all the neighbours came running out.

'Manuela!' he shouted to his wife. 'It's me, Jacinto!'

She didn't know what to do. It was definitely Jacinto's voice. Just to make sure, though, she went over to the umbrella, which was still standing there open.

'If you're Jacinto Onega Ribas, married to Manuela García Verdes, prove it!'

And that was when Jacinto stuck out his tongue for the first time.

'That's him!' said his wife. 'I'd know that tongue anywhere.'

For Jacinto had a very long tongue, which would loll out of his mouth when he was distracted, and which had got him into a lot of trouble when he did his national service in the 8th Zamora Regiment in Lugo. And since becoming an umbrella, or, rather, since living inside an umbrella, his tongue had grown even longer because he was always having to stick it out to declare that he was there, and having to lick his relatives too, and even the cows, for he drank directly from their udders, suckling away to his heart's delight.

'Why don't you take him round the fairs?' asked Guerreiro, who was already regretting having thrown that peseta into the beret presented to him by Jacinto's brother-in-law.

'My sister won't let me, I mean, she even sleeps with the umbrella. Well, he is her husband after all!'

Jacinto's brother-in-law said he was going to take a nap, and bade farewell to Guerreiro, who continued on his way. The two brothers-in-law stayed behind, talking. The umbrella must have said something that displeased the other, because the little man with the moustache gave the umbrella a sharp slap. The umbrella shouted something that Guerreiro couldn't hear. The argument continued, and Guerreiro hurried on, not wanting to get involved. It was raining up there on Aris, and the sky over Arneiro was growing dark. Before beginning the descent to Lombadas, Guerreiro climbed onto a rock, and saw the man with the umbrella struggling to open it, then climbing inside. The umbrella began to fly over the flowering gorse. It was flying into the wind, with the brother-in-law mounted on the handle. Guerreiro could not help crying out as loudly as he could:

'Señor Jacinto!'

Something red appeared on the handle of the umbrella, between the legs of Jacinto's brother-in-law – presumably Jacinto's tongue. Then Jacinto leapt into the air, and set off, heading, according to Guerreiro, in the direction of Guitiriz or La Coruña.

PERE CALDERS

Feat of Arms

One day, in mid-battle, I got separated from my comrades and was left unarmed, alone and utterly helpless. I felt rather humiliated, because everything seemed to indicate that I would certainly not be playing any vital role in the battle that continued to rage on without me, and with a clamour and a loss of life that would make your hair stand on end.

I sat down at the roadside to ponder this state of affairs when, lo and behold, a parachutist wearing a very strange uniform landed right beside me. Underneath his cape he had a machine gun and a folding bicycle, all very well disguised of course.

He came over to me and in a very strong foreign accent asked:

'Could you please tell me if this is the way to the town hall of this small village?'

(The previous week, there had been a village nearby.)

'Don't be such an ass,' I said. 'Anyone can tell a mile off that you're an enemy, and, if you go to the town hall, they'll take you prisoner.'

This caught him completely off guard, and, after snapping his fingers to show his anger, he replied:

'I knew they couldn't have thought of everything, but what in particular gives me away?'

'Well, that uniform's completely out of date. Our general got rid of it

Pere Calders (1912–1994) was born in Barcelona and started life as a commercial artist. In 1936, he published his first collection of stories, *El primer arlequí*. When the Civil War broke out, he enlisted as a military cartographer on the Republican side and, following the Nationalist victory, spent twenty-three years in exile in Mexico. There he found work as a graphic designer and continued to write and publish in Catalan, writing mainly novellas and short stories, often with a fantastical or satirical edge.

over two years ago, saying that times had changed. You lot are obviously very ill-informed.'

'We found it in an encyclopaedia,' he said glumly.

He sat down beside me, clutching his head, apparently in order to think more clearly. I looked at him and said:

'What you and I should do is have an argument. If, like you, I had a gun on me, it would be different, but . . .'

'No,' he said. 'There's no point. We're not on the actual battlefield, and, whatever the outcome, it wouldn't get official recognition. What we need to do is try and get back into the fray, and, if the opportunity arises, we could fight each other then.'

We tried more than ten times to re-enter the battle, but a wall of bullets and smoke prevented us. Hoping to find an opening, we climbed a hill overlooking the scene. From there, we could see that war was proceeding vigorously, just as the generals would have wanted.

The enemy said to me:

'Seen from up here, I have the distinct impression that, even if we did manage to rejoin the battle, we'd probably just be in the way.' (I nodded my agreement.) 'And yet you and I still have unfinished business.'

I felt he was absolutely right and suggested helpfully:

'What if we had a fist fight?'

'No, that won't work either. We owe progress a certain degree of respect, for the sake of your country and mine. It's difficult,' he said, 'very difficult indeed.'

Then, thinking I'd found a solution, I said:

'I know, why don't we play a game of noughts and crosses? If you win, you can wear my uniform and take me prisoner, and, if I win, you'll be the prisoner and that machine gun and bike will belong to us. What do you think?'

He agreed, we played, and I won. That same afternoon, I returned to camp, carrying my booty, and when the general, very pleased with my work, asked how I would like to be rewarded, I told him that, if it was all the same to him, I'd keep the bike.

ALONSO ZAMORA VICENTE

On a Visit

Whenever we get to go to Aunt Plácida's apartment, we're always really pleased. It'll either be on a Thursday afternoon, when there are no classes, or on a Saturday, when there's no need to get up early the following morning. Aunt Plácida is always well prepared for our visit, after various phone calls postponing it – she has a cold or a headache, or perhaps unexpected visitors – but, finally, the definitive call comes: she's expecting us. We set off. Now, don't you go touching the walls with those grubby hands of yours, and didn't you notice you'd stepped in a puddle. We have to enter Aunt Plácida's house as if we were newly made, freshly ironed, combed and brushed to perfection. She doesn't miss a thing, and will say at once: What have you done to your trousers, or else, Children, however did you get such filthy hands? It makes no difference if we touch the walls or not, because that's what she'll say anyway and then blithely escort us to the bathroom, savouring her role.

Aunt Plácida lives in a large, spacious apartment, in a new building opposite the Museum. Yes, it is rather on the expensive side, but it's a very good neighbourhood, besides, at my age, one needs a little comfort and warmth, and it's so central. When we arrive, the smart, blue-uniformed

Alonso Zamora Vicente (1916–2006) was a philologist, lexicographer, dialectologist and writer. Born in Madrid, his studies were interrupted by the Civil War, but he graduated in 1942 with a Ph.D. on the dialect of Mérida, which was a pioneering work in the field of dialectology. He wrote many books on this subject, as well as literary criticism and scholarly editions of many classic and modern writers. He went on to teach at many of the major universities in Spain and was visiting professor at many others in Latin America, North America and Europe. He had a particular liking for the short story, and published several collections, notably *Primeras hojas*, *Smith y Ramírez, S. A.* and *Mesa, sobremesa*.

porter greets us and tips his cap, addresses us respectfully as *señoritos*, and solicitously ushers us into the lift. The lift, a mirror-lined cage, begins its ascent. Paco makes some disparaging remark about the porter, saying he was rude, thus clashing with Elisa, who finds the porter very distinguished. As for me, I also feel a certain respect for him. Our aunt is waiting on the landing to greet us, and, although she says nothing to me directly, I can feel her kindly hand nearby, and the inevitable question: And what about your father? although she never waits for an answer, because she knows he'll come and fetch us later. Inside, there's a vague smell of mothballs and disinfectant, mingled with the odour of cakes, custard, vanilla, a whiff of puff pastry, the sweet waft of melted sugar, and of now-unusable perfumes and of clothes long closeted in wardrobes – a mixture of patisserie and mustiness. It seems a shame to walk on the gleaming floors; stealthy maids appear behind us, righting anything we've overturned or made crooked, then zigzagging out of sight like a cool breeze. The afternoon passes slowly, slowly, but it's never boring, as we listen to our aunt seamlessly asking questions, speaking, explaining her furnishings and fittings. We have tea in the parlour, we're not allowed in the other rooms, where all the furniture is swathed in white and red, the enormous gilt-edged mirrors and the lamps covered in gauze, as if the apartment were half darkly dozing, half filled with the scent of fried bread and assorted cakes – every visit a surprise – and the murmurings of the music box, of seashells, a souvenir from Sorrento, 1890, oh, we went back to Santa Lucia time and again, what with the volcano and the port being so nearby.

They were one long, extended marvel, the endless afternoons we spent with Aunt Plácida, those exquisite teas where we were treated like royalty, and where, as a reward, we were allowed a glimpse of the other rooms, one at a time. Our uncle's library, it's just as he left it, I haven't even emptied the inkwell, and we would earnestly study the inkstand, a plump angel perched on a lion, all in gold, and a thermometer on one corner of the desk, its mercury evaporated, for ever frozen and absent. My uncle's many titles hung on the wall: a Knight Bachelor of something or other, two Grand Crosses – one from San Hermenegildo and another from the Queen – a very special decoration that one, a medal from the sieges of Cádiz and Zaragoza, as well as the Order of Civil Merit. Our aunt would stand very stiff and erect when she told us this, her necklace tight about her throat, and she would point threateningly at each object as she told us what it was: the glass cabinet containing our uncle's last uniform, when he was a Colonel in the Royal Guard, and which he wore for the first time at the King's wedding – I'd never seen him so elegant. And the portrait of him standing rather awkwardly, as if not quite sure what to do with his gloves, but how dashing he looks, well, he *was* dashing, of course, Ramón Casas painted him when he was in Santander. The reception room full of old paintings, the dragon represents hell below, with the Virgin and Child above, and all those people, the fortunate ones, sheltering beneath her blue and white mantle, and the Child holding out his hand to a woman up to her waist in the flames, and in between the paintings a cane pedestal table, and a small Japanese lacquer chest of drawers, and a marble sculpture in one corner, a wedding present from my sister-in-law, hideous I know, but I can't possibly get rid of it, and a cabinet containing fans, ivory carvings, rosaries from the Holy Land, miniatures from the Retiro Palace. A small wooden box containing a sprig of orange blossom, which our aunt would take out, smile, then lovingly put back again. And always a vase of freshly cut flowers. Her bedroom, full of photographs, a vast wardrobe (I always look inside before I go to bed, just to check no one's hiding there) and more boxes containing medals of various Virgins – de la Montaña, de Rocamador, de Montserrat, del Buen Suceso – and the scapular of Nuestra Señora de los Llanos, and Christ on the Cross, and, on top of the chest of drawers, a wooden image of the Virgin, fully clothed and with a lot of hair (what are you sniggering at?), and she would always give us a religious picture or a medal or a relic, all of which had miraculous properties and were warmly recommended. We were almost never allowed into the room off the corridor, full of saints, old and new and large dark paintings, no, you might break something, and don't ask me again what's in there. And the long corridors, and the kitchen and the bathroom, a room full of pipes and taps, all very strange and complicated, half-fishmonger's, half-hospital, where our aunt always seemed particularly pleased and smug. And then that stream of sweets, titbits, fancies, cakes, caramels, chocolate, the occasional toy, a veritable torrent of happinesses, while, outside, night was coming on, and the red or green screens made the vast apartment seem colder and smaller, the apartment where my aunt lived alone in almost celestial and inevitably motionless privacy.

Every day when it grew dark, Agustín the chauffeur would arrive, slightly out of breath, good evening, Señora, at your orders, Señora, and always the same answer: thank you, Agustín, you go and rest, and when Agustín left, rather bent now, with his huge, black nostrils and large side whiskers, my aunt would tell us how, once, she had owned an English carriage, but all that's long gone, these days I don't even have a landau, but he's such a good fellow, Agustín, and he still comes faithfully every evening. And we were amazed at the idea of having a chauffeur but no car or carriage, a mere phantom, struggling to catch his breath.

Yes, there's always an empty feeling about our aunt's house, a clamour suddenly silenced, rather dim lighting, something almost mutilated about her broad, commanding gestures, delicately indicating that afternoon's special cake, her wrinkled face soft above her jet necklace. Aunt Plácida's apartment, always full of that strange smell – part-patisserie, part-church, part-mothball – where we felt so comfortable and yet which always had a secluded feeling about it, something tangible yet, at the same time, desperately remote. I can see my aunt on the landing, waving goodbye with her small, white handkerchief, the lift coming up, a sudden, bright light as the doors open, now hold each other's hands, the porter ready with a greeting, Paco bursting to say something rude, to jump up and down, the list of the presents we'd received, all of us talking loudly, Elisa looking smug, what did she give you, show me, and did you see that photo of Uncle on the table, well, the woman with him was the one he was living with when he died, he had two wives, you see, and what did she give you, it's cold now, it's always cold as we walk past the Museum, then the balcony light goes on, she comes out to watch us cross the road, and I clutch my gold coin so hard it hurts, aren't you the lucky one, a gold coin, and I refuse to swap it, not for that antique fan or that scrapbook, not my gold napoleon coin (don't give it to one of your siblings), wow, what did you do to deserve that, and I clutch it still harder amidst the growing amazement, by now, we can't see the house, and in my memory the balcony is empty again, a widening desert, the coin in my eager hand, and our aunt combing her hair, perhaps even singing, alone in her vast bedroom.

JULIÁN AYESTA

At the Beach

In the late afternoons, the beach was full of orange sun and there were lots of white clouds and everything smelled of potato and onion omelette.

And there were crabs that hid among the rocks, and we children were put in charge of burying the bottles of cider in the damp sand to keep them cool.

And everyone said: 'What a glorious afternoon,' and the young couples sat apart from the rest of us, and, when it began to grow dark and everything was lilac and purple, they would sit very silently with their faces pressed close, as if they were in confession.

But the best part was the late afternoon swim, when the sun was going down and was huge and kept getting redder and redder, and the sea was first green, then a darker green, then blue, then indigo, and then almost black. And the water was *so* warm, and there were shoals of tiny fishes swimming in and out of the reddish seaweed.

And it was fun diving down and pinching the women on their legs to

Julián Ayesta (1919–1996) was born in Gijón, in the northern Spanish province of Asturias. His father was a lawyer, a Republican member of parliament and editor of two local newspapers. At the age of fifteen, despite his father's allegiance to the Republic, Ayesta joined the Falange, the fascist movement founded by José Antonio Primo de Rivera, and fought on the Nationalist side in the Civil War. However, he soon became disillusioned with the Nationalist victory and, after studying at the University of Madrid, he opted to become a diplomat and subsequently spent long periods abroad. Alongside his diplomatic duties, he wrote articles, poems, short stories and plays and became fiercely critical of the Franco regime. In 1952, he published *Helena o el mar del verano* to great acclaim. It is not so much a novel as a series of interlinked stories very much based on his own childhood experiences. Critics praised the author's evocation of innocence and joy, and, when one considers what a very grim, joyless place post-Civil War Spain was, it is hard not to experience *Helena* as a deeply subversive book.

make them squeal. And then Papa and Uncle Arturo and Aunt Josefina's husband would lift us up onto their shoulders and let us dive into the water from there. And then two of them would grab one of us and hurl us through the air, saying: 'In he goes, squirming like a cat!' and the women, bottoms bulging in their antediluvian costumes, would say: 'Stop messing around with the kids.' And then the men would say to us: 'Come on, let's give 'em a fright,' and we would chase Mama and our aunts and the other ladies and they would scuttle screaming out of the water and up the beach until we caught them and dragged them back, captive, to the shore, and there they would sit on the sand, terrified, and Aunt Honorina, close to tears, would say to her husband: 'No, please, Arturín, no.' And we kids would kill ourselves laughing when she called Uncle Arturo 'Arturín', and for at least an hour afterwards, until we got tired of it, we would all call him 'Arturín'. But then we would join hands (the women's hands would be shaking) and run into the water together and plunge in, not the women though, they would sit down where the water was only about two inches deep, laughing like a lot of broody hens. And stupid Albertito would always open his mouth and gulp down lots of water and sand and then vomit it up and be left with a bitter, burning sensation inside.

And it was so funny to see Aunt Josefina's legs under the water, they seemed to swell and shrink and were the same disgusting greenish white as a toad's belly.

And there was an older girl who had just arrived from Madrid, very pretty and very tanned, with really big eyes and smelling of a perfume that made you feel all funny.

And she had a very clear, sad sort of voice and she used to say to us boys: 'Which one of you is brave enough to swim with me out to the Camel?' but no one ever dared, not Papa, not Uncle Arturo, not Aunt Josefina's husband, not us, and then she would swim all alone out to the Camel, which was so far off you could hardly see it, and she didn't care if the sea was rough or if it was one of those grey days when you felt afraid even to go in the water. And she swam wearing the bracelets that she always wore, and we would watch as one arm then the other emerged shining and wet, the bracelets glinting in the sun, and because she was swimming crawl, her feet left behind them a wake of foam.

And there was a bald German gentleman, who wore white bathing trunks and always had two dogs with him, and his skin was burned red, almost black, from spending all day in the sun, fishing and reading the newspaper, with a white towel over his shoulders. And we would have our afternoon snack on the beach, and for the children there were the lunchtime leftovers, tuna, omelette and cutlets fried in breadcrumbs, and for dessert we had a choice of oranges, apples, pears, grapes, cherries or peaches. And there were bananas too, and we used to have fun squeezing them at one end so that the flesh popped out the other and then showing them to the grown-ups; it always made the men laugh, though we never knew why.

And the slices of omelette and the cutlets were all gritty with sand, and the little girls' wet hair stuck to their faces, and their eyes shone, and they would scream and leap about among the dogs, who would leap about too and bark and run to fetch the bits of dry seaweed that were thrown for them, and then the girls would give them any scraps that were left over, and there was always loads: omelette, cutlets, tuna, and the dogs would lick the empty sardine tins until the tins shone like mirrors, and King would even eat the peel from the fruit, although he was the only dog that did.

And because the men said that we mustn't leave a scrap of paper or any rubbish on the beach, 'because we had to set a good example', we would pile up the cardboard trays and the bits of greasy paper and the peel and set fire to it all and then bury the ashes along with the cans that wouldn't burn in the fire.

And then we would go and get dressed behind the rocks. And the sand was really cold, and a cold wind came whipping through, making us shiver because, by then, it was growing dark.

And then everyone – apart from the ladies – would pick up a bag and we would set off home. And we would walk along singing and picking blackberries, which were still warm from the sun.

And our backs were all sticky and stinging, and a great, fat moon would be coming up.

And the frogs and the toads would be singing too.

And everything smelled of thyme.

And then we would have to go past the cider-houses and the bars, which were full of men drinking and playing skittles and pitch-and-toss.

And it was good to hear the sound of wood on wood or the clink of metal on metal.

And there was a man who sang really well, and Papa said why didn't we sit down at one of the tables and rest a while, and he ordered cider for everyone, including the children, and it tickled and bubbled as it went down.

And that was when the stars would come out.

And from time to time, you'd notice a very dark patch of sea, so dark that just the thought of swimming there all alone made you feel afraid.

And Papa and Uncle Arturo asked Aunt Josefina to sing 'I've got three little goats', but she turned bright red and said how could she possibly sing in front of all those people, and everyone laughed.

And suddenly a man came over, stinking of wine, and he clapped my father on the back and said something I couldn't hear.

And Papa gave him a nasty look, then immediately paid the bill, and we left.

You could hear music coming from a Sunday dance somewhere.

And by the time we reached Gijón, we were all very quiet, almost sad.

And the lights in the streets were sad too.

And on the beach, you could see the Yachting Club decorated with coloured lights.

And there were lots of people in the street, and a band marched past, playing.

And cars with white wheels went by.

And the streets were all newly washed and shining and black.

And everything smelled of hot tyres and cologne and sea.

All because the Prince of Asturias* was visiting Gijón.

---

* The Crown Prince and heir to the Spanish throne.

MIGUEL DELIBES

On Such a Night

I don't know what a man's supposed to do when he's let out of prison on a freezing cold Christmas Eve with just two *duros* in his pocket. If, as in my case, he finds himself alone, probably the best option is to go and sit on a park bench, start whistling a nursery rhyme, and watch other people hurrying past, eagerly making plans for the evening. Because the worst of it isn't being alone, it isn't the cutting wind or just having got out of prison, it's finding yourself a complete wreck at the age of thirty, with your left shoulder racked with rheumatism, your liver completely shot, and not a tooth in your head. Being alone is bad too, especially when the air around you is alive with excitement, an excitement that never actually touches you. All these things are bad, so is having to feel them; on such a night, it's even more stupid and absurd to harbour any hope of transforming yourself from head to toe, when your left shoulder's racked with rheumatism and you've only two *duros* in your pocket.

It's a cold night, the sky is overcast, heavy with the kind of uniformly grey clouds that threaten snow. That's to say, it might snow or it might not, but, snow or no snow, it won't help my rheumatism or my toothless

Miguel Delibes (1920–2010) was born in Valladolid. Only sixteen when the Civil War broke out, he enlisted in the Navy on the Nationalist side, returning to Valladolid when the war ended and doing a course in business studies. However, he began his career as a caricaturist, columnist and journalist, gradually becoming a full-time writer. He was passionate about the natural world, about hunting and rural life. In 1947, he published his first novel, *La sombra del ciprés es alargada*, which won the prestigious Premio Nadal. His third novel, *El camino*, became an instant classic. From then on, he published almost a novel a year, among them *Mi idolatrado hijo Sisí*, *Diario de un cazador*, *La hoja roja*, *Cinco horas con Mario* and *Las ratas* to name but a few. He was awarded Spain's highest honour, the Premio Cervantes, in 1993.

state, or the awful emptiness in my stomach. And so, when I heard music and decided to find out where it was coming from, it led me to a man wearing a tattered, threadbare suit, but with his face almost covered by a beautiful scarf. He was sitting on the pavement outside a brightly lit café and, between his legs, on the ground, lay a black beret full of loose change. I went over to him and stood beside him without saying a word, because, at that moment, the man was playing a tune on his accordion, 'The Blue Danube', and it would have been a real crime to interrupt him. Besides, I felt as if he were playing just for me, and I felt touched that, on such a night, one needy man *should* be playing for another needy man. When he finished, I said:

'What's your name?'

He looked at me from beneath half-closed lids, like a dog begging not to be kicked. I asked again:

'What's your name?'

He got to his feet and said:

'My name's Nicolás.'

He picked up his beret, put the coins in his pocket and said:

'How do you fancy going for a walk?'

And it seemed to me that we needed each other, because on such a night one human being needs another human being, and we all need the warmth of company. And so I said:

'Do you have any family?'

He looked at me and said nothing. I asked again, saying:

'Do you have any family?'

At last he answered:

'I don't understand what you're saying. Speak more clearly.'

I thought I'd been quite clear enough, but said:

'Are you alone?'

And he said:

'Well, right now, I'm with you.'

'Can you play and walk at the same time?' I asked.

'I can,' he replied.

And I asked him to play a Christmas song as we walked along, and the few stragglers we passed eyed us warily. While Nicolás was playing, I thought of my dead son and about Chelo, wondering where she would be now and where my dead son would be. And, when Nicolás finished, I said:

'Do you know "O to be high in the sky like the moon"?'

I really wished Nicolás would just keep playing without me having to ask, that he would play all the songs that awoke in me some distant echo or some precious memory, but Nicolás stopped after each piece, and I had to beg him to play something else and to do so meant being forced to return to my memories and to my present sorry state, and each return to the past made me shudder and filled me with grief.

And so on we walked, away from the town centre, and ended up in a place much more to our taste, among workers and other needy people. Besides, it was so cold by then that even the accordion's breath froze in the air like a wisp of whitish mist. Then I said to Nicolás:

'Let's go inside. It'll be warmer.'

And we went into a shabby, deserted bar, furnished with a long, grubby pine table and a few equally long benches. It was warm inside, and Nicolás took off his scarf. I saw then that half his face was missing, that his lower jaw was broken, and the skin of his cheek was wrinkled and ruched into a horrendous scar. He had no eye on that side either. He saw me looking at him and said:

'I got burned.'

The landlord came over to us, a massive, bull-necked man with very coarse features. He wore his shirtsleeves rolled up and was doubtless one of those enviable types who never feels the cold.

'I was just about to close,' he said.

And I said:

'Go ahead. We'll be better off on our own.'

He looked first at me, then at Nicolás. He hesitated. I said:

'Go on, shut up shop. My friend here will play music and we'll drink. After all, it is Christmas Eve.'

Nicolás said:

'Three glasses.'

Without a word, the burly fellow bolted the door, lined up three glasses on the damp zinc counter and filled them with wine. I drank mine down in one and said:

'Play, Nicolás, play "Mambrú went off to war", will you?'

The landlord looked slightly put out. Nicolás stopped. The landlord said:

'No, play "Our last night together". That was the last tango I danced with her.'

And a shadow seemed to cross his face. And, while Nicolás was playing, I said:

'What happened?'

He said:

'She died. Three years ago now.'

He refilled our glasses, and we drank, then he filled them again and we drank again, and he filled them again, and again we drank, and then, without me saying a word, Nicolás began playing "Mambrú went off to war" with great feeling. I felt a lump in my throat and said:

'My son used to sing that song every day.'

The landlord refilled our glasses and said in some surprise:

'You have a son who can sing?'

I said:

'I had.'

He said:

'My wife wanted a son too, but she died before she could have one. She was a real gem, you know. I wasn't a very good husband to her, and then she died. Why is it always the best people who die?'

Nicolás stopped playing and said:

'I don't know what you're talking about. When I got my face burned by the cooking oil, people were dancing to "My best girl". That's all I can remember about it.'

He downed another glass of wine and played the opening notes of 'My best girl', then played the whole tune. The landlord once more refilled our glasses and leaned on the bar. The cold and damp of the counter didn't seem to penetrate the skin of his bare forearms. I looked at him, and I looked at Nicolás, and I looked at the rest of the deserted bar and I sensed in it something that was both inexplicable and oddly familiar. Nicolás's one eye glinted strangely. The landlord's gaze softened and, after another glass of wine, he said:

'At the time, I didn't much care for her. It seemed to me that was just the way things were, and sometimes I loved her and sometimes I beat her, but it never occurred to me she was anything extraordinary. Then, when I lost her, I said to myself: "She was a real gem." By then, of course, it was too late. We buried her, and the son she'd always wanted never arrived. But that's life for you.'

While he was talking, I drank a couple more glasses of wine, not that I was intending to get drunk that night, I just wanted to feel a little of God's warm, healthy joy and a firm intention to mend my ways. And the music Nicolás drew from his accordion was a further stimulus to those honest impulses and filled me with love for him and for the landlord and for my dead son, and filled me with forgiveness for Chelo too for having gone off and left me like that. And I said:

'When my little boy fell ill, I told Chelo to go to the doctor, and she said a doctor would cost ten *duros*, and I said: "That's not much, is it?" And she said: "I don't know whether it's a lot or a little, but I don't have ten *duros*." And then I said: "Neither have I, but that still doesn't make it a lot of money."'

Nicolás's one eye, wild with wine, drilled into me. He had stopped playing, and the accordion hung limply about his neck, resting on his belly, like something that had come to nothing or else died a premature death. The handles and the keys and the folds of the bellows were thick with grime, but the sound was good, which was all that mattered. And when Nicolás drank another glass, I said as much to him, although without saying it, because it seemed to me that he wasn't drinking wine, he was drinking music, life and a need for more music. I said:

'If you're not too tired, play "Silent Night", will you?'

But Nicolás didn't hear me, or perhaps didn't understand. His one eye suddenly took on a retrospective look. He said:

'Why have I always had such lousy luck? One day, I saw the number 21 in the window of the shop selling lottery tickets, and I said to myself: "I'm going to buy that ticket, because the number 21 is sure to come up some time." At that moment, though, a neighbour happened by and said: "What's so special about the number 21, Nicolás? The small numbers never come up." And I thought: "He's right. The small numbers never do come up on the lottery." And so I didn't buy number 21, I bought number 47,234.'

Nicolás paused and sighed. The landlord was looking hard at Nicolás. He said:

'Did number 21 win the jackpot by any chance?'

Nicolás's one eye glittered feverishly. He cleared his throat and said:

'I don't know, I only know that I didn't even get my stake back on number 47,234. Yeah, I've always had really lousy luck.'

There was a silence, and the three of us drank in order to forget Nicolás's dreadful luck. Then we drank another glass in order to fend off any more such terrible luck in the future. An almost visible sense of solidarity was beginning to grow between the three of us. Suddenly, the landlord turned and took another bottle off the shelf. I felt my knees almost give way beneath me and said:

'I'm tired. Why don't we sit down.'

And Nicolás and I sat on the same bench, while the landlord sat across the table from us. As soon as we were seated, the landlord said:

'I don't know what was so special about that woman. She had fair hair and blue eyes, and she was a good mover in her day. A real gem she was. She'd say to me: "Pepe, you should sell this bar and get a better job." And I'd say: "Yes, sweetheart." And she'd say: "We might manage to have a child then." And I'd say: "Yes, sweetheart." And she'd say: "If we have a boy, I'd like him to have blue eyes, like me." And I'd say: "Yes, sweetheart." And she'd say . . .'

I interrupted him.

'My son had blue eyes, and I wanted him to be a boxer, but Chelo put her foot down and said that, if he became a boxer, she'd leave me. And I said: "You'll be too old by then, and no one will want you." And she burst into tears. She cried when the boy fell ill too. I didn't cry, but I felt a terrible pain inside. Chelo told me off for not crying, but I think not crying is worse, it leaves your feelings kind of shrivelled up somehow. And when we called the doctor, Chelo cried again because we didn't have the ten *duros* and I said again: "That's not much, is it?" By then, our son no longer had blue eyes, they were pale, the colour of water. When the doctor saw him, he frowned and said: "We need to operate at once." And I said: "Go ahead and operate." And Chelo took me to one side and said: "Are you mad? Who's going to pay for that?" And I got angry: "What do you mean, who's going to pay? I am," I said. And they brought an ambulance, and that night, I didn't go to the club to play cards, I stayed at my son's side, watching over him. And Chelo sat weeping silently in one corner, never leaving him for a moment.'

I paused and drank another glass of wine. Outside, the bells were ringing for Midnight Mass. They sounded dull and distant, and Nicolás got up and said:

'There's snow in the air.'

He went over to the window, opened the top part of the door, then closed it again and fixed me with a triumphant look.

'I was right,' he said. 'It's snowing already.'

And we remained silent for a time, as if, from the safety of our shelter, we wanted to listen to the soft sound of flakes falling on streets and roofs. Nicolás sat down again and the landlord said angrily:

'Play!'

Nicolás put his head on one side and opened the accordion wide. He began playing 'Farewell, lads, friends of my youth'. The landlord said:

'If she hadn't insisted on spending that day with her mother, she'd still be here with me. But that's life for you. No one knows what might lie ahead. If there were no bars, the driver wouldn't have got drunk and what happened would never have happened. But he did get drunk, and she would insist on going to see her mother, and she and the driver had to arrive at that particular corner at the same time, and that's all there is to it. Some things are just meant to be, and there's nothing you can do to change them.'

Nicolás stopped playing. The landlord shot him an angry glance and said:

'Will you play!'

'One moment,' said Nicolás. 'The fact that I didn't buy that lottery ticket had nothing to do with bad luck, it was entirely my fault. That's the truth of the matter. And if I got burned that's because I chose to lie down underneath the fryer. The woman in charge blamed me right enough and said, so what if I got burned, she could just as easily have caught a chest infection from my accordion. Anyway, it's all nonsense, a way of complicating matters. I said to her: "As far as I know, no one has ever caught a chest infection from an accordion." And she said to me: "And no one has ever burned anyone with the oil from a frying pan." I got angry then, and said: "Damn it, woman, you've just burned *me*!" And she said: "Yes, and I could easily have caught an infection from your accordion."'

Nicolás's one eye glittered as if he were about to cry. The landlord seemed annoyed by Nicolás's confession.

'Play,' he said. 'It's Christmas Eve after all.'

Nicolás put his fingers on the keys and asked:

'What shall I play?'

The landlord closed his eyes, gripped by a feeling of intense, troubling nostalgia:

'If you don't mind playing it again, play "The last night I spent with you".'

He listened with rapt attention to the first few bars. Then he said:

'When we used to go dancing, she'd put her arms around my waist rather than putting one hand on my shoulder. I don't think she could even reach my shoulder, because she was really tiny. That didn't hold us back, though. She and I even won a tango competition once. She danced the tango with such feeling that one of the judges said: "Young lady, your feet can talk." And she came over to me then and let me kiss her on the lips, because we'd won the competition, and because being good at the tango was the most important thing in life for her, second only to having a child.'

Nicolás appeared to wake from a dream.

'Don't you have any children, then?' he asked.

The landlord frowned.

'I already said that I don't. Apparently I was going to have one, but then my wife died. That's why she went to her mother's house. I knew nothing about it.'

I downed another glass of wine before speaking. My dead son felt so close to me then, it was as if, since his death, the earth hadn't turned once on its axis. My voice almost breaking, I said:

'My son died that same night, and Chelo left without even saying goodbye. I don't know what the stupid cow was afraid of, because her son certainly wasn't going to end up being a boxer, but, anyway, she left, and I haven't heard from her since.'

Nicolás's accordion filled the room with notes as soft as caresses. Perhaps that's why we seemed to be lifted into the air on those notes, all of us, the landlord, Nicolás and me, all filled with longing for those lost caresses. Yes, perhaps that was the reason, perhaps it was the accordion, or perhaps the evocative power of such a night as that. The landlord was now sitting staring into the dark space under the table, his elbows digging into his knees.

Nicolás stopped playing and said:

'My mouth's dry.'

He drank two more glasses of wine, then rested the accordion on the edge of the table to give his neck a rest. I shot him a sideways glance and noticed a rash on the back of his neck. I said:

'Does it hurt?'

But Nicolás ignored me. He had more important matters to consider. He didn't even look at me when he said:

'My bad luck was so bad that a slut like her could burn my face and I didn't get a penny in compensation. My neighbours said I had a right to compensation, but I just didn't have the dosh to take things that far. I was left with only half a face and that was that!'

I thought again of my dead son, and Chelo too, and I asked Nicolás to play 'Sweet flows the stream'. Then I took a sip of wine to fortify myself and said:

'Over the past few months, I've had time to think and I know now why Chelo left me. She was worried about the doctor's bill and so she left me in the shit. She didn't love me. She put up with me because of the boy. Otherwise, she would have left me sooner. And that's why she dumped me, leaving me to pay the doctor's bill and to grieve alone over my son's death. And everything else just followed. To fill a hole I had to dig another hole, and I got caught. That was my mistake: stealing instead of working. I won't do that again . . .'

The pain in my left shoulder had got worse, but I found a kind of relief in just talking. That's why I drank another glass of wine and added:

'What's more . . .'

The landlord looked at me with his dull, weary eyes, like the eyes of an ox:

'You mean there's more?' he said.

'There is,' I said. 'In prison my rheumatism got much worse, and to "cure" it they pulled out all my teeth, including my wisdom teeth, and then removed my tonsils. The rheumatism didn't go away, of course, and when there was nothing left for them to take from me, they said: "Give number 313 some aspirin."'

'Ah!' said Nicolás.

I explained:

'You see, up until the day before yesterday, I was number 313.'

And then we all fell silent. From the street came the jolly rattle of tambourines and I thought of my dead son, but said nothing. Then the bells of many churches rang out in unison, and I thought: Goodness, it's Christmas Eve. We should be happy! And I drank another glass of wine.

Nicolás had his head on the table by then and was fast asleep. His breathing was irregular, full of false notes and whistles; worse even than his accordion.

CARMEN LAFORET

The Return

It was a very bad idea, thought Julián, his face pressed against the windowpane, feeling the damp, cold surface cool him right down to his bones, the bones that stood out so clearly beneath his pale skin. Yes, it was a very bad idea sending him home on Christmas Eve, and, what's more, sending him home for good, completely cured. Julián was a very tall man and was wearing a really quite decent black overcoat. He was fair-skinned, with prominent eyes and cheekbones, which only seemed to emphasize his thinness. And yet Julián looked very well now. Whenever she visited, his wife would exclaim at how well he looked. There had been times when Julián was nothing but a bundle of blue veins, with legs like elongated toothpicks and huge, gnarled hands. That was two years ago, when he was first admitted to the place which, strange though it may seem, he was now reluctant to leave.

'I bet you can't wait, can you? They'll soon be here to fetch you. The four o'clock train is due any moment. Then you can both catch the five o'clock train and be home in time to celebrate Christmas Eve . . . And, Julián, I would so appreciate it if you would take your family to Midnight Mass, as an act of thanksgiving. If we weren't so far away, it would be

Carmen Laforet (1921–2004) was born in Barcelona, but went to live in Gran Canaria when she was just two, and spent her childhood there. She studied philosophy at Barcelona University, then moved to Madrid to study law but abandoned her studies in order to write. Her first novel, *Nada*, written when she was twenty-three, won the very first Premio Nadal, and the book remains a classic to this day. It describes a young girl's arrival in a sordid, poverty-stricken post-Civil War Barcelona to live with her very strange relatives, now fallen on hard times. Laforet went on to write four more novels and several collections of short stories, but she remains best known for *Nada*.

lovely to have you all here tonight. You have such delightful children, Julián. One of them, the youngest, looks like the Baby Jesus, or a little St John, with his curly hair and blue eyes. I think he'd make an excellent altar boy, because he's obviously bright as a button . . .'

Julián was listening closely to the nun's chatter. He was very fond of Sister María de la Asunción, who was small and plump, with a smiling face and apple cheeks. He'd been so absorbed in his own thoughts that he hadn't heard her enter the vast, cold visiting room where he was waiting, ready to leave. No, he hadn't heard her arrive because those women, despite the voluminous habits and headdresses they wore, somehow managed to walk very lightly and silently, like ships in full sail. He felt quite overcome with joy to see her there; the last time he'd feel such joy at this point in his life. His eyes filled with tears, because while he always had been easily moved to tears, lately, his sentimentality had become almost a sickness. 'Sister, what I'd really like is to hear Midnight Mass with you and the other sisters. I'm sure I could stay until tomorrow. After all, I'll still be able to spend Christmas Day with my family. And, in a way, you're my family too. I . . . I'm just so very grateful.'

'Don't talk such nonsense, child. Your wife is on her way to fetch you now. Once you're home with your family again and back at work, you'll forget all about this, it will seem like a dream.'

Then she left too, and Julián was alone again with the bitterness of the moment, because he was genuinely sorry to be leaving the asylum, that place of death and desperation, which, for him, had proved to be a real refuge, a salvation. Indeed, in the last few months, when everyone considered him cured, it had been a place of happiness. They'd even allowed him to drive! Seriously. He'd driven the Mother Superior and Sister María de la Asunción into town to do the shopping. He knew how brave those women were to entrust their lives to a madman or, rather, an ex-lunatic, but he didn't let them down. The car behaved perfectly in his expert hands. The ladies didn't even notice the potholes in the road. When they arrived back, they congratulated him, and he'd felt himself blush with pride.

'Julián . . .'

Standing before him now was Sister Rosa, who also had round eyes and a round face. He wasn't so fond of Sister Rosa though; in fact, he didn't like her at all. She reminded him of something unpleasant in his life, he didn't quite know what. He'd been told that, during his first days there, he had more than once been put in a straitjacket after trying to attack her. She seemed perennially frightened of him. Now, suddenly, he realized who it was she reminded him of: his poor wife, Herminia, whom he loved dearly. Life is full of such enigmas. Sister Rosa looked just like Herminia. Nevertheless, or perhaps for that very reason, Julián could not stand Sister Rosa.

'Julián, there's a long-distance call for you. Do you want to come to the phone? Mother said you should answer it yourself.'

Mother was the Mother Superior. Everyone called her 'Mother'. It was an honour for Julián to be summoned by her to the phone.

It was Herminia, her tremulous voice at the other end asking him if he wouldn't mind getting the train on his own.

'It's just that your mother's not feeling well, no, it's nothing to worry about, it's her liver again, still, I wouldn't feel happy leaving her to look after the children on her own. That's why I couldn't phone earlier . . . because I didn't want to leave her alone when she was in such pain . . .'

Even though he still had the phone in his hand, Julián was no longer thinking about his family. He was thinking only that this was an opportunity for him to stay there another night, that he would be able to help put up the lights on the crib, enjoy the marvellous Christmas Eve supper they always served, and sing carols with everyone, all of which meant so much to him.

'In that case, I probably won't come home until tomorrow. No, don't get alarmed, it's just that, if you're not coming today, I'd like to give the sisters a bit of a hand this evening. They're so busy at this time of year. Yes, yes, I'll be there for lunch tomorrow . . . Yes, I'll be home for Christmas Day.'

Sister Rosa was standing next to him, observing him with her round eyes and her round mouth. She was the only one of the sisters he disliked, the only one he would be glad to leave behind. Julián lowered his eyes and asked humbly to speak to Mother, because he had a special favour to ask of her.

Next morning, a train was carrying Julián through a grey, sleety Christmas Day towards the city. He was crammed into a third-class carriage along with turkeys and chickens and their owners, all of whom seemed to be brimming with good cheer. Julián's only luggage was a small, battered suitcase and that good-quality black overcoat, which was keeping him snug and warm. As they approached the city, his nostrils were filled with its smells, and, as his unaccustomed eyes took in the grimness of the vast industrial areas and the workers' houses, Julián began to feel guilty for having enjoyed the previous night so much, for having eaten so much and so well, for having sung in that voice which, during the war, had brought some relief to his comrades in the trenches from all those hours of boredom and sadness.

Julián had no right to such a warm, cosy Christmas Eve, because, in his own home in recent years, those festivities had been utterly meaningless. Poor Herminia would have made some kind of nougat out of potato paste and artificial colouring, and the children would have eagerly devoured this once they'd eaten a meal that would have been identical to the one they ate every day. That, at least, is how it had been on the last Christmas Eve he'd spent at home. By then, he'd already been out of work for many months. It was the time of petrol shortages. He worked as a chauffeur, and, until then, had always earned good money, but that year had been truly dreadful. Herminia scrubbed other people's stairs for a living. Day after day, all she did was scrub stairs, and, in the end, all the poor thing could talk about were stairs, with which she became as obsessed as she was with the food she couldn't afford to buy. Herminia had also been pregnant again at the time, and had a monstrous appetite. Like Julián, she was tall, thin and fair, but naturally cheerful and much too young for the pebble glasses she had to wear. Watching her gobbling down their daily diet of watery soup and sweet potatoes had entirely put Julián off his food.

During that winter, watery soup and sweet potatoes had been their unremitting daily diet from morning till night. Only the children ate breakfast. Herminia would stare greedily at the hot, almost bluish milk they would drink before going to school. Julián, who, according to his family, had always been a big eater, stopped eating completely . . . This proved disastrous for everyone, because it was then that he began to lose his grip on his sanity and become aggressive. One day, when he'd already spent several days convinced that their humble home was a garage and that the folding beds filling the rooms were luxury motorcars, he came close to killing Herminia and her mother, and was taken from the house in a straitjacket and . . . But that was some time ago . . . although still not that long ago. Now he was returning home cured. He had, in fact, been well for several months, but the nuns had taken pity on him and let him stay a little longer . . . until that Christmas. He suddenly realized how cowardly he had been in wanting to stay.

The street leading to his house was bright with shop windows, with glittering cake shops, and he stopped in one of them to buy a cake, spending what little money he had. He himself couldn't really face anything sweet after all he'd eaten at the asylum over the last few days, but his family would feel differently.

He struggled up the many stairs to their apartment, suitcase in one hand and cake in the other. He suddenly felt eager to arrive, to embrace his mother, that cheerful old lady who never complained about her various ailments, or did so only if she was in real pain.

The four doors on the landing had once been painted green, but the paint was now chipped and peeling. One of those doors was his. He knocked.

He found himself instantly surrounded by childish shrieks and Herminia's scrawny arms. And by the smell of a warm kitchen and a good stew.

'Papa, we've got a turkey!'

That was the first thing they said to him. He looked at his wife. He looked at his mother, who, although she had aged greatly and was still rather pale after her latest bout of illness, was wearing a new woollen shawl. In the small dining room stood a lavish hamper full of sweets, titbits and ribbons.

'Has someone won the lottery?'

'No, Julián. When you left, some ladies from the local benefit society came round and they've been so good to us. They found me a job and they're going to find work for you too, in a garage . . .'

In a garage? Needless to say, it would be hard to find anyone willing to take on an ex-madman as a chauffeur. Perhaps he could work as a mechanic. Julián again glanced at his mother and saw that her eyes had welled up with tears, but she was still smiling, always smiling.

He suddenly felt all the old responsibilities and anxieties bearing down on him, like a lead weight on his shoulders. He had come home to save that whole family gathered around him from the grasp of the benefit society, and would probably lead them once more into starvation . . .

'Aren't you pleased, Julián? Here we are together again on Christmas Day. And what a Christmas, eh? Look!'

She again pointed to the hamper of presents, to the children's greedy, excited faces, pointing all this out to him, that poor skinny man with his black overcoat and his sunken eyes, whose face was the very picture of sadness, because for him it was as if, on that Christmas Day, he had once more emerged from childhood in order to see, underneath those gifts, life in all its bleakness, ordinary life marching inexorably on.

IGNACIO ALDECOA

Come Twelve o'Clock

'Yesterday, at a quarter to twelve, a house
on a construction site collapsed.'
A newspaper report.

It was so cold that it hurt to breathe. The factory sirens pierced the white morning air. The garbage trucks were heading for the rubbish dumps. Pedro Sánchez blew on his fingers.

Antonia Puerto woke up. Her little boy was crying. She opened the window a little, and the cold air flew in like a bird, fluttering about the room. The child coughed. Antonia immediately closed the window again, and the cold shrank back into nothing. Juan woke up too then, his eyes like those of a frightened hare. He turned over in bed, waking his older brother.

When Antonia closed the window, the room smelled terrible. She ran her calloused fingertips over the windowpane, over the glass scabbed with ice. She had a sour taste in her mouth from a rotten tooth. She looked down at the street, at the frozen puddles and the piles of gravel embroidered with frost. Her youngest child was crying. Pedro had already gone to work. Married for ten years, they'd had a child every two years. The first was born dead, but she never even gave him a thought; she didn't have time. Then along came Luis, Juan and the little one. She was expecting another in the summer. Pedro was a construction worker. He'd had

---

Ignacio Aldecoa (1925–1969) was born in Vitoria, but lived in Madrid for most of his adult life. He was part of a group of writers who began to publish in the late 1940s, a group that included Rafael Sánchez Ferlosio and Carmen Martín Gaite. He began by writing poetry, then went on to publish six novels, among them *El fulgor y la sangre* and *Gran Sol*, which won the 1958 Premio de la Crítica. He also published several collections of short stories, notably *El aprendiz de cobrador*, *Pájaros y espantapájaros* and *La tierra de nadie*. His work is concerned above all with the under-privileged and the forgotten. He died when he was only forty-four of a stomach ulcer. His wife was the writer Josefina Aldecoa, who also features in this anthology.

better jobs before, but you know how it is . . . He didn't earn much, and they had to get by. That's where she came in, apart, that is, from grumbling and keeping the house in order. She sewed shirts for the army.

The little one's crying finally woke up both his brothers. Luis, the oldest, jumped out of bed in his shirt and hurriedly pulled on his trousers. Juan lay there, pretending that his knees were a range of mountains and imagining possible disasters.

The folds in the blankets set him dreaming; he would invent landscapes, imagine rivers where he could go fishing, stone by stone, for crabs of course. Crabs cooked with rice, because those were the best things about their summer Sunday outings.

Luis had now washed, and the little one had stopped crying. A neighbour came in to borrow some milk; for some reason theirs kept curdling. Antonia gave her some, and the neighbour, one arm folded across her chest and the other clasping a battered saucepan, began talking. Their voices reached Juan only indistinctly. The neighbour was saying:

'When babies are born, the bones in their head are like this . . . Then they have to grow on both sides to be normal . . . If they only grow on one side . . .'

'Juan!'

His mother's voice startled him. He wanted to remain immersed in his daydream.

'Coming.'

'Get up now or you'll get a good hiding.'

Juan had no choice: he got out of bed. The bedroom was right next to the kitchen. He was nice and warm there, but, once he'd been into the kitchen, there would be no going back. It made him shiver.

Juan picked up the chamber pot. His mother's voice reached him bearing a new threat.

'Don't be such a lazy slob. Use the toilet.'

He didn't want to go to the toilet because it was so cold, but he went. The toilet was in the courtyard. By the time he returned, the neighbour had gone. His mother grabbed him by the neck and dragged him over to the sink:

'When are you going to learn to wash yourself properly?'

Finally, he had breakfast.

Feeling warmer, with some food in his stomach, he went out into the courtyard. His friends were playing at being street-sweepers. They traced semi-circles in the dust with their brooms, making swishing sounds as they did. He stood watching for a while, hands in his pockets, a scornful look on his face. He stood on one leg for a moment to scratch his ankle, but without taking his left hand out of his trouser pocket. Then his brother Luis came racing out with an errand to run. He decided to go with him.

It was fun climbing the piles of gravel, stopping to look at a puddle and break the ice with your heel, picking up an empty matchbox or a sad, damp piece of paper.

Antonia was sitting by the window in a low, wide chair, busily working. The light from the courtyard is a bitter light, an oppressive light that makes her bow her head to do her sewing. A saucepan is rattling away on the stove. Antonia puts the shirt down on her lap and pokes her tongue into her cheek, feeling for her rotten tooth. The boys don't come back until ten o'clock, either because they got distracted or because they preferred the cold of the street to being shut up indoors. Antonia tells them off in a voice at once harsh and affectionate. Luis gets the blame for them staying out too long. Juan pouts indignantly.

'And as for you, Juan, don't you play the innocent either. You don't fool me.'

Then Antonia launches into her usual monologue, which is always the same, but which has a soothing effect on her. The boys stand watching their mother, until she sends them out into the street again.

'Off you go, you're no use here.'

Juan walks slowly over to the door. He opens it and is just about to take a leap into freedom when his mother calls him back:

'Now don't go running about too much. You might start sweating and catch a cold, and then it'll be the hospital for you, because we don't want any sick people in the house.'

The hospital and the orphanage are the two threats she uses on her sons, to no avail. And, when neither appears to work, she resorts to their father:

'Just you wait until your father gets home . . . He'll sort you out. If you do it again, then, come twelve o'clock, you'll pay for it right enough.'

A shudder runs down Juan's spine whenever his mother threatens him with his father, because he knows his father will be tired when he gets home and, if he does give him a beating, he'll do it indifferently and unthinkingly. Not like his mother, who beats him conscientiously and vociferously.

A ray of sunlight gilds the façades of the houses now that the mist has burned off. The sparrows puff out their breasts like a child blowing out his cheeks. A dog lies down in the sun, tongue lolling. The milkman's horse stamps its hooves and twitches its ears. The morning yawns with happiness.

Juan wanders off to an empty plot of land. He whistles to himself and sees how far he can throw stones.

The windows of the house opposite are tinged blood-red, just like the water when you rinse out your nose after you've been picking it too much. The walls of the house next to the empty plot are grey, like when you lick your finger and leave your fingerprint on the whitewashed partition wall. Juan is good at making out clown's faces in the damp stains on the walls. He remembers that, when he had a cold once, those faces on the wall had been his sole entertainment.

Antonia leans out of the window and bawls:

'Juan, come here.'

'Coming, Mum.'

But Juan the dreamer lingers for a while longer, rooting around for something or other on the ground.

He finally reaches the front door and goes upstairs. His mother says:

'Take this to the shop for me, will you? And say I'll drop by later on. Then you can carry on doing whatever it was you were doing, and I won't say a word.'

She shoots him an ironic glance:

'You've got until twelve o'clock to do whatever you want.'

Luis is sitting with his little brother on his lap. He smiles because he feels he's being rewarded for being virtuous. Juan is startled. It's been a long time since she said anything like that to him. Yes, he can do what he wants now, but not for very long, only for an hour or an hour and a quarter if his father stops to have a drink with his friends, which seems unlikely given that it's Friday and, on Fridays, there's no wine for his father and not much food for them. What bad luck. Juan can't tell the time, so, when he reaches the shop with his mother's basket, he asks the shopkeeper:

'Could you tell me what time it is, please?'

'Ten past eleven.'

'This is from my mother; she'll drop by later on.'

'Thanks, lad. Here, have some almonds.'

The shopkeeper is a kindly man and gives all his customers' children almonds. Juan mumbles his thanks and leaves. He's not much interested in almonds today, and so he just bites into one of them, then stuffs the others in his pocket, while he considers how soon twelve o'clock will come.

Juan sits down on the front step and ponders what he could do with that time. He could go back to rooting around on the empty plot; go upstairs and apologize for being naughty; go over to the corner of the street and watch some men digging a ditch; go upstairs and crouch in a corner and wait; play in the courtyard and make just enough noise for his mother to know that he hasn't gone far and is playing like a good little boy. Yes, that's what he'll do.

In the courtyard, the boys who had been playing at being street-sweepers are now playing with an old packing case. Juan stands by watching with a pleading look in his eyes. One of the boys, sweating and panting, turns and asks:

'D'you want to play?'

'All right.'

Juan generously shares out his almonds. Antonia Puerto continues her sewing. Now and then, she gets up to go over to the stove, where the saucepan continues to rattle and moan. Every time she picks up the lid, she burns her fingers, and has to use the folds of her apron as an oven glove. Luis is helping her, while the little one babbles happily away. From downstairs they hear Juan's voice; pleased, Antonia looks out of the window, and Juan turns round at that very moment and sees her there. It's a quarter to twelve and Juan has triumphed.

A neighbour comes in from the street and hurries across the courtyard. When she sees Juan, she asks:

'Is your mother in?'

Juan nods and follows her upstairs. When they reach their apartment, the neighbour knocks at the door, anxiously, quickly, telegraphically. Like a strange kind of SOS. The ring on the bell, the rap on the door, the pounding on the knocker that makes the inhabitants of a house rush out, hearts beating fast. Antonia comes to the door.

'What's wrong, Carmen?'

'Wait a moment, and I'll tell you. In you go, Juan. You're needed on the phone, Antonia. It's the foreman at the building site. Something's happened to your Pedro.'

Taking off her apron, Antonia races down the stairs.

'Take care of the kids, will you?'

'Of course, don't worry.'

Juan has heard everything and starts to cry loudly. Frightened, Luis does the same. The neighbour picks up the little one and tries to calm them all down. She closes the door.

Antonia rushes into the shop which has the only telephone in the street. She finds it hard to speak.

'Hello . . . yes, it's me. Is it bad? Yes, right away.'

The sun comes in through the shop window, setting the red ball of cheese on the marble counter glinting.

The factory sirens rise up to the clear, transparent, midday sky. It's twelve o'clock.

ANA MARÍA MATUTE

Conscience

She'd had enough. She was convinced she wouldn't be able to bear the presence in her house of that hateful tramp a moment longer. She was determined to get rid of him once and for all, whatever the consequences. Anything was better than having to endure his tyranny.

She'd been wrestling with this problem for nearly two weeks. What she couldn't understand was why Antonio put up with him; that was the really strange thing.

The tramp had asked if he could stay at the inn, just for one night, he'd said, Ash Wednesday it was, when the wind was sending up whirling clouds of blackish dust that battered and shook the windows. Then the wind dropped. A strange calm descended, and, as she was closing the shutters, she thought: It's too quiet. I don't like it.

Indeed, she hadn't yet bolted the front door when the man arrived. She heard him knocking at the kitchen door, calling:

'Señora!'

Mariana started. There he stood, a ragged old man, hat in hand, head bowed like a beggar.

Ana María Matute (1925–2014) was born in Barcelona, but, after she fell seriously ill when she was four, her parents took her to live with her grandparents in a small village in the mountains in La Rioja. The people she knew there coloured all her writing, as did the Civil War and its aftermath. She wrote many novels and even more short stories, and many are haunted by the traumatic effect of war and its consequences on children. Among her most famous novels are *Los Abel, Fiesta al Noroeste, Pequeño teatro, Los hijos muertos, Los soldados lloran de noche* and, above all, *Primera memoria* (translated into English as *School of the Sun*). She was awarded Spain's highest literary honour, the Premio Cervantes, in 2010.

'May God preserve you, Señora,' he began by saying, but his beady tramp's eyes looked at her strangely, so strangely she didn't know what to say.

Men like him often asked for shelter, especially on winter nights, but there was something about this man that, for some reason, frightened her.

He launched into the usual spiel: It would only be for one night. He could sleep in the stable. A crust of bread and a night in the stable, that's all he was asking for. A storm was brewing and . . .

And, outside, Mariana could hear the rain lashing the wooden door. A dull, heavy rain, a foretaste of the storm to come.

'I'm on my own,' said Mariana brusquely. 'I mean . . . when my husband's away, I don't want strangers in the house. Off you go, and may God preserve you.'

But the tramp just stood there, looking at her. Slowly putting his hat back on, he said:

'I'm just a poor old man, Señora, who never harmed nobody. I'm not asking for much, just a crust of bread . . .'

At that moment, the two maids, Marcelina and Salomé, came running in from working on the vegetable patch, shrieking and laughing, their aprons over their heads. Mariana felt unusually relieved to see them.

'All right,' she said. 'All right, but just for one night. When I come down tomorrow morning, I don't want to find you still here . . .'

The old man bowed and smiled, rattling off an extravagant string of thank yous.

Mariana eventually went upstairs to bed. During the night, the storm beat against the bedroom windows and she slept badly.

The following morning, when she went down to the kitchen, the clock on the dresser was striking eight o'clock. What she saw both surprised and annoyed her. Seated at the table was the tramp, calmly and contentedly eating a sumptuous breakfast of fried eggs, a big slice of fresh bread, and a glass of wine . . . Mariana felt a flicker of anger, mingled perhaps with fear, and she turned to Salomé, who was quietly labouring away over the stove.

'Salomé,' she said, and her voice sounded harsh, severe. 'Who told you to give that man breakfast . . . and w-why didn't he leave at first light?'

She was so furious, she stumbled over her words. Salomé stared at her open-mouthed, the slotted spoon in her hand dripping oil onto the floor.

'But I . . .' she began. 'He said . . .'

The tramp had got to his feet now and was carefully wiping his mouth on his sleeve.

'Don't you remember, Señora? Last night you said: "Give the poor old man a bed in the attic and as much food as he can eat." Isn't that what you said last night, Señora? I heard you with my own ears. Or are you having second thoughts?'

Mariana was about to respond, but suddenly her voice froze. The old man was staring at her with his small, dark, piercing eyes. She turned and petulantly flounced out of the kitchen door into the vegetable garden.

The sky was overcast, but the rain had stopped. Mariana shivered. The grass was drenched, and in the distance the road had disappeared beneath a subtle mist. Hearing the old man's voice behind her, she involuntarily clenched her fists.

'I'd like to talk to you about something, Señora . . . nothing of any importance.'

Mariana did not move, still gazing across at the road.

'I'm just an old vagabond, but sometimes we old vagabonds find things out. Yes, I was there, Señora. I saw it with my own eyes.'

Mariana opened her mouth, but no words came out.

'What are you talking about, you wretch?' she said. 'I'm warning you: my husband will be back with the wagon at ten o'clock, and he takes no nonsense from anyone!'

'I know, I know he doesn't!' said the tramp. 'That's why you wouldn't want anyone finding out about what I saw the other day. Isn't that right?'

Mariana spun round, all her anger gone. In her confusion, her heart began beating still faster. What does he mean? What does he know? What did he see? But still she said nothing. She merely looked at him full of fear and loathing. The old man smiled at her with his grubby, toothless gums.

'I'll be staying here for a while, Señora, yes, for a while, until I've recovered my strength, until the sun returns. Because I'm an old man now and my legs are tired.'

Mariana broke into a run. She could feel the wind cutting her face. When she reached the well, she stopped. She felt as if her heart were going to leap out of her chest.

That was the first day. Antonio arrived home later with the wagon. He brought goods from Palomar each week, for, as well as being innkeepers, they kept the only shop in the village. Their large, spacious house, surrounded by a vegetable garden, stood at the entrance to the village. They lived well, and the other villagers considered Antonio to be a wealthy man. A wealthy man, thought Mariana angrily. Since the arrival of that hateful tramp, she had grown pale and listless. Would I have married him otherwise? No, of course not. It wasn't hard to understand why she had married that brutish man, fourteen years her senior. A sullen, solitary, rather intimidating man. She was pretty, as everyone in the village would agree. As did Constantino, who was in love with her. But Constantino was a sharecropper like her, and she'd had enough of hunger, hard work and poverty. Yes, she'd had enough. That's why she married Antonio.

Mariana felt a strange shudder run through her. It was nearly two weeks now since the old man had arrived at the inn. He slept, ate, and, when the sun was out, sat by the door to the garden, shamelessly picking the lice off his clothes. On the first day, Antonio asked:

'What's that fellow doing here?'

'I felt sorry for him,' she said, fiddling with the fringe on her shawl. 'He's so old and the weather's so dreadful and . . .'

Antonio said nothing. It seemed to her that he was about to go over to the old man and throw him out, and so she fled upstairs. She was genuinely frightened. What if the old man saw Constantino climbing up the chestnut tree under my window? What if he saw him climb into my room on one of the nights when Antonio was away with the wagon, on the road? What else could he mean by that 'I saw everything with my own eyes'?

She could stand it no longer, no, not a moment longer. The old man wasn't content now just to live in the house. He'd even started asking for money. And the odd thing is that Antonio never said another word about him. He just ignored the man, whereas he did occasionally look at her, and, when she felt his large, dark, shining eyes fixed on her, she would tremble.

That afternoon, Antonio was again heading off to Palomar. The mules were being hitched to the wagon, and she could hear the voices of the stable boy and of Salomé, who were helping him. Mariana felt cold. I can't stand it any longer. I can't go on living like this. I'll tell him to leave, to go. I can't live with this threat hanging over me. She felt sick. Sick with fear. She had stopped seeing Constantino out of fear. She couldn't bear the sight of him now. The mere thought of him made her teeth chatter. Antonio would kill her if he ever found out. Of that she was sure. She knew him well.

When she saw the wagon disappearing down the road, she went downstairs to the kitchen. The old man was sitting by the fire, dozing. She looked at him and said to herself: 'If I was brave enough, I'd kill him.' The iron tongs were there within reach. But she wouldn't do it. She knew she couldn't. 'I'm a coward. I'm a great coward and I love life too much.' That was her downfall, her love of life.

'Old man,' she said, and, even though she spoke very softly, the tramp opened one mischievous eye. So the sly old fox wasn't really sleeping, thought Mariana.

'Come with me,' she said. 'I have something to say to you.'

The old man followed her to the well, where Mariana turned to face him.

'You can do what you like, wretch. You can tell my husband everything if you want, but you have to go. You must leave this house now.'

The old man fell silent for a few seconds, then he smiled and said:

'When will your husband be back?'

Mariana had turned deathly pale. He observed her lovely face, the dark circles under her eyes. She had lost weight.

'Leave,' said Mariana. 'Leave now.'

She was determined, and the tramp could see this in her eyes. She was determined and desperate. He had long experience of such eyes. There's nothing more to be done, he thought philosophically. The good times are over. No more lavish meals, no more soft mattress, no more shelter. Off you go, you old dog, off you go. Time to hit the road.

'All right,' he said. 'I'll go. But he'll find out everything . . .'

Mariana maintained her silence, although she did perhaps turn still paler. Suddenly, the old man felt a tremor of fear: She's capable of doing something drastic. Yes, she's the sort who might hang herself or something. He felt sorry for her then. She was, after all, still young and beautiful.

'All right,' he said. 'You win, Señora. I'll go. I don't really have any choice. I knew it couldn't last. I've had a very good time here, though. I'll never forget Salomé's stews or your husband's wine. No, I won't forget, but I'll go.'

'Now,' she said hurriedly. 'Go now. And if you run, you might catch up with him. Yes, run after him with your smutty stories, you old dog.'

The tramp smiled sweetly. He picked up his staff and his leather pouch. As he was about to leave, when he had already reached the picket fence, he turned.

'Of course, Señora, I didn't actually see anything. I don't even know if there was anything to see. But I've spent many years on the road, far too many, and I know there isn't a soul in the world with a clear conscience, not even kids. No, not even kids, dear lady. Look a child in the eyes and say: "I know everything! You'd better watch it . . ." And the child will tremble, just like you, my lovely.'

Mariana experienced a strange sensation, a sound as if her heart were cracking. She didn't know if it was bitterness filling her heart or violent joy. She moved her lips and was about to say something, but the old tramp had closed the gate behind him and again turned to look at her. With a malicious smile, he said:

'A word of advice, Señora. Keep a close eye on your Antonio. He, too, has his reasons for letting old beggars stay in his house, very good reasons, I'd say, given the look he gave me!'

The mist hanging low over the road was growing thicker. Mariana watched the man until he had disappeared from sight.

MEDARDO FRAILE

Berta's Presence

It was Lupita's first birthday. Lupita was an amorphous, attractive being, at once yielding and terrible, whom no one had ever seen in a theatre, a cinema or a café, or even strolling down the street. But she was plotting in silence. She imagined great things, engaged in vigorous movement and was convinced that she would triumph. She smelled delicious in her night attire. She smelled like a little girl about to turn one. Her parents had invited their friends over for a bite to eat. 'Do come. It's Lupita's first birthday.'

Jacobo rang the bell and heard familiar voices inside. When the door opened, he said loudly: 'Where's Lupita? Where's that little rascal?' And the child appeared, squirming about in her mother's arms, her small body erect, excited, attentive. Lupita, in her own strange, personal language, had managed to convey to her mother the idea of tying two small, pink bows – like wide-set miniature horns – in her sparse, perfumed hair. It hadn't been her mother's doing at all. The suggestion had come from Lupita herself, aware of her charms and her flaws. 'So what have you got to say for yourself, then, eh? What has Señorita Lupe got to say for herself?' And Jacobo produced a little box of sweets from his pocket and

Medardo Fraile (1925–2013) was born in Madrid, but, from 1964 onwards, he lived in Scotland, where he was Professor of Spanish at the University of Strathclyde until his retirement. As a student he was very involved in the theatre, but abandoned that world to devote himself to writing – almost exclusively – short stories. He was part of the same group of writers as Ignacio Aldecoa, Carmen Martín Gaite, Rafael Sánchez Ferlosio and Ana María Matute. As well as nine collections of stories, he wrote six children's books, one novel, seven volumes of essays and one memoir. His work brought him many prizes, notably the Premio Nacional de la Crítica. A collection of his stories is available in English, *Things Look Different in the Light*.

showed it to her. 'Baaa!' said Lupita joyfully, showing the visitor her pink uvula and waving her arms and legs about as if fearlessly leaping over each 'a' she uttered. She liked Jacobo.

A bottle on the table reflected the branches of the chestnut tree outside the window. It was a warm evening, with the windows open, full of the distant murmurs and melodies set in motion by the departing sun. One of those evenings on which the scented, rustling countryside suddenly enters the city, as if the countryside had left itself behind for a few hours in order to set the city-dweller humming a tune, whether at a birthday party, in a bar or at home. One of those evenings when the factory siren sounds like the moan of a large, friendly animal gone astray and where the frank, rustic kisses of the soldier and his sweetheart sound like pebbles in a stream. One of those evenings of high, long, tenuous mists, so that, when the first stars come out, they will not appear too naked.

Every now and then, the doorbell rang and new friends came into the room. The engaged couple, bound together by a prickly sweetness, the wounding words recently and rapidly spoken on the landing outside not yet forgotten and transmuted instead into delicate, social irony. The tall friend, in a dark, striped suit, who keeps looking at his watch only immediately to forget what it said, with the look of someone who has left some poor girl standing on a corner. The newlyweds, inured by now to everyone's jokes, strolling in as if fresh from a gentle walk, he in an immaculate shirt and she full of solicitous gestures. The desperate young woman, who can never persuade her fiancé to accompany her on visits, and whose stockings always bag slightly and who has one permanently rebellious lock of hair. The sporty friend, always fresh from the shower, slightly distant and smiling and as if fearful that the great lighthouse of his chest might go out. And Berta, the outsider, the surprise, the one they had not expected to come.

They all got up again when Berta arrived. She greeted everyone – Jacobo rather coolly – and then immediately turned all her words and attention to Lupita. 'Look, Lupita, I've bought you some earrings. Do you like them?' Jacobo was put out. He had been just about to speak to Lupita when Berta arrived. He had gone over to her, and Lupita was already looking at him. He was about to say: 'Aren't you getting old! One year old already!' But, when he heard Berta speak, his words seemed pointless and unamusing. They seemed hollow and, therefore, entirely dependent on intonation and timing. He allowed them to die on his lips, and that death was an almost insuperable obstacle to all the other things he subsequently said and thought.

Jacobo knew how difficult it was to speak to children. You had to have something of the lion-tamer about you, or else limitless wit and spontaneity. Children demand a lot of those who speak to them and, unless they instantly succumb to the charm of a phrase, they regard their interlocutor circumspectly and occasionally harshly. They can tell when the words are sincere and when they falter in any way. They cry in terror at clumsy words or words full of twisted intentions or falsehood. And Jacobo, who had, on occasions, spoken to children quite successfully, fell silent, profoundly silent, listening to the river of efficacious words that flowed from Berta to Lupita.

That was one of Berta's qualities, knowing how to talk to children. With her subtle, imaginative intonation, Berta came out with the most wonderful things. Children stood amazed as they, intently, pleasurably, followed the thread of her voice. It was as if they had before them a fine-feathered, perfumed bird with an attractive, kaleidoscopic throat, like a grotto full of stories and legends. And Berta didn't change her voice in the least, she was just herself. That voice – thought Jacobo – emerged from clean, colourful depths, it bubbled gently and was, like water, sonorous and fresh, rich and profound. More than that, Berta knew the language of children, knew which syllables to cut out and in what innocent moulds to reshape words so that they could be understood. How could one speak to them using the serious, rule-bound words used by grown-ups, words that have been through the hard school of Grammar?

'So, Berta, what are you doing here? What happened?'

And while Berta was explaining that she was spending a few days in Madrid before leaving again for Seville, where she had been sent by her company, Lupita was momentarily ignored and she remembered that, before Berta had arrived, someone else had been about to speak to her. And she turned her head, looking at everyone there, one by one, until she found him: Jacobo. Eyes wide, gaze fixed on him, she urged him to say his sentence. Jacobo noticed and grew still more inhibited. For her part, Lupita's mother, smiling sweetly, followed the direction of her little girl's eyes. Lupita even uttered the usual password: 'Baaa!' But Jacobo, who, when he arrived, had managed some quite acceptable phrases, now nervously crossed his legs, stared into his glass of wine or grimly studied a painting on the wall, or shot a fleeting glance, which he intended to appear casual, at a newspaper or some other object. Lupita felt suspicious, and her gaze grew more searching and persistent. 'What a strange man. It was so hard to know what he was thinking.'

Jacobo refused, after much hesitation, to compete with Berta. As everyone knew, her presence always made one more aware of one's own absurdity and the need to make a good impression. Not that he made much of an impression with his familiar long silences, his all-consuming shyness that showed itself in the form of an affected seriousness and slightly tactless, brusque remarks. He could never, with any naturalness, manage those strange verbal deviations of Berta's, those clean leaps from one word to another. 'How's my little babbler, my baboon, my bouncing bean!' And it worked perfectly. Lupita – like all babies – did babble and could certainly shriek like a baboon and, at certain moments, she actually did resemble one of those neat little butter beans, all creamy and soft.

'What's so fascinating about Jacobo, sweetie? Why do you keep looking at him like that?' said Lupita's mother.

'Yes, she won't take her eyes off him,' said the others.

And Jacobo gave Lupita a faint smile, accompanied by a determined, almost aggressive look that asked the usual nonsense one asks of children. But his shyness, crouching in his eyes like two dark dots, censured the words it occurred to him to say, pursued and erased them, leaving only a charmless, bitter void. There was a dense silence. Everyone was waiting for something to happen, for Jacobo to speak to Lupita. Half-hidden in a corner, Berta was watching and smiling imperceptibly, curious and silent.

'It's awfully hot, don't you think?' he said.

And he said this as a warning to the others. He meant to say: 'Yes, it's true, children do sometimes stare insistently at some grown-up, it's a habit they have, but we shouldn't pay them too much attention, we should simply talk about our own affairs. And it is awfully hot today. Unusual for the time of year. That's what we should be talking about.'

'Baaa!' cried Lupita defiantly.

'It's usually getting cooler by now.'

'Say something to the child! Can't you see she's looking at you?'

Yes, the moment had arrived. The silence and the expectation thickened. Eyes flicked from Jacobo to Lupita and back again. Slowly and terribly shyly, almost regretfully, Jacobo finally managed to say:

'Hello! How are you? Why are you looking at me like that? What's up? What do you want? What did I do?'

As if he were talking to a moneylender.

'What do you *think* she wants? Say something funny, man. Pay her some attention. That's what you want, isn't it, Lupita?'

Lupita burst into tears. She had seen the scowling black cloud advancing towards her across the room. And she hadn't wanted things to go that far. The words had left a dramatic aftertaste in the air, threatening and exciting. Lupita was crying because she had ventured innocently into unknown territory, where the somewhat stiff words exuded a certain bitterness, and where situations crystallized into impossible shapes. The daylight blinked, and the room filled with loud, laborious, rhythmical words of consolation. Lupita pouted and sobbed and wept bitterly. It lasted a long time.

The evening succumbed meekly. The clock struck the hour. Jacobo made his excuses, saying that he was expected elsewhere, then got up and left. He was walking slowly down the street, not sure where he was going. It felt slightly chilly. He was thinking about Berta – to whom he still felt attracted – about Lupita, so friendly and funny and lovely, and about his friends, his old friends. How nice it would have been to have stayed with them to the end.

CARMEN MARTÍN GAITE

Behind the Eyes

It was simply a matter of finding a safe place, a kind of refuge, for your eyes. Francisco had finally come to this realization. And, as a vague, insecure man of few resources, he was proud to have arrived at this truth on his own, at this small solution to so many situations. People could board you through your eyes and climb inside. He couldn't bear these sudden, inconsiderate assaults by other people, which obliged you to step outside yourself, and, as if drawing back a curtain, reveal words and smiles, whether you wanted to or not.

'She was so funny that lady from Palencia! Do you remember, Francisco?'

'Francisco, tell them that story about her little dog.'

'We weren't there when she came, were we, Francisco?'

'You mean Margarita? Oh, Francisco will know all about that. That's his business. Now, come on, don't play the innocent. Anyone would think you didn't even know who Margarita was. Look, he's blushing.'

Was he really blushing? No, he wasn't, they just imposed their own interpretation on everything, creating complicated stories that only confused matters more. He might have been looking at them partly in

---

Carmen Martín Gaite (1925–2000) was born in Salamanca but lived most of her adult life in Madrid. She was largely home-educated by her father, who wanted her to have a secular education. She did her first degree in Romance languages at the University of Salamanca, then moved back to Madrid where she met other young writers, such as Ignacio Aldecoa, Medardo Fraile and Rafael Sánchez Ferlosio, whom she married in 1953. She wrote poetry, novels, short stories, plays and children's fiction, as well as essays on a variety of subjects. She also worked as a translator, translating such works as *Wuthering Heights* and *Madame Bovary*. Her work has been widely translated (*Variable Cloud*, *The Farewell Angel* and *The Back Room* are all available in English).

bewilderment, because he couldn't remember who Margarita was, and partly out of embarrassment at his failure to remember and his desire to fob them off with some answer or other just so they would leave him in peace with his own thoughts. Although, if someone had asked what his own thoughts were or why they should take up so much time, he wouldn't have been able to explain. He had a sense, though, that returning to his own thoughts was tantamount to freeing himself from those tenacious pairs of hands that kept insisting on dragging him onto the stage to perform pirouettes beneath a troublesome, faltering, intermittent light, before a battery of footlights that threatened at any moment to focus once again on his eyes. It was like freeing himself from those grasping hands, reaching his own front door again, pushing it open and sitting down quietly to resume whatever it was that he had left unfinished, and with not a sound to be heard.

Some people launched into long, complicated dissertations on some minuscule, barely perceptible subject, which slipped and slid away from their words, and he had the devil's own job to follow the thread and find a path through all that mist. Others preferred to recount amusing incidents that he was obliged to find delightful; still others waxed indignant – any topic would do – and proved terribly repetitive and incoherent, their talk full of interjections and ups and downs, sharp jabs to provoke the others, to get them worked up into the same state of indignation, and, until they succeeded and could then rest easy for a while, they would return to the charge again and again, incapable of calming down. Most alarming of all, though, and from whom there was no escape, were the sort who would throw down an implacable question followed by a silence: 'What do you say to that?' or 'What do you think of that?' And they would stand there, watching and waiting, chin slightly lifted.

Francisco flailed about like a drowning man among these other people's conversations, caught up in them all and unable to cut himself off, with everyone waiting for him to put in his twopenny-worth. And, even if he didn't, there he was, trapped. He felt he was being forced to join in, obliged to endure conversations that neither consoled nor concerned him, unable to detach himself from the words circling around him.

Then, one day, he discovered that the answer lay in the eyes. You listen through your eyes, and only your eyes commit you to keep on listening.

For those people who caught him before he had time to put his eyes safely away, this was tantamount to hailing a cab and never letting it go; you were defenceless. It was your eyes that you needed to isolate, it was your eyes that others always addressed. Francisco learned to fix them firmly on lamps, pedestal tables, rooftops, groups of people looking elsewhere, on cats or carpets. He gazed insistently at objects and landscapes, drinking them in along with their colours and shapes, with the time and the respite they allowed him. And he would hear the conversations going on, but as if he were disconnected from them, looking down on them from a great height, caring not a jot about their conclusions or their intentions, distracted and lulled by the odd snippets that reached him. He would occasionally smile in order to pretend that he was actually listening, a pale flicker of a smile that someone always noticed; and he could even utter the occasional brief, uncompromising sentence. People began to say of him: 'He's sad,' but they didn't ask him anything because they could never catch his eye.

Everyone spoke well of him.

'Your son, Señora,' they would say to his mother, 'has a very rich inner life.'

'Well, he's studying for his civil service exams, you see. I think he might be studying too hard.'

Francisco wasn't studying particularly hard, nor did he have much of an inner life. He shut himself up in his room, studied what he needed to study, then spent his time making little birds out of paper and drawing very slowly. He would go to the café, to the club, or stroll around the streets near the cathedral. His sister's friends would say to her:

'He's amazing. He listens so intently to everything people tell him. I don't care if he doesn't know how to dance.'

Francisco's parents lived on the first floor of a house in the main square. In summer, when it was dark, they would leave all the balcony doors open, and from the street you could see the red tassels on the curtains, a few dark pieces of furniture, some portraits, and the glow of an oil lamp. At the far end, there was a big mirror that reflected the lights from outside.

'It must be such a great apartment!' the youngsters in the street would say.

And sometimes Francisco would watch them from the balcony of his bedroom. He would see them standing around, hair all dishevelled, in a break from their running about and their games; indeed, he would spend so much time looking that they would end up looking at him too and start nudging each other and laughing. Then Francisco would come inside.

One day, his mother called to him from the little room next door to his.

'Listen, Francisco, as long as your father and I are alive, you don't need to worry about anything. We were talking about it just last night.'

There was a brief pause, like those you get in dialogues in a play. Francisco fidgeted uneasily on his cushion; he always found such preambles extremely disconcerting, and he was less and less prepared to hear things that affected him directly. He looked over at the moon, which had appeared above a roof opposite, and it was so white, so silent and so remote that he found it really consoling. He opened his eyes very wide and withdrew into himself, imagining the two tiny moons that would be forming in his pupils. His mother spoke again, and this time it was less painful to him. She was talking now about some complicated deal which had, apparently, gone rather badly, and about which Francisco should have known. He realized this because of the precise way in which she mentioned names, dates and details that he should probably have been familiar with. And he did recall hearing them talk about the matter earlier, over lunch.

'Anyway, you're not to worry. Don't worry about your exams either. That's all over. I don't want to see you looking sad again. Regardless of whether you pass your exams or not, you can marry whoever you like.'

So that's what it was about! Francisco stared still harder at the moon. His mother presumably thought he was in love. Perhaps he was. Had one of the girls he'd spoken to recently left a more indelible image than usual on that stockroom behind his eyes? Was there one of them he could take by the hand and say: 'Shall we?' He began to feel very anxious. There, behind his eyes, in that back room, in that old warehouse, where everything accumulated over the days and evenings, he had stored away the faces of various girls. There was one who sometimes appeared in his dreams and who looked at him without saying a word, just as he was now looking at the moon. It was always the same girl: she had long, dark hair caught back with a ribbon. He would ask her urgently: 'Please, speak,' and she was the only person in the world he would have wanted to listen to.

Francisco's mother waited, as if some great battle were going on inside her. He had already forgotten that he should have replied to what she had said before. He only looked away from the moon when he heard his mother say:

'Oh dear, I don't want you to feel sad again. You can get married whenever you want. And you can marry whoever you want, all right? Even Margarita.'

Francisco sensed his mother eyeing him furtively and felt a wave of emotion. He made his decision right there and then. He didn't care if he wasn't quite sure who Margarita was or where he had seen her for the first time. People had mentioned this Margarita person many times already (and he was too obtuse to have noticed), this humble young woman who appeared in his dreams and who probably loved him. She must be some rather insignificant person, a casual acquaintance of his sister's, but inferior to them, for they measured everyone according to whether or not they came from 'a good family'. She must have come to the house one day. A shop assistant perhaps. After all, his mother had said: 'Even Margarita.'

Yes, he would marry her and no other. He felt in a hurry now to look at her and to allow himself to be looked at, to surrender his eyes to her, with their jumbled store of nostalgias, silences, chairs, lights, vases and rooftops. Yes, he would give his eyes to Margarita, for they were all he had, containing as they did everything he might have thought and missed. He wanted to go with her to some as-yet-unknown city. To deposit in Margarita's gaze his own shifting, rootless gaze. The eyes alone open the door into a person, letting in the air and transforming the house. He stood up.

'Yes, mother, I will marry Margarita. I would marry her even if you disapproved. I'm going to see her now. Yes, I must see her.'

He said this resolutely, looking his mother in the eye and speaking in a determined, rebellious tone he'd never used before, as if he were shaking off the shackles. Then he strode out of the room.

JOSEFINA RODRÍGUEZ ALDECOA

Madrid, Autumn, Saturday

It was the same every Saturday, the anxiety she always felt on waking, which appeared along with the light filtering in through the slats of the half-open shutter, and, as usual, she leapt up to abruptly close the slats. Then she pulled the curtains tight shut, and darkness filled the room. She closed her eyes and tried to go back to sleep. 'It's Saturday.' And she ordered herself not to think, not to remember, not to be assailed by any of the usual weekday worries. Timetables, appointments, phone calls, snippets of information that were rapidly replaced by others. Plans, problems. 'It's Saturday. I need to switch off. I can't afford the luxury of getting a head start on whatever I have to do on Monday. Or Tuesday for that matter . . . Oh no, I've got to give that lecture on Tuesday. There's no way I can go back to sleep now.' She sat up in bed and turned on the light. 'I'll just take a quick look at my lecture, mark the pauses and underline any key words in red . . . Then this afternoon, I'll answer some of the more urgent letters. That way I'll have Sunday completely free . . .'

She drew back the curtains and pressed her face to the glass. Stretched out below, like an English landscape painting, lay the Botanical Gardens, wrapped in a thin mist transparent enough to allow a glimpse of the treetops.

Josefina Rodríguez Aldecoa (1926–2011) was born in León, and came from a family of teachers. She wrote her Ph.D. on the relationship between children and art, going on to found the Colegio Estilo, a secular school focusing on literature, writing and art. While studying in Madrid, she got to know other writers such as Carmen Martín Gaite, Rafael Sánchez Ferlosio and Ignacio Aldecoa, whom she married, only taking his name after his death in 1969. She then concentrated on her teaching career but returned to writing in the 1980s with novels such as *Los niños de la guerra*, *La enredadera*, *Porque éramos jóvenes* and *El vergel*.

Hours later, when the Madrid sky was aglow with the autumn sun, the garden would reveal its treasure trove of dry leaves, transformed into gorgeously coloured fabrics: yellow gauze, brown velvet, golden satin, orangey-red wool with a tracery of greyish veins. The fragile stems attaching the leaves to the branches surrendered easily to the onslaught of wind or rain. On some mornings, they would appear around the tree trunks in untidy piles that extended as far as the sandy paths. In spring, the green leaves, attached to their stems with invisible hooks, staunchly resisted the most violent of storms, but these lovely, decaying leaves fell wearily to the ground, in the knowledge that they had reached the end of their life cycle. Then they would swirl around the tree for a moment, forming indecipherable arabesques . . .

Julia walked through to the living room and opened the balcony door. She gazed out at the autumnal scene and listened to the chirruping of the birds, a sound obscured only by the occasional whoosh of a passing car, one of the few cars driving along the Paseo del Prado at that hour on a Saturday morning. Julia gave a sigh of satisfaction: 'This is where I always dreamed of ending up. With this view over the Botanical Gardens and its lush vegetation changing with the seasons.'

When she went into the kitchen, she turned on the light and saw the tray on the table with all the ingredients for her breakfast neatly laid out. María always left it there on a Friday afternoon before she went home for the weekend. The air of comfort that María so painstakingly cultivated throughout the week, with everything carefully organized and Julia's clothes all neatly stowed away, meant that Julia could enjoy her weekend in peace and quiet without the hassle of housework. Her day began with a leisurely breakfast and the newspaper, which was delivered first thing, then silently conveyed to her apartment by the caretaker. A day to savour the pleasure of choosing from among her various weekday temptations: an exhibition, shopping, or going to an early showing of a new film, then home early to read, listen to music, relax. She had long ago decided to reserve weekends for herself. During the week, she might go to a lecture, a cocktail party, meet useful contacts, arrange an interesting lunch somewhere or have supper with friends. Her life was thus a balance between work, socializing and these absolutely vital periods of solitude.

Those hours spent alone were not without their dangers. They were vacant hours, free of any external stimuli or the inevitable demands placed on her by others. However, they could also prove troubling, unleashing a storm in Julia's otherwise tightly controlled universe by allowing a sudden nostalgia for another time to surface or for some insignificant event to spark a far more significant memory.

Right now, as she looked up from her desk beneath the window and gazed out at the Botanical Gardens already bright with midday sun, she paused briefly to study the small square full of tourists, the off-duty people wandering idly past the Prado Museum or heading for one of the gates to the nearby Parque del Retiro. A couple with a pram were trying to get into the garden. The mother removed the child from the pram while the father went over to the ticket office and disappeared. The sight of that woman alone with the baby in her arms provoked in Julia a flood of memories that were usually safely buried in the depths of her mind. Bernal's childhood, her solitary walks with him during that first interminable year. They lived far from there then, in a lively new part of town, in a quiet street with broad pavements planted with a line of plane trees that protected you from the summer sun. Bernal had been born in June, and his first months had been spent being pushed up and down those pavements. While he slept, Julia would use that brief respite to sit with him on the terrace outside a bar and try to catch up on her reading. She recalled that first year as being one long walk through a dense mist. Days and nights blurred into one, and her mind was totally taken up with bottles, walks, bathtimes and bedtimes . . . By the end of the day, she would be totally exhausted, as if she had climbed a mountain or returned from a long journey. It was an exhaustion that had gradually accumulated through the pregnancy, the birth itself and those first few months of constantly broken sleep. It was different from any she had known before. That year had been a kind of somnambular year filled with a permanent sense of being in limbo, as if bonding with her child had been a prolongation of the whole prenatal stage, when somnolence was the main characteristic of those nine months of waiting. A whole year. Then Julia had gone back to work. Finding Ramona, that delightful young woman who could spend all day there and was genuinely fond of Bernal, had been her salvation . . .

That boy was now a young man and lived far away. They were long gone, those luminous childhood days when the three of them, Diego and Bernal and her, would laugh and play together when they weren't at work, or at the weekends when they were free . . .

In a way, that memory cast a cloud over her Saturday morning. 'Best forget about it by doing some work,' thought Julia. And she had barely settled down with her papers spread out on the desk, when the phone rang, and she asked in a slightly irritated tone: 'Hello?' and a familiar voice asked: 'Julia? It's Cecilia . . .'

'How lovely to hear from you, Cecilia,' said Julia, but she said this rather too enthusiastically, as if to make up for her initial reserve, her coolness and her obvious displeasure at having someone intrude on her Saturday privacy.

'I'm here in Madrid and staying just around the corner from you, in the Palace Hotel,' said Cecilia.

And Julia couldn't help asking:

'But what are you doing here?'

'I'll tell you later. If you're free, we could meet after lunch. I can't before . . .'

'So what do you think of my secret?' Cecilia asked. 'Did you ever imagine me having an affair?'

Julia hesitated before replying. To avoid saying No, she said:

'Do you see any future in this affair?'

'Any future, Julia?' Cecilia smiled and then grew serious. 'Do we have much future left? We did once, a long time ago. When we were children, our mothers were always talking about tomorrow, and everything seemed to depend on that mysterious day somewhere on the horizon. You couldn't do anything without thinking about the consequences your actions might have on that distant tomorrow . . .'

The two fell silent, then Julia said:

'Tell me more about how it happened. I know who you mean now. He was that boy you were so keen on before you met Matías. And I remember how keen he was on you too. And, of course, you chose someone else, because, as you say, what kind of tomorrow could you expect with a dull young man who wanted to study medicine? Your mantra was always: "I don't want to end up stuck in a village somewhere. Anything but that!"'

'All right, here goes. One day, I read in the paper, in the list of upcoming events, that Dr Javier Valverde Díaz had given a lecture, that he'd just arrived back from the States, where he works in a famous hospital. I was astonished. Had I been completely wrong about him? And when choosing between the modest son of an obscure vet and rich kid Matías, had I chosen the wrong one? Now it's Matías who lives in the country, and my poor medical student is a bigwig in America. Anyway, as you can imagine, things would have gone no further if I hadn't been in such a state ever since Matías did the dirty on me, running off with my daughter's best friend. I'm sure you haven't forgotten that. And he's still with her, living on a farm somewhere fifty kilometres from us. They're always off travelling somewhere, and she's always dressed to kill. Matías comes to see me once a month, asks how I'm getting on and gives me some money. He asks about the kids, as if he cared . . . When he left us, our youngest still wasn't married. Oh, it's been just awful, Julia. And of course when you think about how we girls were brought up . . . You soon sloughed it all off, but I . . . well, I married young and ended up trapped with a patriarch straight out of the nineteenth century. Mind you, he's certainly proved to be a quick learner. He took to the new fashion for second marriages like a duck to water. Because, while our fathers might have had a mistress, they rarely left their legitimate wife . . .'

'Yes, but tell me how you managed to get in touch with Javier.'

'Very easy. I phoned round a few of the best hotels in Madrid and found him almost at once. I knew he wasn't living here because of what I'd read in the paper, about him being over from America to give some lectures. He was completely taken aback. He couldn't even speak. Then he asked me all kinds of questions about my life, and I asked about his. He married an American woman, but they've since divorced. We immediately discussed meeting up. I lied and said that, as it happened, I had to come to Madrid on family business. And so I came. I didn't phone you then, of course. That was two and a half months ago. Since then, Javier has been to Europe twice, and we met both times. And this weekend is the third time. You could call my story *Brief Encounter in Madrid* . . .'

Ah, Cecilia, always stuck fast in an unresolved adolescence, in a longed-for, but impossible independence. And now, suddenly, this complete change, with no thought for the family prejudices that had always been her real guide. An adolescence that passed without her having 'killed off' her father, her mother and the boyfriend she'd always had . . .

Cecilia had started talking again. She said:

'And what about you?'

Julia said:

'Me? Affairs, you mean? Oh, I've reached the stage in life when me and all my friends are passionately involved in our careers. We're in our prime. We're all forty-seven, forty-eight, touching fifty. You too. So what can I tell you about me? I live a life of daily solitude and peace. I've left behind any dreams and hopes and wishes. I have my son. He lives a long way away, but I still have him. I visit him in London sometimes, and he sometimes comes here, and, of course, we talk on the phone. Both of us have a good relationship with Diego. And Diego continues his nomadic lifestyle, flitting here and there, separated now from his second wife and his second son. I imagine *he* has a few fleeting affairs. And I'm lucky because I really love my job, and spend my time between the university and the council and all the thousand and one other organizations I'm involved in, some professional, others not. I write articles and the occasional book. And I like living in Madrid.'

After a brief silence, Julia felt the need to go on.

'When I came to study here, Madrid for me meant freedom, coming and going by day or by night with whoever I chose. Even at the beginning, when real freedom was still a long way off, even then, Madrid represented freedom. The morality police can't find you in the big city, nor can the politicians . . . And I'm happy now in this apartment. I've found the landscape I want, a bit of nature in the middle of the city. Maybe I'm yearning for my childhood in the village where my grandparents lived and which you know well . . .'

Cecilia said nothing. She was listening to Julia and looking down at the garden below, at the golds and reds and greens that were beginning to fade with the coming of twilight. Julia stopped talking and sat for a while apparently absorbed in thought. Only for a moment though. Then she sprang to her feet and said:

'Let's go and have a drink in a fabulous bar I know just near here, before it gets dark. I say of *madrileños* what Dorothy Parker said of New Yorkers: "As only *madrileños* know, if you can get through the twilight, you'll live through the night."'

RAFAEL SÁNCHEZ FERLOSIO

The Recidivist

Old, almost toothless, grizzled and bedraggled, worn-out, sick, tired of living and of going hungry, the wolf felt that the hour had come for him, finally, to go and rest his head on the Creator's lap. Night and day, he travelled along ever remoter and more godforsaken tracks, ever craggier mountains, ever steeper and more precipitous hills, to the place where, suddenly, the fearsome roar of the hurricane, up among those ridges carved out of ice, became, as he entered the thick cupola of mist, like a voice muffled in soft cotton wool: the white silence of the Eternal Heights. There, no sooner had he raised his eyes – his sight blurred, partly because of age, partly because his eyes were still stinging after the recent blizzard, partly because they were filled with tears that were a mixture of self-pity and gratitude – no sooner had he glimpsed the golden gates to the Mount of Beatitudes than he heard the piercing, crystalline voice of the guard saying:

'How dare you even approach these sacrosanct gates with your mouth still bloody from your last cruel repast, you murderer.'

Dumbfounded by such a reception and plunged into unbearable grief, the wolf turned tail and walked back along the path it had cost him such

Rafael Sánchez Ferlosio (1927–2019) was born in Rome to a Spanish father – Rafael Sánchez Mazas, a founder and leader of the Falangist movement – and an Italian mother, Liliana Ferlosio. He wrote two novels, *Industrias y andanzas de Alfanhuí* (1951), a strange blend of the picaresque and fantasy, and *El Jarama* (1955), a realistic novel describing sixteen hours in the lives of eleven young friends. He then wrote nothing for twenty years. Some believe this was a kind of silent protest at the Franco regime, but he himself never gave a reason. He returned to writing in the 1980s, writing one more novel, *El testimonio de Yarfoz* (1986), and several volumes of essays and aphorisms. In 2004, he was awarded Spain's highest literary honour, the Premio Cervantes.

pain and effort to travel, returning to the earth, to his usual haunts and hunting grounds, except that now he behaved quite differently: he no longer slew sheep or even lambs, something which the loss of his teeth had, besides, long since prevented him from doing; he even abstained from eating carrion or gnawing at bones that younger wolves with better teeth might have thought unworthy of their attention. Now, determined not to touch any food that even remotely resembled meat, he was forced to become a pillager of villages and farmhouses, a snapper-up of lunch packs and picnics. His few remaining teeth, albeit almost worn down to the gums, did, however, allow him to chew bread, fresh bread when fortune smiled on him, but more often than not the dry, stale variety. Under this new regime, in the fields and the vast woods of his native hills, he continued to cling on to life for another whole cycle of winters and summers, until, doubly exhausted and doubly desirous of rest after this second round of what had already been a very long existence, he again felt that the time had come when he deserved, finally, to rest his head on the Creator's lap. If the climb up to the Eternal Heights had been hard the first time, how much harder must it have been now, had it not been for the fact that the decrease in his physical strength was compensated for, to a greater or lesser extent, by an increase in his yearning for rest and beatitude. And he did once more reach the Eternal Heights, although, by then, his sight had become so poor that he didn't even notice he had reached the golden gates when the hoped-for voice of the angel on guard rang out:

'So you're back again, intent on offending by your mere presence the dignity of those who, by their merits, have made themselves worthy of passing through these gates and enjoying Eternal Beatitude, as if you, too, were a worthy candidate. How dare you? You burglar of bakeries, you plunderer of pantries, you looter of larders. Get out of here! Skedaddle as you usually do, since you've more than demonstrated your talent for skedaddling, undaunted by traps or fences or dogs or rifles!'

Who can gauge the desolation, bitterness, abandonment, wretchedness, hunger, frailty, illness and mange of the many long, miserable years that followed? Now he dared only nibble, with his now entirely toothless gums, the curly tops of lettuces, or use the tip of his tongue to lick off the syrup-sweet drop hanging from the bottom of figs still on the tree, or lap up, one by one, the circular stains left by the cheeses on the shelves of an empty pantry. When he walked now he left no mark, like a shadow, for he was so thin and light that the weight of his paws was not enough to crush anything underfoot. Another long procession of years went past and, as was perhaps inevitable, the day dawned for the third time when the wolf considered that the hour had come for him, finally, to rest his head on the lap of the Creator.

He set off then, invisible and weightless as a shadow, and he was, indeed, the colour of a shadow, except in the few parts where the mange had not caused his fur to fall out; and where some fur remained, it was completely white, as if his whole body had turned to mange, to shadow, to nothing, leaving in those white hairs only the call of the snows, the pressing, inextinguishable longing for the Eternal Heights. If the climb had been almost too much for an old wolf on those two previous journeys, you can imagine the urgency of the impulse that set him on that path again for a third time, bearing in mind that the first and, one might say, natural old age of that first journey was now overlaid with a second and even a third old age; imagine, then, the superhuman effort required for him to make the journey yet again. Treading gently, softly, humbly, he could now only just make out the gates to the Mount of Beatitudes; leaning his chest on the threshold, he first lowered himself down on his haunches, stretched out his front legs, so that they were parallel with his chest, and rested his head on them. Just then, as he suspected would happen, he heard the metallic voice of the angel on guard and the very words he had so dreaded hearing:

'Well, thanks to your own stubbornness, you have reached a situation that could and should have been avoided and which is equally undesirable for us both. You knew this perfectly well the very first time or surely you must have guessed; you knew this even better the second time and were proven right; and yet, despite all, you have insisted on coming back a third time! So be it! If that's what you want. Now you will leave as you did before, but this time you will never return. Not because you're a murderer. Not because you're a thief, but because you're a wolf.'

JUAN BENET

Reichenau

Years ago, the man had said to him:

'If you need anything, you only have to ring the bell. I'll come at once.'

He hadn't said this in the bored tones of someone accustomed to repeating the same formula over and over; he probably had very few guests, and wanted to suggest some meaning which, at the time, he himself didn't quite understand, anxious as he was to get to bed and too troubled by the feeling of unease provoked by the arrival of that stranger.

It happened one night when the traveller took a wrong turning at a crossroads and ended up on a rough, potholed mountain track, and then didn't get back onto a proper road for another couple of hours, only to find an ancient signpost on which the lettering was so eroded that he couldn't decipher it in the light of his headlights. Unable to see where he was on the map, he set off blindly in one direction and, after quite a few kilometres, came upon a dark, deserted village consisting of a dozen or so ramshackle houses on either side of the road and a single lightbulb dangling from a cable, too dim even to illuminate the road, and, despite his tiredness and the lateness of the hour, he felt he had no option but to drive on in the direction indicated by a sign saying: 'Región 23 km'. And so when, shortly afterwards, as he came round a sharp bend, he saw a big

Juan Benet (1927–1993) was born in Madrid. He was unusual among writers in that he combined the profession of engineer with the practice of literature. A friend introduced him to the work of William Faulkner and this, he said later, was what prompted him to start writing. His first novel, *Volverás a Región* (1967), created a mythical place, Región, much like Faulkner's Yoknapatawpha County. His style is generally considered to be difficult, but many of his contemporaries considered his work to be groundbreaking, opening up new possibilities for the Spanish novel. He wrote novels, short stories, essays and plays, including an adaptation of four plays by Beckett.

rambling house by the roadside with a gloomy sign bearing the one word: 'Rooms', he didn't think twice.

When he knocked for the second time, a light came on in a window on the floor above, and a man – making it abundantly clear that he had been woken up and dragged from his bed – asked what he wanted, then, having agreed to take him in for the night, brusquely ordered him to park his car behind the house. He took some considerable time to actually open the front door and was still fastening his belt under his pyjama jacket when, without asking any further questions or demanding any documentation, he picked up a large key bearing the number 9 stamped on the metal tag attached to it by a ring.

The hotel was an antiquated, cheaply built edifice that smelled faintly of damp, and was furnished with such rigour and economy that every inch of it revealed an evident disdain for superfluous details: the bulbs hung bare and bereft, the walls were unadorned by any pictures from calendars and the only piece of furniture in the bedroom – apart from the metal bedstead, the bedside table and a tiny basin with no running water – was a flimsy wooden chair. As for the owner, which he clearly was, his only discernible quality seemed to be his apparent distaste for his chosen job, as if he had sought refuge in it more for reasons of security than anything else, in order to squirrel away a little money who knows where or how. Once he had shown the traveller the room and handed him the key, he pointed to the switch hanging above the bedhead and said:

'If you need anything, you only have to press the switch to ring the bell. I'll come at once.'

The traveller fell asleep immediately, determined to make that spartan night as brief as possible, but he soon woke up again, bathed in sweat and sweltering under the weight of the blankets. He began to toss and turn, incapable of shrugging off the intense smell of poverty; then he heard the sound of voices, of people whispering beyond the walls and the empty corridors, beyond the deserted kitchen and neat storeroom, the muffled words and suppressed laughter that seemed to correspond to the conversation of maids anxious not to be heard by the master and mistress of the house.

Anxious and unable to sleep, he turned on the light, and the voices stopped. He assumed that the light from his window shining onto the road had served as a warning to those imprudent chatterboxes, and, feeling calmer, he switched it off, although he feared he wouldn't easily be able to convert that sense of calm into sleep. The voices soon returned, nearer now and more insistent, sibilant, long-drawn-out sounds and repeated consonants which, just as they seemed about to crystallize into an intelligible word, would vanish into thin air like a soap bubble, sounds that seduced him with their improbable proximity, with an intensity that belied their remoteness, with the suspicion that they were directed at him precisely because he would never be able to understand them. No, they weren't coming from any precise place, they weren't being spoken anywhere, but existed somewhere beyond the furniture and the walls of his room, in a soundscape defined by that concatenation of feminine whispers and laughter – older women exchanging evil, malign secrets, mingling and drawing apart in a whirlwind of gestures and movements that came to nothing and vanished at the very instant they appeared in the silvery glint of the shadows, not carried on the ether, but immersed in and inseparable from the all-enveloping darkness.

He again turned on the light, but not for long. The bulb fused with a fizzing sound that was the signal for the women to resume their hubbub, excited by their victory over the light and ready to make the most of the impunity that was now theirs.

He sat up, dripping with sweat, but, since it was so cold in the room, immediately lay down again. He drew the blankets up over his head and it was as if the whispered conversation did actually grow more muffled, as if it were taking place in some corner beneath the sheets, simultaneously near and far. He emerged from under the blankets and felt for the switch above his head, but, when he found it, he couldn't bring himself to press it and ring the bell. Or, rather, he was held back by his fear of having to ask the owner for help, by that and by the man's smug expression, his papier-mâché head. He grabbed the switch with both hands and, in the grip of fever, even raised it to his lips and licked it, unable to control either his tears or his bladder in the face of the unbearable crescendo of voices that subsided only with the coming of a dawn that would find him drenched in sweat, panting and exhausted, his head pressed against the bars of the bedhead and a crazed look in his eyes, as he clung with both hands to the electric flex of the bell, feeling nevertheless proud to have survived the night without having to resort to that offer of help.

The following morning when he paid the bill – a risible amount – he said as little as possible to the owner; perhaps a feeling of confidence had taken hold of a mind oppressed at the time by all kinds of difficulties, but still capable of ignoring the landlord's oblique gaze, which doubtless – with a little scorn added in for good measure – was telling him: that he could easily have saved himself all that trouble if only he had rung the bell; that this wasn't intended as a reproach or a warning, merely a statement of fact; that he couldn't claim to have been deceived because what he had been through was entirely due to his rejection of that offer of help; and that, should he ever find himself in a similar situation again, he should act very differently, because he could have avoided it altogether simply by ringing the bell. Exactly as he had told him to do the previous night.

This happened in the early days of his hard, difficult, solitary profession, trying to sell in hostile lands products for which, in those days, people had no need. However, by dint of sheer self-belief and perseverance he soon achieved professional independence, financial stability, became a representative for makers of foreign goods, and was transformed into a businessman and an inveterate smoker who, once a year, was obliged to take a rest cure. Those early days were long gone when, driving a little van laden with luxury goods, he had arrived one night at a roadside inn – in the heart of a nocturnal desert – which, had he not completely forgotten it, would constitute the lowest point in those difficult years, and which, if he ever had recalled it, would only have provided the obligatory preamble to his present prosperity.

The tickle in his throat and the tightness in his lungs woke him again late one night, but in very different circumstances. It was a silvery night, not far from Lake Constance, accompanied by a murmur that seemed to be hiding behind the serene, solemn murmur of the fir trees and the timid clapping of the lime trees and larches, as if they were applauding – out of politeness, not enthusiasm – the foolish, nonsensical remarks made by a hidden nocturnal animateur inaccessible to the man's senses. Within these murmurings, though – among the dense woods flanking the path leading down to the lake – was hidden the sound of feminine laughter, louder, more audible, resonant and agitated when the wind dropped and the leaves ceased their clapping, intent on what might happen next.

He closed the window, and the room was instantly filled, apparently out of nowhere, with the tumultuous whispering of those elderly women, laughter that grew steadily in intensity and moved ever closer, about to take physical shape in hands and gestures directed at him, in winks and glances, which, blotting out the bogus shadows cast by the furniture, emerged into abject nakedness, stripped bare even of the darkness into which they would dissolve before – although only a moment before – he turned on the light and called for the chambermaid.

And then he understood that he was no longer as brave as he once had been, that he had succumbed. And, when he realized this, he understood that the other man had been waiting for and following him ever since their first encounter in remote, timeless Región many years before, until, as he had intimated with a look, this night in Reichenau, in Württemberg, not far from Lake Constance; that he had been watching him ever since they parted and had become convinced that, in these new circumstances, the traveller would prove incapable of clinging on to his self-belief, and would instead succumb to asking for the help promised by the bell. For, at that very moment, he recognized the man's footsteps coming down the carpeted corridor and knew that he would have no difficulty in opening the door; that the man who had, quite rightly, warned him then not to hesitate to call him if he needed help was now taking his revenge with an arrogance accumulated over years of being disdainfully forgotten simply because the conditions on that other occasion had not been quite right. The traveller did not move from his bed. Sitting up, leaning on the pillow and pressing his back against the wall, he recognized the man's hand, his papier-mâché head, by the slow way in which he turned the door handle.

JUAN MARSÉ

The Street of the Sleeping Dragon

The beggar stopped in the middle of the deserted street and clenched his fists. He hadn't noticed anything as yet. The sun was beating down hard on his head and shoulders, and he was swinging his arms back and forth in front of his belly as if they were pendulums, but he stayed right where he was, leaning slightly forward. It was a Sunday. The sky-blue convertible was parked behind him. As if some sixth sense had alerted him to this fact, the old man slowly turned his head and stared brazenly at the car with his dull eyes.

There was apparently nothing unusual about what was about to occur between the old man and the car in that deserted street in a poor part of town. Beggars and drunks had no need to justify their actions there. The sight of the absurd duel about to take place between beggar and car would at least give the people living in Calle del Dragón Dormido – a wretched, forgotten, dusty street sloping down to the beach – the chance to experience, however briefly, the deep-seated, thrilling certainty that they were alive and free . . .

After studying the car with a pensive, slightly astonished air – you'd think he'd never seen a car before in his life – the old man cocked his

Juan Marsé (1933–2020) was born in Barcelona. He worked initially as a jeweller and did not begin publishing stories until 1958. His first collection, *Nada para morir* (1959), was awarded the Premio Sésamo. He lived in Paris for a few years, working as a Spanish tutor, translator and laboratory assistant at the Pasteur Institute. On his return to Spain, he worked as a journalist, newspaper editor and scriptwriter. He published *Últimas tardes con Teresa* in 1966 and has since published many more novels and short stories. All are set in Barcelona, in particular in the area known as El Guinardó, where he spent his childhood, and often describe the bleak post-Civil War period. In 2008 he was awarded Spain's highest literary honour the Premio Cervantes for his life's work.

head and fixed his eyes on the ground between his feet. He was about five metres away, to the right of the handsome vehicle. He again looked at the car and then at the ground, and continued to do so until, finally, he raced over to it and began kicking one side. He did this furiously, head down, as if in the grip of a fit of temper, his body tense and his expression fixed, but minus the tearful, gentle deliquescence of a childish tantrum. With every kick, he saw his own battered shoes reflected in the gleaming blue body of the car, which stood sleek and solid and magnificent in the street bathed by the noonday sun.

Men and women stood watching the old man from the doorways of their small houses ingenuously painted in pinks and greens and blues, from the tiny windows and from over the tops of walls. At first, they all made fun of the beggar, and someone even shouted at him, assuming he was drunk. But he wasn't drunk. Still keeping his head down, he looked at them rather sadly and as if offended.

'What's wrong?' he said. He was a ragged old man, with a collarless shirt and a sparse, limp beard, the colour of slush. 'Ah, I thought . . .'

And then he resumed his frenzied attack on the car. His little eyes were half-closed like badly healed wounds.

The blows could be heard from inside the small courtyard. The blinding light of the sun was there too, beating down on empty cans of food and shoe polish, on olive stones and the remains of vegetables and flowers, on a disparate pile of objects all blithely drained to the last drop, then discarded. A little girl was bent over a doll without arms or legs, a piece of crumpled cardboard, but still a doll: easy enough to do on that hard, grubby piece of ground.

'Carmela!' her mother called from the kitchen. 'What are you breaking now?'

'Nothing, Mama.'

'What's all that banging, then?'

The woman went out into the courtyard. She stood utterly still, looking at her daughter. Then she peered over the wall, only to withdraw at once and stand motionless again, deep in thought, her gaze fixed on the detritus and the sunlight. Her daughter, who was observing her intently, heard her murmur: 'Not again, not again!'

After taking another peek over the wall, the woman went back into the kitchen, pressing the palms of her hands to her apron. Walking slowly and without turning round, she asked the girl that question so full of the old, unmistakable taste of nights spent sleeping in metro stations beneath rough blankets, with the sound of bombs echoing down the tunnel, the taste of meals eaten in the dark and in silence, the taste of waiting and of death, or simply of an autumn morning without a ray of sunlight on the window. It was like a whisper: 'Where can your father have got to? Why is he so late coming back?'

The two young people were sitting on the rickety old bed in the blue corner. They were sitting slightly apart, gazing into each other's eyes and occasionally kissing. Above their heads, on the adobe wall, hung photos of the film stars the girl had pinned up there with drawing pins and a secret thrill of excitement. The bulb, wrapped in fine blue paper and hanging from a nail, gave off a pale light that slid over the mud floor as if over a lunar landscape. The radio was on, they were holding hands, their mouths seemingly bursting with words that are always inadequate, always impotent:

'Do you really love me?' she was saying.

'Yes.'

'How much?'

'How much? I don't know.'

Her gruff father and brothers, all of them in vest and trousers, kept pacing up and down, whistling and rubbing their arms and necks, occasionally looking at the pair of lovers without actually seeing them. The couple continued to gaze at each other.

'We can go walking in the rain when autumn comes . . .'

'Yes. Can you hear that banging out in the street?'

'. . . because then I'll be able to leave the building site early. Like that other afternoon when it rained, do you remember?'

'Can't you hear the banging? What's going on out there?'

The brothers went and stood in the doorway, leaning against each other. Then slowly and cautiously the father joined them: 'Let me see, let me see . . .'

'He must be mad,' said the older of the brothers, looking at the beggar.

'Mad as a hatter.'

'Don't you know who he is?' yelled someone down below. 'I do, and he's the sanest of us all.'

The father cleared his throat, and everyone drew closer, looking at each other with questioning eyes, then, suddenly, as one person, they began to feel a strange, furtive, minuscule wave of joy rising up into their throats. And they smiled beneath the fierce sun and proudly lifted their heads.

In the blue corner, the couple, indifferent to anything else, were still drowsily kissing each other.

'Whose car is it?'

'I don't know.' The person who said this was a small, dark young woman with large, bright eyes. She was listening to the noises reaching her from the other side of the sacking hanging over the door of the house. The only room. The sun was cheerfully pouring in through the holes in the cloth, and she, leaning against the wall, her hands behind her back, was looking at her husband sitting at the table, eating.

'How should I know, sweetheart?' she added, smiling strangely.

He turned and looked at her and thought: She's mad. A poor, mad, useless creature like me, which is hardly surprising . . . 'Go on,' he said out loud. 'Go and see.' He was a short, scrawny, swarthy fellow with a narrow forehead and hard, piercing eyes.

His wife drew aside the sacking and peered out, leaning over and raising one knee as she did and resting one foot on the wall. The man pushed away his plate and looked up at her. For a moment, he gazed at her long-forgotten legs, the grubby cloth covering thighs ravaged by the monotony of the day-to-day, and then he continued chewing, his thoughts impenetrable, his baleful, eagle brain once more asleep.

'He's still at it,' she said. 'Still kicking that car. Come and look.'

He got up, went over to her and rested one hand on her shoulder. They were both watching in silence, and suddenly he began to feel stronger – he puffed out his chest and tightened his grip on her shoulder – and she, in turn, felt protected – tenderly, strangely protected.

'Whose car is it, do you think, sweetheart?'

'Who knows? But don't you get involved.' And he screwed up his eyes against the furious sun and against recollected past violence. 'It doesn't really matter whose it is. I'll go across and see what's going on, but don't you leave the house.' And he gave her a hard stare. 'Do you understand, you ninny? This isn't women's business,' he said, adding: 'You ninny.'

Further down the street, towards the beach, stood a house a little taller than the others, the pink stucco walls streaked with black by dripping water. You couldn't honestly say it was a bar; it was more like a greengrocer's or an impromptu corner shop or simply a place where you could swap novels about the Wild West. In one corner stood a small marble table on which lay a pack of cards and a newspaper permanently open at the sports pages. A place full of coarse, warm wine and a few drowsing men, all of whom woke up enough to go out and take a look at the mad old man attacking the car.

And no one laughed. The sun obliged them to screw up their eyes and keep their gaze fixed and still, their hands resting on their legs, their stiff, scrubbed-clean Sunday hands. As if they had all suddenly started thinking.

Beneath the blue light of her dreams, the girl fidgeted and felt for her boyfriend's hand. She observed the muscular backs of her brothers standing at the front door. She could clearly hear the loud clang of metal being struck. Nothing else. New, bronzed muscles appeared on her brothers' backs whenever they changed position.

'I sometimes think I'd like to be a man and not be afraid of anything,' she said. 'You can do lots of things in life, lots, if you're a man . . . Did you hear that? Now someone's shouting.'

She stood up, her small mouth open, her moist, pink, shining lips like two fishes biting each other's tails. Her boyfriend clasped her hand more firmly, her hand soft with washing-up water, his rough with whitewash and dried cement, and he looked up at the wall, at a blond film star, smiling and remote.

'Don't be so silly,' he whispered in her ear. 'You're always so silly.'

But he squeezed her hand, as if it were a bird he had trapped.

Three men went over to the beggar. They were wearing white shoes and summer-weight suits. One of them got into the car, while the other two pushed the old man away, surprising him with the strength and logic of their questions: – What are you doing? Why? What for? What do you want? – for which the old man had no answer, and never had had an answer.

They pushed him away with their cold, dignified gaze. The neighbours watched in silence, not moving. They all wore the same tense, contained expression, and all were now leaning slightly forwards. Panting and muttering, all his strength gone, the beggar moved off and disappeared. Then the two men got into the car, the third man started the engine, and they left.

The dust rose up, then settled slowly down again, and the street resumed its long Sunday silence.

Everyone drifted back into their small white, pink and blue houses, and everything fell asleep again.

ESTHER TUSQUETS

Summer Orchestra

Summer was already well advanced – more than halfway through August – when the decision was made to begin renovating the smaller dining room in the hotel and to move the children, together with their governesses and their nursemaids and their mademoiselles, into the grown-ups' dining room. Throughout the whole of July and the first two weeks of August the children had formed a wild, unruly and increasingly uncontrollable gang that invaded the beaches, raced through the village on bikes with their bells ringing madly, prowled with restless curiosity around the stalls at the fair, or slipped – suddenly surreptitious, silent, almost invisible – into secret places among the reeds. Year after year they built the huts there that housed their rarest treasures and where they initiated each other into marvellous, secret and endlessly renewed transgressions (smoking their first cigarettes, often communal, crumpled and slightly damp; getting enmeshed in poker games played with a ruthlessness that would have astonished the grown-ups – games so intense and hard-fought that the participants often preferred to play on rather than go down to the beach – and venturing into other stranger and more ambiguous games, which Sara associated obscurely with the world of grown-ups and the forbidden, and to which, during that summer, she had reacted with both fascination and shame, eager to be a spectator but very reluctant to take

Esther Tusquets (1936–2012) took over from her father as director of the publishing house Editorial Lumen, and remained in charge there for forty years, publishing both Spanish and foreign-language authors such as Beckett, Woolf and Sontag. Her first novel, *El mismo mar de todos los veranos*, was published in 1978, three years after the death of Franco, and was the first volume in a trilogy, focusing very much on a female view of life, love and sensuality. She went on to write twelve more novels, as well as short stories, essays and four volumes of autobiography.

part. She – possibly alone among all the girls – had been astute or cautious enough when playing forfeits and lucky enough at cards to get through those days without once having to let anyone kiss her on the mouth or touch her breasts or take her knickers down), transgressions that were doubly intoxicating because they were the culmination of that parenthesis of temporary freedom provided by the summer and would be unthinkable once they were all back in the winter environment of schools and city apartments.

But within a matter of two or three days the summer community had broken up and with it the band of children, some being transported inland to spend what was left of their holidays in the mountains or in the country, most of them going home to prepare for the September results. And Sara had stayed on as the one female straggler among the decimated gang of boys (Mama and Mademoiselle had promised consolingly that, at the end of August, four or five of her best friends would be allowed to come up for her birthday), but the atmosphere had changed, it had grown suddenly tense and unpleasant, the general mood of irritability and discontent aggravated perhaps by the frequent rain and the shared feeling that all that remained now of summer were a few unseasonable, grubby remnants. One thing was certain, the boys' pastimes had grown rougher and Sara had simply had enough of them, of their fights, their games, their practical jokes, their rude words and their crude humour, had had enough of them spying on her through the window when she was changing her clothes, of them upending her boat, of having three or four of them corner her among the reeds. That was why she was so pleased about the change of dining room: there, at least during mealtimes, the boys would be forced to behave like civilized beings. And they must have had the same idea, for they protested and grumbled long and loud, complaining that, now there were so few of them and the rain deprived them not only of many mornings at the beach but also of almost every afternoon previously spent among the reeds, it really was the end to be expected now to sit up straight at table without fidgeting, barely saying a word, eating everything that was put in front of them, being required to peel oranges with a knife and fork and, to crown it all, wear a jacket and tie to go into supper.

But Sara was radiant and so excited on the first night that she changed her dress three times before going down – opting in the end for a high-necked, full-skirted organdie dress that left her arms bare and which her mother did not much approve of, saying that it made her look older than her years and was inappropriate for a girl who had not yet turned twelve – and then caught up her long, straight, fair hair with a silk ribbon. What most excited Sara that first night was the prospect of getting a good look at the adult world, until then only glimpsed or guessed at, since during the long winters the children's lives were confined to school, walks with Mademoiselle, and the playroom. There was hardly any contact between children and parents during the summer either – not this year nor in any previous year. (Sara had overheard Mademoiselle making a comment to one of the chambermaids about the delights and charms of the family holiday, at which they had both laughed, only to fall silent the moment they realized she was listening, and the whole episode had filled Sara with a terrible rage.) For the fact was that, while the grown-ups slept on, the children would get up, have breakfast, do their homework or play table tennis and be coming back from the beach just as their parents would be finishing breakfast and lazily preparing themselves for a swim; and, when the grown-ups were going into the big dining room for lunch, the children would already be off somewhere, pedalling down the road on their bikes or queueing at the rifle range at the fair. It was only occasionally, when Sara – quite deliberately – walked past the door of one of the lounges or the library, that she would catch sight of her mother sitting, blonde and evanescent, among the curling cigarette smoke. She would feel touched and proud to see her there, so delicate and fragile, so elegant and beautiful, like a fairy or a princess hovering ethereally above the real world (the most magical of fairies, the most regal of princesses, Sara had thought as a child, and in a way still thought), and for a moment her mother would stop playing cards or chatting to her friends to wave a greeting, call her over to give her a kiss, or pick out a liqueur chocolate from the box someone had just given her. At other times, her father would come over to the children's table and ask Mademoiselle if they were behaving themselves, if they did their homework every day, if they were enjoying the summer. And, of course, they did coincide at church on Sundays because there was only one mass held in the village and the grown-ups had to get up early – relatively speaking – but even then they would arrive late and sit in the pews at the back, near the door. Although they did wait for the children on the way out to give them a kiss and some money to spend on an ice cream or at the rifle range.

So Sara dressed with great care the first night the children moved into the big dining room – where they occupied only four tables – and she entered the room flanked by her brother and Mademoiselle, both of whom looked bad-tempered and morose. Her own face was flushed and her heart was beating fast, and she was so excited and nervous that it was an effort to finish the food they put on her plate, and she felt she could see almost nothing, that she was unable to fix her gaze on anything, such was her eagerness to see and record every detail: the women in their long dresses, with their shoulders bare and their hair up and the earrings that sparkled on either side of their neck; the men, elegant and smiling, so different from the way they looked in the morning on the beach or on the terrace, and talking animatedly – what about? – amidst the laughter and the tinkling of crystal glasses. The unobtrusive waiters slipped furtively between the tables, treading lightly and barely uttering a word, so stiff and formal and impersonal that it was hard to recognize in them the rowdy, jokey, even coarse individuals who, up until yesterday, had served them in the children's dining room. And no one, neither the waiters, nor the other diners, took the slightest notice of the children, so that any attempts by governesses and mademoiselles to stop the children fidgeting, make sure they left nothing on their plates and used their knives and forks properly were futile. As was the music played by the orchestra (hearing it as she crossed the foyer or from far off on the terrace, Sara had imagined it to be larger, but now she saw that it consisted only of a pianist, a cellist and a violinist, and the pianist, it seemed to her, had terribly sad eyes), for no one appeared to be listening to it, or even to hear it. People would merely frown or raise their voices when the music increased in volume, as if they were obliged to superimpose their words over some extraneous noise. There wasn't a gesture, a smile, even any pretence at applause. That surprised Sara, because in the city, parents and their friends attended concerts and went to the opera (on those nights her mother would come into their room to say good night, when the children were already in bed, because she knew how Sara loved to see her – the way she was dressed now in the dining room – in beautiful, long, low-cut dresses, fur coats, feathered hats, jingling bracelets with the little gold mesh bag in which she kept an embroidered handkerchief and opera glasses, and all about her the sweet, heavy perfume that impregnated everything her mother touched and that Sara would never ever forget). But in the library there were several shelves full of records which, on some nights, when her parents were not at home, Mademoiselle would play so that Sara could hear them from her bedroom and drift off to sleep to the music. But here no one paid the least attention and the musicians played for no one and for no reason, so that when Sara went over to her parents' table to kiss them good night, she couldn't help asking them why that was, at which they and their friends all burst out laughing, remarking that 'that' has little to do with real music, however hard the 'poor chaps' were trying. And that remark about 'poor chaps' wounded Sara and, without knowing why, she associated it with the jokes the boys told and the stupid acts of cruelty they perpetrated among the reeds. But she immediately discounted the thought, since there was no possible connection. It was as irrelevant – she had no idea why this came back to her now either – as Mademoiselle's tart, sarcastic comment about the delights of family holidays.

Nevertheless, the following night, because she still thought the music very pretty and because it infuriated her that the grown-ups, who did not even bother to listen, should then condescendingly pass judgement on something to which they paid not the slightest attention, she said to Mademoiselle: 'The music's lovely, isn't it? Don't you think they play well?' And Mademoiselle said yes, they played surprisingly well, especially the pianist, but in the dining room of a luxury holiday hotel in summer it made no difference if you played well or badly. It really was a waste of good musicians. Then, screwing up all her courage, with her cheeks flushed and heart pounding but without the least hesitation, Sara stood up and crossed the empty space separating her from the orchestra and told the pianist how much she enjoyed the music, and that they played very well. She asked why they didn't play something by Chopin, and the man looked at her, surprised, and smiled at her from beneath his moustache (although she still thought he looked terribly sad) and replied that people there didn't normally expect them to play Chopin, and Sara was on the verge of saying that it didn't matter anyway since they wouldn't be listening and wouldn't notice and then she felt – perhaps for the first time in her life – embarrassed by her parents, ashamed of them and of that glittering grown-up world, all of which seemed suddenly rather less marvellous to her. Before returning to her table, without quite knowing why, she apologized to the pianist.

From then on, Sara put on a pretty dress every night (alternating the three smart dresses that she'd brought with her and not worn all summer, because, up until then, she had gone around in either jeans or swimsuit) and she did her hair carefully, brushing it until it shone and tying it back with a silk ribbon. But she still felt awkward and self-conscious when she entered the dining room (the boys made angry, spiteful, possibly jealous comments, but Sara no longer heard them, they had simply ceased to exist) and she would mechanically eat whatever was served up to her because it was easier to eat than to argue. She still observed the women's lovely dresses, the new jewels and hairstyles, their easy laughter and chatter among the clink of glasses; she still noticed how elegant the men looked and how gracefully they leaned towards their wives, smiled at them, lit their cigarettes and handed them their shawls, while a few waiters, as insubstantial as ghosts, bustled about them. The music played on and, outside, the full moon shimmered on the dark sea, almost the way it did in Technicolor films or advertisements. But her eyes were drawn more and more towards the orchestra and pianist, who seemed to her to grow ever sadder, ever more detached, but who, when he looked up from the keyboard and met Sara's gaze, would sometimes smile and make a vague gesture of complicity.

Suddenly Sara felt interested in everything to do with the pianist and discovered that the pale, thin woman (though she was perhaps faded rather than pale, like the blurred copy of a more attractive original) whom she must often have seen sitting on the sands at the beach or strolling along the farthest-flung and least frequented parts of the garden, always accompanied by a little girl who would hold her hand or be running about nearby, this woman was the pianist's wife and the little girl was their daughter. Sara had never seen a lovelier child, and she wondered if at some time in the past the mother had also been like that and wondered what could have happened since then to bring her so low. And, having definitely broken off relations with the gang of boys, and Mademoiselle having raised no objections, Sara began to spend increasing amounts of time in the company of the woman and the little girl, both of whom inspired in her a kind of transferred or displaced affection. Sara loved the pianist – she discovered this on one of those nights when he looked up from the piano at her and their eyes had met; it was a discovery that brought with it no surprise, no confusion or fear, it merely confirmed an obvious reality that filled her whole being – and, because the little girl and the woman were part of him, Sara bought the child ice creams, candied almonds, bright balloons and coloured prints and took her on the gondolas, the big wheel, the merry-go-round, to the circus. The little girl seemed quite mad with joy, and when Sara glanced at the child's mother, perplexed, the mother would always say the same thing: 'It's just that she's never seen, never heard, never tried that before', and here her look would harden, 'We've never been able to give her such things.' And then Sara felt deeply troubled, as if she were somehow in danger – she would have liked to ask her forgiveness, as she had of the pianist one night, long ago now it seemed, though she did not know for whom or for what – perhaps because she could not understand it or perhaps because something within her was doggedly coming to fruition – and because when it did finally emerge and spill out of her, she would be forced to understand everything and then her innocence would be lost forever. The world would be turned upside down, and she would be shipwrecked in the midst of the ensuing chaos with no idea how best to adapt in order to survive.

At nightfall – by the end of August it was already getting darker earlier – while the woman was giving the little girl her supper and putting her to bed in the servants' quarters, Sara almost always met the pianist in the garden, and they would walk up and down the road together, holding hands, and the man would speak of everything he could have been, of all that he had dreamed in his youth – his lost youth, even though he couldn't have been much more than thirty – of what music had meant to him, and how much he and his wife had loved each other and of how circumstances had gradually caused everything to wither and crumble, forcing him to abandon everything along the way. It was a bleak, terrifying speech and it seemed to Sara that the man wasn't talking to her – how could he unburden such stories on a child of eleven? – but perhaps to himself, to fate, to no one, and on the road, and in the darkness of the night, they couldn't see each other's faces, but at certain points the man would hesitate, a shiver would run through him, his voice would tremble and then Sara would squeeze his hand and feel in her chest a weight like a stone, whether pity or love she no longer knew, and she would have liked to find the courage to tell him that there had doubtless been some mis-understanding, that fate had conspired against them, that at any moment everything would change, life and the world could not possibly go on being the way he described them. And, on a couple of occasions, the man stopped and held her tightly, tightly to him and, although she had no way of knowing for sure, it seemed to Sara that his cheeks were wet with tears.

Perhaps the woman felt subtly jealous of their walks alone together in the dark, or perhaps she simply needed someone to whom she could pour out her own anguish, someone she could justify herself to (although no one had accused her of anything) because she sometimes alluded bitterly to 'the things my husband has probably told you' and, however hard Sara tried to stop her, tried not to listen, she would go on. 'Did he tell you that, now there are fewer guests in the hotel, the management won't even pay us the pittance they originally promised us, something he simply doesn't want to know about?' 'Did you hear what the manager did to me the other day, right in front of him, and did he tell you that he didn't say a word in my defence?' 'Did you know that I've borrowed money from everyone, we don't even own the clothes on our backs, that we have nowhere to go when the summer season ends in a few days' time and that he just stands on the sidelines as if none of this had anything to do with him at all?' And one day, she grabbed her by the shoulders and looked at her with those hard eyes that left Sara defenceless and paralysed: 'Yesterday, I felt so awful I couldn't even eat, but do you think he cared or bothered to ask me what was wrong? No, he just picked up my plate and, without a word, finished off both our suppers. I bet he didn't tell you that.' And Sara tried to explain to her that the man never talked to her about real events, about the sordid problems of everyday life, about what was going on just then between him and his wife; he talked only, in melancholy, desolate tones, of the death of love, of the death of art, of the death of hope.

The day of Sara's birthday came round, the last day of the holidays, just before the hotel was to close and they were all due to go back to the city and, just as Mama and Mademoiselle had promised, her best friends travelled up especially and even the boys behaved better, wearing their newly pressed suits and their Sunday smiles, and she got lots of presents that she placed on a table for everyone to see, including a new dress and, from Papa, a gold bracelet with little green stones that had been her grandmother's and which signalled that Sara was on the threshold of becoming a woman. There were sack races, lucky dips, fireworks, mountains of sandwiches, a vast cake and a fruit punch with lots of champagne in it, which, because it was the first time they'd ever been allowed to drink it, got them all a little merry and was just one more sign that they were leaving childhood behind them. And the whole afternoon Sara was so excited, so happy, so busy opening her presents and organizing games and attending to her friends that it was only when night fell, when the party was over and some of the guests were already leaving to go back to the city, that she realized that the musician's little daughter had not been among them, and, however much she tried to deny what to her seemed at once both obvious and inconceivable, she knew instantly what had happened. She knew even before she grabbed Mademoiselle by the arm and asked, shaking her furiously: 'Why didn't the little girl come to my party? Tell me!' and there was no need to specify which little girl she was talking about, and Mademoiselle blushed, she did her best to act naturally, but instead blushed to the roots of her hair and, not daring to look at Sara, said: 'I don't know, Sara, really I don't, I think it must have been the doorman who wouldn't let her in,' adding, in an attempt to placate her, 'but she is an awful lot younger than all your other friends . . .' She knew before she confronted the doorman and screamed her bewilderment and spat out her rage at him, and the man simply shrugged and explained that he'd simply done as he was told, that her mother had issued instructions about who should be allowed into the party; and she knew before she went over to her mother, swallowing back her sobs, her heart clenched, and her mother looked up from her book with surprised, unflinching eyes and said in a slow voice that she had no idea they were such good friends and that anyway it was high time Sara learned the kind of people she ought to be associating with, and then, seeing Sara's eyes fill with tears, seeing that she was shaking, said: 'Don't cry now, don't be silly. Maybe I was wrong, but it's not so very important. Go and see her now, take her a slice of cake and some sweets and it'll all be forgotten.' But in the musician's room, where she had never set foot before, the woman gave her a hard look, a look, thought Sara, that was now fixed, a look the woman had been rehearsing and learning throughout the summer, but her voice quavered when she said: 'The worst thing, you see, was that she didn't understand, she saw you all having tea and playing games and didn't understand why she couldn't go in; she cried a lot, you know, before she finally went to sleep.' But the woman didn't cry. And Sara dried her own tears and did not ask forgiveness – now that she knew for whom and for what, she also knew that there are some things for which one does not ask forgiveness – and she took them no cakes or sweets, made no attempt to give them presents or to make anything better.

She went up to her room, tore off the ribbon, the dress, grandmother's little bracelet and threw them all down in a heap on the bed, then she pulled on her jeans and left her tousled hair hanging loose over her shoulders. And when she went into the dining room, no one, not Mademoiselle or the boys, her parents or the head waiter, dared say one word to her. And Sara sat down in silence, without even touching the food they put on her plate, sitting very erect and very pale, staring at the orchestra and repeating to herself that she would never ever forget what had happened, that she would never wear a long, low-cut dress and a fur coat and jewels or allow men in dinner jackets to fill her glass and talk to her of love, that she would never – she thought with surprise – be like the rest of them, that she would never learn what kind of people she ought to be associating with, because her place would always be at the side of men with sad eyes who had had too many dreams and had lost all hope, at the side of hard-eyed, faded women, old before their time, who could barely provide for their own children, not after this terrible, complicated summer in which Sara had discovered first love and then hate (so similar, so intimately linked), not after this summer in which, as the grown-ups kept telling her in their very different ways, she had become a woman. She repeated all this to herself again and again while she looked and looked at him and he looked at no one but her, not even needing to look down at the piano on which, all through supper, he played nothing but Chopin.

ÁLVARO POMBO

Luzmila

Luzmila was tall, thin and very ordinary. She had proved to be a good worker in her days as an errand girl for the nuns, but, long before the sparse, diffuse point at which her earliest memories began, she had been at the beck and call of swarms of errant people: her parents, who each went their respective ways, her bedridden grandmother reaching out to her with the blind, confident voracity of all trapped creatures, her siblings and, finally, the nuns, who, unintentionally, but with the infallible egotism of the angels, kept Luzmila with them for nine or ten years, letting her believe that one day she would enter the convent as a novice – as a lay sister, which is what she wanted. They sent her running back and forth on their footling errands, only to declare at last that she had no 'true vocation' and that, in the mother superior's words, 'she would be far better off working for a good family'.

'Dear Jesus, in whom I firmly believe,' Luzmila would whisper each night, lulling herself to sleep, 'it is for my sake that you are there on the altar, that you give your Body and Blood to the faithful soul as heavenly nourishment.' And Luzmila would repeat, in the same faint murmur as the choir of nuns at the Convent of the Most Pure Conception: 'To the faithful soul as heavenly nourishment.'

Álvaro Pombo (b. 1939) was born in Santander, did his first degree in Madrid and for eleven years lived in London, where he studied at Birkbeck College. A resident of Madrid since then, he writes poetry, short stories and novels, two of which have been translated into English as *The Hero of the Big House* (which won the very first Premio Herralde in 1983) and *The Resemblance*. He won the 1990 Premio de la Crítica for what is now considered his finest novel, *El metro de platino iridiado*, the 2006 Premio Planeta for *La fortuna de Matilda Turpin* and the 2012 Premio Nadal for *El temblor del héroe*.

The nuns at the Convent of the Most Pure Conception were known as the 'Most Pures', partly because it was shorter and partly because the Holy Founding Mother, the Blessed María Antonia de Izarra y Vilaorante, devoted herself to saving girls from a life of licentiousness; and partly, too, because of the exquisite bobbin lace and embroidered sheets and tablecloths they produced. The girls from the 'Most Pures' slept in a blue-and-white painted dormitory in twelve identical beds, separated by six very rickety wardrobes, one for every two girls, and which were frequently broken into and the cause of many arguments. The sisters taught the girls to get up early, to mend clothes – using the invisible mending technique, almost like a spiritual emendation, which was the pride of the convent – to say, 'Yes, Madam', 'No, Madam', and 'As you wish, Madam', and the brighter, keener girls were taught to cook the whitish stews that the nuns had invented (for purity, as they say, is in all things) and the recipe for *yemas de la Beata* – sweets made from egg yolk and butter – much-sought-after by the pious ladies who tended to predominate in the area. And having thus equipped the girls, the convent would find positions for them later on as cooks and maids in the select households of families who regularly attended Nocturnal Adoration. The girls were fond of Luzmila because she would swap their novels for new ones, but, among themselves, they all considered her to be both holier-than-thou and slightly crazy.

When Luzmila left the convent, the nuns found her a post as a nanny, and thus she began a long peregrination through houses and more houses, through jobs that always ended in the same way: when the children left primary school and began to dress themselves, her employers would tell Luzmila that she should start looking for another post.

And so Luzmila would start looking and sooner or later (usually sooner, because she was always given excellent references), she would find another post. Each time she left, she did so very early in the morning, when the refuse collectors could be heard up the street; she would say goodbye to the concierge, think fondly of the children she was leaving, then set off carrying her wooden suitcase.

Her hair was caught back in a thick, greying plait which she coiled up each morning in a bun at the back of her neck. She wore brown cotton stockings. She worked with eyes downcast. She spoke without raising her voice. She always had in her bag a pair of check slippers to wear around the house. She walked about the households where she was employed as she walked about the convent, never prying into anything, never looking at the pictures in the nuns' prayer books, never leafing through the master's newspaper before the master had read it, never filching food from the pantry. At the age of sixty-five, she ended up in Madrid, and since, by then, there was no demand for nannies, she found work as a cleaning-woman.

Luzmila had saved a few thousand pesetas, and, wishing to avoid banks or savings accounts, she always carried these with her in an envelope, along with the Infant Jesus's box. She had a very clear idea of the Kingdom of Heaven. It was – she firmly believed – the home of the Infant Jesus of Prague. And the Glory was like the six o'clock Benediction held by the Carmelites, only without the need to brave the indifferent evening rain, the penetrating solitude of the streets, or the walk past the assault guards posted at the door of the police station opposite the church. Luzmila never went to the cinema or read the newspapers or listened to the radio. With the years, and after all that travelling from one end of Spain to the other (because, in her days as a nanny, Luzmila had travelled frequently from provincial capital to provincial capital), she had ceased to have a fixed church, that is, a fixed place where she could worship. Her family had dispersed years before, when her mother and her grandmother died, and Luzmila, who had loved her brothers and sisters dearly, could now barely remember them. Or, rather, she remembered only the dirty overalls, the Sunday suits hanging lifeless in the wardrobe, the sour smell and the masculine disorder of her brothers' bedroom. Indeed, she remembered that disorder as a clear, enduring, oppressive, unpleasant fact. Perhaps, without her realizing, this was what had drawn her to the refined world of the convent and to the nuns, as pretty as pictures, with their firm, eternally young faces framed by their wimples. She found the unreal sayings and manners of the nuns as captivating as a fairy tale. And she wanted to be the lay sister who polished the parlour and kept the tiles in the corridors as bright and shining as a wall of mirrors.

The vagueness with which Luzmila recalled her own family was transformed over the years into a precise, detailed image of the Holy Family. St Joseph returning from the carpenter's shop in the evenings; the Virgin spinning or else sewing some trousers for the Infant Jesus; the Infant Jesus eternally playing with the doves (which were always white and of which there were always five). Luzmila did not vary the movements of her characters very much; on the contrary, the little they did, they did in the same way and almost without moving. The mystery and the charm of imagining something consists precisely in it being *tota simul et perfecta possessio* – and utterly motionless.

Luzmila took communion every day very early in the morning and then went for a walk, killing time until nine o'clock, when she would arrive at whatever household currently employed her. To take communion is to eat and drink the body and blood of the Infant Jesus of Prague. Luzmila always found this idea slightly terrifying: the sacred gruesomeness of the feast, the empty stomachs and the souls without a stain or fleck or particle of sin. Luzmila made a point of removing her false teeth before taking communion, reasoning that then she would not risk biting the Holy Shepherd as he entered the fold, the soft, sweet, pink, newly washed cave of her mouth. Luzmila had a horror of all those gaping mouths at the communion rail, those gullets crammed with sacrilegious teeth. In the end, the very thought of that sacrilege, of biting the Holy Infant, provoked such anxiety in her that, in order not to have to witness it, she began attending the half-past-five mass in the church in Plaza de Manuel Becerra. In winter, Luzmila, still warm from her bed and from walking, would kneel down in the dark church which was – or so it seemed to her – entirely hers, and she would contemplate, enraptured, without praying or thinking, the bright butterfly flame of the lamp burning in the sacrarium and the devout, sour, composite smell of the church as it lay bathed in the submarine lightness of near-dawn that dazzled the figures in the stained-glass windows in the side chapels.

One day, the combined unreality of the deserted church and her own state of mind fused into one, and Luzmila found herself taking communion twice, in order to feel again the magical presence of that *panis angelicus*, the hard, bland, round wafer that tickled the palate and stuck to the cheek like an ice-cream cone. The next day, however, Luzmila felt that consuming two hosts one after the other demonstrated quite unprecedented greed, and so, when she returned to her pew, she pretended to cough and spat out the second host into her handkerchief. She felt uneasy all day, eager to finish work and get home in order to put the Infant away in a safe place.

She kept looking at the handkerchief, although without daring to unfold it for fear that the defenceless wafer, the Infant Jesus, might catch cold. After work, she went into a haberdashery and bought a jewellery box, the biggest and best they had. It was decorated with enamelled shells and had a view of La Concha beach on the lid and an inscription that said: 'A souvenir of San Sebastián'. This sacrarium, this nest, gradually filled up with a collection of Infant Jesuses, and occasionally Luzmila saved both hosts, which began to warp and grow yellow from her dried saliva. It came to be Luzmila's reserve fund, far more real in its sheer unreality than the thousands of pesetas in the envelope. And it comforted Luzmila, as the impossible always comforts our impossible desires.

Luzmila lived in Madrid in an attic room with a right to use the kitchen. This 'right' meant that Luzmila could go down to the concierge's kitchen – on the landing below – 'to warm up a bit of food'. From the very first day, though, it was clear that the concierge – who occupied a bedroom next to the said kitchen – had very particular views on what constituted a 'right'. She deemed that mere legality does not do justice to the real complexity of each individual case and that it was therefore wisest to temper the august impersonality of the law with a prudent application of her own law, enriching the concept of 'a right to use the kitchen' with the infinitely more subtle concept of being allowed to use it as a special favour. In this way, whenever a new tenant took up residence in the attic room, the concierge would give a little speech intended to impress on the new tenant that the only reason the 'right' remained in force was down to the concierge's peculiar goodness of heart (she had always been pretty right-wing, as any tenant could tell from the painting above her bed of the Sacred Heart of Jesus, adorned with a palm from Palm Sunday, and the photos of José Antonio and the Caudillo placed together, slightly askew, in a frame on top of the radio). Years had gone by since Luzmila last enjoyed the favour of using the kitchen. And this fact, along with everything else, disconnected the little of Luzmila that was still connected to the outside world. All that was left to her then was her professional identity, and she did her best to make herself a cleaning-woman through and through, taking that role as far and as deep as necessary. This was the point at which Luzmila began to go so unnoticed in the world that the visible and the invisible met seamlessly in her.

A year after Luzmila's 'disappearance', the concierge was joined by a young niece from her village, the daughter of a younger sister, Rosa, who had died after being kicked by a mule (or by her husband, it was never quite clear). The niece had just turned twenty, although she could easily have passed for sixteen. Her name was Dorita, like the concierge, and she looked like a rather intelligent boy. It was precisely because she was intelligent and because she looked like a boy that she had got a job in the village working in an incubation shed. The wife of the owner would never have allowed a more alluring female anywhere near her husband, but Dorita was such a little slip of a thing that she slipped into the job at once, and that ability to slip into places became part of Dorita's character from that time on. Working with the incubators was an easy enough job (apart from the broken sleep), and a natural affinity immediately sprang up between Dorita (who had something strangely larva-like about her) and the hygrometric vicissitudes of the eggs lined up in their thousands on trays. Everything went well until an agricultural products representative appeared on the scene, a rather plump, slimy, middle-aged fellow, who gave her a hundred pesetas and a packet of cigarettes for letting him get his leg over. From then on – although no one ever quite understood why – things went from bad to worse, and, when her mother died after being kicked either by the mule or by her husband, Dorita came to live in her aunt's house in Madrid.

Dorita hung around the streets of Madrid thinking vaguely about getting a job and thinking rather more about *not* getting a job and simply enjoying seeing the sights. One day, in a cinema in Calle de Carretas, she met a man who rather resembled that agricultural products representative and, right there and then, she earned her second one hundred pesetas. And, in pursuing that resemblance from cinema to cinema and from trick to trick, Dorita was soon left with no time to think, even vaguely, about finding a job. The men she picked up were always similarly gentle, paternal fellows, somewhat broad in the beam, who did not entirely understand themselves and invariably felt thoroughly ashamed when it was over. They always seemed frightened or lonely. They always said 'I can't give you very much', but nevertheless paid promptly the little they had promised at the start. Afterwards, they vanished without trace. This, among other things, was what made it the perfect job for Dorita. She would think proudly:

The things that happen to me you wouldn't even read about in *El Caso*. Dorita read *El Caso* every week, looking in vain for some case similar to her own. Dorita and her companions had a shared belief that theirs was the one invincible reality.

In that unreal, sourly picaresque Madrid, which covers the real Madrid like a second skin, Dorita spent her money like water on anything she saw, on the odd little things sold in the street, on bottles of nail varnish, of which she managed to collect hundreds. She still looked like the same Dorita of the incubators, except that now she had exchanged her overalls for a kind of loose shirt and trousers. When she wore trousers, she looked even more like an intelligent boy, and was occasionally pursued by queers, who mistook her for precisely that. Her aunt said of her that money simply slipped through her fingers, which was true, and, in a sense, Dorita slipped through life as well; you barely saw her come and go. This fluidity would impregnate her entire existence. According to the concierge, it was an advantage having her in the house because 'she's sharp as a tack and brings in a bit of money too'. And Dorita did pay a weekly sum for bed and board. And, to anyone who asked, her aunt would say: 'It's nice having a bit of company of an evening.' Dorita then became firmly established at her aunt's and was – to all appearances – learning to become a hairdresser at a salon in Calle de Atarazanas. This careful, exact lie had, as Dorita hoped, reassured her aunt completely.

Dorita and Luzmila met one night at the door of the lavatory. This was purely by chance, because they could easily never have met, and Luzmila's story doesn't depend on this meeting being anything other than accidental.

The lavatory gave onto a landing two steps down from Luzmila's attic room and three steps up from the concierge's kitchen. It was a high, narrow room, with a small window at roof height and a single, fly-spattered light bulb that appeared to be gazing down at its own reflection in the funereal toilet bowl. Luzmila was in the lavatory when the door handle turned from outside. She quickly got up to leave and mumbled an apology as she emerged, a tall, gaunt figure with her coat on over her long nightdress, not bothering to look to see who was there; and she would have walked straight past, but for Dorita, who was naturally sociable and who had, out of pure curiosity, attempted to approach Luzmila before. She grabbed Luzmila's arm and said: 'Sorry to rush you. I don't know what it was I ate, but it's given me the runs.' Luzmila went up to her room, feeling agitated and content. The following night, Dorita slipped into Luzmila's room and said: 'I just thought I'd pop in for a chat. I'm fed up to the back teeth with my aunt.' It then became the custom for Dorita to visit every night. And Luzmila grew accustomed to the custom, and the custom, as always happens, became a trap. Dorita would sit at the foot of the bed and chat away, interspersing her chatter with some of her adventures, enjoying watching her own life pass before her as she spoke. 'Don't get the wrong idea, I don't like sex at all,' she said. 'Some men want to plate you or grope you and others just want to tell you about their life, and some of them could talk the hind leg off a donkey, and then there was one guy who gave it to me very gently up the arse like a suppository, claiming he didn't know how to do it any other way. I tell you, horror movies have nothing on life.'

Dorita told these stories in the same tone of voice in which one recounts gossip or tittle-tattle, and Luzmila grew accustomed to them as well, although without entirely understanding them, much as we grow accustomed to our neighbours without ever understanding them.

Around that time, Luzmila suffered a mishap that made her life still narrower, were such a thing possible, and made her entirely dependent on the uncertain companionship of Dorita. Don Antonio, the priest, was known as *el Comulguero* because all morning, every morning, at the chapel of Our Lady of Perpetual Succour, he gave communion every ten minutes. Wearing his stole and a rather creased half chasuble that emphasized his stooped shoulders, he said mass early and then remained by the kneeler at the main altar. For this reason, there was always a long queue of communicants waiting for him, like the queue outside the butcher's. With practice, Don Antonio had developed both an abbreviated way of saying the *Corpus Domini Nostri* – reducing it to one word – and a series of conditioned reflexes that enabled him to leap up and offer communion as soon as he saw some vaguely human shape kneeling down before the altar of Our Lady of Perpetual Succour. Since Don Antonio reacted more to shape than face, it was easy for Luzmila to take communion along with everyone else at mass and then again, once or even twice, with Don Antonio. However, the time came for Don Antonio to retire, and he was replaced by a very earnest, learned, inquisitive priest, who was studying to be a canon and used every spare moment between masses, benedictions, confessions, novenas and rosaries to prepare for his exam. He used to sit in one of the more central confessionals that was lit by a large light bulb, which made the little cabin resemble nothing so much as a puppet theatre, and, in between studying his books and his index cards, he would observe his parishioners. He came to know them all, one by one, and, since he had a naturally good memory and an eye for detail, he reached the stage where he had to make regular examinations of conscience, more like purges really, in order to wipe his mind clean of all the minuscule idiosyncrasies that he had, quite unwittingly, absorbed and remembered along with the articles of the *Summa Theologica*, and that he could not get out of his head. The gentleman with the grey hair who looked like a clerk at the Banco de Vizcaya; the wealthy lady who came to mass without her make-up on (God bless her) and who had said three rosaries in the time it took him to say the *lavabo* and read from the gospel; the widow who spent the entire mass trying to find the words of the mass in the missal; the little girl in Wellington boots; the young lad as handsome as St Stanislas, who piously attended mass every morning apart from Fridays and always knelt down before the Seventh Station of the Cross. And then there was that tall, rather stooped woman who took communion twice. The first time, he let it pass, thinking he must have been mistaken. The second time, however, he pounced on Luzmila like a devil. In her fright, Luzmila swallowed the second Infant Jesus and fled the church in terror, without hearing a word the priest was saying. Luzmila has never been seen twice by anyone and no one has ever taken a really good look at her. When the day comes and we hear no more of her, she will be neither more nor less invisible than before.

One evening, Luzmila arrived home early. When she tried to open the door and found it bolted from the inside, she began to shout. She pounded on the door and kept shouting, and eventually Dorita opened it. Luzmila went in and found a man hurriedly pulling on his clothes. He escaped, entangled in the jacket and raincoat he just had time to throw over his shoulders. Dorita ran after him. Luzmila sat down on the bed without removing her overcoat. The room was filled with the murmur of the urban dusk and the wild, yellowish, Castilian winter. She could see the greenish tiles of the roof very close to the head of her bed, like a precipice. Dorita did not come and see her for two whole weeks. And Luzmila's feelings were as disparate and confused as ants in an ants' nest. She grew thinner and seemed ever more sunk in herself, ever greyer. It's hard to say whether Luzmila was visibly losing colour, corporeality, being or bulk. Maybe she wasn't even suffering, because, for Luzmila, pain, perhaps, has the same tenacious structure of those material objects to whose inescapable weight we become accustomed from birth and which we do not even consider to be obstacles.

After those two weeks, a tearful Dorita returned, saying something about being in a terrible fix and how it had been the first and only time and how much she loved Luzmila. Dorita believed her own lie so completely that she wept bitterly, sobbing: 'Look, Luzmila, I'm crying', as if to say that anyone who cries must have some good in them. This was a complete waste of time really, because, in Luzmila's mind, Dorita and the Infant Jesus of Prague were beyond judgement (our beliefs, after all, are the structures by which we judge real objects, whether possible or impossible). They were both part of the last strand of identity left to Luzmila. Besides, how could she judge Dorita's story when she barely heard it? The only thing she really saw and heard was that Dorita was asking forgiveness, although Luzmila didn't know why (because the incident that had occurred two weeks before was not connected causally in her imagination with the incident she was witnessing now). She had been greatly confused by Dorita's absence, not because it upset some particular plan or project of hers, but simply because she found it confusing. However, that feeling of pure confusion was immediately cancelled out by the pure objectless joy of having Dorita back, just as two quantitatively and qualitatively equal things cancel each other out. 'Forgive us our debts as we forgive our debtors.' Luzmila had always found those words surprising because she had never been able to work out who in the world her debtors could be. She didn't think anyone owed her anything. Neither debtors nor enemies can penetrate true solitude. Only the enmity that knows no enemies and the offence that has no guilty parties can enter therein. Luzmila, then, felt no need to forgive Dorita. Indeed, on that occasion, she gave her three hundred pesetas, and that afforded Dorita her first glimpse of the envelope stuffed with banknotes. So taken aback was she that Luzmila's room seemed to fill with a kind of bent-backed silence and the showers of dust in the room shone like snowfalls of ghostly pins.

When Luzmila went to the lavatory the following night, Dorita took another two hundred pesetas, and for the first time she experienced shame, the shame that, for everyone apart from Dorita herself, would later become shamelessness. And out of that shame was born, like a good feeling, or, rather, an easy and immediate feeling, the idea of compensating Luzmila in some way, because, in the imbalance that follows a fall, the idea of compensating someone is always instantly present, as a possibility. And so, to compensate Luzmila for the theft, Dorita began to trace on Luzmila's unsatiated skin and need for tenderness the ambiguous lines of love. It was like a bad performance at a puppet show. But, every evening, Luzmila would return home thinking joyfully of Dorita's sweet, moist body. And, in Luzmila's dreams and dozings, Dorita became the Infant Jesus – well, an incarnation is an incarnation – sleeping, exhausted, in the Infant Jesus's box along with the other crumbling hosts. In Dorita's imitation of love, cruelty lurked, with its tiny, translucent suckers. For two weeks, possibly longer, Luzmila experienced the accelerated pulse of blood threading the oblique needles of a late, empty spring. Sexuality adds nothing to an interpersonal relationship that is not already contained in the mere concept of that relationship. What it adds (and which is not contained in the concept) is a meaningless animation, a somnambular acceleration, the ultimate snare. During that time, Luzmila's pious imaginings became keener, more perfect and more absurd than usual. She even started talking about them to herself in the street and, when she got home, she would describe them to Dorita.

'Once, the Infant Jesus wouldn't go to sleep,' she said, 'and, even though they held him and rocked him, he just wouldn't go to sleep, talking all the time about the Passion and how painful the crown of thorns would be. Then the swallows came and plucked out the nails.'

And she was assailed again and again by the same image: the Infant Jesus, plump and fair, so unlike the children of her siblings, who, having been born in the years of shortages, were old before their time, bow-legged, irritable and crotchety, and with greenish-yellow skin, like the colour of the bread then. It was different with the Infant Jesus, who began life with the Annunciation and with the Angel's clear words, with the moon beneath his feet and a crown of twelve stars about his head. The Virgin lived in a clean street in a little white house with green doors neatly

painted by St Joseph. The windows were decorated with pots of gera-
niums, and there was a garden at the back, with marble columns holding
up the porch, and a marble fountain in the same colour with a little spout
of water that never ran dry. The Virgin kept everything spotless. At the
bottom of the garden were some pear trees that bore ripe pears all year
round, and a bed of maize with cobs whose glowing red-gold kernels the
Infant Jesus husked each evening.

These stories alarmed Dorita. She's a bit cracked, she thought to herself,
and this thought reassured her in the sense that one need not treat a mad
person with the same consideration as one would someone normal. A
madwoman is, after all, a joke, like the village idiot, sometimes petted
and sometimes beaten. Initially, Dorita found the stories amusing, but
then she got fed up with them. One night, after they had recited 'Dear
little Baby Jesus', the prayer Luzmila had taught Dorita, and once Luzmila
had fallen asleep, exhausted, Dorita shot out of bed like an arrow, opened
Luzmila's bag and made off with the envelope. When Luzmila woke the
next morning and went to put the Infant Jesus's box next to the envelope
as she did every day, she found the envelope missing. Carefully, calmly,
she searched the room, as one might search for a lost thimble; there were
not many things in the room and Luzmila inspected them all, one by one,
like someone checking a very simple sum. She experienced a slight dizziness that resembled the emptiness of life in that it was entirely smooth,
in that it did not hurt or cause anguish or anxiety in any precise sense, in
that it had no causal connection with any event past or future. The only
thing Luzmila did not do – as if she had suddenly broken the habit of a
lifetime – was go to work that morning. Instead, she walked the streets
and, in Plaza de Manuel Becerra, went into the dusty provincial park
behind the church, where she sat down on a bench and remained there,
motionless, for several hours. Then she felt a need to urinate and walked
up Calle de Alcalá to the Retiro Park, where she knew she would find
some public toilets. Then she walked very slowly back to Manuel Becerra.
Then she went back home and slept until the next day. And the following
morning, she began again or continued as usual, as a cleaning-woman.
And she put away more than half her wages in an envelope that she kept
alongside the Infant Jesus's box.

JOSÉ MARÍA MERINO

The Deserter

Love is something very special. That's why when she saw the shadow by the door – in the faint moonlight, it looked more like a flat, ominous stain – she wasn't at all frightened. She knew he had come home. The sweet air of that St John's Eve, the diaphanous sky, the fresh smell of the grass, the murmuring stream, the singing of the nightingales, were suddenly combining all that was most benign in nature with that newly restored presence.

They had only been married for about five months when war broke out. He was called up, and, in the brief letters he wrote to her from the front, she could read between the lines, despite all the words crossed out by the censors, about the hardships of life in the trenches. Those letters, though, which, at first, made somewhat confused reference to events and places, became more and more a simple record of longing and a desire for home. When they started to arrive uncensored, they were so steeped in a stark yearning to be home that they always made her cry when she read them.

She had been less alone at first. His mother was still living in the house at the time, and, even though she was ill, her mere presence had kept her company, filling the days with minor chores, daily conversations and shared comments on his letters and on the other grim news from the war. A year later, the old lady was dead. She died right there in the kitchen, sitting on the bench with a bunch of grapes in her lap and still holding a

José María Merino (b. 1941) was born in A Coruña, Galicia. He lived for several years in León and currently lives in Madrid. He is a master of the short story and has a particular penchant for the fantastic. He is also a poet, novelist, children's writer, travel writer and teacher of creative writing. His work has brought him various prizes, including the 2013 Premio Nacional de Narrativa for *El río del Edén*.

grape in her right hand. In another letter from him, she learned that, when news of his mother's death had finally reached him, his officers didn't consider it necessary to give him leave because the funeral had already been and gone.

Then she was left alone in the house and spent most of the day in silence, except when she dropped round to her sister's for a brief chat, and the village – from which the young lads and the young husbands were all absent – was equally silent, as if stunned.

She immersed herself in household tasks, willing herself to forget. And, setting herself a rigid timetable, she performed the daily chores of cleaning and cooking, doing the laundry and mucking out the barn, and keeping to the strict calendar required by work in the fields: harvesting and transporting the hay, hoeing the vegetable patch and around the fruit trees, grinding the barley. Absorbed in the task of the moment – the sheer physical effort establishing its own rhythm – she even came to think of his absence as a vague daydream from which she would soon wake up.

Time, however, continued to pass, and still the war did not end. She didn't really understand the reasons for the war. From the pulpit, the priest described the enemy as some terrifying, diabolical evil, as contagious as the plague. The war and the enemy ended up seeming something quite unreal, as if the war effort were a fight to the death with monstrous beings come from a distant, deadly land. So much so that when, one day, a convoy arrived bringing prisoners, and the intensely curious villagers went out in the street to watch the spectacle, one particularly stout woman exclaimed: 'But they don't have tails', expressing her surprise and disappointment at finding that these enemies in no way resembled what they'd been led to expect from the priest's diatribes and from other sources.

No, they had no tails, no hooves, no horns. They were men. Sad, dark creatures, wearing filthy capes and threadbare jackets, with balaclavas or field service caps covering their shaven heads. Almost all had thick beards and gaunt faces, although some were lads too young to have even started shaving.

The sight of those battered soldiers made her imagine her own husband who, perhaps at that very moment, was also being driven along in some muddy truck, shivering beneath a khaki cape. Caught up in a state of anguished confusion, she even thought she could recognize her own beloved's face in those other men's faces.

Time passed. Another year. The village continued to lose men until the only remaining inhabitants were the children, the women and the elderly. The evenings were no longer happy occasions for telling stories and remembering the past; the only reason to get together now was to pray. Rosaries and litanies, novenas and masses occupied any hours spent together.

When that particular St John's Eve* arrived, they found it hard to believe in a time when the young lads, and the one appointed king for the night, would light the traditional bonfire on top of the hill. It was the children who revived the memory of that ancient fiesta, building a big fire in the square. The fire attracted the grown-ups, who gathered around it. It was a warm, clear night, with not a breath of wind.

The children ran in circles round the fire, shouting and enjoying the warm glow. The grown-ups recalled other St John's Eves, when their sons would fill the night with noise and laughter. They now missed the very thing they had accepted at the time with the obligatory mixture of indulgence and annoyance called for by such an inevitable ritual; it was as if a part of their life had been amputated. That year, there was no need to keep an eye on eggs or sausages or kettles, as had been the case in the past. No one would creep in at night to steal them. Nor would anyone trample paths or scatter the embers in the hearth.

The village had no young men, and, in the sweet night air, that fact, made still more painful by the circumstances, felt particularly melancholy.

When the fire burned out, the improvised gathering broke up. She went to her sister's house, briefly greeted her other family members, then went home. That was when she saw the shadow by the door. She recognized him at once and ran to fold him in her arms.

He had changed. He was thinner, paler, and his face had taken on a kind of pensive quality. She realized at once that he had deserted. He had

---

* The veil between the living and the dead was thought to be particularly porous on certain nights of the year, and St John's Eve (23 June) became one of those days when the dead were believed to walk abroad.

been admitted to hospital after being wounded by shrapnel from a grenade, and had decided, once he recovered, to escape and go home. It had been a gruelling journey, lasting weeks. But there he was, silent and smiling.

Secrecy was of the essence. She concealed her happiness and went about her life as usual. During the hours of daylight, he remained hidden somewhere in the house. At night, under cover of darkness, they went out into the garden and sat next to each other, conscious of the pulsating stars, the murmuring stream and the birds calling to each other in the invisible canopy of the trees.

She rediscovered both the savour of the early days of marriage and the anguish of their final kisses and embraces. And, because love is something very special, all the problems – the war, having to cope on her own, the constant bartering to get enough food to survive – became very secondary considerations.

Her one fear was that he would be discovered. One afternoon, when she returned home after scavenging for firewood, she found two Civil Guards waiting for her. They brought news of his desertion – for he had apparently announced his intention to desert while delirious in hospital – and searched the house. They failed to find him, but that unexpected visit filled her with anxiety, fearing that one day they might find him and take him away again and perhaps punish his desertion with death.

And so the summer oscillated between fear and the joy of having him home. She would sometimes spontaneously burst into song, which, in that glum, silent village, seemed positively shocking.

And yet a strange feeling would sometimes wake her in the middle of the night, and, even though she could still feel his body next to hers, a whole flock of sombre fears would come crowding into her mind, as if the future were already decided and all kinds of terrible omens were about to come true.

When she woke on the first day of September, he was no longer beside her in bed. It was a damp, grey day. She looked for him everywhere, in the house and in the yard, but he was nowhere to be found. His absence, reviving memories of her long solitude, aroused in her a sense of foreboding.

At the hour of the angelus, she saw the two Civil Guards again approaching the house. It had started raining hard, and their oilskin capes were dripping water.

They had found his body on the top of the hill, lying among the rocks, as if he had been straining every sinew to get a glimpse of the village. His wound had presumably opened again on the long journey home, and his body was as withered as a shed snakeskin. The guards said he must have been dead since at least St John's Eve.

MARINA MAYORAL

Then He Began to Forget

It was only when I tried to tell the story, and convert it into a series of events that happened in real time with a cast of characters who each behaved in a certain way, that I realized there were certain aspects of the story that I hadn't noticed when it was actually happening.

It's just like *The Immortal Story* said my sister. I'd thought exactly the same to begin with, because my initial impression was that it was just some extraordinary, fantastical tale. As it unfolded, though, I became more aware of the ways in which it differed from the Orson Welles film and the original Isak Dinesen story. I have absolutely nothing in common with that ignorant, ingenuous sailor. Yes, I'm young like him and I'm not exactly ugly, but I would certainly never have chosen myself for such a role. I would look for someone with a more impressive physique, what you might call a fine figure of a man, or perhaps a man of superior intelligence, a celebrated scholar or an artist of undoubted talent. On the other hand, that might only complicate matters. Famous people tend to be suspicious and mean about money. They might perhaps fear some kind of blackmail, or feel they were being used: many won't even allow themselves to be photographed, still less donate a part of their actual person. Not that they were being asked for a kidney or an eye, but they would be far less receptive than me, and the results would possibly be the same, or worse. Everyone knows that genius can't be inherited. There were, besides,

Marina Mayoral (b. 1942) was born in Mondoñedo in Galicia and writes in *galego* and in *castellano*. She taught Spanish Literature at the Complutense University in Madrid until her retirement. She writes short stories and novels, and many of her novels take place in an imaginary place in Galicia called Brétema. Since 1990, she has written a weekly column in *Voz de Galicia*.

other arguments that she used to justify choosing me: extremes are always dangerous and it was preferable to choose someone in the middle, a sensible fellow, in good health, well set up in life and with no attachments. There was also the question of affinities: it had to be someone to whom she felt attracted, because, if it was a case of having to submit to something rather unpleasant, she might as well opt for the operating table, as it would be more hygienic. All this seemed perfectly reasonable.

I'd be terrified, said my sister: some complete stranger appearing mysteriously out of nowhere, like the sailor in the legend: a dark, foggy night in some remote port, a figure beckoning you to follow her . . . But it had, in fact, been a bright sunny morning on the beach, and we weren't in India or Hong Kong. She had thought this place would be exotic and romantic, and, having hesitated between here and the Greek islands, she chose to come here because it was where she'd spent her honeymoon, and the memory of those marvellous days, she told me, had made the decision for her. She came straight over to me, there was no silent beckoning, and she spoke fluent English and French and a little Spanish.

She really was like someone out of a legend, not because she was mysterious, but because she was so beautiful: blonde hair, deep blue eyes, luminous, golden skin, slender body, high, firm breasts, curvaceous hips, long legs . . . An erotic fantasy, said my older brother, the classic 'gorgeous Swede' we all used to fantasize about. But Nora really did look like that, and she wasn't particularly tall, nor did she resemble a pretty boy in drag. She was absolutely lovely, and I suppose that was the main reason why I agreed to collaborate with her in an act that seemed to me both marvellous – at least the way she told it – and, at the same time, perfectly normal. Nora wanted to have a child, but her husband, who was considerably older than her, was infertile. They both thought that rather than opting for artificial insemination they would resort to a process more in tune with nature. They just had to find the right person and keep their identities secret so as to avoid any subsequent problems. This explained her natural reluctance to reveal her nationality and her name, as well as her husband's profession and any other information that could be used by the child's biological father should he want to track them down in the future and attempt some form of blackmail. This seemed to me a very prudent position to take and far more practical than having me sign a legal document renouncing all claim, something that would only serve to further complicate the situation, although, as she herself said, what really mattered was my moral commitment to accept this agreement, because unless I gave my word of honour she would not pursue the matter. I gave her my word and consequently made no attempt to find out anything about her. In other words, I behaved like a true gentleman, according to my sister. Or like an arrogant bastard, according to my sister-in-law.

My older brother sees things differently. The idea of elective affinities and mutual attraction seems to him a very banal chat-up line: Nora didn't choose me because I was a promising, reasonably talented young man, in good health and from a well-to-do family; she chose me because I'm stupid. The word he actually used was 'ingenuous', but I could tell that he meant 'stupid'. Nora might well be a con artist, intending to use this story about wanting a child to get money out of me at a later date. I had obviously explained myself badly, otherwise he would never have thought such a thing of her. There might also be a touch of envy in his remark. He's always been one of life's winners and can't understand why on earth Nora would choose me, when he had been there with me on the beach. It's also clear that I failed to convey Nora's air of utter confidence. She's not the classic femme fatale or a man-eater; if she were, I would have steered well clear, and would certainly never have agreed to help her out. Nora loves and respects her husband, she's a good wife and will be a good mother to the child: she's affectionate, cheerful, calm. She'll give him security. She has a real talent for listening and for inspiring trust. When you're with her, you feel like talking and telling her your problems. My brother still can't understand it: what you mean is that you didn't ask any questions, you just told her all about yourself, he says. I bet you talked about the whole family. No, not all of them, but almost all. I did talk about his wife. Nora asked me why I hadn't married; she felt that a man with my good qualities, as she put it, wasn't made to be a bachelor, and that's why I talked to her about my sister-in-law. At first, Nora didn't ask out of curiosity, but because she was interested to know more about her child-to-be's family; she wanted to know anything that might affect him in the future – if any illnesses or peculiarities ran in the family, if we had a special talent for some particular activity or art. She was very pleased to know I was a writer, and congratulated herself on her good taste, her clinical eye, as she put it. And so we gradually moved on to more personal subjects.

The thing I find hardest to understand is that she left without saying goodbye. The night before, she said 'see you tomorrow', but when I went back the next day, the house was all closed up: the gate, the front door, the windows, everything. She's obviously a very careful woman, said my sister-in-law. She must have realized that you'd fallen in love with her, which is why she vanished. A man in love doesn't listen to reason, doesn't respect promises. Had the relationship gone any further, I might have started making enquiries, tried to find out who she was, where she came from, how I could meet her again. Perhaps I'd already tried that. Or had I perhaps revealed the intensity of my desire, my growing love for her, my sadness that the child, our child, would become another man's child. Perhaps I'd already begun my emotional blackmail. I don't know where my sister-in-law got all this, I don't know if it was there in the story I told her or if she's drawing on another, different story known to both of us. She may well be right, and this might explain Nora's sudden departure with no goodbyes. But perhaps there's something more to it. Perhaps Nora has fallen in love with *you*, says my sister. She wouldn't want to betray her husband, the same husband who, to spare her suffering, allowed her to give herself to another man; a husband who so trusts his wife, her loyalty and her love that he felt able to allow her to choose as the father of her child any man she wanted. She obviously wouldn't want to disappoint a man like that, says my sister. He must be a fool, a pushover, says my older brother. She's come here on holiday, and, when she goes back, she'll pretend the child is his, the scheming hussy! She's used you both. I wonder if there's any hint of that in what I told him. Perhaps my disappointment, my rage, my pain at her unexpected departure were all there in my words. Or perhaps my older brother is projecting onto them certain dark suspicions about another story that he'd prefer not to be told.

My story, the one I experienced, ends outside that closed door, but everyone has come up with the ending he or she likes most. She might well come back, says my sister. Her husband will realize she's in love with another man and won't allow her to make such a sacrifice. He's a kind man, and generous, quite a lot older than her, and very understanding. Nora will be able to tell him everything that happened and what she feels, because she knows he'll understand, he always has. He'll tell her that, for the moment, she must keep calm and rest, so that she gives birth to a healthy baby. There'll be time later on to resolve the matter, she's free to decide, as always. Meanwhile, he'll look after her, spoil her, put his hand on her belly to feel the baby moving, they'll laugh together and decide on a name. And, after nine months, you'll be nothing but a romantic memory, said my sister-in-law. And when the child grows up, and their friends start saying how much he resembles his father, they'll exchange wry, knowing looks. Tender looks, says my sister, and they'll remember you with gratitude, so why are you so down about it, you got laid by a really gorgeous woman and who knows who the child's father might really be, says my older brother, and, if that's the end of the story, then I can hardly complain, the trouble is I'm a writer and try to make literature out of everything, to dress things up, to show off, I'll probably end up making a novel or a story out of it, says my sister-in-law. But it's too much like *The Immortal Story*, says my sister, you'd have to find a different ending, that she comes back, for example, or steals the guy's credit cards, says my older brother, that it was all a dream, says my sister-in-law. Or a lie.

When I finished telling the story, it was quite different, whether closer to the facts or more removed I don't know. I don't really care. I needed somehow to get some distance from it, to make it into something I could manipulate. To say: I was sunbathing on the beach, minding my own business, when a young blonde woman came over to me. And six pages later say: the house was all closed up, the gate, the windows, everything. Now it's not me who's filled with despair, the one trying in vain to summon up a ghost or at least understand what happened. It's my character. I read his story again and make changes to the structure and style. I read it to my sister, who says she doesn't like the ending, and to my sister-in-law, who smiles and says: I knew it was just a story. You wanted to make me jealous, didn't you? And to my older brother, who says I'm a fool to agonize about a situation that isn't going to benefit me.

The sailor must have agonized about it too. He would tell it first to his shipmates: she was a really beautiful woman, with golden hair and eyes as green as the sea, like no other woman he'd ever seen before. Then, when he was no longer working as a sailor, he would tell his wife: the arrival in port, the mysterious figure beckoning to him, the luxurious house. And to his children when they grew up: her husband was a very rich and powerful man, but he couldn't have children. And also to his grandchildren: many years ago, in a far-off land . . . Then one day, in a bar in the port, he would hear another sailor just back from sea telling *his* story: the servant beckoning to him in the dark night mists, the palace, the beautiful woman, her jet-black eyes and her long hair as black as the night . . . Then he began to forget.

CRISTINA FERNÁNDEZ CUBAS

A Fresh Start

Translated by Simon Deefholts and Kathryn Phillips-Miles

She had decided to make a fresh start. She had to make a fresh start. And as soon as she arrived at the small apartment-hotel, chosen at random and booked in Barcelona through a travel agent, she thought it was the ideal place to allow her to stop wondering 'How do I go about it?', 'Where do I begin?', 'What's the recipe for starting a new life?' The room was large and bright. There was a kitchenette, a big bed and the bathroom had everything she needed. There was a sofa, armchairs, a dressing table attached to the wall and a large window looking out onto Gran Vía. The fact that there hadn't been one single room available for these particular dates at her usual hotel in the Paseo del Prado, the one she always went to, had been a stroke of luck. The same thing had happened with all the other alternatives she resorted to whenever her usual hotel told her on the phone, 'I'm very sorry. We're full up.' Something had to be going on in Madrid during those first few days of spring – a particularly important conference, trade fair or symposium. Now she was glued to the window, protecting her eyes from the sun behind dark glasses and watching the activity in the street, fascinated. It was as if she were watching a silent film with a huge budget. There were thousands of extras, all the colours of the rainbow and lots of action. Some of the actors were trying to attract more attention and play a bigger role. She had seen one

Cristina Fernández Cubas (b. 1945) was born in Arenys de Mar, Barcelona and studied law and journalism. She worked as a journalist until she decided to devote herself entirely to literature. She has written three novels, but is best known for her short stories, which are heavily influenced by the stories she was told as a child. There is a marked fascination with the fantastic and the otherworldly. She is widely recognized as one of Spain's finest writers of the short story, and her most recent book, *La habitación de Nona* (*Nona's Room*), brought her the Premio de la Crítica.

stylish passer-by cross the road at least four or five times. Where on earth was that man going – if indeed he was going anywhere? She moved away from the window and opened her suitcase. Two nights. She would be there only for two nights. But perhaps she would stay longer another time, for a week or a month. She turned on the television and put on the music channel. Then she switched on the air conditioning. For a minute she thought this really was her usual hotel and felt a hankering for what she had lost a long time ago – the urge to read, write, turn the dressing table into a writing desk, cook, stock up the fridge, go to the theatre and the cinema. More than anything, she wanted to come back. She wanted to come back to that bright room every evening and, given the choice, she wouldn't change a thing. It was hers. She had been given a room that belonged to her.

She looked at the key. Room 404. She had liked the number straight away. Four plus four equals eight. The symbol for infinity, she remembered, is a figure 8 on its side. An isolated zero, she thought, in principle has no value. It's nothing. Or perhaps it is something. Perhaps it's not a number but actually a letter. An O for oxygen, for example. She took a deep breath and turned off the television, the music channel and the air conditioning. Then her mind went back to the figure 8, to the key she was still holding in her hand. Four plus four equals eight. Eight months had already passed since *he* had gone. Eight months that time hadn't measured in the usual way. Sometimes those eight months seemed like an eternity, just like the figure 8 on its side. And sometimes they simply seemed like smoke rings jauntily colliding in the air between puffs on a cigarette. That's what her eight months had been like – interminable and empty.

She went out, and now she was part of the film, too. She was one more extra, one among many thousands. Perhaps at that very moment, someone from a double-glazed window, from a soundproofed room in some hotel, was watching her among the crowd. She liked the thought that whoever was watching her – whether it was a man or a woman – would suddenly feel strangely relaxed and happy, just like she did now. She walked down Gran Vía and thought how lucky she was – the room, such a beautiful day, wanting to get down to work again, to start living again. She'd barely walked a block when she stopped in a square. She was surprised that what she thought was a square actually had a street name, Calle de la Flor Baja.

But that morning wasn't like any other. She'd decided that it wouldn't be like any other. She sat down at a table outside a bar, opened her diary and wrote 'Flor Baja'.

She ordered a beer. She was sure she would never go back to the old hotel in Paseo del Prado. Flor Baja could very well be the starting point for a new itinerary. She would have new interests, start new habits, perhaps her new life was beginning just at that very moment. She looked through her diary. She had arranged to have dinner with a friend that evening and had to go to an office to sort out some paperwork the next day. Suddenly the very idea of the dinner felt like torture, and it seemed as if the paperwork had just been a pretext to spend a few days in Madrid and have a change of atmosphere. She wrote down, 'Cancel dinner and send documents by post.' She looked at the things she had written down on previous days. There were sayings, suggestions, reminders to be optimistic and how to behave. She smiled as she noticed that, in a fit of fury, she had ended up striking them all out for being useless. Only two of them had escaped the carnage: 'Live for the day', and Einstein's words of condolence to a friend's widow: 'Your husband has departed this world a little ahead of me, but you know that for me, as a physicist, neither the present nor the past exist.' She couldn't remember the friend's name or his wife's, but she did remember how many times she had read those words in amazement, as if they were meant exclusively for her. The past, the present . . . of course the past existed! The only problem lay in what exactly the past was. Sometimes it insisted on disguising itself as the present. Voices, laughter, whole sentences often made her turn around hopefully in a cinema or in the middle of the street. Just as they would make her toss and turn anxiously when waking up from a dream. But now . . . she called the waiter over and quickly paid for the beer and didn't wait for the change. What was happening now?

She had just seen him. Him. The man who had left this world almost eight months earlier. The man with whom she had shared her whole life. He was wearing an old beige jacket. That beige corduroy jacket! He was absent-mindedly crossing the square in the middle of Calle de la Flor Baja. She followed him cautiously. She was right. Although the similarity was remarkable, she knew it could only be an illusion. But that morning, she'd decided, wasn't like any other. She'd felt that immediately, as soon as she'd walked into room 404 and felt it was hers. It was a morning unlike any other and he was now walking down Gran Vía, and she was following in his footsteps like a shadow, at a sensible distance. A few seconds later, he stopped at a news-stand. She saw him hand over a few coins and pick up a packet of cigarettes, and then he moved off again. No, she said to herself, that's not possible. He gave up smoking years ago. Although 'neither the present nor the past exist', she remembered, and it was only then that she thought she understood the reason why she'd once written down that sentence to which she repeatedly returned. Perhaps, in her new life, she would do nothing more than follow any stranger who looked like him. She had no time to feel sorry for herself, to turn around or even to realize that she was behaving like a madwoman. He, whoever he was, had suddenly turned round as if her eyes were burning into the back of his head, and she had no option but to hide in a doorway. She was quick. He didn't see her. But the look on the doorman's face made her realize that she was acting ridiculously. Or was she? She told herself that she wasn't. What was wrong with following someone you love? The man who, defying all the laws of nature, had reappeared in Madrid in the full light of day one sunny morning, delightfully confounding his own past.

She walked into the street again and for the second time in a few minutes felt as if she were taking part in a film, but now she wasn't just another extra, someone to make up the numbers. She was walking surprisingly nimbly and she had an objective: not to lose sight of that old jacket; to follow it at a distance. And for a few moments she thought that the people walking around and about her realized what she was doing and were aware of her objective. That was why they were looking at her, falling into step with her, spurring her on. But were they really spurring her on? She wasn't young any more and had passed through the doors of invisibility some time ago. She could move around comfortably without anyone paying her any attention. And now, when she needed to be more anonymous and invisible than ever, she was the target of comments, remarks, flirtatious compliments, outrageous proposals. What was happening that morning on Gran Vía? Before she had time to answer her own question, he suddenly headed off taking great strides and she had to run to keep up with him. She no longer cared that people were looking at her or that some idiot jokingly tried to block her way. She couldn't lose him. Those great strides of his – that was how he walked, with great strides. Then he stopped dead in his tracks. He often used to do that. When he remembered something important he would stop dead in his tracks. She took a deep breath and stopped in front of a perfume shop. Just for a few seconds, she thought, until he moves off again and I can follow him without being noticed. But the glass in a mirror reflected her face back at her, and she just stood there fascinated, astonished, and not moving a muscle.

Because it really was her. Who could say how many years ago, but it was her. She was wearing a very short skirt, and her long, shiny chestnut hair was loose. She thought she looked pretty. Very pretty. Had she ever been so pretty? She wanted to think she was in a dream, someone else's dream. Wherever the man she loved was, he was dreaming about her and now she was looking at herself through his eyes. That's how he must have seen her around the time they met; that time, so long ago now, when anything seemed possible. She took a great big breath and had the feeling she had already experienced that moment. The shop window, the mirror, her girlish reflection, Gran Vía one sunny morning. A mirage or simply an optical illusion. The sun, her reflection, a trick of the mirror, the objects and posters in the window becoming entwined with her own reflection.

'Where did you get to?' she suddenly heard.

She put her hand out to stop herself from falling over. He was there – tall, slim and just as young as when they first knew each other. There was no longer any doubt. The boy in the beige jacket was right there, behind her, and he'd just put his hand on her shoulder.

'Come on, we're late. Don't forget, we're meeting up with Tete.'

He put his arm around her waist and she let herself be led away like an automaton. Tete Poch. Tete Poch had died years before. Tete was the first of their friends to disappear, to abandon this world. But now it seemed as if none of all this could have happened yet. Tete was still alive. He had not yet departed for the place from which there is no return, and she was a girl with long hair who wore amazingly short skirts. She took a deep breath, and once again thought she might faint. She bit her lip until it bled. It wasn't a dream. This was really happening. She gradually recognized streets, shops and bars. They went into one which seemed surprisingly familiar. She knew the place. There was a time she used to go there regularly, although she couldn't now remember its name. A blotchy mirror reflected back her face. She was still pretty. And there he was beside her, very, very young, wearing that nice corduroy jacket he never wanted to take off and which she still (without knowing why) kept in the wardrobe.

'Tete's borrowed a car off someone. We could go to Segovia for the day.'

'Great.'

'What's up? You've hardly said a thing all morning.'

She shook her head.

'You were walking so quickly . . .'

Tete hadn't arrived yet. It was better that way. She needed some time to take in what was happening. He had just taken out a book from his pocket.

'I found it in an old bookshop yesterday. It's a real gem.'

She looked at the cover. *The Oresteia* by Aeschylus. She was surprised that she could read the title without her glasses. Her sight was still good back then. Perhaps, but she'd recognized the book immediately. It was still at home too, on the bookshelf in the study. She hadn't dared take anything out of that room, even though he had gone.

'It's a trilingual edition,' he said proudly. 'Classical Greek, Modern Greek and English.'

'Yes.'

He took her hand.

'Something's up with you. Or are you worried about the exam?'

The exam? What exam?

'I'm sure you've passed. Don't worry.'

She suddenly began remembering: Tete, a beaten-up old car, the three of them in Segovia, the journalism exam. That's why they'd gone to Madrid. She had to take an exam in journalism and *he'd* gone with her. They went everywhere together, almost from the first time they met at the Faculty of Law in Barcelona. They were never boyfriend and girlfriend. They didn't like those words. They hated them. They were friends. That's what they used to say. 'FRIENDS' in capital letters. No one was surprised that some years later the friendship turned into marriage, although they didn't like the word 'marriage' either and 'husband' and 'wife' even less. They thought they sounded formal and boring. If anyone had asked them what they were back then, at the time when Tete was around and when they used to go to Madrid and when she was taking the journalism exam, they would have said 'FRIENDS'.

'I'm just going to the toilet,' she said, and he stroked her cheek.

Her cheek, my God, her cheek was burning! She was scared she would burst into tears, get emotional, say something out of place and spoil the marvellous encounter. She got up and added, 'I'll be back in a minute.'

She didn't need to ask where the toilets were or stop and look at the sign ('TOILETS. TELEPHONE') because she knew exactly where she was. It was as if she had been there just the day before. She went down a couple of steps and turned back to look at the table. Tete had just arrived, and they were giving each other a hug. They were giving each other a hug! Then she did burst into tears. Tears of joy, tears of forgotten joy. Her mascara had run into one eye and she had to almost feel her way down to the toilets. She splashed some water on her face when she got there. She needed to clear her head and sort herself out. She had to look happy and carefree and think there was still a whole life ahead of them. If they were surprised at how she looked or guessed that she'd been crying, she would simply say, 'Bloody mascara. I don't know why I bother with make-up.' She suddenly remembered that this was exactly what had happened. She remembered it clearly, word for word. 'Bloody mascara. I don't know why I bother with make-up.' She also clearly remembered that, on that morning she'd miraculously been allowed to relive, her eyes had stung for a long time and they went to a chemist's and bought eye drops (which brand was it?). Then they all got into the borrowed car and sang songs the whole way. Back then it was quite a journey to get to Segovia. They sang war songs, anthems, banned lyrics that were just as forbidden as the fact that she, a girl of twenty years of age at the time, should be in a car with Tete and him, as free as birds, happy and carefree, while her parents in Barcelona thought she was taking an exam or studying. What a charmed life they'd led before mobile phones. She dried her face with a towel (paper towels still hadn't invaded the toilets) and went up the steps two at a time. She was ready. She knew the script and she was happy. She was the happiest girl in the world, even though her mascara was still running and, for a moment, when she rubbed her eyes, she could see only a grey mist. Bloody mascara!

For a second, she thought she'd made a mistake and that the bar had another room or that the toilets were shared between two different premises. But there was only one staircase and upstairs there was a soulless bar with an enormous counter, a few customers and a dozen tables piled up any old how in a corner. 'Where are the young men who were here a short while ago?' she asked a waiter in a quavering voice. The man shrugged and didn't understand. She leaned against the wall. Where had they gone? How could they leave her behind?

A young woman offered her a seat and asked, 'Are you OK?'

She shook her head.

'She seems confused,' said the waiter. 'She came in a while ago and went straight to the toilets.'

The young woman spoke to her gently, very slowly and in a loud voice as if she were a foreigner who found it difficult to understand. 'What's your address? Shall we call a taxi for you?'

She didn't reply. She opened her handbag and took out a small mirror and looked at herself in it for a moment. She wasn't surprised. In the distance she could hear a hum of voices wondering what was going on and the young woman asking for a napkin with some ice cubes and talking to the onlookers.

'It's all right. The lady doesn't feel very well.'

She went back to the hotel, to the apartment-room she had liked so much that morning. The past, the present, she remembered. There is no past and there is no present. Today, the present had slipped into her past. Or was it the other way round and fragments of her past had surfaced in the present? She opened her suitcase. By this time they would already be on the way to Segovia. Once more she wondered how they could have left her behind. But taking the high-speed train would mean she could overtake them and get there before they did. The present racing against the past. Not everything was lost yet because, once again, she remembered everything perfectly well: the restaurant, as much wine as you could drink, searching out a cheap hotel for the night. The names and the exact locations didn't matter. She would go to each and every restaurant, inn, tavern or hostelry until she found them. It would be best to leave her suitcase down at reception and travel without any luggage. There wasn't a second to lose. She would take a taxi and go to Chamartín station. She'd catch up with them and would reappear in that delightful day from so long ago. Tete, him and her, with their whole lives ahead of them.

The key slipped out of her hand and clattered on the floor. She saw the number on the key fob and smiled. 'Eight months, oxygen, four plus four, infinity.' She knelt down, picked up the key and couldn't help recalling her own thoughts from just a short while ago, her frustration or despair at her question: 'How could they leave me behind?' But also, as she was leaning against the bed to help herself get up, she was grateful for the miracle of time travel: the hope that, if *that* (whatever it was) had happened, it could happen again; clinging to Einstein's words, which had become a mantra: 'There is no past and there is no present.' Suddenly she understood that she'd made a mistake about something very important. They hadn't left her behind. How could she have thought something so ridiculous? Of course they hadn't left her behind. There they were, the three of them, together on the road in an old banger someone had lent them, singing and laughing. They were free! That day from years and years back, that she had experienced again just for a few moments, was not over. She squeezed the key as if it were an amulet. 404. Oxygen. Four plus four equals eight. Infinity was a figure 8 on its side. She opened her hand without realizing it; the key slipped from it once more and clattered on the floor. But now she thought it was mocking her. *A fresh start. A fresh start. A fresh start.*

She sat down at the dressing table and looked at herself in the mirror. She wouldn't go anywhere. The past had a cast-iron script and there could be no improvisation. Whatever Einstein said, the past and the present were two irreconcilable spaces. She had been on the verge of doing something crazy; the whole morning had been completely ridiculous. If she closed her eyes she could still see and hear them – the songs, the car and the road – but if she opened her eyes she saw her tired old face again. That's what her new life was offering her. It would be no use trying to cheat the clock and steal back times that didn't belong to her any more. For a moment she saw herself, exhausted and in a sweat, finally finding the bar where the three friends were cheerfully chatting away, and discreetly sitting down at a nearby table to watch them and to wait for the miracle to work its magic once again. But now she felt ridiculous. She felt like an intruder, an interloper, a gooseberry, because those three were twenty years old; they were young and living for the moment. And what was now clearer than ever: they didn't need her for anything. They didn't need a sixty-year-old woman staring into a mirror who sometimes, occasionally, didn't feel very well.

JUAN JOSÉ MILLÁS

She's Everywhere

When my second marriage collapsed, I knew that it marked the end of my romantic biography. In future, I might have a few semi-passionate affairs, but there was bound to be something artificial, something false about all of them, completely at odds with the degree of commitment that, in my view, was necessary to sustain any long-term relationship. I hate to generalize, but men *are* very strange, by which I mean that they lack emotions or are more or less incapable of communicating them. They relate best to objects – a car, a gold watch, a leatherbound diary, a credit card – and it may be that, through them, they're trying to say things too profound for us women to understand; we, on the other hand, have a much closer relationship with the abyss, with the void, with absence. You can't have a conversation about life with a man or, if you do, there's always something rather coarse or vulgar about his words, and that fills me with a kind of atavistic revulsion of which I've tried in vain to cure myself. It's funny, because when you see fathers with their daughters, they do seem to develop genuinely tender feelings for them, as if they were their ideal girlfriends or something. As I say, all this is a massive generalization; there *are* men capable of peering into the abyss on the edge of which we women sit permanently perched, although I've yet to meet such a man, and am unlikely to do so at this stage in my life. Anyway, I'm not prepared to hang around waiting for such a rare event to happen.

Juan José Millás (b. 1946) was born in Valencia but moved with his family to Madrid in 1952. He worked in a bank and then for the airline Iberia, writing short stories and novels in his spare time. Since winning the Premio Sésamo with his second novel, *Cerbero son las sombras*, he has written ten more novels and several collections of short stories, and he contributes a weekly column to *El País*. His most recent novel to be translated into English is *From the Shadows*.

Not that my relationships with other women have been easy either. I seem to arouse feelings of intense rivalry in them, and, while I found this rather flattering when I was younger, I absolutely loathe it now. So I don't have any close women friends either, and, of course, none with whom I could consider sharing my life. That's why, when my second husband left me, I began to embrace solitude in the belief that, in future, this would be the norm. I quickly acquired the habits of a singleton, little routines with which I gradually fortified my existence, until I had come to a proper understanding with the walls of my apartment and with my sheets, and, generally speaking, this worked very well until, that is, I met Julia.

I met her in a café where we both used to have lunch. The first time I saw her and our eyes met, I knew there was something about her that touched me deeply. We only had to exchange a few words for that dis-quieting feeling to be confirmed, a feeling that continued to grow apace in the weeks that followed. It was the beginning of autumn and I was beset by a vague but persistent melancholy, which found meaning and direction in Julia's company. I began to depend on her, but without having to pay the high price that comes with depending on a man. I would never have dared say this to her, but I felt as if she were a part of my being that had long ago been plucked from me, leaving a subtle wound that had now found sweet relief.

Meanwhile, autumn was sliding into winter, and I was beginning to think of life as a home in which the evening was the most pleasant room to sit in. I even began to lose my fear of Sundays and rediscovered the old pleasure of going for walks alone and viewing myself from the outside as if I were some kind of spectacle, like a flame that would burn for a finite, but unknown period of time. On rainy days, I would take refuge in a café and enjoy watching people crossing the street, dodging the cars and the puddles, in order to go nowhere at all, like in those nature programmes where the animals wander from one place to another with no apparent objective, but with admirably precise movements.

Julia began to come to my apartment on a fairly regular basis. We would spend the evenings talking about things that didn't concern us directly, avoiding delving into any personal matters, not out of respect for what is usually called 'privacy', but rather because it seemed unnecessary to indulge in such exhibitionism. Meanwhile, our relationship grew imperceptibly, building between us a bridge connecting the two parts of a single country split in two by some catastrophe.

One day, I remember, it snowed and, from the living-room window, I saw Julia get off the bus and run over to the street door below. Her feet were soaked, and I had to lend her a pair of woollen socks and some slippers that fitted her perfectly. Then I made some tea, and as it began to grow dark, and using the cold weather as an excuse, we each drank a glass of brandy.

'Would you like to stay for supper?' I asked.

'Well, if the weather carries on like this,' she said with a smile, 'I'll have to stay the night.'

'There's plenty of room,' I said, trying not to betray my feelings.

She asked me to show her some photos, and I brought out the various albums that summarize my life. I'm not a particularly organized person, but, when it comes to photos, I've developed a kind of mania, with an eye to the future. I've arranged the photos according to the date and the event they commemorate, and under each one I've written a few lines summing up how I was feeling when the photo was taken. We sat at the small, round table I'd recently placed in the living room, opposite the window, and we began turning the thick leaves of the first album, while, on the other side of the window that was keeping us safe from the harsh world outside, the snow continued to fall in indolent flakes. I think it must have been the brandy – which I hardly ever drink – that encouraged me to talk.

'This is me at my first communion.'

'Why so serious?'

'My mother had told me not to smile because I had two teeth missing.'

'And who's that?'

She was pointing to a girl the same age as me standing to the right of the photo, in profile, observing me with a kind of ironic aloofness, as if she disapproved of my dress or my hairband or my general attitude to the whole occasion. But I didn't know who that girl was, I never have, just as I've never been able to identify another girl (possibly the same one) who is there in a school photo observing me from one corner, as if disapproving of the special sash I'm wearing. I couldn't help myself then and I shared my first confidence with Julia.

'Look,' I said, focusing my gaze on the album, 'that girl gets everywhere. She's always different, but she's always looking at me as if reproaching me for something, or mocking me.'

Indeed, throughout my whole photographic career, at all the most important events in my life, you can see a girl growing up at the same rate as me and who is always there, in one corner, eyeing me impertinently. I noticed her recently, one Saturday evening when I was adding dates to my latest albums. I asked my mother and my siblings if they could identify the woman who appears in the photos of both my first and my second wedding, in the photo taken during my first trip abroad, or on my birthday, but no one knew who she was. I only know that she's observing me, sometimes affectionately, but almost always with a hint of sadness, as might the most disillusioned part of my own self.

And while I was explaining all this to Julia, trying to avoid her eyes, her smile, I knew that this same woman was now sitting next to me, contemplating my life, while the snow continued to cut us off from the world, sealing a pact that would bind us together for ever now that we'd finally met each other outside a photo. The brandy was warming my veins, and in the next-door apartment I could hear the music of the cutlery being irritably plonked down on the table for the family supper. And Julia said that, yes, she would definitely stay the night.

So there we are.

VICENTE MOLINA FOIX

The Real Hairdresser

When I started out as a homosexual, I only ever slept with hairdressers, but this wasn't some kind of weird obsession on my part, it was just the way things were at the time, which will give you some idea how old I am. It would be a long time before there were any gay engineers, or gay councillors, sportsmen or butchers. The word 'gay' didn't exist as such. Homosexuals were simply queers, and the queer crowd who frequented the same pick-up joints as me all worked with hair.

They were lovely, slender boys, bottle blonds most of them, and since highlights (or even layers) hadn't yet come in, their blondness was a pure, uniform gold. To me – bespectacled, plump-verging-on-fat, with dark hair and dandruff – they were the very epitome of sexiness. True, I did sometimes fantasize about being stopped in the street one night by a policeman demanding to see my ID and who, instead of beating me up for not renewing it, would surrender his body to me in some homo-friendly police station; in my imagination, I also screwed the occasional baker or tram driver, but that doesn't mean I found hairdresserly sex sad or staid. On the contrary, I liked everything about those boyfriends from the world of hair, even the permanent smell of lacquer.

I slept with both graduate and apprentice hairdressers, with one guy who claimed to have spent time in Germany studying pre-Romantic ringlet techniques, and a lad whose sole job was shampooing the customers' hair

Vicente Molina Foix (b. 1946) spent three years at Oxford University teaching Spanish literature. He has written poetry, novels and short stories, and his work has brought him many prizes, notably the 2007 Premio Nacional de Narrativa. In 2001, he began directing films and has since made two: *Sagitario* and *El dios de madera*. This story comes from his 2009 collection, *Con tal de no morir*.

in the barber's on the corner. With some, I even suggested converting our one-night stand into daily love. Such relationships, however, never lasted for more than four weeks, not for lack of commitment or desire on my part, but because all the hairdressers I became involved with seemed to be suffering from some kind of identity crisis, and at bedtime they would offload their neuroses onto me, leaving me sleepless and anxious. Hair wasn't enough for them – that was the problem – they all longed to be classical ballet dancers or models, to make it as a singer or as an interior designer to the wealthy or, at the very least, as hairdresser to various Hollywood actresses rather than to the local medusas – the local silly moos – who really didn't deserve the care lavished on taming their wiry locks.

Then one 20th of August, Graham swayed into Madrid, scandalized to find that a capital city, famed throughout Europe for being the city that never sleeps, was unable to provide him with supper at half past midnight, even in the Gran Vía. I had left my apartment at seven that evening to go out hunting and, feeling about as arid as the city itself, I was returning home after visiting two deserted pubs, a rather drab doggers' park, and exchanging a few fruitless glances in the street. Graham, walking along as briskly as if death were at his heels, was accompanied by an even more wasp-waisted friend, and both would have killed for a Big Mac. Graham's left ear was pierced by a silver pin, at a time when boys in Spain had not as yet learned to pierce any body part. I stopped to look at his lovely, tortured earlobe, and my evident curiosity encouraged him to approach and ask for help in an English mingled with Italian. They had arrived on a charter flight from Luton at eleven, and room service in their three-star hotel in Plaza del Carmen had finished for the night. '*Londras*', '*jamburguesa*', '*vacazzione*' and '*mio nome Graham*' were the words that came closest to resembling Spanish. Then, wishing to explain what he did for a living, he put on his best smile, raised one hand to his hair – which was blond without a hint of forgery – and snipped at his long locks with his fingers. 'A hairdresser?' I asked in English. '*Peluquero. Mi amico e io.*'

I immediately invited them back to my apartment in Campamento to dine on sliced bread and tinned pâté. After the third slice, his friend Patrick went back to their hotel to sleep. Graham and I finished off the bread – without pâté – and a bottle of white wine, and, since he had turned twenty-two the week before, he insisted on giving me twenty-two kisses, starting at my feet, commenting that he found my hairy legs terribly *gitano*. He got no further than my belly button, and spent the night in my bed.

Going anywhere with Graham, even in the inhospitable August heat of Madrid, was a truly sensational experience. With his blond hair caught back in a mother-of-pearl slide, his swaying six-foot-two body made still more unstable by his platform shoes, and his arms like the sails of a windmill in a hurricane – there simply were no equivalently striking, restless Spanish bodies, and, when we passed the few Madrid natives left in the city, they all turned to stare and continued to scrutinize us until we were out of sight. I sometimes think I followed him to London – where no one is ever surprised by anything – more out of shyness than love.

We were together for the entire ten days of his Spanish vacation (spent, because of me, wholly in Madrid; they didn't even bother with the weekend in Sitges they had booked and paid for), while poor Patrick, being both ugly and very picky, had no luck at all; he liked fat men twice his age, and all the gay discotheques we visited were packed full of handsome, willowy younger guys. Patrick wanted 'a real man' and, under the influence of several potent Spanish gin-and-tonics, he would announce this on the dance floor in a shrill, hysterical voice, to the complete indifference of the gorgeous guys dancing alongside him, every one of whom was doubtless a hairdresser.

Because of the heat and because we always fucked at night, Graham and I tended to get up late, although I did manage to take them both to the Prado and, one Sunday at noon, to the Museo Lázaro Galdiano, so that they could view English art in a Spanish context. They whizzed round the room containing Goya's black paintings in one minute and sixteen seconds, a record worthy of that well-known British book of extraordinary feats. Not that Graham was necessarily uncultivated (he knew by heart whole paragraphs by the Brontë sisters, all three of them, because they, like his mother, were from Yorkshire, and he loved Italian opera, preferably in translation); he was simply very impatient. Convinced that he would die young, like all the men in his family, he felt that spending more than a quarter of an hour in a Spanish museum subtracted too much time from the brief sum of a life under sentence of death.

He declared the Egyptian temple of Debod 'very authentic' (his father, a mercenary in the Middle East, had taken him to Cairo once, where the rosy-cheeked boy's doubtless already equivocal beauty had provoked looks, desires and even bids in the bazaar). However, a Madrid family picnicking in Christian fashion near the temple were offended by Graham's undulating gait, by his skin-tight T-shirt with the cropped sleeves, and by the hint of make-up on his naturally long-lashed eyes. Realizing that I was Spanish, they directed their rancorous looks at me from the bench where they sat, passing round meat pasties and a Thermos, as if they blamed me for the outrageous effeminacy of that foreign import.

On the 1st of September, Graham went back to London, to his elegant ladies' hairdressing salon in Mayfair, and I, having nothing to lose, decided not to lose him. I was thirty-four years old, the ideal age for committing an adolescent folly. I left the one thing that bound me to practical life, the private classes I gave in history, Spanish and (in theory) English, and, two weeks later, went to join him. My train arrived in Victoria Station at the busiest time for him at the salon, and so he couldn't come to meet me himself, but Patrick came instead. Since his return from Spain, he had met the love of his life in the English countryside, in the form of a dairy industrialist who weighed in at more than two hundred pounds and was, so Patrick told me, equally loaded with dosh.

Graham lived in Kentish Town in an apartment that was small but replete with furniture in a cacophony of styles, with drapes, wall lights, hand-painted wallpaper, exotic rugs, antimacassars on all the chairbacks and runners on the side tables. Patrick had to rush off to see his fat rich boyfriend and left me alone among that superabundance of objects, like an interloper in Ali Baba's shopping mall. Graham arrived at eight o'clock that night, laden with flowers and Harrods bags.

The unmistakable sound of his platform shoes on the stairs, the clink of keys, his face concealed behind packages plastered with ribbons and brand names, my lone scuffed, fake-leather suitcase in the hallway; this was the first time we had seen each other on English soil. Would he still be the beautiful blond androgyne who had so astonished us in Madrid? Would I still be his romantic idea of a Spanish gypsy? That first look was fraught with danger. He lowered the tower of packages slightly, revealing his eyebrows. I took a few steps towards him, to make myself more visible. Eyes, skin.

That look seemed to last for ever, with me, the poor, empty-handed southerner, and Graham peering out from behind the finest products Knightsbridge could offer. Suddenly everything fell to the floor. Among the beribboned packages and bags and my fake-leather suitcase, our two bodies met in the hallway, incapable of resisting the headlong impulse to embrace, once we had both assured ourselves that I was the same swarthy *madrileño* and he was my angel of ambiguity.

For the first six months, I lived a contented life as hairdresser's consort, although I did not entirely waste my time. Apart from doing the house-work (I may have been a complete slob in my Madrid home, but I kept Graham's apartment spotless, with all its bits and pieces dusted, polished, brushed, perfumed and in their designated places), I enrolled in some English conversation classes. I also visited the museums for which Graham had neither the time nor the interest, and, on some Saturdays, he would drag me off to see Italian operas sung in English, which I could barely understand. He would sing whole arias to me afterwards, in an excellent singing voice, and explain Puccini's plots, Puccini being his favourite; he preferred operas with sad endings. However, he barely mentioned the refined Mayfair salon where he worked – out of natural professional discretion.

I didn't want to live at his expense and suggested looking for a job so that I could earn some money, but the idea irritated him. He earned quite enough for both of us ('or is it that you need more pocket money?') and I was his man, his guest, his gypsy fantasy. To cut short this vulgar con-versation, he took from the bag that he wore slung across his shoulder a present he had bought for me: two records of operas '*loqueados*' (his trans-lation of 'located' perhaps?) in Spain: *Carmen* and *The Barber of Seville*. Before playing them for me, though, he took a few lengths of fabric and some combs and created for me, right there in the living room, the Anda-lusia of his dreams.

Then came the London winter, as harsh as any winter you'll have seen in films: the inevitable raincoat, the electric fire that devoured the coins we kept feeding it, the uninterrupted melody of the rain. I had finally managed to persuade Graham to allow me to contribute to the conjugal coffers by giving a few Spanish lessons to English families wishing to spend the summer on the Costa del Sol with the benefit of a little vocabulary. Shivering and swathed in scarves, I spoke to them of the warming qualities of sangria, about the bullring in Ronda, and added a few invented attractions of my own.

On the last Sunday of every month, Graham used to get dressed up as a girl and take me to the competitions held at the civic centre in Notting Hill Gate, where the men were more genuinely womanly than the women. Drag balls they were called, not to be confused with drag queens, a later invention and, at least in their Spanish version, coarsely folkloric. Heavily made up and with his eyebrows plucked, wearing a dark wig caught back in a net (in deference to me, he often dressed up as a Goya *ma-ha*, as he pronounced it, bravely grappling with the Spanish '*jota*'), Graham was always rewarded with one of the top prizes and with the leering admiration of the men who went to the ball in search of the eternal feminine in other men.

Stilettos in hand and mascara singeing his eyes charcoal black, Graham always liked to play the man in bed when we returned home from one of those drag balls. And, with a few more whiskies than usual inside him, he would allow himself the odd xenophobic joke: I was the invincible Spanish Armada and he the hard cliffs of Dover. I let him break through the Spanish ranks without a patriotic flicker.

On one such Sunday, Patrick came to the ball with us (he was going to open his own salon in Brighton, paid for by the dairy industrialist), together with his milky boyfriend (who had evidently piled on the pounds since living in married bliss) and two young hairdressers hired for the new business; all four were done up as pop stars. Patrick was supposed to be Barbra Streisand, but failed to convince, despite a ghastly false nose. His plump boyfriend was Shirley Bassey, bursting out of a leather mini-skirt decorated with buckles and straps. The youngest of the young men, barefoot and trailing puppet strings, was Sandie Shaw, and the other a bewildering mixture of David Bowie, Lulu and himself. They all looked extremely vulgar and overdone beside Graham, who, that night, was authentically Carmen (Bizet's not Mérimée's). While those four caricatures of queens took to the floor and danced (very badly) to the music of Tina Turner, Graham sat beside me, the very embodiment of *duende*.

What a difference between those servile slaves to women's hair and my boyfriend, I thought at home that night, while the cigar-maker was screwing her Don José.

During those early days of spring I was so in love with Graham that I began to imagine a far better career for him. I spent many hours alone, either at home or engaging in some high-grade tourism in the City, having set myself the task of visiting all of the Baroque churches built by Wren, the architect of St Paul's (I left the great cathedral itself until the final day), and, during that time, my brain never ceased toiling away at finding a better future for my boyfriend. 'Graham may be a hairdresser, but he could just as easily be a sculptor or a set designer. And he's so witty, with that dry, mordant sense of humour of his, not unlike Oscar Wilde's. He makes being a pansy – so offensive to the middle classes of Madrid – into a kind of Expressionist statement. If Susan Sontag were to meet him, she'd know what "camp" really meant. Graham is far too brilliant to spend his days building castles in the air out of backcombed hair.'

'You're an artist, Graham, and you're wasting your talents on those empty-headed women.'

'An artist? Well, yes, I am. You should see my clients when I've finished with them. They're transformed, beautiful, happy. After I've done their hair, their husbands probably treat them like princesses – at least for one night.'

'But it's so ephemeral, Graham. With your exquisite taste and instinct, it seems a positive sin to . . .'

'Speaking of sin, why don't you and I go and do a little sinning right now, Es-ca-meel-yo?'

That was how he eluded my first attempt at artistic evangelizing, with the taurine call of sex, which I never refuse. However, a few days later, I returned to the fray.

'Graham, why don't you study design at the Royal College, the birth-place of pop art?'

'Become a student – now? When I'm earning good money at the salon and am as happy as Larry among what you call those "empty-headed women" – and with you of course. Honestly.'

I brought him information about some courses in landscape gardening that the ICA was putting on; I mentioned Robert Wilson's next show, for which he was auditioning young men who were at ease with their bodies – 'like you,' I said – and Graham listened respectfully, meekly, but, when I had finished dangling these temptations before him, he came over and kissed me.

'Silly boy.'

Graham forgave this intrusion into his life, and, to prove it, he tried to dazzle and daze me with kisses, as he had that first night in Madrid; this time, he gave me thirty-five, to celebrate my recent birthday. He could even create works of art on my skin with his kisses.

That year, summer in London was bizarre in the extreme. In the middle of June, cars driving into the city on the motorways coming from the Midlands had snow on them, and a week later, on the 23rd, St John's Night, there was a heatwave and the English were going completely crazy. In London's parks and gardens, there was not a single clothed torso to be seen, and the maddest of the mad plunged into public fountains or into the Serpentine, where some drowned. Graham only succumbed to the madness for one Sunday, but after his day-at-the-beach on the grass of a local cemetery his skin was bright red, and he had a third-degree burn on his forehead. In July, the northern climate took its revenge, because it rained for days on end and the temperature plummeted twenty degrees.

I didn't know what to do, aside from sweating profusely and catching cold after cold. I think all those drastic changes in the weather caused me to let myself go physically too. Fewer showers, less shampoo, large amounts of ice cream and Coca-Cola. Sometimes, I would look in the mirror and notice a few extra pounds padding out my trousers – fat, not money. At other times, I looked like some pale Nordic ghost.

This conspiracy of the elements, however, did not divert me from my attempts to rescue a genius like Graham from the underworld of unruly female British heads of hair. Several months before, in a second-hand bookshop, I had bought a lavishly illustrated catalogue of work by the Pre-Raphaelites, to whose simultaneously Christian and effeminate paintings I had felt so drawn in the Tate Gallery. One sultry day, which ended in a hailstorm, I sought it out in the pile of books I had been accumulating in one corner of our bedroom, and that night, when Graham arrived home, exhausted, from the salon, I was waiting for him with the book open on my lap like a loaded gun, cocked and ready.

I let him have a shower and poured two glasses of the white wine he liked to drink before supper. Once he had sat down on the floral sofa in his bathrobe, with cigarette and wine glass in hand, I began my attack.

'Look at this book, Graham.'

'Ah, Rossetti. Yes, it's odd how those very unhomosexual Pre-Raphaelites painted the most homosexual pictures ever.'

'Look at those women. Those heads. That hair.'

'Yes, I know, they're gorgeous.'

'Is that all you see?'

I started leafing swiftly through the book, showing him the reproductions I had chosen beforehand: Rossetti and Burne-Jones's dangerous women with their long, curly hair, either dark or as red as a fruit.

'You . . .'

'I . . .'

'You could do this. Instead of spending your time combing out tangled mops of hair, you could be making paintings of women.'

'But I can't paint, sweetheart.'

'You painted that lovely wallpaper in the hall and the ceiling in our bedroom.'

'Yes, but I was copying a design from a magazine. I don't have any ideas of my own. I've just got a bit of a knack for making women's hair look nice.'

Then it began to hail outside, and Graham revealed a jumpy side to his nature I had never seen before, nervously stubbing out his cigarette, dropping his glass and spilling most of the wine on the Indian rug, before coming over to snuggle up to me. Fear made him seem more like a little boy or like a little girl and more precious too. He refused to look out of the windows and stuck his head under my sweater. The hail stopped and was followed by another sort of storm, with lightning falling close by and twice causing a localized power cut. This time, the English fleet did not leave port, while the Spanish Armada valiantly withstood the elements. I kept these thoughts to myself, however, so as not to make him feel still more intimidated.

In the last week of July, Graham turned twenty-three, and our apartment filled up with friends, most of them hairdressers (some with their consorts, although none as foreign as me). It was a party which, like the storm, called for lightning conductors, because, once English queers get some booze inside them, they give off sparks and flashes, especially if they're synchronized. Despite the physical havoc wrought by the summer, I think two of the guests, retired Welsh manicurists, rather fancied me, but the person I was most attracted to was still Graham. There were more-handsome boys than him, with better bodies, but none had his conversation, his exquisite fingers, his elegant, gravity-defying way of walking. Although he was clearly tipsy, he remained in charge of the party until the end, and, when he noticed that some of his guests were starting to leave after a particularly inept rendition of 'Cabaret' given by Patrick, his lacteal boyfriend and their two chubby rustic friends (drawn to the city by the recent successes achieved by certain other plump bodies), Graham immediately launched into some popular songs from Yorkshire, the land of his mother. The effect was quite miraculous. Gnarled and ancient queens shed tears on the rugs, and I, despite my drunken state, felt indignant to hear that great lyrical voice being wasted in the name of *haute coiffure*. I can't remember now when or how the party ended.

The following day, I was woken by a thunderclap in a dream storm and opened my eyes to find Graham standing there holding a glass of orange juice, and the midday sun streaming in through the bedroom window. I sat up in bed, drank half a glass, gave him a sloppy kiss full of orange pulp, and went back to sleep. My second awakening on that Sunday was equally electric, and the explosion came from close by. I opened my eyes. The room was filled now by the light of a cloudy day, and Graham was sitting beside me in bed, staring at my head.

'Oh, Graham, it's you. You gave me such a fright.'

'You're losing your hair, my love.'

'Losing it?'

'Your hair is falling out.'

That present continuous tense had a threatening tone to it and, when I sat up, I immediately put my hand to my head, but my fingers found no hair in the actual act of falling.

'It's the weather we've been having. One day I'm sweating and the next I'm having to pull on a woolly hat before I leave the house, so as not to freeze. That and the drink. We've been drinking too much . . .'

'This is something different, love. It's alopecia.'

I knew the word, of course, but when I heard him pronounce it like that, *alopissia*, full of sibilant esses, it sounded less like a seborrhoeic disorder and more like a sinuous reptile lurking beneath the pillow. That night, I had my first nightmare: a plague of alopecias, centipedes and other slimy creatures were licking my hair, coating it with a poison for which there was no antidote.

Graham finally began to take up my suggestions, although not in order to follow the lofty, creative, pictorial path I had traced for him. He broadened his horizons, but without abandoning those wealthy, empty-headed Mayfair women. He arrived home from work laden down with specialist books borrowed from the local library, having enrolled in a weekly evening class entitled 'Psychism and cultural custom in male hair loss' given by some American expert on Ayurvedic medicine. I didn't know what 'Ayurvedic' meant and had to look it up in the *Encyclopaedia Britannica* at the same library that had supplied him with the books. It had something to do with legendary Hindu kings and gods, and I was deeply troubled by the number of snakes that appeared in the accompanying illustrations and symbols. Graham, however, returned from each Ayurvedic evening more convinced than ever of the truth of this curative principle.

And all to remedy the invasion of alopecias and other hair-eating things gnawing away at my dark Spanish thatch (although, personally, I didn't think my hairline was receding as much as he said), with my head as the experimental desk on which Graham carried out his capillary studies, applying to my (continually falling) greasy hair state-of-the-art lotions and organic serums, which he massaged into my scalp with the artistry so prized by the *grandes dames* of Mayfair. One day, he asked if he could try out an unguent made from aloe vera and tangerine recommended by the Ayurvedic expert as a way of preventing trichomycosis, an illness to which, given my ethnic origins, I was apparently more than usually prone. (In English 'trichomycosis' sounded even worse than *alopissia*, evoking not so much insects and small reptiles as murderous bacteria ending in -osis: tuberculosis, salmonellosis, brucellosis, phimosis. Terrifying, ominous words.) The sticky, evil-smelling unguent had to be left on for two hours in order to work its way into the roots of my hair. I let him rub it into my scalp and, in the process of being plastered with this orange substance, I caught sight of myself in the bathroom mirror and realized that I resembled nothing so much as a kind of Pre-Raphaelite *madonna fatale*.

By late October, Graham had become an intellectual of the hair world, and the English families to whom I gave conversation classes had dispensed with my services until the following summer. Ever since Graham had arrived home from his evening class declaring that we could not continue our normal sexual activities, life in our Kentish Town apartment had been run according to the strict rules of medicine and chastity. I needed to calm my male hormones, he said, and to retain as much semen as possible, because, as the Ayurvedic doctor had demonstrated so graphically in class, excessive arousal and consequent seminal spillages dry up the follicles that nourish the hair. My hair, in this case.

'It's just a temporary preventive measure, my darling.'

Now, without sex, I'm worse than I am without hair, but there was no way I could make Graham shift from his scientific doctrine. We would sit on the floral sofa and he would caress me and allow me to touch him up within the confines of his underpants, but, as soon as my rebellious manhood began to loom large inside my trousers, he would call a halt to the game and suggest a massage – of the head.

'Look at my comb, Graham. Not a single hair. It's stopped falling out.'

'That's because of the treatment, which is precisely why we must continue. I want you to be as strong and handsome as a matador.'

Meanwhile, Patrick, in his empty Brighton salon, had been abandoned by his boyfriend, who, following acupuncture treatment, had lost a miraculous amount of weight and promptly hooked up with a Cambridge undergraduate, who was better-looking, younger and even blonder than Patrick. Graham, who was seriously considering taking a part-time course in trichology, spoke to his friend – only partly to console him – about opening a hair clinic together. London was starting to get suffocatingly Christmassy, and we had spent six whole frigid weeks in bed.

Graham was still very much in love with me, although he was more concerned about my hair than my desires. I was still very much in love with him, but I missed that other Graham: the *señorita* of the Notting Hill drag balls, who deployed his wrists – made more flexible with the application of a few gin-and-tonics – to send out a crazy code of nautical signals that would lure me later into sweet shipwreck in our bed. He lost the art of applying make-up and, one night, even donned some reading glasses to read his medical books. One Saturday, we went to Patrick's birthday party, but it was such a glum, tense affair that Graham drank in order to keep his friend company in his distress. When we got home, his mouth was still full of scientific talk, but as soon as we reached the bedroom door, lust put paid to science.

'Oh screw the green pomade! There's no treatment today! Who cares if your hair is falling out!'

He started getting undressed and then began undressing me. But nothing happened. Was it lack of practice or the clothes he was wearing? *His* hair was as long and truly golden as ever, as it had been on our first night in Madrid, but, in keeping with the funereal mood at poor Patrick's party, he was wearing it caught back in a rather unkempt ponytail, secured by an elastic band; and no lacquer. His heavy flannel trousers sagged over his feet, no platform heels this time, and he had on some intellectual-looking glasses that consisted solely of prescription lenses without even the adornment of metal frames.

We were in the bedroom by then, and Graham kissed me and repeatedly stroked my timid cock; he even hummed the 'Habanera' from *Carmen*, but to no avail. I tried to rise to the occasion, but failed abjectly, like a bullfighter quailing before the bull. He did all he could. Soft lights, the warm air of a hairdryer, which he wielded like a gun, to steal my soul away. But that didn't work either. On the one night when I was allowed to let my hair down, I couldn't get it up.

Fucking had never failed us before in our relationship. It was our recruiting flag in the amorous war between two contrary powers, which is what love always is. In bed, we signed no treaties and were oblivious to time or frontiers. Or, indeed, fatigue. Sexual appetite had brought us together for a one-night stand, which had then turned into a holiday romance and, finally, had made a stable English couple of us. Then came love, which is different for everyone. Unusually, though, love did not put an end to the desire to fuck, not until Graham imposed that Ayurvedic prohibition. My failure to perform that night had the effect of a lethal delayed-action bomb.

Christmas was already unbreathably thick with lights and carols in Oxford Street, and I invented a familiar duty: a family. I had no mother (dead) or father (partnered up with a woman I loathed) or siblings (never born), but at Christmas any tie can bind, and like a good, sentimentally dutiful Englishman, Graham fully understood, even suggesting giving me a home-made Christmas pudding to take back to my nearest and dearest.

I returned to Madrid, with my receding hairline having receded no further, with my apartment in Campamento looking an utter tip, and with no celebrations at all. I phoned a few friends, who invited me to a couple of New Year's Eve parties, but what I really wanted was to lie in bed pondering what was the sexiest profession for a man and running my fingers through my hair. I never went back to Kentish Town, although I do sometimes feel a twinge of nostalgia for that encouraging hairdryer and the crazy maritime signals of Graham's hands.

'Have you never been back?'

'Never, but Graham and I write to each other, and I'm very fond of him. A year later, he met another Spaniard who was living in London, a bank clerk, younger than him and fair-haired, from Almería. They're still together. Without me there, Graham has probably lost his scientific curiosity and abandoned his experiments. He's now co-owner, with Patrick, of a small unisex salon, where he does the hair and Patrick does the manicures. Afterwards, I lurched from one boy to another, and, while I've had boyfriends who did the most sophisticated and dangerous of jobs, I've never realized my dream of fucking a policeman. Until . . .'

'. . . until you met me last night at the disco.'

'That's right.'

'And?'

'Well, that's it really. I think I've told you almost my entire life story. I didn't bore you, did I? And here I am.'

'Naked.'

'And you really like me? You have no idea how old I am, of course. And then there are all the things I have too much or too little of . . .'

'You mean this . . . and this? I love it.'

Julio was the handsomest boy at the disco last night and has just turned twenty-two. He has blond highlights in his naturally dark hair, a stud in each ear and beneath his lower lip, and he dresses in a half-male, half-female way. He likes, or so I think he said, minimalist art, Wagner operas and the contemporary Spanish novel. And now he's happily nibbling at the rolls of fat around my waist and stroking my head, which is now definitively hairless.

'I find the billiard-ball look a real turn-on.'

'You *like* bald men?'

'Oh, yes.'

'You haven't told me yet what you do for a living.'

'That's a long story too.'

'Tell me.'

'Now?'

'Why not?'

'Wouldn't you rather have another fuck?'

'Of course, Julio. In a while.'

'I'm dying to lick your bald head.'

'First, tell me the story.'

'Well, I've just graduated in classics, but what I'd really like to be, and you're going to love this, because it has nothing whatsoever to do with my degree . . . have you noticed my hands, by the way?'

'Kiss me!'

'What? Now? I thought you wanted me to . . .'

'I'd rather you kissed me. I'm suddenly in the mood. Do you really like bald heads?'

'I told you I did, and it's true.'

'Well, it's all yours. Kiss it. You can tell me your story later. Another day perhaps.'

SOLEDAD PUÉRTOLAS

Traffic Jam

Trapped in the stream of cars clogging up the La Coruña–Madrid motor-way, still quite a way from Puerta de Hierro, I tell myself that I couldn't possibly have foreseen this situation, while, at the same time, telling myself that I really should have realized there was sure to be a morning traffic jam before I headed off to the suburbs yesterday evening, straight from work, to see my friend Laura simply because I felt like having a good old moan, simply because I needed a bit of company and comfort. At this hour in the morning, yesterday's annoyance and sadness signify nothing, or almost nothing.

All I care about now is that I'm stuck in the car with Laura's unbearable husband. I'm driving the car, *my* car. He announced to me last night, once I'd accepted Laura's invitation to stay over at their place, that he would take advantage of my return to downtown Madrid and come with me, because a work colleague, a near neighbour of theirs in the suburbs, could drive him back. Another obvious fact that completely slipped my mind yesterday evening was that Laura is actually married, and now here beside me, on this exasperating journey, sits this awful man, this pretentious music lover, who sways to the rhythm of the music as if it were rising up from his very soul, as if, at this critical moment, when the rest of us are driving to work and cursing our fate, nothing, absolutely nothing in the world, mattered apart from those harmonious notes of the *Sonatensatz* by

Soledad Puértolas (b. 1947) was born in Zaragoza and studied in Madrid. When she became heavily involved in student politics, she was obliged to leave university and moved to Trondheim in Norway for a year. She also lived for three years in Santa Barbara, California, where she gained an MA in Linguistics. She has published many novels and short stories, and her book of stories *Adiós a las novias*, from which this story comes, won her the 2001 Premio NH.

Schubert. Schubert's piano trio in B-flat major, D.28, he'd said, along with some other detail I've already forgotten. And he said it with a disdainful, superior little smile, having first played a guessing game with me. He caught me off guard and, like an idiot, I joined in the game, and my answers – because I gave several – were, inevitably, all wrong. That faint, irritatingly superior smile grew wider. But I'm not going to give him any reasons for my answers, I'm not going say anything about not knowing a lot about music – besides, I bet he doesn't know as much as he makes out – and so here I am, silent and staring straight ahead, stuck on this motorway, envying the harmony that I imagine reigns in other cars. Most of all I envy those drivers who are on their own. O blessed solitude!

I observe the occupants of the cars nearest to mine. I imagine their lives. There are a few couples, married I suppose. They barely talk. Each one seems to be turned inwards, thinking his or her own thoughts. They all seem accustomed, resigned, to this morning traffic jam. They don't even look fed up. Bored perhaps. I imagine each of them getting to the office, imagine the moment when this whole slow journey is forgotten, when it disappears without trace and the man or woman goes over to his or her desk, as if suddenly filled with energy, still fresh from the shower and with the smell of cologne not yet entirely dissipated in the stuffy air of the car.

And what about us? Do we look like a married couple? This hideous thought almost makes me laugh in sheer horror. Me? Married to this ghastly, presumptuous man? Poor Laura, I still can't understand it. I still sometimes have to listen to her telling me how handsome she thinks he is, when they've been married for fourteen years, this man listening now to that Schubert sonata, nodding his head slightly, as if the music were pouring into him, possessing him; he seems completely indifferent to the fact that the rest of us are all desperate to reach our destination and escape from this jam once and for all.

Then the very brief sonata ends, and he emerges from his trance. People simply don't make the most of their time, he says suddenly, they don't organize themselves, and he launches into a sermon in praise of the usefulness of these morning traffic jams. Needless to say, he doesn't listen to the radio, not even to the classical music station – which is the one I have on now – no, no, he compiles his own personal playlist. On Sunday, he chooses the music he'll play for the next week, and thus leaves home every morning with his two or three cassettes, ready to enjoy his hour-long journey. Now we're listening to another Schubert piano trio; this time, though, he doesn't test my knowledge, because the voice of the presenter has just told us the answer. That's a relief.

And the music continues for another half an hour, by which time we've reached the corner where I was to drop him off, as he told me the moment we left his house. He repeated it more than once on the way, in case I should forget, he even directed me, get in the left lane, now the middle one, now the right one. Careful, there's a four-wheel drive coming up very fast, better let it pass first.

I'm beginning to dislike this man more and more, a man so far-sighted that he spends his Sundays preparing the music he's going to listen to in the weekday traffic jams, and there are doubtless many other things that he plans and prepares, oh how he irritates me, this lucky man who has carried Laura off to live on the outskirts of Madrid, to a quiet suburb of large houses with large gardens and who – at last! – is saying goodbye to me with a self-satisfied smile on his face. I can see him in the rearview mirror, in his impeccable suit, subtle colours carefully co-ordinated, walking along in his English shoes. Poor Laura, still in love with the fortunate man who this morning hitched a ride with me into Madrid. I bet he calculated precisely how much petrol he's going to save today.

And here I am alone again, back in Madrid, having spent the night at my friend Laura's house, because I felt sad and didn't know who else to turn to, didn't know what would help me shake off my sadness. I listen to the end of the piano trio written by that tormented man Schubert. I sit alongside him, sharing the abyss.

CARME RIERA
The Return Home

I was woken in the early hours of a rosy-fingered dawn by the anxious voice of my mother, who has never really come to terms with the time difference between Europe and the US. 'Your father's gravely ill and is asking for you.' Twenty-four hours of travelling proved more than enough for me to put my memories in order. I banished the worst and clung on to the more pleasant ones, determined to confront with good grace the painful experience of seeing my father, possibly for the last time, after ten years of silence. Neither he nor my mother had felt able to accept that I'd given up my job at the bank in order to devote myself to writing, and had certainly never forgiven me for marrying a foreigner (and with no church wedding either) and then, when I eventually got divorced, had chosen to stay on in the States rather than returning home to recover – to use their words – a smidgeon of common sense. I hadn't told them when I would arrive and didn't even phone them from the airport. I wanted to surprise them and to avoid, at the moment of that much-postponed reunion, the presence of other relatives whose curiosity would have made them rush solicitously to meet me at the airport. And so I hired a car.

When my father retired, he decided to leave the city and, accompanied by his stamp collections and my very reluctant mother, shut himself away in Son Gualba, the only one of his properties in the countryside that he'd never wanted to sell, perhaps because he felt he could still hear in its rooms

Carme Riera (b. 1948) was born in Mallorca and writes her novels and short stories in Catalan and her essays in Spanish, translating her own novels and stories into Spanish. Her historical novel *Dins el darrer blau* (1994) brought her the Premio Nacional de Narrativa, the first novel in Catalan to win that prize.

a faint echo of his childhood games, something that, to some extent, might help mitigate his inexorable descent into old age.

The bleak, tortured landscape that surrounds the property – a chalky terrain of razor-sharp ridges that gives way to dense pine forests interspersed with dark holly oaks reaching all the way down to the cliffs – was also the landscape of my solitary childhood summers and of nearly every weekend of my bored-rigid adolescence, the landscape that, in my dreams, always ended up imposing itself on other, very different landscapes: motorways racing towards other parallel motorways that ran perpendicular to still more motorways to which I'd simply had to accustom myself. Indeed, I'd become so used to the flicker of neon advertisements and fluorescent hoardings, to the brightly lit signs of petrol stations and motels that, when the moment came to leave behind the tarmac highway for the dusty road to Son Gualba, I felt as if I were entering the pages of one of my own children's stories, in which I nearly always include an enchanted forest.

I took the first bend on a perfectly anodyne evening as the sun, surrounded by clouds, was sinking behind the mountains. There would be another twenty-five bends to negotiate before I reached the house, which I imagined would have all its lights lit and smoke curling up from the chimney, even though it wasn't really cold and even though my mother had become very penny-pinching since she sold all her shares. That imagined smoke, dense and white as cotton wool, took me back to the cosy Christmas holidays when the surrounding land was still being worked and Father Estelrich still celebrated matins in the chapel. A fine drizzle began to leave a melancholy tracery on the windscreen while I mentally reviewed old photographs from a time which, oddly enough, I no longer found distasteful. On the contrary, I enjoyed them and, without a hint of a blush, even allowed myself to be filled with nostalgia. When I was halfway there, the drops grew thicker, more violent and lava-like. Worried that the storm would break before I reached the house, I accelerated. My headlights startled the motionless eyes of an owl. The rain grew heavier, and the car was occasionally shaken by a fierce, hostile, vulpine wind.

I know every centimetre of the three kilometres that separate the main road from the rough track that leads to the house; I know exactly where the woods end and the vine terraces begin, where the road crosses the stream or where a solitary stone pine grows. I remember with stubborn precision the view that appears after each and every bend in the road and the exact point at which the estate walls, surrounded by fruit trees, become visible from the final bend. I know every corner of Son Gualba, in every season and at every time of day, and that is why, however heavy the rain and even in almost zero visibility, I cannot possibly have gone wrong.

The rain obliged me to drive slowly. I reduced my speed still more because, between bends ten and eleven, there's a very steep slope that can be really perilous when it floods, because then the embankment on the left, with no protective wall, seems about to plunge over the precipice. I admit that panic was beginning to take hold. A still worse fear was added to my fear of the storm. I had a sudden keen sense that all my efforts would prove futile, that I wouldn't get home in time to embrace my father before he died, that there would be no final reconciliation.

The windscreen couldn't cope with the dense curtain of rain that seemed intent on drenching the car bonnet and the roof. In the darkness I was assailed by the grim image of my dying father, his gaunt face. There was no room on the blue rictus of his lips for kisses or words. At that moment, I would have given anything to find him just as he was when I left, even if he continued to reject me.

I tried desperately to exorcise these images and replace them with other, more pleasant ones, as I had succeeded in doing up until then, and I almost felt my father's strong hand gently taking mine when I was a frightened little girl and we got caught in a storm in the woods, and I tried to summon up his voice telling me stories of fairies and magic spells that I would later go on to recreate in my own books, and which I never heard him finish because I always fell asleep just as things were starting to go wrong for the wicked witch. But once again my mother's voice brought me back to the present: 'Your father's gravely ill and keeps asking for you.' A particularly deep pothole almost made me lose control of the car and, when I made the mistake of braking suddenly, I stalled the engine. I tried to start it again, but in vain. I tried once, twice, three times, twenty or fifty times, but to no avail. At first, it responded with a faint, dying stutter, then not even that. I vented my fury by pounding on the steering wheel with my clenched fists. According to the clock, it was seven o'clock exactly and already pitch-black night. The face of my moribund father rose implacably before me. I could imagine his almost expressionless eyes searching for me in every corner of the room. I was utterly convinced that he could sense how close I was to home and that he wanted to speak to me. In response to this summons, I got out of the car and started walking. My feet sank into the mud as if I were walking through a quagmire. The sound of the stream's rushing waters told me that I was only one kilometre from Son Gualba. I struggled on, feeling my way and trying to hang on to branches as I waded through the torrents, while at the same time trying to avoid getting scratched. Suddenly, I tripped on something and fell to the ground. When I finally clambered to my feet, my left ankle was throbbing. I could feel it swelling up inside my boot. Dragging my injured leg, I managed to advance a little further only to fall again. I must have passed out from the pain.

I don't know how long I was lying there, but it must have been quite a while because, when I stood up, my clothes were almost dry. The rain had stopped completely, and my ankle hardly hurt at all. From far off came the fresh, intoxicating smell of oranges and lemons, diluted by a breeze so faint it barely stirred the leaves of the trees. The night had taken on a troublingly diaphanous air. By the light of an almost full moon, I realized that I was very close to the house, next to the first wrought-iron gate, the one that opened onto the path that goes around the orchard and into the main courtyard. The hinges creaked when I opened the gate, but no dog barked. The lights were on upstairs on the first floor, the only floor occupied by my parents, and smoke was rising up from the chimney. So great was my need to arrive, that I didn't even stop to consider just how I had reached that point. As I crossed the courtyard, the scent from the cherry blossom impregnated every pore of my skin, and I could smell it with the same intensity as on the day I left. For ten years I had tried and failed to find that smell again, now, finally, I could take in whole gulps of it. When I paused on the landing, my legs were shaking. I didn't have to knock because the door stood ajar. Nothing had changed. The monkish armchairs stood in precisely the same positions. The portraits of gloomy ancestors covered the walls right up to the ceiling as they always had, and the brass fastenings on the large chests gleamed as they always had. Even the keys I had put down when I left were still there on the same tray. I couldn't resist picking them up and putting them in my pocket. As I pushed open the door, the wall clock welcomed me with a single chime. I heard my mother's voice calling to me from the kitchen.

'Is that you, María? How wonderful! I thought it was you.'

I ran to her side, and we embraced. She hadn't changed at all. Time had been very kind to her. She looked her usual impeccable self, with her hair neatly caught back, and she was even wearing the same blue flannel suit she'd worn the day we said goodbye.

'And Papa?'

'Oh, he'll be so pleased to see you. Bernardo! Bernardo! María's here. She's come back.'

The clock gave its final chime. It was seven o'clock on the dot, just as it had been on the day I left.

'Come along, dear. Your father's got the TV on too loud and can't hear us. The doctors are saying he won't last the day, so he's waiting for news.'

Too bewildered to ask any questions, I followed my mother into the living room. My father was indeed quietly watching the TV. A grave-faced newsreader was reading out the headlines '. . . the health of His Excellency the Head of State has now entered a critical phase.'*

I violently pushed my mother out of the way, scratching her face as I did so, and, before my father could get up from his chair, I ran to the door, convinced that neither of them really existed and that they were mere shadows, mere projections of my own desires, the ghosts that each night occupied their respective bedrooms, just as they often occupied my mind despite the ten thousand kilometres and ten years of misunderstandings separating us. But I was wrong and made an unforgivable mistake. I was timorous to the point of cowardice, foolishly rational at a time when only feelings should have counted, incapable of accepting that miracles do actually exist outside legends and that it isn't only in fairy tales that impossible wishes are granted. If I had accepted what was happening as perfectly normal and slipped casually back into an evening that took place ten years before, my father would probably have died ten years later and my mother would have many more years of life ahead of her. But I refused to do this, and with disastrous consequences.

My father died an hour after my arrival in Palma de Mallorca at around

* A reference to General Franco's long-drawn-out death in 1975.

seven o'clock on the evening when the pain of my sprained ankle had left me lying unconscious on the muddy road. The doctor insists that everything that happened afterwards was the result of an hallucination and that I never got as far as Son Gualba, however often I show him the keys – my keys – the keys I picked up from the tray, and however often I assure him that my mother is looking at me in hostile silence while she runs her index finger over the unexplained scratch marks on her left cheek.

ENRIQUE VILA-MATAS

Sea Swell

I had a friend once. Indeed, at the time, I only had one friend. His name was Andrés and he lived in Paris and, much to his delight, I travelled to that city to see him. The very evening of my arrival, he introduced me to Marguerite Duras, who was a friend of his. Unfortunately, that evening, I had taken two or three amphetamines. This was my regular daily dose, for I was convinced they would help me to imagine stories and become a novelist. I don't know why I was so convinced that this was true, since I had never written a word in my life, and the amphetamines were largely to blame for this. They were also to blame for me losing all my money in secret gambling dens in Barcelona.

I was completely bankrupt when I travelled to Paris, where my friend lent me some money and introduced me to Marguerite Duras. Andrés was one of those people who believes that the company of brilliant writers helps to improve one's own writing.

'One of my attic apartments has just become vacant,' Marguerite Duras said as soon as we met.

If I hadn't taken those wretched pills, I would have responded at once and said that I would very much like to rent it. However, the amphetamines always had a bad effect on me. I would fix people with mad, staring eyes, as bright as fog lamps. There seemed no point in giving expression

Enrique Vila-Matas (b. 1948) was born in Barcelona and studied law and journalism. His first job was writing for a couple of cinema magazines, and he made a few forays into acting and making films. He has published many novels and short stories, and his work often blends essay and fiction, with frequent references to other writers' work. He is a regular contributor to the Spanish daily newspaper *El País*. His work has been translated into over thirty languages, including English, notably *Bartleby & Co.*, *Dublinesque* and *Mac's Problem*.

to any of my thoughts because I had already thought them. On top of that, I lost my appetite and, needless to say, any desire to write.

We were standing opposite the Café de Flore. Hearing me babbling a few syllables that stubbornly refused to cohere into words, my friend Andrés made a series of friendly gestures in my direction and came to my aid in his curious, heavily accented French, making clear that I would love to rent that attic apartment situated in the highly desirable location of Montparnasse. And so it was that, without my having uttered a single word, Marguerite expressed her willingness to become my landlady. The rent was very reasonable and included an invitation to dine at her house the following evening. In fact, the rent was purely symbolic. Marguerite liked to help young writers in need of accommodation.

I went to the supper with Andrés, and with two or three amphetamines inside me. An act of sheer youthful recklessness, bearing in mind that behind that invitation lay Marguerite's desire to get to know me a little and find out if I would make a suitable tenant. Unfortunately, I only realized this when it was too late. Andrés told me when we were already standing outside her house. I panicked and roundly cursed the amphetamines. But, as I say, by then, it was too late.

The person who opened the door to us was Sonia Orwell, who had also been invited to supper. We went into the kitchen and said hello to Marguerite, who was embroiled in an unlikely struggle with some baby squid being cooked in their own ink and which – although I never knew why – were leaping and dancing about in the frying pan. With a cigarette clamped in one corner of her mouth, Marguerite seemed entirely occupied with these rebellious squid. One of them leapt out onto the kitchen floor and, quick as you like, Marguerite bent down and immediately restored the squid to its proper place in the pan. In doing so, her cigarette fell in among the other squid and was instantly fried to a crisp.

We went into the living room, leaving Marguerite to finish preparing supper. Sonia Orwell offered us a cup of coffee, and I wondered if it was the custom in Paris to begin suppers at the end. Sonia Orwell soon cleared up this mystery by explaining that she was feeling really exhausted and was hoping the coffee might perk her up. In an attempt to be nice, I made a supreme effort and said:

'Thank you very much. I love coffee.'

I actually disliked coffee intensely, but saying these words cheered me up, even though I felt that I would find it as hard to drink the coffee as to utter another word. Fortunately, Andrés again came to my aid, proving what a good friend he was. Knowing the deleterious effect that amphetamines had on me, he began speaking for both of us. He did so by embarking on a discussion of the huge advances made by feminism in the modern world. I merely nodded now and then. Then he spoke about General de Gaulle and how fed up he was with seeing him governing France. Then, suddenly, he began to talk about me. He explained that I had only been in Paris for one day and that he was the only person I knew.

'The thing that has surprised him most about the city is seeing so many Japanese people,' Andrés said, with a smile on his lips, indicating that, while he considered me to be a friend, he also thought I was a complete hick.

Then he told her about the striptease club. He explained that, as soon as I had arrived in Paris, I had headed straight for the Quartier Pigalle, where I spent the little money I had staring at naked women and feeling bored.

'On the other hand,' said Andrés, 'a whore from Alsace told him that he was very handsome and complimented him on his sweater and, above all, on the colour of his trousers.'

I felt pretty embarrassed but, at the same time, unable to correct anything he had said because I was incapable of speech.

'Speaking of whores,' said Sonia Orwell, downing her second cup of coffee, 'Marguerite suggests that we go to the Bois de Boulogne tonight. She wants to find out if it's true what they say in the newspapers.'

'And what do they say?' asked Andrés.

'Oh, nothing much, just that some of the prostitutes there are dressed as if for their first communion.'

Marguerite came into the room and said that we would soon be able to sit down to eat and that she just had to finish making the curry sauce. I thought this odd. Octopus doesn't need any sauce. What was I saying? It was squid not octopus I'd seen in the kitchen. I realized to what extent those wretched amphetamines were addling my brain. I glanced at Andrés, hoping he would continue to help me out and speak for me, but he clearly wasn't up to doing that just then. He rather resembled a coffee pot. A few words that appeared to be coming to a boil immediately behind his eyes were bubbling up towards his brain. Suddenly, his head began bobbing frantically up and down, as if it were about to explode, until, pointing at me, he said to Marguerite:

'Do you know, until he came to Paris, he had never seen a Japanese person?'

'Not even at the films?' she asked.

I swallowed hard, recalled several films about Hiroshima that I had seen, but was incapable of saying anything.

'But how is that possible?' she insisted. 'Are there no Japanese people in Barcelona?'

I cursed the fact that Andrés occasionally forgot I could not speak. And, since he again failed to rescue me, I made a supreme effort and, attempting to be comical, said:

'No, Franco has banned them.'

Instead of accompanying these words with an ironic smile, my face became fixed in a harsh, horrific grimace. To conceal this, I tried to take a sip of coffee, but my hand was shaking so much that I nearly spilled coffee over Sonia Orwell's skirt. They all pretended not to have noticed. I listened to them talking for a while. Then Marguerite announced that she was going back into the kitchen to finish making the curry sauce and carried the coffee pot away with her. I understood this to mean that she would be adding coffee, not curry sauce to the squid. So much for squid ink, I thought. God, I was in a state. I shot Andrés another pleading glance, a cry for help, but, instead, my face creased into a crazed scowl, which Marguerite saw as she left.

'We don't eat people here, you know,' she said, coming back into the living room, this time bearing a tray containing a dish of rice with curry sauce, which was, apparently, to precede the squid cooked in their ink. I felt Sonia Orwell's eyes fixed on me, and had the distinct impression that she was beginning to view me as if I were a Martian.

'Help yourselves,' said Marguerite.

When it was my turn, I piled my plate with rice.

'You're obviously hungry,' said Andrés, knowing full well that I had no appetite at all. I thought this was because he wanted to draw attention to me and my piled-high plate. I forgave him, though, because it seemed to me that he was actually trying to draw me out and, like any good friend, was worried about what would happen if I didn't start behaving rather more normally – and soon. I knew that, deep down, he was acting out of the best possible motives.

I tasted the sauce and could barely keep from pulling a face. As for the rice, I knew, right from the start, that I wouldn't be able to eat it. When they had all cleared their plates (even soaking up the sauce with a great deal of bread), all eyes were turned on my plate, which remained scandalously intact. Luckily, this time, Andrés rode to my rescue. He said that, only half an hour before, I had succumbed to the charms of some Tunisian cakes.

'You're making all kinds of discoveries,' said Marguerite. 'Eating Tunisian cakes, seeing Japanese people for the first time.'

'Yes, that's true,' I replied laconically.

I assumed I had lost any chance I might have had of renting that attic apartment. I couldn't have been less charming. However, just then, someone rang the doorbell. Sonia Orwell suggested it might be Louis Jacquot, an actor who wanted to adapt one of Marguerite's books for the stage. He was, I learned, a poor wretch who had played so many different roles that he no longer knew who he was. We heard Marguerite talking to someone in the hall and, when she returned to the living room, she confirmed that it had indeed been the actor.

'He's gone now,' she said.

'That was quick. What did he want?' asked Andrés.

'Oh, nothing. The usual thing,' Sonia Orwell said. 'He wanted to know who he is.'

There was a brief silence, then Marguerite poured herself a glass of wine and declared:

'Poor man.'

Andrés took charge of the bottle of wine and drank four glasses one after the other, almost without pausing for breath. Marguerite was obliged to open another bottle of Beaujolais.

'So you're from Barcelona?' Marguerite asked, as if giving me one last chance to say something.

Then, as if the question had been addressed to him, Andrés stepped in and said:

'Yes, he's from Barcelona, whereas I, on the other hand, come from Atlantis.'

At first sight, one might have assumed this was the result of those four glasses of wine, but he hadn't really drunk that much. Knowing him as I did, it was more likely that he had finally decided to behave as the most heroic of friends should behave in the most difficult of circumstances. It could be that he had chosen to adopt a diversionary tactic, which involved behaving like a mad eccentric in order to focus attention on himself and thus divert those dangerously perplexed and probing looks away from me. If so, it must be said that Andrés was a very good friend indeed.

'So, you're from Atlantis, are you?' asked Sonia Orwell, with a smile on her lips.

'I am,' responded Andrés succinctly, and tears welled up in his eyes. When we saw this, we all froze. A heavy silence fell. For a while, as we ate the main course, we listened to him talking about that lost continent. Gesturing dramatically, he summoned up certain marine images which, according to him, were ancient memories from when he used to live in his real homeland. I had never before heard anyone describe with such precision the unknown world of the seabed. He spoke of paths carved out of the rocks, of the giant skeletons of fish, of shells and stones as pink as mother-of-pearl. He talked and talked, oblivious to the food on his plate, oblivious to the evening and to us. At one point, Marguerite suggested that he had perhaps drunk too much.

'I read somewhere,' he said, 'that when you've drunk a little, reality grows simpler, you can leap over the spaces in between things, everything seems to fall into place and you can say: yes, that's it. Well, that is what has happened to me tonight. You might think me mad or that I'm making it all up, but you're wrong. For me, tonight, everything has suddenly fallen into place. Ever since I was a child, I've always had a sense that, in another life, I used to live in Atlantis. Now, at last, I feel absolutely sure I was right.'

And, with that, Andrés finished off the second bottle of Beaujolais.

'Everything you've told us – and you told it very well indeed – is curious in the extreme,' Marguerite said, 'but it's very hard not to think that you've either drunk too much or are simply having us on.'

Andrés did not bat an eyelid.

'And would you believe me,' he continued, 'if I were to speak to you of a sea that was always so calm that its waves barely rippled when they touched the foot of the cliffs? I remember, too, flocks of seabirds resting on the bluest waters that have ever existed. I remember the profound happiness of all my compatriots, because we lived on the very margins of history or, rather, entered into it only very superficially. We stored up energy in all our cities. So much so that the cosmos threatened to be transformed into pure energy. I remember vividly the pieces of white tin-plate with the top part painted in red lacquer and that we used as bait to catch the sumaje fish, our only enemies.'

He did not appear to be inebriated. True, he had drunk quite a lot, but he spoke with utter serenity and with a nostalgia that appeared genuine.

Perhaps trying to change the subject, Sonia Orwell pointed at me, still locked in my rigorous silence, and said:

'Your friend is so shy that, not only has he barely uttered a word all evening, he hasn't even dared to open his mouth to eat.'

'My friend,' said Andrés furiously, 'is not in the least shy.'

His sudden fury seemed to indicate that he wanted to keep their attention from falling on me. However, what he said next did not exactly confirm that impression.

'My friend,' he added, 'has taken a few amphetamines and is constantly thinking about his novel.'

I was horrified. He had just produced out of nowhere a novel that did not exist and about which I was probably going to be obliged to talk. This proved unnecessary, however, because Andrés went on to explain that I was writing the memoirs of a ventriloquist.

'Unfortunately,' he added, 'this very evening, he lost the manuscript. He left it in a taxi. The memoirs could be read as a novel, although the plot was not in any way conventional; it was a fractured, uncertain thing and, unlike nineteenth-century plots, was in no way tyrannical, making no attempt to explain the world, far less embrace a whole life, but only a few episodes in a life.'

'And what kind of person was this ventriloquist?' asked Sonia Orwell.

'I don't know,' Andrés went on, 'the kind of man who is always considering leaving everything behind, saying goodbye to Europe and following in Rimbaud's footsteps. I think, in the end, he did leave Europe, but the real cause of his departure did not appear in the memoirs.'

'Why not?'

'Because, before he fled, he committed a murder, and he could hardly confess to that in his memoirs. In the Lisbon night, having bade an unexpected and final farewell to the stage and to his public, he had gone in search of the barber who had stolen from him the woman he loved, and, in a deserted alleyway in the port, he stabbed him through the heart with the sharpened point of a sunshade from Java. He could not, of course, write about that in his memoirs and so he fled Europe. In his memoirs, though, he disguised what was repugnant and cowardly as something beautiful, cultivated and literary.'

I was lucky in that, once Andrés had invented this story, he promptly forgot all about me and plunged back into his eager search for his origins, and spoke about certain still, hot summer days, when the torrid heat weighed on the waters of the river, and it was easy to fall into a sleep so deep it resembled death, and thus retrieve that most distant of past lives on Atlantis.

'Even as a child, I had a sense that I came from there,' he went on. 'One day, I fell into the Manzanares river. I was a clumsy boy and didn't know how to swim, and, to be honest, I've never learned. I went right under, and then I noticed I was being transported to remote places that suddenly seemed very familiar, as if I'd been there before. It took three or four minutes for me to resurface, time enough for me to see, at the bottom of the Manzanares, the old palaces of my true homeland. I remembered them as soon as I saw them. The light had a silvery tinge to it. And that was where my real life went on, the streets, houses, stones, the footsteps of my true compatriots. And there was I, too, telling stories to a rapt and loyal audience. I was a storyteller recounting the stories of people who had migrated from their bodies in order once more to inhabit their ancient lands.'

Someone commented that it was getting late. We were certainly surprised by what he said, but also somewhat weary and weighed down, although I was still grateful to my friend for coming to my rescue like that. That's what friends are for, I thought, pleased with his efforts on my behalf. I preferred to think that he had acted selflessly rather than assume that he was simply drunk or mad.

'I would suggest,' said Marguerite kindly, 'that we postpone this conversation until tomorrow. It really is very late, and I'm beginning to feel sleepy. I wanted to go to the Bois de Boulogne, but I'm too tired now.'

It really was very late, but Andrés seemed not to notice. He started talking about underwater currents stronger than life itself, currents that dragged one inexorably back to the lost continent.

'Perhaps the day will come,' he said, 'when I won't come back. My old suit is already very worn, I need to change it, I don't feel comfortable in it any more. I am, I believe, in the same state as a snake just before it's about to shed its skin: the daylight becomes bothersome and then, like any good snake, it withdraws to its lair.'

He paused so briefly that we did not have time to interrupt. He went on to describe the fires that burned in every hearth in his homeland.

'The flames,' he said, 'used to rise straight up and gave off no smoke at all. They were fed by dry juniper branches that exuded an acrid odour. On every mantelpiece in Atlantis there were always shields in the form of candelabra, whose candles gave out a powerful blue light, like the deep, deep blue of our seas.'

Someone said again that it was getting late.

Andrés agreed to put his coat on over his old suit, but first polished off whatever alcohol was left in the house. I put a friendly arm about his shoulder.

'Come on,' I said, leading him gently to the front door.

'The attic is yours,' Marguerite said, much to my surprise. 'I'll show you round tomorrow. There's only a mattress, so you may have to buy some more furniture. Yes, I think there's just a mattress and a poster. A poster of Venice showing a very fine reproduction of a crystal chandelier. That's what the concierge told me anyway. You'll see.'

I said goodbye, feeling very pleased at this unexpectedly happy ending. Then Andrés and I went out into the street. All the cafés in Paris were closed and, beneath the starry sky, they resembled silent mausoleums on the moon. It would, I thought, be a difficult night to forget. And so it has proved to be. That night, walking home with Andrés, he told me that we would never see each other again, that he kept remembering with irresistible nostalgia a valley of streams and mauve waterfalls and that he wanted, without further delay, to disappear by his own hand.

I did not quite understand what he meant by this, but I assumed that 'by his own hand' must be some reference to suicide. I thought that perhaps he was talking about a disappearance that belonged not so much to the realm of necessity, but to the domain of freedom. I was still pondering this when Andrés repeated those same words and, in one bound, leapt into the icy waters of the Seine and vanished from sight. My first thought was that he really was taking things too far; then I realized that it was up to me to save him, because there was no one else around to help. I took off my overcoat and, with no further hesitation, jumped into the Seine and soon managed to locate him beneath the waters. He was in a near-ecstatic, I would almost say blissful state, as if he were allowing himself to be carried by those underwater currents back to his original homeland.

I grabbed him by one arm, but he struggled violently, as if I had interrupted his journey. I had no option but to punch him hard and render him unconscious. Then came the worst part, because never have I done anything requiring such an enormous physical effort. When I finally managed to drag his body up onto the quay, there was still no one else around. I covered him with my overcoat and waited for him to regain consciousness. When he did, he looked at me in bewilderment, felt his chin, and asked what we were doing there, soaked to the skin.

'Can't you remember anything?' I said.

'To be honest, no . . .'

I thought for a moment. I felt confused and exhausted. I was afraid I might have caught pneumonia and, deep down, I was very angry.

The water had wiped my head clean of the effects of those amphetamines.

'Do you really not remember?'

'No, I told you, no.'

'You mean, you can't even remember where we've come from?'

I immediately regretted asking this question, fearing that he might say: 'I don't know about you, but I'm from Atlantis.' But he really didn't seem to remember anything. I was glad I hadn't mentioned Marguerite Duras, a name he might have associated with the lost continent.

'Let's go home,' I said.

And again I regretted my words, fearing that he might recall the humble home of that storyteller back in Atlantis. But no, he remained in a state of utter bewilderment. The problem was that I couldn't say a word, because anything I said might trigger a memory. Alas, I was so angry with him that anger overcame both prudence and silence. I asked him why he had done all that.

'All what?' he said with his most beatific smile.

'What do you think?' I said very loudly, my eyes wild.

He lay there, half-confused and half-thoughtful, until suddenly he gave signs of having recovered his memory.

'Ah, yes,' he said.

I feared the worst.

'Why *did* I do all that?' He was clearly thinking deeply. 'Well, the truth is, it really doesn't matter. I would say that I had to do it, do you see?'

I can still remember the hard look in his eyes when, shortly afterwards, he stood up and walking slowly backwards, as if about to take part in the hundred-metre backstroke, he said:

'That's what friends are for.'

And he again leapt into the river, this time taking my overcoat with him, as if he wanted to find out just how far our friendship would go.

JAVIER MARÍAS

A Sense of Camaraderie

I went outside to smoke a cigarette, well, the priest *was* going on a bit. I stepped out onto the mirador, where the whole Ronda landscape lay before me, a vast expanse seen from on high, although not so very high, more a vision in cinemascope where one was conscious more of breadth than of height, similar to the view I'd seen on other occasions from the famous Ronda hotel which has, in its gardens, a dark, incongruous statue of the poet Rilke – they'll even show you the room where he stayed and which they've turned into a minuscule museum. I rested one foot on the lower part of the balustrade, my foot slightly raised, and lit a cigarette despite the unfettered wind, or perhaps it was just a strong breeze, stimulating rather than irksome, the kind of breeze you get on a bright, early March day, when it's still winter, according to the calendar.

Another man came out after me, barely ten seconds later, as if I had encouraged or infected him, because it's rare for just one person to leave a public event, others usually take courage from such a departure and follow suit, even right in the middle of a concert or a lecture, and the poor abandoned scholar or musician stumbles and feels momentarily disheartened and, despite himself, his words or his notes waver and, for a second, falter. Like me, that other man placed one small foot on the balustrade,

Javier Marías (b. 1951) is considered to be one of Spain's foremost novelists. He has also worked as a translator, translating works by Conrad, Sir Thomas Browne and, notably, *Tristram Shandy* by Laurence Sterne. He has published sixteen novels, among them *A Heart So White*, *Tomorrow in the Battle Think on Me*, *The Infatuations*, *Thus Bad Begins*, *Berta Isla* and *Tomás Nevinson*, as well as several collections of short stories and essays. His work has been translated into forty-six languages and won many literary awards, both national and international, including the International IMPAC Dublin Literary Award. He writes a weekly column for the Spanish newspaper *El País*.

about three paces to my left, took out a shiny lighter, the rechargeable kind, and cupped the flame with his hand.

'That priest is going on a bit,' he said, 'and he looks set to talk for a good while yet.' I immediately noticed his Andalusian accent, although it wasn't very pronounced, as if he corrected and controlled it, he was doubtless someone who could disguise it almost completely when not in Andalusia and easily recover it when he returned, an imitative, indecisive fellow. 'I really don't see the need for such a long homily.' I felt sure that 'homily' wasn't the right word for that verbose priest's semi-matrimonial meanderings addressed to the bride and groom, but I haven't been to church in a long time and don't know the exact terminology, was it admonishment or admonition, or is that something that happens before the couple are married, I've no idea really. I said:

'He has to make the most of his opportunities; he won't often have a full church.'

'You'd be surprised,' the man answered. 'Here in the South, churches aren't as depopulated as they are elsewhere. My name's Baringo Roy, by the way. Are you on the bride's side or the groom's?'

I again wondered if he had intended to say what he said and if 'depopulated' was the right word. Had he meant 'unpopular'? He had given his two surnames naturally and unemphatically, as if he were accustomed to giving both, like a football referee for example, or García Lorca or Sánchez Ferlosio. Although with such an unusual first surname, Baringo, it was hard to see why he would need a second.

'Neither I suppose. I've just driven up from Madrid, giving a lift to a friend of mine who doesn't drive. She's a cousin of the groom, but I'd never seen either bride or groom until now. I still haven't seen their faces, not properly, or only when they each walked down the aisle, otherwise I've only seen them from behind as they were standing at the altar.'

Up until then he had only imitated my posture, placing one foot on the lower part of the balustrade and gazing out at the broad, pleasant fields; now he turned towards me, tilting his head very slightly when he introduced himself.

'Ah, the pretty little cousin from Madrid, yes, I've met her already,' he said. 'Her name's María, isn't it? I was introduced to her just a moment ago.'

'Yes, the pretty little cousin,' I said and thought how María would have hated that diminutive. I would tell her about it later on, just to tease her. 'And you're on the bride's side,' I stated rather than asked, although I only did so purely out of politeness, I really didn't care, I felt no curiosity whatsoever about these people, I was just doing María a favour, she goes to a lot of weddings, which I never do – in fact, whenever I'm invited, I tend to sneak off and send a nice present in my place.

'Well,' answered Baringo, 'I'm on both sides, since I know them both. But I'm more on the bride's side really. I met her first, before I met him. Not much before, but a bit. And before him. I mean, before *he* met her.'

I wasn't really paying attention and so what he said seemed extremely confusing, but I didn't particularly want him to clarify the matter, I wasn't interested to be honest, people often give overlong explanations without being asked, they seem to feel it's vital to provide complete strangers with a clear, detailed explanation of the most insignificant aspects of their life, they have time on their hands, at least idle Andalusians do, although some are very silent and you practically have to drag the words out of them, while others are very quick and nimble. He's the idle kind, I thought, and for the first time I turned to face him too and looked at him more closely. He was of average height and rather burly and square-set, not enough to suggest that he worked out at the gym every day, perhaps it was simply his natural build. He was wearing glasses with very pale tortoiseshell frames, which made his eyes seem smaller – he was obviously seriously myopic – and gave him a vaguely professorial air, which fitted ill with his very tanned skin, the same colour as his thick lips, as if both skin and lips formed a continuum of colour. I noticed that he was very smartly dressed even for a wedding, and I tried to identify what it was that seemed so excessive. This proved fairly easy: the cut of his suit (and his tie) – both in rather too light a grey considering that it was still winter – inevitably made one think of a morning coat, a fake or approximate morning coat, which, in turn, gave him the appearance of being a reserve or deputy groom, rather than a mere guest.

'I see,' I said, more as a response to his silence and to avoid having him launch into an explanation of his previous brainteaser of a sentence.

When I turned towards him, he changed position again and stood facing the church, leaning his elbows on the balustrade. He gestured with his head toward the church, as if pointing it out to me with his eyebrows.

He repeated this gesture twice more before he spoke again, as if taking a run-up to what he was about to say.

He said: 'I've had it off with the bride, you know.'

I have to say that this comment rather amused me, and I may even have thought: Ah, the thwarted lover. But his remark wasn't so much scornful or boastful as utterly childish, a quality I hate in men, even in myself sometimes. I don't like men who boast about such adventures, which usually have no basis in truth, but in what he said, at least initially, there was more a note of possessive revindication than mere bombast. I thought: It's one of two things: either no one else knows about this and, when he saw her getting married and thus moving irrevocably away from him, he just couldn't stand it any longer and simply had to blurt it out to someone – and he made a good choice in me, a non-threatening stranger; or else everyone knows about it – they were engaged once or a couple, for example – and he couldn't bear the fact that there was someone here, someone from Madrid, completely indifferent to and uninformed about his past connection to the bride. And because his assertion amused me, I couldn't help but respond in a somewhat jokey fashion – I often find it hard to keep my humorous remarks to myself.

'Oh really,' I said, 'I can't imagine you're the only one.'

'What do you mean by that?' he said, immediately on his guard. 'Don't get me wrong now, there aren't many men who can say what I just said.'

I had besmirched the good name of the bride, which, according to certain ancient traditions, he had already besmirched in the presence of a complete stranger and in the middle of the marriage ceremony. How things have changed, I thought. Here we are at the beginning of the twenty-first century and already ninety per cent of twentieth-century Spanish literature is completely outdated, as remote as Calderón de la Barca, at least as far as sexual mores are concerned. Valle-Inclán and Lorca and all the others who came after them will soon be relegated to the museum, pure archaeology.

'No, as I said, I don't know the bride at all, I'm just here as a favour to a friend. But given that the bride is in her thirties, it's only normal that, like everyone else, she'll have had some experience. Although nothing to compare with you, I'm sure,' I said, unable to resist that final comment. 'Does the groom know?'

Baringo Roy adjusted his glasses with the middle finger of his left hand, meanwhile offering me one of his cigarettes with his right. I accepted, and he didn't respond to my question until we had both lit up, again using that ostentatious lighter, the flame cupped this time by our four hands against the Ronda wind that continued to blow untrammelled.

'Well, he does and he doesn't,' he said, again leaning his elbows on the balustrade, his back to the view. 'The man's an idiot. He does know, but at the same time he can't really get his head around it. His bride, who'll be standing there now with her veil and her bouquet making him all kinds of promises . . .' and again he indicated the church, perhaps with just one eyebrow this time, not two, 'well, I've had her every which way. Kneeling, on top, underneath, from the front, from the back, from the side, at an angle. She's a real tiger, when she's with me, that is.' And he circled one index finger twice in the air, as if drawing a spiral.

I was beginning to like Baringo Roy. Perhaps he really was angry as well as being somewhat cocky, but that was apparent more in what he said than in the tone in which he said it. There wasn't any real anger in his voice, nor any desire to humiliate the bride and groom. That wasn't what was impelling him to talk; his lack of discretion seemed to respond rather to a desire to establish the truth of the situation, to set the record straight, at a crucial, albeit inopportune moment. Not that he expressed himself dispassionately (he had pronounced the word 'tiger' with a certain vehemence, but also with a degree of respect), but his tone did not denote rage or a desire for revenge either, nor a desire to discredit the ceremony that was taking place at that very moment, nor any feelings of rancour towards the bride, or even towards the groom. He was quite clear that the groom was an idiot, but that was all, and he had said this as if stating a self-evident, widely known fact, not his own personal opinion or a private insult, but a commonly held idea. And now that I had taken a liking to Baringo, I allowed myself to be carried along by the same jokey tone, fostered by the sense of camaraderie that immediately springs up between men who are neither attacking each other nor competing, a camaraderie that is somewhat frowned upon these days. We men tend to know at once what other men are like because we've been observing them all our life, ever since we were children, at school and in the street. We often dismiss or even detest certain men on sight for the same reason, because we can see straight through them, we can understand or recognize them or recognize ourselves in them, because we know that it would not take much for us to be like the worst of them, on the contrary, we constantly have to make an effort not to be like the worst of them. And so I said:

'Well, if she is such a tiger, perhaps you're wise to pass her over to the groom. We wouldn't want you dropping with exhaustion.'

He looked at me as if I were nothing but a little squirt, even though I was about an inch and a half taller than him. His expression was so unequivocal that I thought he was about to give full vent to his cocky self and say: Watch your mouth, buddy, or some such thing. He didn't go that far though, perhaps because it wasn't my possible impertinence that astonished him, but my ingenuous concern for the groom.

'The groom? That idiot? He sleeps with bedsocks on.'

'Do you mean he's inexperienced? That tiger of a bride might get him to take them off.'

He continued to regard me as if I were a mere worm.

'No, I mean that he's an idiot, incapable of learning anything. Anyway, I said she was a tiger when she's with me, right? With me, you understand. I'm a very sexual guy, you see. I've even been with transvestites.'

I couldn't quite see the connection here, although, out of politeness more than anything, I tried to find one:

'Ah, I see,' I said. 'They do say that it's mainly heterosexual men who go with transvestites . . .'

'You're damned right,' he said, cutting in.

I found this strange digression distinctly embarrassing and didn't really know what to think. I felt more comfortable talking about the tiger, and so I turned the conversation back to Baringo and to her.

'What I don't understand, then, is why you're not there in church instead of the guy with the bedsocks. Or are you already married? I don't wish to be indiscreet, but after what you've told me . . .'

Baringo Roy gave a short, sharp, emphatic guffaw, as if to make it perfectly clear that this was a sarcastic laugh. Then he twice puffed out those thick, flesh-coloured lips of his.

'I've never been seen in a church and never will be, I wouldn't let myself, no, I'm your typical outsider. Like I said, I'm a very sexual guy, and for that very reason I choose never to be too available. To anyone. I'm the guy who can't be relied on to be there, I'm the exception, the impromptu party. I would hate to find out one day that the party was going on somewhere else, and I'm not referring just to sex now, but to everything, to fun, excitement, the unexpected. And sex as well, of course, that goes without saying, don't you think. What that idiot doesn't know is that I screwed his bride just two weeks ago, and right under his nose too. We were having supper with a big group of friends in a restaurant in Seville, and the two of them were there too. After the meal, I left the table and went to the toilet. Two minutes later, she joined me, we bumped into each other in the corridor, her coming and me going back. Anyway, I had her right there, quick as a flash, in the gents' toilet, we shot the bolt on the door and away we went.'

'It would have to have been as quick as a flash.' I couldn't resist making that remark either, although this time I think I was genuinely taken aback.

Baringo Roy ignored my comment, he still had more to say.

'And what he can't know either is that in another couple of weeks' time, when they're back from their little honeymoon, the same thing will happen again. Not necessarily in a toilet, of course. But no amount of willpower can control a thing like that. She may not even know it herself at the moment, and I'm not saying she's behaving like a sly bitch, not at all. That happened two weeks ago and, when I phoned her a week later, she didn't even want to speak to me: That's all over, she said, which is perfectly normal, considering that all this was just about to happen.' And he again made that gesture towards the church with his eyebrows, although with less expression this time, less brio, in fact, he may only have used his eyelashes. 'I can understand that, because you have to prepare yourself mentally for something like this, otherwise it's really hard work. But two weeks from now, she won't be able stand it any longer, you'll see.'

'I doubt very much if I will see actually,' I said, unable to resist making yet another wry comment. 'We drive back to Madrid tonight, after the post-wedding revels.'

'No, of course you won't *see*, that was just a manner of speaking. But I'll see and so will she. Some things you just can't fight, as I'm sure you know. What you *will* see is the way she looks at me when she comes out of the church, even if she is the newly-wed, the bride. You can't hide feelings like that, you can tell by the look in someone's eyes. The thing is, though, that so few people know how to interpret looks.'

I immediately turned to see the look in his eyes, which wasn't easy and certainly not interpretable behind those glasses that made his eyes seem smaller anyway. My curiosity was growing, I wanted to see the faces of the idiot and of the tiger, who, as Baringo put it, was capable of bolting the door and having it away as quick as a flash. I had only glimpsed the couple briefly, and from the side, when they each walked down the aisle. My impression of the groom had been one of elegance and good looks. María said that her cousin was by far the best-looking of all the cousins, and she, who is also a 'pretty little thing', was including herself when she said that. But that had nothing to do with what Baringo was talking about.

'Don't worry, I'll be watching,' I said.

And, when I said that, I already knew that I would do the exact opposite, that I would do everything I could not to look and not to watch what was sure to happen. I knew this because of Baringo Roy's desperate certainty. He lit another cigarette with rather more agitation and impatience than before – impatience with himself – this time even neglecting to offer me one too. I think this was because at that precise moment we began to hear murmurings indicating that the ceremony was over and, immediately afterwards, guests began to emerge from the church door, gradually, step by step, although there would still be many guests inside greeting each other or dragging their weary feet, the traffic jam would have to ease before the bride and groom could come out, and then the people hanging around outside would cheer and throw flowers. I very much hoped that the prosaic custom of throwing rice had not yet reached the South.

Baringo Roy had moved away from the balustrade and stepped forward as soon as he saw the first guests appear. He wasn't looking at me now and he didn't look at me again, he had immediately, seamlessly forgotten about me and our conversation. He took a few more steps towards the church, and by then I could see only his back. The false morning coat suited him quite well, but it still seemed inappropriate. He discarded the cigarette he had just lit, still almost intact, and moved a little closer, although not so close that any acquaintances would come over and incorporate him into their small groups and distract him with their talk. He only joined the other groups when we both saw them turn, as one, towards the door for the long-awaited appearance of the newly-weds, the tiger and the idiot or the idiot and the tiger. I noticed that, as soon as they appeared, smiling and arm-in-arm, Baringo Roy burst into applause along with all the other guests, except that he applauded more loudly, one certainly couldn't accuse him of a lack of enthusiasm, which seemed quite genuine, not put on, or perhaps it was an expression of his devotion for her. Then I turned away and gazed out at the broad, pleasant fields and allowed the unfettered breeze to strike me full in the face. I wasn't even going to try and make eye-contact with María, whom I had left behind in the church some time before. I didn't want to run the risk of looking at the bride and seeing with my own eyes that, at no point, did she direct her gaze at Baringo. I knew she would be cheered all the way to the ribbon-bedecked car and would get in, together with her idiot husband and her long train, without even once remembering that there among the guests was Baringo, abruptly relegated to the past. Not that he would care if I saw the absent female gaze that failed to linger on him, no, Baringo Roy had already forgotten all about me. But it mattered to me and I preferred not to see it, because, by then, my sense of camaraderie had become too entrenched, too deep.

BERNARDO ATXAGA

Teresa, *poverina mia*

Teresa had something wrong with her right knee, which meant that she had a slight limp, a fact that had been the cause of great sorrow to her ever since she was an adolescent. Although there was nothing very noticeable about the way she walked, and although, with time, her body had grown pretty and her face, 'with the golden eyes of a goat', had become particularly attractive, she was unable to rid her memory of the words which – on 12 August 1978, her fourteenth birthday – had emerged from the mouth of an Italian tourist who was a regular guest at her parents' boarding house: 'Teresa, *poverina mia*!' Those three words had been spoken with such feeling, sympathy and pity that Teresa – finding a new, darker meaning to the mocking remarks made by classmates and by her playmates on the beach, and suddenly fully aware of her situation – burst into inconsolable tears, just as, when a jug shatters, the water spills out onto the floor. When those around her asked what was wrong – her mother, if her knee was hurting; her brother (two years older than her), if her tears were due to the excitement of the moment and the fact that she was still a silly little girl; her father (glancing at the Italian woman who spent every summer at the boarding house), if this was any way to behave with their friend and guest, Signora di Castri, making such a fuss;

Bernardo Atxaga (b. 1951) is the pen name of Joseba Irazu Garmendia, who was born in the small village of Asteasu, in the Basque Country. He is the best known of contemporary Basque writers and has done an enormous amount to promote the Basque language and its literature in post-Franco Spain. He has written short stories and novels for children and adults, as well as poetry and songs. Eight of his novels have been translated into English, as well as into many other languages. His children's book *The Adventures of Shola* won the 2015 Marsh Award for Children's Literature in Translation. In 2019 he received the Premio Nacional de las Letras Españolas for his whole body of work.

Aunt Magdalena (looking angrily at her father and at the others), if she felt like going away and never seeing any of them ever again – she spoke of a school friend who had drowned in the sea that spring after slipping on the rocks below the jetty, and who, had she lived, would also have been fourteen, and how, when she had thought of her, she had all of a sudden felt terribly cold and that this was the reason for her tears. They all accepted or pretended to accept this explanation and went out onto the balcony with the slices of cake hurriedly handed round by Aunt Magdalena. There were lovely views from the balcony: you could see the jetty, part of the beach and, beyond it, the blue of the sea.

That night, Teresa added a new chapter to the five – entitled 'The Boarding House', 'The Workshop', 'My Parents', 'Aunt Magdalena' and 'My Brother' – that appeared in her secret diary, and, at the top of the page, she wrote Signora di Castri's words: Teresa, *poverina mia*! Teresa devoted four pages to analysing the problem of her lameness from a point of view which was intended to be totally objective. She should not feel resentful towards Signora di Castri, but, on the contrary, she should be grateful to her for revealing so clearly, in just three words, the true extent of her misfortune. It was true, there was no hope. Because of her disability, she would have to renounce many of the good things in life. Love, of course, would be denied her. She had already noticed that the boys at school took no notice of her or, if they did, it was only in order to make fun or to play cruel jokes. But what did that matter? Wasn't the misfortune of the girl who had slipped on the rocks and drowned in the sea far greater? Besides, if things got worse, she could always take that way out – wait until the tide was in, climb down into one of the gaps in the jetty and let herself slip into the sea.

Fifteen years later, this melodramatic confession in her diary was almost forgotten, but not Signora di Castri's words. These continued to live in some fold in her brain, and sometimes, like a nagging refrain, like the cricket's song as it moves its wings in the darkness of its nest, they would suddenly appear in her thoughts – Teresa, *poverina mia*! – with exactly the same pitying tone and intention of fifteen years before. It could be anywhere, at any time: when she was having a shower, going through some invoices at work, or when she was sitting on one of the benches along the jetty, smoking her last cigarette of the day. At such moments, her mind noticed what she described in her diary as 'a resurgence of the message', and she dreamed of being able 'to drive away once and for all' the cricket that had crawled inside her when she was fourteen; although, sometimes, with barely contained sarcasm, she would forget about the anxiety provoked by this memory and would, instead, admire its durability, its vividness and perpetual freshness, qualities notable by their absence in the other chapter titles in her diary. These – 'The Boarding House', 'The Workshop', etc. – had lost their real meaning and were now like entries in an antiquated dictionary, sad voices, names that spoke of the precariousness of life. The boarding house, for example, the seven-room house in which she and her brother had been born, was now a modern hotel with two hundred bedrooms. As for the workshop, the place in the Old Harbour where Aunt Magdalena once repaired the fishermen's clothes and nets, had become one of a chain of cafés. 'We'll show them we're no fools, Teresa,' her aunt had said to her on the day when Teresa had been told she would inherit the workshop. 'As soon as I reach retirement age, and I no longer have to work for the fishermen, we'll take all this junk and throw it in the sea. Then we'll talk to some big company about setting up a restaurant here or a café, and ask for twenty per cent of the profits in exchange for the site. We might as well take advantage of being in the Old Harbour. It's a favourite spot for tourists to come and sit.' And that is exactly what they had done.

The changes to Aunt Magdalena's workshop and to her parents' boarding house had, ultimately, been positive ones. True, she had left behind part of her life so that some truck could come and carry it off to the dump, along with the chipped partition walls and the broken-down furniture; on the other hand, that loss had put her in a most unusual economic position, one that allowed her to be different. For, thanks to her money, she, who knew she was different – irredeemably, eternally different – had found another more gratifying way of demonstrating this difference, in the way that she dressed and adorned herself. She didn't wear a lot of jewellery, but what she did wear was always of exceptional quality. She got through about forty outfits a year and had an amazing collection of shoes. 'You've got a real treasure house stashed away in your wardrobes and drawers. Aren't you forgetting that true beauty comes from within?' her brother said mockingly when they were still living with their father in an apartment on one of the top floors of the hotel. But she was immune to such remarks. Even the word 'brother' was no longer what it once was. It lacked the glow it had had in the early pages of her diary.

'Some years ago, when I was still a little girl,' said the entry for 2 September 1977, 'I saw a little orange bottle near the stone steps of the harbour and I went down the steps to try and catch it. But the water kept carrying it just out of reach. Then my brother appeared and, when he saw what was happening, he jumped into the water, got the bottle and swam back to me with it. It wasn't worth anything, it was just a discarded bottle of sun lotion that the sea had brought from Biarritz or some other French beach, but for me, at the time, it was something precious, and I thought my brother was the best boy in the world.' That childhood incident, however, was a long way off, in every sense. Her brother was very different now. He had become a mean, materialistic person, incapable of imagining a situation in which money did not play a central role. 'I've been told that you're to have the workshop in the Old Harbour,' he had said to her very aggressively on the day when she and Aunt Magdalena had been making plans for their future. 'Why are you so upset? And what's so very odd about it, anyway?' she had retorted. 'You didn't say a word when Father sold you the shares in the hotel for a nominal price, with the one proviso that you should give me a job in the office. It seemed fine to you then that you should get everything and that I should be your employee!' Her brother replied: 'That's got nothing to do with it. Father had very fixed ideas about the business. I had no alternative but to accept his proposal!' Before this discussion ended, she said to him: 'Do you know what we're going to build in place of the workshop? The best café on the coast!'

Teresa, who led a solitary life and whose sole refuge was her family, had felt the rift with her brother deeply, and she pondered the reasons for this transformation, pondered the secret force which, little by little – with all the determination of something organic, of something that is in the blood and can only manifest itself in silence – had made of her brother an exact copy of their father. She found no answer, but what had happened seemed to her a great misfortune, the second great misfortune of her life. She hated her father with all her heart. 'We're not going to Barcelona now,' she had written in her diary on 2 May 1979. 'My mother and my aunt had everything prepared, but my father came home at midday and said we couldn't go, that this year we had to open the boarding house early and that we could go to Barcelona another time. My mother burst into tears and I got angry and went to spend the night at Aunt Magdalena's house. Fortunately, my aunt took us to the circus. My brother didn't enjoy it very much, but I did. Especially the tightrope walker. His name was Monsieur Gabas and, with only the help of a balancing pole, he walked along a high wire that ran the whole length of the big tent. I thought it was really thrilling.'

Her father was the son of poor fisherfolk, who, having been taken on at the boarding house as a kind of factotum, ended up marrying the owners' eldest daughter and becoming sole manager; he was a man, however, who never lost his servant's heart and who lived with his head permanently bowed before his clientele; yet he was also a man who, like a bad dog, showed no respect for his own family. 'Is that any way to behave towards our friend Signora di Castri? Fancy making such a fuss!' was all he could think of to say when she was sobbing inconsolably and those three words were still echoing in her mind: 'Teresa, *poverina mia*! Teresa, *poverina mia*!' 'So you'd like to come and spend the first two weeks in May here. No problem at all, we'll be expecting you,' he had said to some unknown customer, knowing full well that this would put paid to the trip that her mother and her aunt had been planning for months, knowing too that her mother was ill and that this might be her last chance to travel. And now his son, her brother, behaved in exactly the same way and shared precisely the same values.

After her mother died – in 1981, two years after the ill-fated trip to Barcelona – Teresa had the feeling that she was walking a tightrope, just like Monsieur Gabas whom she had seen at the circus. And yet she had never felt afraid or dizzy or desperate, because her Aunt Magdalena was always there at the other end of the high wire, holding out her hand to her and keeping her from losing her balance. In the bad times, in the really bad times – when there was some problem at the hotel, or when on Sundays and public holidays her single state became more obvious, or when she chanced to hear some malicious remark about her limp that 'woke up the cricket' who would repeat Signora di Castri's words – the mere presence of her aunt made her feel far safer than all the poles in the world. Alas, shortly before Teresa turned twenty-nine, on 15 July 1993, the person she loved most in the world, apart from her mother, died.

'This morning we buried Magdalena,' she wrote in her diary on 16 July. 'The church was full of people and many of them came up to me afterwards to say how sorry they were. In a way, it helped me. It was awful weather, very rainy. There was a seagull perched on the mast of a yacht moored in the Old Harbour, and when we passed by with the coffin, it started to scream. Later that afternoon, I shut myself up at home and started cleaning shoes. I must have cleaned at least twenty pairs. Then, for the first time in a long while, I went down to the beach and swam until it was dark. There was a seagull there too. It never left my side, and when I turned on to my back in the water to rest, it seemed to do the same and to hang quietly in the air. It occurred to me then that I was like that bird. Up until now, whenever I've thought about my life, I've always thought of the tightrope walker at the circus, Monsieur Gabas, but perhaps the moment has come for a change of image. The bird hanging in the air more accurately reflects the situation I find myself in.'

Teresa, blinded by the death of the person she had loved, was wrong. She could not be like the bird that had accompanied her as she swam; she could not, as the seagull could, with a simple tilt of its wings, fly up from the waves to the clouds, fly back down from the sky to the rocks or to the roofs of the town. She lacked the strength, the power to triumph over the heaviness of the world, and, very soon, she found that she had to make a real effort not to fall into the void. What got her through these times was the monotony of life and the regularity of routine, and she applied herself to this with rigour: from ten until two, she worked in the office at the hotel; between two and three she went to the café in the Old Harbour and had a sandwich, a no. 10, the vegetarian option, at the table reserved for her; until seven o'clock, she stayed at what used to be Aunt Magdalena's apartment, above the café, then returned to the hotel where she worked until nine, spent an hour having supper at the café, ten minutes on the jetty smoking a cigarette, and then went back home, where she would pass what remained of the day watching television or reading a fashion magazine.

When monotony and routine were not enough, when she needed more protection or more diversion, Teresa would go across the border to Biarritz or Bayonne to buy shoes or to have clothes made. For the same reason she had tried to be more sociable and to go to the movies or out to supper with a friend of her brother's who used to phone her occasionally, or to resume, with as much enthusiasm as she could muster, her visits to the beach to swim, something which had always done her so much good. However, she found the latter particularly difficult. The jetty had been built in such a way that getting to the seashore meant trudging across 300 yards of beach, which proved both irritating and painful. Long before she reached the water's edge, her right leg would keep sinking into the soft sand, thus exaggerating her limp. Then the cricket would start to sing again, and Signora di Castri's words would go round and round in her head: Teresa, *poverina mia*! Teresa, *poverina mia*! Teresa, *poverina mia*!

The page she had written on 16 July 1993, the day after Magdalena's death, completed the sixth volume of her diary, and at the time, in the despair of the moment, she decided that she would not write any more, that she would live in silence, without the relief of that private confession. Nevertheless, exactly forty days later, on 25 August, she bought her seventh notebook and continued writing. The new chapter bore the name of a character who had long been with her: Monsieur Gabas. This was not a reference to the tightrope walker, however, or even to her personal situation.

'Last week, something surprising happened,' began Teresa's entry for that day, a longer entry than usual. 'There was a craft fair on in town, and in the evening, instead of going straight back to the office, I decided to go for a stroll around the Old Harbour where the stalls were set up. After buying a few knick-knacks, I was just about to go back to work, when I noticed a stall right at the end of the jetty, one that I hadn't noticed until then; it seemed to be selling wooden toys, and so I went over, thinking that I would just have a quick look. There was a slight breeze, and from the jetty, the sky looked like marble veined with red and green and blue. It was a really lovely evening.

'Next to the stall was a man in a white shirt, standing with his back to me and looking out to sea, and, at first, I thought he must be a visitor. But when I started looking at the toys, he turned round and said: "Take your time, there's no hurry." I don't know why, but I felt a kind of shock, as if a bolt of lightning had struck the ground immediately behind me. He was about fifty, with curly, greying hair. He looked rather like the kind of actor who gets cast as Jesus in American movies.

'I thought the toys were really lovely, the kind my mother or my aunt would have had when they were children, and I set about choosing one, rather hurriedly, because it was getting late. "If you haven't got time today, come back tomorrow," he said. He had a French accent, I realized then, and this was perhaps why he spoke so slowly, almost sweetly. "Yes, you're right. Your toys deserve more time. I'll come back tomorrow," I said. "About six o'clock?" he said. Again I felt that flash of lightning behind me. The way he said these words didn't sound like a business appointment. I said six o'clock would be fine. Then he held out his hand and introduced himself. His name was André and he was from Bordeaux. I did the same. I shook his hand and told him my name too.

'Our conversation had evolved in such a strange way, as if the jetty in the Old Harbour had provided us with a peculiarly intimate atmosphere, ideal for this quiet exchange, but the most surprising thing of all occurred just as I was leaving. "What name would you give to this doll?" asked André, putting his hand into a box and drawing out . . . a tightrope walker! It was a doll in the form of a spinning top which, because of its long arms, could remain balanced on a column without falling off. "I'd call it Monsieur Gabas," I replied without a moment's hesitation. "The perfect name," he said, and I had the feeling that there was a thread between us, something binding us together. "I'll expect you tomorrow, then," he said, putting the doll in my purse. I thanked him for the present and walked very slowly and unhurriedly away from the stall.

'The following day, as soon as André saw me appear on the jetty, he closed his stall and invited me to go for a walk. "We lame people don't tend to go in much for walking," I said in a steady voice. I felt odd and strangely energized. "What caused it?" he asked. "Infective arthritis?" "Don't tell me you're a doctor as well," I said. "I am actually," he replied coolly. "But I gave it up seven years ago. I used to work in the hospital in Bordeaux." Then he offered me his arm, saying: "If you hold on tight, you won't get tired." I felt slightly giddy, as if I were drunk. "Do you want people to think you're my boyfriend?" I said. He looked into my eyes and smiled broadly. "That's exactly what I do want. I'd like to be your boy-friend. And if you'll allow me, that's what I'll try to become." A few seagulls were flying about above the jetty, very excited about something. I waited for them to fall silent. I felt strong and suddenly very aware that

I was from the same stock as Aunt Magdalena. "Why do you want to be my boyfriend, may I ask?" I said. "Because you have the golden eyes of a goat," André replied. Somewhat taken aback by this answer, I insisted: "Is that the only reason?" He smiled again, and looked at me like someone making a calculation. "Well, because of that and because of something Montaigne, the philosopher from Bordeaux, once said," he replied after a silence. "According to Montaigne, a man who has never lain with a lame woman does not know what it is to lie with a woman." He stood still, looking at me hard. For my part, I felt my head becoming considerably hotter than the rest of my body. "I've never heard that before," was all I managed to say. Then I pulled myself together sufficiently to add: "And I've been lame for a long time." In this frame of mind, we walked along the jetty and strolled about for quite a while. We had supper at one of the restaurants with tables on the beach.'

There exists a treatise on love which describes a custom among workers in the saltmarshes of Salzburg that involved lowering the branch of a tree down into one of the pits, then taking it out again in summer when it would emerge covered in thousands of salt crystals, glittering in the sun like diamonds, a marvellous phenomenon which the author of the treatise compares with the effects of love on the beloved: 'Just like that branch in Salzburg,' he writes, 'the beloved becomes brilliant, beautiful and full of fine qualities.'

This statement, which may not be applicable to all cases, perfectly described what happened to Teresa: love – a feeling she had always denied herself and which was mentioned only in the pages of her personal diary – entered her heart as it would the heart of a fourteen-year-old, like a whirlwind, sweeping everything before it, and transfiguring the craftsman she had met on the jetty in the Old Harbour. For her, André was the polar opposite of her father and her brother; he seemed to her intelligent, generous, thoughtful, better even than she herself was, because he was freer, because he lived according to his own values, unconcerned about social position or money. Paradoxically, André's foreignness brought him closer to her, because she too, for different reasons, felt herself to be excluded and obliged to live on the margins of society. Thus this union of extremes came into being: the man who always wore the same sandals and the woman with a hundred pairs of shoes had met on the high wire, in the middle of the void, and had decided to join forces.

'André needs nothing,' she wrote on 5 October. 'He says he had quite enough things when he worked in the hospital in Bordeaux, and that his model now is Diogenes. Apparently, the Emperor Alexander once went to visit Diogenes to tell him that anything he asked for would be given to him. Diogenes' response was to ask him to move out of the way because he was blocking the sun. "So you don't need anything," I say to him sometimes. "Yes, I need a woman with golden eyes like a goat. Oh, and Montaigne, of course," he replies. He's such a wonderful man.'

Generally speaking, when one is happy, one tends to write rather less than when one is unhappy, and Teresa put the seventh volume of her diary away in one of her desk drawers and forgot all about it for nearly two years. On 5 September 1995, the silence was broken. Teresa reopened her notebook and scribbled this:

'André has gone to Bordeaux to teach a course on making toys, and it will be a month before we see each other again. I would go and visit him, but I can't, because my brother is all tied up with sorting out the new golf course, and I've got to take charge of running the hotel. The night before he left, I got angry and was in a foul mood, and he took it badly. My ill temper, he said, struck him as "vulgar". Then he looked very serious and said that ours was a relationship between two free individuals, and that I should have the same respect for the way he lived his life as he had for mine.'

Shortly after André left, Teresa's thoughts grew darker, and her private confessions took on a querulous tone. One day, she wrote about the school friend who had drowned after falling off one of the rocks below the jetty, and how sad that still made her feel; on another day, about her sense of panic at the idea that André might have gone to Bordeaux for good, and how wrong she had been to rest her whole being on one point, just like Monsieur Gabas, 'the doll he gave me on the day we met'; and on another day, about 'how fragile love was', and how it made her suffer. 'I don't know what stories you're inventing for yourself,' André said during one of their telephone conversations. 'Listen to me, Teresa, stop getting things all out of proportion and just try to enjoy yourself as much as possible. Why don't you go to the beach and go swimming? The waves would wash away all those ghosts filling your head.'

For the first time since her relationship with André had begun, Teresa felt misunderstood. Nevertheless – for she was not the same woman she had been two years before – she decided to resist the tendency 'to weep into her diary' and to follow the advice she had been given: she would go to the beach, plunge into the water and let herself be buffeted by the waves. But the day on which she decided to do this – 17 September, a Sunday – was not the most opportune of days. There was a strong wind blowing in from the sea, and she found it difficult to walk. It was also very noisy, and there were lots of children playing football and racing around all over the place, and the sand they kicked up inevitably got in her eyes. Worse still, it was low tide. The waves, the succeeding rows of white lines that the waves made with their foam, seemed miles away.

Teresa decided to turn round and go back to the hotel. The wind was blowing harder than ever, and she was afraid it might knock her off balance and throw her to the ground. Then, just as she was thinking this, a ball hit her on the head. She didn't actually fall over, but the noise on the beach vanished and she felt as if she were floating, like a balloon that someone has thrown into the air, having first put a bit of spin on it with their hand. In the air, in the midst of that silence, the cricket stirred its wings and began to sing. The words of Signora di Castri rang out only once, but louder than ever: Teresa, *poverina mia*!

As soon as she reached the hotel, she called Bordeaux, but André, she was told, was teaching and couldn't come to the phone. She hung up and took out her diary.

'Panic,' she wrote at the top of a new page. 'After two whole years, I have just heard those words again. I thought I was cured, that love had worked a miracle. But the cricket is still there inside me. André told me once that if you wanted to get a cricket out of its nest, all you needed was a twig. However . . .'

Someone was knocking at the door and gently pushing it open, so Teresa broke off her writing. Seconds later, when she had got up from her desk, the door opened fully and she found herself face to face with an old lady. 'Can I help you?' Teresa asked, bemused. The old lady did not reply at once. She began examining Teresa, wide-eyed and open-mouthed. '*Ma che bella!*' she exclaimed at last, taking a step back and opening her arms. '*Ma che bella!*' she said again. These three words were filled with such surprise and admiration that Teresa – finding new, luminous meaning in the compliments and words of praise spoken by Magdalena, André and a few other people, and suddenly fully aware of her situation – burst out laughing, just as, when a jug shatters, the water spills out onto the floor. 'Don't you recognize me, Teresa?' asked the old lady. 'Signora di Castri, it must be years since you were here!' she said, still laughing. '*Ma che bella!*' said the old lady before embracing her. 'But what's that? A cockroach?' she asked, starting back and pointing to an insect that was just crawling in through the door. 'No, it's a cricket, Signora di Castri. It probably lives in the hotel garden,' Teresa told her. It all fitted, everything slotted into place, the ground on which she walked seemed more solid now, with plenty of support along the way.

The phone rang. It was André, concerned about her earlier call. 'I just rang to tell you that I'm really happy and can't wait to see you again,' she said, still looking at Signora di Castri. '*Ma che bella!*' sighed the old lady.

QUIM MONZÓ

The Fullness of Summer

Translated from the Catalan by Peter Bush

They are all related. They meet three or four times a year and this is their summer reunion. They usually arrange to have lunch, and today is no exception. They come from different cities and rendezvous two hours before, in one of their homes, a vast apartment with sea views. There are a lot of them. A genuinely large family from the days when families were really large and not like now, when large is three children. Amid loud shrieks of joy – 'Hellooo!' – they kiss each other and, as there are dozens of them, the rounds of kisses mean the kissing phase is so prolonged that, when they finish, it's almost time to jump into their cars and head to the restaurant where they have a reservation. So, displaying the same joy with which they greeted each other on arrival, they then rush out shouting, 'Follow me!' and 'See you at the restaurant!'

When their cars drive up, it's as if they're reuniting after centuries apart, and they thus repeat their greetings – 'Hellooo!' – and the kisses. Given that, as mentioned earlier, there are dozens of them, it takes ages for them to do the rounds, but the restaurant is no stranger to meals of this nature and, consequently, the waiters are in no hurry to start serving, because, however long they took, they would find everyone still in the pecking phase. The fact is that when they finish kissing they still have a good half hour to wait for the *tapas* first course, and they use that time to take photos. Photos of everybody together in front of the restaurant

Quim Monzó (b. 1952) was born in Barcelona. He has worked as a cartoonist, a scriptwriter for radio, films and television, graphic designer and war correspondent. He writes in both Catalan and Castilian and has won several important literary prizes, the most recent being the Premio de la Crítica Serra d'Or. Six of his books (novels and short stories) have been translated into English, the most recent being *Why, Why, Why?*

entrance. Photos of genuinely married couples. Photos of individuals. Photos of the children by themselves. Photos of the children with the older folk. Everybody smiling, even the two alpha males of the species who are competing to show off their expertise with digital cameras. A rivalry that extends even to the moment when the waiters finally start to serve the meal and the pair walk along the extremely long table, taking fresh photos of all the people who they have snapped outside and who now compete to see who can smile the most spectacularly, and the longest, so much so that some individuals sustain their smiles through the hours that slowly elapse between desserts, coffees, cigarettes, cigars and post-prandial chat until finally it's goodbye time again, with fresh rounds of kisses, and the last photo sessions before they climb into their cars to drive – in one long convoy – to the apartment where they had met before lunch and where, as they arrive, they greet one another – 'Hellooo!' – and kiss anew, before going in for an immediate viewing, on the television screen, of every single photo the dominant males of the species have taken before, during and after the meal. 'Look, there's little Laura!' says Silvia, as if it were a miracle that little Laura is there, snapped while eating her veal and champignons. It is less than three hours since little Laura was eating her veal and champignons (which at this very moment must be a magnificent alimentary bolus coasting through her intestines) and they can already see her on screen! This excites them no end. And provokes reflections like: 'People can say what they like, but before we had digital photos you had to take the film to be developed and you couldn't see the photos of the meal on the same afternoon!' Just the kind of thing to keep them in a frothy state of bliss that lasts until it's time for each and every one to go home, when there is another round of kisses and – as there are dozens of them and the necessary turn-taking so that everybody can kiss everybody is never-ending – it is very late by the time they finish. 'But, since it's summer, it's still light!' says little Laura, radiating happiness, while her husband starts up the car and she smiles and waves and photo-graphs the people smiling and waving and photographing her from all the other cars.

PALOMA DÍAZ-MAS

In Search of a Photograph

For my adoptive grandmother

The carefully waxed red tiles in the hall, the astonishing little staircase up to the skylight on the top floor, a space that has now been transformed into a hothouse for a few almost alarmingly lush green plants, the house with its long corridors and polished wooden floors, its spotless, impeccably ironed cretonne door curtains with a floral print.

The dining room with its fine oak furniture, the sumptuous wrought-iron art-deco gate – with its pink lotuses and blue waterlilies, their translucent, frosted petals all twined about with bottle-green tendrils – that opens out onto the roof garden, where there are more tiles, so glossy they appeared to have been brushed with oil; and, out in the sun, azaleas, petunias, busy lizzies, fuchsias, pelargoniums and purple coleus. And, in the shade, ferns, dwarf ivy, spider plants and what we call *amor de hombre* – man's love – but which the English call wandering Jew and the French *misère*. And in one corner the miraculously flowering cacti and all the scented plants: mint, sage and basil.

And, most important of all, there was the kitchen: a big old kitchen with white tiles and pinewood cupboards painted white, with white curtains at the window and a white marble sink where my grandmother María – among mounds of white soapsuds – would wash the white crockery, then dry it afterwards on a soft white cotton cloth. Outside, there was often snow on the peaks of the surrounding mountains.

Paloma Díaz-Mas (b. 1954) was born in Madrid and has taught at various universities both in Spain and in the United States, her specialism being Sephardic Literature. She has written scholarly books and novels, including *El rapto del Santo Grial* (1984), based on the Arthurian legend, as well as short stories and a memoir of her time in Eugene, Oregon, *Una ciudad llamada Eugenio* (1992). She won the 2000 Premio Euskadi for *La tierra fértil*.

And my grandmother herself, with her pearly white hair and her dresses made of brightly coloured floral prints, seemed to be a synthesis of the white kitchen and the chintz curtains, or perhaps the opposite was true, and the whiteness of the kitchen and the flowery fabrics all emanated from her; I always had the feeling that my grandmother was the house and that the house was my grandmother.

But I did say 'and, most important of all, there was the kitchen', for she spent long hours preparing complicated dishes – duck stuffed with pears and chicken cooked with plums, that meaty Catalan stew *escudella*, salt cod with raisins, or a roast vegetable salad and red pine mushrooms cooked in all sorts of ways, sea bream in a cream sauce, and mouthwatering, still-warm profiteroles – and she would never allow anyone to help. In her pink-and-white check apron (on Sundays she wore a different one in blue piqué with white lace appliqué roses) she remained spotless among the grease and the smoke, and would start very early chopping vegetables and preparing condiments, stoning fruit and slicing meat, caramelizing moulds and stirring sauces, sautéeing onions and weighing out herbs, in a subdued clatter of saucepans and pots, frying pans and casseroles, colanders and piping bags, grinders and graters, mortars and whisks, baking dishes, paella pans and salad bowls.

She knew how to make soap out of sodium carbonate and lard, could make an aioli sauce with just a mortar and pestle; she could create whole mountains of foam out of a single egg white. What's more, she was beautiful, lovelier than any other woman I'd ever met. However, I didn't realize this until I saw the photo. And these, by the way, are not childhood memories. I only met María when she was already an old lady, and I was nearly thirty.

I think it was early one summer morning when she was sitting in her rocking chair on the terrace, stoning prunes for some party dish. I caught her like that, sitting there quietly and yet in constant activity, surrounded by flowers and red tiles. I didn't have that particular roll of film developed for a long time, when I was already living in the city far from that mountain village and the little house of white wall tiles and gleaming floor tiles, and I had completely forgotten ever taking that photo.

And yet, there she was, looking at me with the mischievous expression of someone who, despite all my precautions, knew perfectly well that I was taking her photo, and there was in her eyes, in the faint lines on her forehead and at the corners of her mouth, just the hint of a mocking, ironic smile. In the morning sunlight, her pearly white hair had an almost bluish tinge, her small blue eyes were so bright they looked almost black, one elegant ear stood out above a butter-smooth neck marked by just a single wrinkle, the V of her blue-and-yellow spotted dress coquettishly revealed a surprisingly firm eighty-year-old bust, her strong arms rested on the arms of her chair, and she wore the sweetly energetic expression of one who has had to suffer many things, most of them cruel and terrible, and the mocking smile of one who knows that we've known worse and have survived. And those hands, so touchingly white, with their clean, trim fingernails, hands at once beautiful and distorted by arthritis, an arthritis that did not seem like an illness or a defect, but merely the result of a natural evolution: these were the contorted bones and swollen joints that an ancient tree might have if it had white hands. In the background, the cat is playing, and there's a whole thicket of red busy lizzies.

Ever since that day, I had enjoyed imagining how beautiful grandmother María must have been when young, because such a lovely, golden old age, so immaculate and perfect, so vivacious and venerable, must have been preceded by a splendid middle age and a fascinatingly gorgeous youth. How would she have looked as a little girl, with her hair in plaits, wearing a striped smock and carrying her lunchbox as she walked reluctantly to the village school? I enjoyed imagining her as a delightful pre-adolescent with shiny knees and a neatly ironed collar, with a single, plump, heavy plait like a thick piece of rope, a jet-black plait that was the envy of the other girls in the village. Or post-pubescent, looking rather stiff and starched in her first grown-up dress: the fascinating girl who seems unaware of her own beauty and at whom all the boys stare without daring to ask her to dance, because she seems so terrifyingly beautiful. And then as a married woman, a radiant proud young mother walking around with her baby in her arms, convinced that everyone is looking at the child and not at her. And then as a strong, mature woman, facing up to the hard life of a young widow in what old people now still call 'the bad old days' and, sometimes, 'the hungry years'. How could it have been otherwise?

And thus began my desire, then my wish, then my urgent need, then my obsession with finding a photo of grandmother María when she was young. Because I wanted to see for myself what must have been her unequalled beauty, a beauty beyond compare. Because such a fine, golden old age could only have been the product of a once splendid, incomparable beauty.

Alas, it appeared that grandmother María had never once had her photograph taken. And even though I asked my mother, and asked María herself, even after rummaging through old drawers or searching through family photo albums, I could not find a single photograph from her youth. It was as if, in an unusual, strange display of modesty, time and its protagonists had done all they could to conceal that magnificent image.

It took me years of pleading to get her to show me the one photo she *had* kept from her young days: her wedding photo. She agreed to show it to me on one already rather chilly autumn evening after I had again been nagging her to let me see it. She removed it from a cream-coloured cardboard folder with gilt corners, from between two sheets of airy tissue paper. I prepared myself to see what I had imagined would be a dazzling, fascinating beauty.

Looking out at me from that sepia photo were a provincial couple posing between a truncated pillar and a large bouquet of fake flowers, and beneath a cloudscape worthy of some angelic apparition. Encased in his stiff new suit, he is seated on a rather grand chair, his shoes polished to within an inch of their lives and his hands the coarse hands of someone who works the land; and she is standing behind him, looking equally coarse and dull, her face inexpressive, conventionally oval in shape and rather plain, with her pale eyes and dark hair; she is resting her anodyne and equally inexpressive hands on her husband's shoulders, hands which, having nothing to say, said nothing about either work or pleasure – they could have belonged to anyone. And that was it: a village girl in her cheap wedding dress, with the face of a china doll, a slight figure just like thousands of others, and eyes in which there was not a spark of light. Grandmother María's golden old age was not, then, the product of an exquisitely beautiful youth: her beauty had been forged over the years, like the beauty of certain trees or certain rocks or certain fine buildings, ennobled by the rains and the winds that polished their stones.

JULIO LLAMAZARES

Balancing the World on His Chin

The posters advertising movies or dances were not the only ones that occasionally clamoured for our attention from Olleros' walls and tree trunks. Sometimes, too, a travelling circus would stop there or a family troupe of actors or puppeteers with a tiny cast (I remember one in particular, in which the man not only sold the tickets on the door and played the parts of lion, devil and monk in the play, he also, still wearing his lion costume, organized the drawing of raffle tickets in the interval) and, for a few days, they would pitch their tents and park their trucks in the square and fill the village streets with posters.

They usually arrived around the fifteenth of each month, which was *el día del pago* in Olleros, when the company paid its employees. On that day, which people waited for all month (some with a certain degree of anxiety since prudent household management was not the most common of virtues), Olleros woke in a state of great agitation. The miners let off rockets and exploded dynamite charges, the women crowded into the shops (some to buy and others to settle accumulated debts) and, from noon onwards, when we children would be coming out of school and the miners returned from the first shift, the day became a holiday, regardless of whether it was a Sunday or a weekday. All afternoon and late into the night or, indeed, depending on the weather and the circumstances, into the early hours, people would fill the bars, stroll along the road or rush to visit the many stalls set up

Julio Llamazares (b. 1955) was born in the now non-existent village of Vegamián near León and currently lives in Madrid. Initially he trained and worked as a lawyer, but soon abandoned that career to work as a newspaper, TV and radio journalist. He has written poetry, novels and short stories based on his childhood experiences. Two of his novels have been translated into English: *The Yellow Rain* and *Wolf Moon*.

around the square since the previous day. There were tombolas, carousels, rifle ranges and try-your-strength machines, fairground barkers, photographers, stands selling sweet fritters, itinerant salesmen and bands, and, from time to time, a special attraction that would be announced with much fanfare several days in advance. I remember, for example, The Great Guzzler, a bald, but otherwise extremely hairy man who devoured coins and lengths of metal pipe and who could, he said, corrode a whole motorbike with his own saliva and eat it bit by bit (this was never actually put to the test because no one in the crowd dared take the risk); or Muscle Woman, who claimed to be the strongest woman in the world and who was capable of bearing the weight of nine men on her body and of dragging a truck several yards with just her teeth; or the Pita Brothers, who performed on a tightrope strung between a chimney and the pithead tower and walked along it many feet above the ground, lit from below by a spotlight; but over and above all of them – even Fu Manchu the Chinaman who could trace the outline of his wife's body with knives which he threw at her from a distance while she stood there against a wooden board, breathing fire – I remember the man who was depicted on all the posters with the globe of the world balanced on his chin, the man who, having first balanced a large lamp post, held me and the chair I sat in poised in the air, as this photo of Barbachey the Seal-Man unequivocally shows and records.

He was a burly, fair-haired man who performed before the public naked from the waist up and whose sideburns formed part of his moustache. He travelled in a van with a woman who acted as his assistant and who was in charge of collecting the money at the end of each performance. For me it proved an unforgettable night. Having balanced the lamp post on his chin and held it there for a while, Barbachey dried his sweat, rested for a moment, and then, addressing the audience in his strange, accented Spanish (for Barbachey was French, as was the woman who accompanied him), he called for a volunteer. Several of us offered, but he chose me, perhaps because I was the tallest. Barbachey gave me his hand – a hand, I remember, as rough and hard as the root of a tree – and told me to sit on the chair which his assistant had placed there for the purpose. A silence fell, the woman stood to one side, and Barbachey, after first flexing his muscles, made the sign of the cross, looked up at the sky, planted his feet wide apart, and then, to the astonishment of all, suddenly lifted up the chair, and me with it, and placed it carefully on his chin, on just one of its legs; then he began to turn, keeping his balance with his arms. I don't know how long I was up there, not daring to move or even breathe – still less look down – but I do know that, when he lowered me to the ground again, I could no longer hear the audience's shouts and applause or Barbachey's voice congratulating me. I was still up there, suspended in the air, floating, holding time stopped in my hands just like the globe he balanced on his chin in the posters. It was the most remarkable night of my life and my most vivid memory from those years.

But life keeps turning. Life turns and turns just as the world did on Barbachey's chin while I was up in the air, and, as it turns, it sometimes surprises us, the way old photographs do, unexpectedly lobbing remnants of the past in our direction. Some time ago, in a village in Soria, I came across an abandoned van. It had lost its wheels, was covered in rust and almost entirely overgrown by brambles, but, despite this, I could still just make out the red lettering which continued to announce from amidst the rust and dust: *Barbachey the Seal-Man. Travelling Show.* Someone from the village told me it had been there several years, precisely the same number of years that had passed since its owner was found hanging from a rope slung over the oak tree beside it. It seems that Barbachey, who had for some time been wandering the villages of Castile performing his show alone (the woman who used to accompany him must have either left him or died), had, with the passing of time, lost his strength and, one day, doubtless no longer able to bear the weight of the world on his old chin, had decided to take his own life. He was buried there, in the village's small cemetery, in the nettle-infested corner reserved for suicides and those who die in mortal sin.

I chose not to go there. I left without saying goodbye and without visiting his grave. I did not even turn round when I was some way off, to look back for the last time at the place where he lay buried. Before I left, though, I went over to the van and, unseen by anyone, removed the torn poster that was still stuck to it like a photograph of the past, but from which the sun and the rain had almost completely erased the image, and I took it with me as a souvenir of the man who had unwittingly taught me that sometimes it's more difficult to bear the passage of time than it is to balance the world on your chin, even though the world turns out to be as hard and difficult as the one balanced by all of them, by Barbachey the Seal-Man and by the miners of Olleros, who are still watching us in this photograph.

MANUEL RIVAS

The Butterfly's Tongue

'Hello there, Sparrow, how are things? Now this, I hope, will be the year when we finally get to see the butterfly's tongue.'

The teacher had been waiting some time for microscopes to be supplied to teachers like him in public schools. He had so often described to us the way in which tiny, invisible things grew bigger when looked at through a microscope that we children had actually started seeing them like that already, as if his enthusiastic words had as much effect as a powerful lens.

'The butterfly's tongue is a proboscis as tightly coiled as a watch spring. When the butterfly is drawn to a particular flower, it unrolls this proboscis and pushes it down into the calyx to suck up the nectar. When you wet your finger before putting it in the sugar bowl, can't you almost taste the sweetness already in your mouth, as if the tip of your finger was the tip of your tongue? Well, that's what the butterfly's tongue is like.'

And then we all envied butterflies. How wonderful to go flying around in those bright party clothes, calling in at flowers as if at taverns stocked with barrels full of syrup.

I really loved that teacher. At first, my parents couldn't believe it. I mean, they didn't understand how I could possibly love my teacher. When I was a kid, school was like a terrible threat, a word that thrashed through the air like a cane.

Manuel Rivas (b. 1957) was born in A Coruña in Galicia. He writes mainly in *galego* and is probably the best-known Galician writer. He began work at the age of fifteen, working as a journalist for a local newspaper. After secondary school, he moved to Madrid where he studied journalism. He has published poetry, novels and short stories, notably *¿Qué me queres, amor?*, *O lapis do carpinteiro* and *Os libros arden mal*, all of which have been translated into English. The story included here formed the basis for a film directed by José Luis Cuerda.

'Just you wait till you go to school!'

Two of my uncles, like a lot of other young men, had emigrated to South America so as not to be sent as conscripts to the war in Morocco. Well, I too dreamed of going to South America so as not to be sent to school. In fact, stories were told of children who had fled into the hills to avoid the nightmare of school. They would turn up a few days later, frozen and dumb, like deserters from the disastrous battle of Barranco del Lobo.

I was nearly six at the time and everyone called me Sparrow. Other boys my age were already working. But my father was a tailor and had no land and no cattle. He would rather have me out of the house than cluttering up his tiny workroom, which was why I spent much of the day running up and down the Alameda, the public promenade. Cordeiro, whose job it was to sweep up the rubbish and the dry leaves, was the one who first gave me the nickname, because, he said: 'You look just like a sparrow.'

I don't think I've ever run as much as I did the summer before I entered school. I used to run like a mad thing and sometimes I would overshoot the end of the Alameda and go tearing on, with my eyes fixed on the top of Mount Sinaí, hoping that one day I would sprout wings and fly off to Buenos Aires. But I never got beyond that magic mountain.

'Just you wait till you go to school!'

My father used to describe as a terrible torment – as if his tonsils had been physically wrenched from his throat – the way in which the teacher tried to eliminate every trace of a Galician accent from the pupils' pronunciation of Spanish, and to get them to say 'agua' instead of 'ahua', 'gato' instead of 'hato' and 'gracias' instead of 'hracias'. 'Every morning we had to practise saying: "Los pájaros de Guadalajara tienen la garganta llena de trigo." The canings we got because we kept saying "Juadalagara", not "Guadalajara"!' If my father's intention was to frighten me, he succeeded. The night before my first day at school, I couldn't sleep. Huddled in my bed, I listened to the clock on the wall in the living room with all the anguish of a condemned man. The day dawned as bright as a butcher's apron. I would not have been lying if I had told my parents I was ill.

Fear, like a mouse, was gnawing at my innards.

And I peed myself, not in my bed, but at school.

I can remember it so clearly. Years have passed since then, yet I can still feel the hot, shameful liquid running down my legs. I was sitting hunched at a desk right at the back, in the hope that no one would notice me, until I could leave and race off again down the Alameda.

'You back there, stand up!'

The fate I had been dreading. I looked up and saw with horror that the order was directed at me. That hideous teacher was pointing at me with a ruler. It was only a small, wooden ruler, but to me it looked like the spear of the Berber leader, Abd el-Krim.

'What's your name?'

'Sparrow.'

All the other boys roared with laughter. It felt as if they were clattering tin cans together right by my ears.

'Sparrow?'

I couldn't remember anything. Not even my name. Everything I had been until then had vanished from my head. My parents were two blurred figures rapidly fading from my memory. I looked across at the window, hoping anxiously for a glimpse of the trees in the Alameda.

And that was when I peed myself.

When the other boys realized, their laughter grew louder and echoed round the room like whiplashes.

I fled. I started running like a mad, winged creature. I ran and ran, the way you run in dreams when the Bogey Man is right behind you. I was convinced the teacher was doing just that. Coming after me. I could feel his breath on my neck, and the breath of all the children, like a pack of hounds after a fox. Yet, when I reached the bandstand and looked back, I saw that no one had followed me, that I was alone with my fear, drenched in sweat and pee. The bandstand was empty. No one seemed to be taking any notice of me, but I had the feeling that the whole village was just pretending, that dozens of censorious eyes were spying on me from behind every window, and that gossiping tongues would soon carry the news to my parents. My legs decided for me. They set off towards Mount Sinaí with a determination hitherto unknown. This time I would get to A Coruña and stow away on one of those ships bound for Buenos Aires.

I couldn't see the sea from the top of Sinaí, only another even bigger mountain, with crags that stood out like the towers on some inaccessible fortress. What I did that day I now remember with a mixture of astonishment and nostalgia. Alone, on top of the mountain, sitting on that seat of stone beneath the stars, while in the valley below the kerosene lamps of the people searching for me flickered like fireflies. My name rode through the night on the back of the dogs' barking. I was quite unmoved by it all. It was as if I had crossed the line of fear. That's why I didn't burst into tears or resist when Cordeiro's sturdy shadow appeared by my side. He put his jacket round me and picked me up. 'Don't worry, Sparrow, it's over now.'

That night I slept like a saint, snuggled up to my mother. No one scolded me. My father, just as he had when my grandmother died, stayed in the kitchen, his elbows resting on the tablecloth, as he silently smoked cigarette after cigarette, filling the scallop shell ashtray with butts. It seemed to me that my mother did not let go of my hand all night. And, still holding my hand, she took me back to school, like someone carrying a basket. And this time, my heart was serene enough for me to be able to look at the teacher properly for the first time. He had a face like a toad.

The toad smiled. He pinched my cheek affectionately. 'I like that name of yours, Sparrow.' And the pinch left a bitter-sweet taste like a coffee caramel. But the most extraordinary thing of all was that, in the midst of the most absolute silence, he led me by the hand to his desk and sat me down on his chair. He remained standing, picked up a book and said:

'Today we have a new classmate. This is a cause of great joy to us all, and I'd like us to greet him with a round of applause.' I thought I was going to pee my pants again, but the only moistness I felt was in my eyes. 'Right, we're going to start with a poem. Whose turn is it? You, Romualdo? Come on, then, come over here. Now you know what to do, read nice and slowly and in a good, loud voice.'

Romualdo looked ridiculous in his short trousers. He had very long, dark legs and his knees were all covered in grazes.

'A dull, dark, cold afternoon . . .'

'One moment, Romualdo, what is it you're going to read?'

'A poem, sir.'

'And what's it called?'

'*Childhood Memory* by Antonio Machado.'

'Excellent, Romualdo, off you go. Slowly and in a good, loud voice. And pay attention to the punctuation.'

Romualdo, whom I knew from having seen him carrying sacks of pinecones like other boys from Altamira, cleared his throat like a veteran pipe-smoker and then read in an amazing, splendid voice, the sort of voice you might hear on the new radio owned by Manolo Suárez, who had emigrated to Montevideo and returned a rich man.

> *A dull, dark, cold afternoon*
> *in winter. The children*
> *are studying. A monotony*
> *of rain outside the windows.*
> *It's lesson time. A poster*
> *depicts a fleeing Cain*
> *and Abel dead*
> *beside a crimson stain . . .*

'Excellent. Now what exactly does "A monotony of rain" mean, Romualdo?' asked the teacher.

'That it never rains but it pours, Don Gregorio.'

'Did you pray?' Mama asked me, while she was pressing the clothes that Papa had made during the day. In the kitchen, the supper pot gave off an acrid smell of boiled turnip tops.

'I think so,' I said uncertainly. 'Something about Cain and Abel.'

'That's good,' said Mama. 'I don't know why there's all this gossip about the new teacher being an atheist.'

'What's an atheist?'

'Someone who says that God doesn't exist.'

Mama pulled a disapproving face and energetically ironed out the creases in a pair of trousers.

'Is Papa an atheist?'

Mama put down the iron and stared at me.

'How could Papa possibly be an atheist? How can you ask such a stupid thing?'

I had often heard my father blaspheme against God. All the men did. When anything went wrong, they would spit on the floor and promptly take God's name in vain, or, indeed, the name of the Devil. Goddammit, they would say, or Devil take it. It seemed to me that only women really believed in God.

'And what about the Devil? Does the Devil exist?'

'Of course he does!'

Fervid boiling was making the lid on the pot dance. Steam belched forth from the mutant mouth, along with gobbets of foam and greens. A moth was fluttering about near the ceiling, round the light bulb hanging from its plaited cable. Mama was a bit irritable as she always was when she had to do the ironing. Her face tensed up whenever she did the creases in the legs of the trousers. But now she was talking in a gentle, rather sad tone of voice, as if she were discussing some poor, helpless creature.

'The Devil was once an angel, but he turned bad.'

The moth collided with the light bulb, which swayed slightly and disarranged the shadows.

'Today, the teacher told us that butterflies have a tongue just like us, only it's ever so long and thin and they keep it rolled up like a watch spring. He's going to show it to us on a machine that's being sent from Madrid. I can't believe that butterflies have tongues, can you?'

'If the teacher says they do, then it must be true. There are lots of truths that seem like lies. Did you enjoy school?'

'Oh, yes. And he doesn't hit us. The teacher doesn't hit us.'

No, the teacher, Don Gregorio, did not hit the pupils. On the contrary, his toad-like face was nearly always smiling. If he came across two boys fighting during recess, he would call them over and say 'you're behaving just like a pair of rams' and then he'd make them shake hands. Afterwards, he would sit them at the same desk. That was how I met my best friend, big, kind, clumsy Dombodán. There was another boy, Eladio, who had a mole on one cheek, whom I would gladly have thrashed, but I never did so for fear that the teacher would make me shake his hand and move me from my place beside Dombodán. Don Gregorio's way of showing extreme anger was silence.

'If you won't be quiet, then I will.'

And he would go over to the big window and stare out at Mount Sinaí. It was a prolonged, troubling silence, as if he had abandoned us in some strange country. I soon came to understand that our teacher's silence was the worst punishment imaginable, because he could turn everything he touched into a fascinating story. The story might begin with a piece of paper, then set off down the Amazon and end up with the systole and diastole of the heart. Everything was connected, everything had meaning. Grass, a sheep, wool, feeling cold. When the teacher went over to the map of the world, we were as attentive as if the screen at the Rex Cinema was about to light up. We felt the fear of the Indians when they heard for the first time the neighing of horses and the boom of the harquebus. We rode on the backs of Hannibal's elephants through the snows of the Alps, on the way to Rome. We fought with sticks and stones in Ponte Sampaio against Napoleon's troops. But it wasn't all wars. We forged sickles and ploughshares in Incio's smithy. We wrote love poems in Provence and on the Vigo sea. We built the Pórtico da Gloria. We planted the potatoes that were first brought from South America and we emigrated there when the potato blight struck.

'Potatoes come from South America,' I told my mother at supper time, when she put my plate in front of me.

'What do you mean, they come from South America? There have always been potatoes,' she declared.

'No, before, people ate chestnuts. And corn comes from South America too.' That was the first time I had ever felt that, thanks to the teacher, I knew important things about our world that they, my parents, did not.

The most fascinating lessons at school, though, were when the teacher talked about nature. Water spiders invented the submarine. Ants kept flocks that gave them sweet milk and they also cultivated fungi. There was a bird in Australia that painted its nest brilliant colours, using a kind of oil it made from vegetable dyes. I'll never forget its name. It was called the bowerbird. The male would place an orchid in the new nest in order to attract the female.

Such was my interest that I became Don Gregorio's supplier of insects, as well as his keenest student. On certain Saturdays and public holidays, he would collect me at my house, and we would set off together for the day. We would wander along by the river, through meadows, over rocks, and we would climb Mount Sinaí. For me, every one of those trips was like a voyage of discovery. We would always return with some treasure. A praying mantis. A dragonfly. A stag beetle. And a different butterfly every time, although I can only remember the name of one, which the teacher called an Iris and which glowed beautifully as it rested on the mud or the dung.

On the way back, we would sing as we walked, like two old friends. On Mondays, at school, the teacher would say: 'Right, now we're going to talk about Sparrow's insects.'

My parents felt very honoured by the teacher's interest in me. On the days when we went out together, my mother would prepare a picnic for the two of us. 'There's no need, Señora, I've eaten already,' Don Gregorio would insist. But when we returned, he would say: 'Thank you, Señora, the picnic was delicious.'

'I'm sure he doesn't always get enough to eat,' my mother would say later that night.

'Teachers don't earn nearly as much as they should,' my father would declare very solemnly. 'They're the guiding light of the Republic.'

'Oh, the Republic, the Republic! Lord knows where that will lead . . .'

My father was a Republican, my mother wasn't. I mean that my mother was the kind of woman who went to mass every day and, to her, the Republicans seemed like the enemies of the Church. They tried not to quarrel when I was there, but sometimes I would accidentally walk in on an argument.

'What have you got against Azaña? That priest's been filling your head with stupid ideas.'

'I go to mass to pray,' my mother said.

'You do, but the priest doesn't.'

One day, when Don Gregorio came to pick me up in order to go hunting for butterflies, my father said to him that, if Don Gregorio didn't mind, he'd like to measure him up for a suit.

'A suit?'

'Don't be offended, Don Gregorio. I just wanted to do something for you and the only thing I know is making suits.'

The teacher glanced round him, embarrassed.

'It's my trade,' said my father with a smile.

'Well, I've always had the greatest respect for all the trades,' the teacher said at last.

Don Gregorio wore that suit for a year and he was wearing it on the

day in July 1936 when he bumped into me in the Alameda, on his way to
the town hall.

'Hello there, Sparrow, how are things? Now this, I hope, will be the
year when we finally get to see the butterfly's tongue.'

Something strange was happening. Everyone seemed to be in a hurry,
yet they didn't move. Those who were looking straight ahead, suddenly
spun round. Those who were looking to the right, turned towards the left.
Cordeiro, the sweeper-up of rubbish and dry leaves, was sitting on a bench
near the bandstand. I had never seen Cordeiro sitting on a bench. He was
looking straight up, shading his eyes with his hand. When Cordeiro did
that and when the birds fell silent, it meant that a storm was
approaching.

I heard the roar of a solitary motorbike. It was a policeman with a flag
lashed to the back seat. He drove past the town hall and looked at the
men talking anxiously beneath the arcade. He yelled: 'Long live Spain!'
and sped off again, the bike leaving behind it a trail of explosions.

Mothers started calling to their children. At home it was as if my
grandmother had died all over again. My father was filling the ashtray
with cigarette ends, and my mother was crying and doing nonsensical
things, like turning on the tap to wash the clean plates and putting the
dirty ones away unwashed.

Someone knocked at the door and my parents stared uneasily at the
handle. It was Amelia, our neighbour, who worked for the wealthy Suárez.

'Have you heard what's going on?' she said. 'In A Coruña the soldiers
have declared a state of war. They're attacking the regional governor's
office.'

'Good heavens!' said my mother, crossing herself.

'And here,' Amelia went on in a low voice, as if the walls might have
ears, 'they say that the mayor asked the chief of police to come and see
him, but that he sent word to say he was ill.'

The next day they wouldn't let me go outside. I stood staring out of the
window and all the people who passed by looked to me like shrunken
shadows, as if winter had suddenly started and the wind had blown away
all the sparrows in the Alameda like so many dead leaves.

Troops arrived from La Coruña and occupied the town hall. Mama went out to mass and came back looking pale and sad, as if she had aged in that half hour.

'Terrible things are happening, Ramón,' I heard her say to my father, her voice broken by tears. He too had aged. Worse still, he seemed to have lost all volition. He had slumped down in an armchair and wouldn't move from there. He didn't speak. He didn't want to eat.

'We'll have to burn anything that might compromise you, Ramón. Newspapers, books, everything.'

During that time, it was my mother who took the initiative. One morning, she made my father get dressed up properly and took him with her to mass. When they came back, she said to me: 'Come along, Moncho, you're coming with us to the Alameda.' She brought out my best clothes and, while she was helping me to do the knot in my tie, she said in a very serious voice: 'Just remember, Moncho, Papa was never a Republican. Papa was never a friend of the mayor. Papa never spoke ill of the priests. And another very important thing, Moncho, Papa never gave the teacher a suit.'

'Yes, he did.'

'No, Moncho, he didn't. Do you understand? He never gave him a suit.'

'No, Mama, he didn't.'

The Alameda was full of people in their Sunday best. People had come down from the villages too, women all in black, local men in waistcoats and hats, frightened-looking children, preceded by blue-shirted men with pistols in their belts. Two lines of soldiers were opening up a path from the town hall steps down to some trucks with covered trailers, like the ones used to transport cattle to the big market. But the Alameda was filled not with the bustle of market days, but with a grave silence, like during Holy Week. Nobody said hello. They didn't even seem to recognize each other. All eyes were on the front of the town hall.

A policeman half-opened the town hall door and scanned the crowd. Then he flung the door open and made a gesture with his arm. Out of the dark mouth of the building, escorted by other policemen, came the detainees. They were silent, bound hand and foot and roped together. I didn't know the names of all of them, but I knew their faces. The mayor, the men from the labour union, the librarian from the workers' club, Charli, the singer with the Sol y Vida Orchestra, the stonemason everyone called Hercules and who was Dombodán's father . . . And at the end of the line, hunchbacked and ugly as a toad, came the teacher.

A few shouted orders and isolated cries echoed along the Alameda like firecrackers. Gradually, a murmur began to emerge from the crowd, a murmur that finally took up those insults:

'Traitors! Criminals! Reds!'

'You shout too, Ramón, for God's sake, shout!' My mother was gripping my father's arm, as if it took all her strength to keep him from collapsing. 'Let people see you shouting, Ramón, make sure they see you!'

And then I heard my father saying in the faintest of voices: 'Traitors!' And then, getting louder and louder: 'Criminals! Reds!' He freed himself from my mother's grip and approached the line of soldiers, his furious gaze fixed on the teacher. 'Murderer! Anarchist! Monster!'

Now my mother was trying to hold him back and tugging discreetly at his jacket. But he had lost all control. 'Bastard! Son of a bitch!' I had never heard him call anyone that, not even the football referee. 'Not that his mother's to blame, Moncho, remember that.' But now he turned his maddened, threatening gaze on me, his eyes filled with tears and blood. 'You shout too, Monchiño, you shout too!'

When the trucks drew away, laden with prisoners, I was one of the children who ran behind them, throwing stones. I searched desperately for the teacher's face, so that I could call him traitor and criminal. But the convoy was already just a distant cloud of dust, and as I stood in the middle of the Alameda, my fists clenched, all I could do was to mutter angrily: 'Toad! Bowerbird! Iris!'

CARLOS CASTÁN

The Usher

My Uncle Avelino wouldn't let me go to the cinema. It seemed that I was living with them purely in order to study, which, according to him, I should be doing at all hours. Who did I think I was? 'Life's no picnic,' he would say, 'someone back there in the village is slaving away just so you won't turn out to be a complete dickhead.' And so it was only on those afternoons when he stayed late at the office that – with the connivance of Aunt Feli, who reluctantly turned a blind eye in order to avoid any unpleasantness – I was able to sneak off to the warm refuge of one of the local cinemas, balconies onto a technicolour paradise of bandits and girls, battles and oceans, that made me forget for a moment the grey monotony of days spent in a state of dull hopelessness.

Then my uncle fell ill, and I had to sit in his dim, fever-filled bedroom reading the paper to him. Aunt Feli would keep interrupting us with glasses of milk or lemon juice and spoonfuls of a viscous syrup that impregnated everything with the smell of death and always dripped onto the sheets, leaving a few black drops, which, for me, were like a hint of something terrible to come.

Obviously, the absence of someone who has died isn't something tangible, but it almost is. It isn't just the shadow that seems to glide along corridors and hide in the wardrobes where his empty suits still hang, along with a pair of black shoes that always look as if they were about to start

Carlos Castán (b. 1960) was born in Barcelona, graduated in philosophy from the Universidad Autónoma in Madrid, and has worked as a teacher in various secondary schools. He has always specialized in the short story and his stories have appeared in many literary reviews and anthologies in Spain.

walking, with the slight limp acquired in his days in the army, and once again pursue me through the apartment, shouting: 'I'll teach you, you little bastard!' It isn't that old business of hearing coughs in the middle of the night echoing forth from the half-open door of what used to be his bedroom or of transparent ghosts or groaning pipes or the wind shaking the shutters. The absence of someone recently deceased is, above all, a scrap of air slightly denser than the rest, and which retains his smell and alights on objects like the shadow of a cloud.

Before he died, Uncle Avelino had asked me to take care of his wife, poor Aunt Feli, who was left behind, a broken woman, with nothing but her futile needlework and her radio programmes. He gripped my arm hard and told me there were to be no trips to the cinema, no leaving her alone; we were to have afternoon tea together and then I was to do my homework with her at my side, doing her sewing. And that is what I did. I'd get back from school without lingering on the way and spread out my homework and my comics on the kitchen table, resigned to a homely evening of radio and Aunt Feli, of serials and sighs, boredom and a bit of bread and chocolate.

But I needed those double bills like a starving man needs food, and I began occasionally to leave my aunt on her own and lose myself in those temples of remote dreams – the local cinemas. One afternoon, in the darkness of the Savoy, it seemed to me that the usher smelled just like my uncle, of old soup and tobacco, that he had the exact same limp, the same foul breath. I managed to overcome the trembling in my legs and escape out into the street, which, at that hour, was a reassuring explosion of traffic and light.

I never went back to that cinema, but the same thing happened later on in the Metropolitan and, days later, in the Montija, and again in the Lido: the dark figure of my Uncle Avelino, torch in hand, the unmistakable smell, the dead eyes peering into the dark of the theatre, possibly seeking me out among the rows of threadbare seats, calling me to account for my broken promise, for leaving his widow to eat her afternoon tea alone.

One night, after the final showing, I dared to wait outside for that figure to emerge. I crouched on the pavement opposite, waiting for him to come out, with the collar of his overcoat turned up, like in a spy movie, in the faint hope that it was all in my imagination, mere glimmerings from the well of guilt I sometimes felt inside me. In the darkness, I thought I saw his shape heading off along the street. For a while, I followed those weary steps, which didn't pause once outside the brightly lit shop windows or at the pedestrian lights on red. We never know where they come from, the forces that lead us to perdition, and, for a moment, I considered running to catch him up, demanding to know what was going on, to ask his forgiveness, to take that hand which, on a few rare occasions, had stroked my head as I read out the news from a world that was already ceasing to be his. For some reason, though, I slowed my pace and ended up losing sight of that figure among a whole blurred legion of lame men walking along in the rain, all with their backs to me, all wearing identical overcoats, all crossing the bridge that led to the cemetery.

TERESA SOLANA

The Second Mrs Appleton

Translated from the Catalan by Peter Bush

There wasn't a day in the last eighteen months when Mr Appleton hadn't rued divorcing the first Mrs Appleton in order to marry the second Mrs Appleton (who rejoiced in the first name of Paige). Mr Appleton was a career diplomat and had met his second wife in the offices of the British Embassy in Rome where he was the ambassador and she was a part-time, low-level temp. Mr Appleton was fifty-six when he made the acquaintance of the second Mrs Appleton, who was twenty-five.

Mr Appleton was born in Woodstock, a small town located next to Blenheim Palace, the country residence of the Duke of Marlborough, and was privileged to be one of the cohort of distant relatives of the first duke of the tribe – the famous 'Marlborough's gone to war' – and the illustrious Winston Churchill. He had been a contemporary of Violet, the first Mrs Appleton, at Oxford, where they were both students, and married her shortly before taking up what was to be his first diplomatic posting abroad and packing their bags to go to Kampala.

Mr Appleton had come to the embassy in Rome thirty years after beginning that life as a vagabond bureaucrat in the capital of Uganda, heralded by a much-vaunted series of successes and a marriage that had lasted thirty years and given him two children. Little did Mr Appleton imagine his life would be turned upside down in the Italian capital, that

Teresa Solana (b. 1962) was born in Barcelona and now lives in Oxford. She writes in Catalan and Spanish, translating her books both ways. She did her degree in philosophy, then became a literary translator, directing the National Translation Centre in Tarazona, Spain, for seven years. Her first novel, *A Not So Perfect Crime*, won the 2007 Brigada 21 Prize for best *noir* in Catalan and *A Shortcut to Paradise*, her second, was shortlisted for the 2008 Salambó Prize for Best Novel in Catalan. This story comes from *The First Prehistoric Serial Killer and Other Stories*.

he'd divorce and re-marry, let alone that he'd soon be regretting replacing the competent, discreet first Mrs Appleton with the young, scatty Paige.

As a man of austere character and rigid persuasions, Mr Appleton disapproved of extramarital entanglements, which he criticized in private. Nevertheless, the arrival on the scene in Rome of the second Mrs Appleton caught him at a moment in his life when the past seemed to stretch out like a piece of chewing gum and the future to shorten like the days of winter, and he decided to make an exception. He so liked the exception that what was meant simply as a weekend fling – a weekend when the first Mrs Appleton was visiting their children in London – finally turned into a torrid affair that would lead him back to the altar.

The second Mrs Appleton liked to tell people it had been love at first sight, and although *he* wasn't so happy to recall that moment – for when the spark ignited he was still married to the first Mrs Appleton and their audience would be sure to compare dates – the fact was that Mr Appleton had suffered a *coup de foudre* in the Italian capital and had been knocked for six.

The lack of an attractive physique certainly wasn't among the second Mrs Appleton's defects, and that was a decisive factor in triggering their affair. The second Mrs Appleton was a freckle-faced English woman with wild, blonde hair, a green-eyed lioness with a come-on smile and moist lips and all the necessary curves and bra sizes to make headway in life without nurturing any other talents. Mr Appleton's sex life, it has to be said, had never been characterized by fireworks, but the first Mrs Appleton's encounter with the menopause had reduced it to the category of a damp squib he was hard pressed to ignite half a dozen times a year. Unlike Violet, the second Mrs Appleton possessed all the splendour of the best pyrotechnics on New Year's Eve, and the diplomat was so dazzled by her display of rockets, bangers, Roman candles, crackers, yellow rain and multicoloured fountains that, when the first Mrs Appleton returned from London, he quickly gave her a new credit card and sent her off to holiday by herself in New York.

For a couple of weeks, while the first Mrs Appleton went to concerts and emptied the shops in Manhattan, Mr Appleton and the second Mrs Appleton had a ball filling embassy annexes and Rome's hotels with a fug of pheromones. However, the second Mrs Appleton, unwilling to play a secondary role in that *ménage à trois*, wasn't slow in confronting Mr Appleton with a choice between transforming the first Mrs Appleton into the ex-Mrs Appleton or returning to a diet of damp squibs. Overwhelmed by a second rush of adolescence to his groin – which only lacked a spate of acne – Mr Appleton didn't think twice: he asked Violet for a divorce and regaled the soon-to-be second Mrs Appleton with a diamond-and-emerald ring to put a seal on their betrothal.

Shortly after marrying the second Mrs Appleton in a discreet ceremony in Rome, Mr Appleton was appointed ambassador to Washington, and the couple began to experience problems. The second Mrs Appleton had always looked forward to living in the United States, but her enthusiasm soon waned when she discovered that Washington wasn't as entertaining as Rome and Americans weren't as dishy as Italians. Unlike the first Mrs Appleton, the second Mrs Appleton wasn't used to the slavish restrictions of protocol, and soon tired of performing like a dummy at banquets and interminable receptions. Her ignorance in any area that wasn't covered by the glossies made her stick out like a sore thumb, and, forced to remain silent most of the time, she was bored stiff. Tedium led her to chase the waiters and seek refuge in champagne, and champagne liberated her tongue and encouraged her to say the first thing that entered her head.

The first Mrs Appleton had set very high standards, and Mr Appleton made comparisons. The first Mrs Appleton had a degree in French literature, was the cousin twice removed of a second cousin of the queen and completely mastered the art of etiquette. In the case of the second Mrs Appleton, she had a degree in interior design from Buckinghamshire New University – a university that at the time enjoyed the dubious honour of hovering near the bottom in the British universities league table – and lacked the pedigree that equips one's DNA with the ability to match flowers, tablecloths and cutlery, and she was, above all, incapable of keeping her mouth shut. If the first Mrs Appleton knew when to be quiet without Mr Appleton having to give her a wink or kick her under the table, the second Mrs Appleton was an expert at putting her foot in it at the most inglorious of moments.

Mr Appleton soon had to spend more time keeping an eye on his wife than on international politics. However, this didn't curtail the second Mrs

Appleton's indiscretions or prevent the provocative dresses she wore –
she'd begun to shorten her skirts and lower her necklines dangerously – from
becoming a matter of gossip in Washington, and the jokes about the lack
of know-how of the ambassador's ever-so-young wife soon crossed the
pond and came to the attention of Downing Street. Realizing the risks
his brand-new wife's inexperience was exposing him to, Mr Appleton
began to long for the professional *savoir faire* of his first wife and to regret
divorcing her.

Rock-bottom was reached when they'd been in Washington for six
months, and the minister in charge asked him to organize a banquet to
conclude a summit meeting. Mr Appleton saw this as a test of his ability
to represent Great Britain in the United States and was conscious of what
was at stake: he decided to take the bull by the horns and leave the second
Mrs Appleton on the periphery of all the preparations.

With the subtlety that was the stock-in-trade of the profession he had
chosen, Mr Appleton asked the second Mrs Appleton to offer her apologies on the day of the reception on the excuse that she had flu, and she
readily agreed. However, she soon regretted acquiescing so meekly to her
husband's peculiar request, and on the day of the dinner she had second
thoughts and asked the waiters to add another place at the top table. What
sense did it make, she told herself, for Mr Appleton to have such a young,
pretty and amusing wife and keep her under wraps?

While he was waiting for his guests to arrive at the embassy, Mr Appleton had to suppress a panic attack when he saw his wife slink into the
reception room, where the aperitifs were being served, in a figure-hugging
black satin dress that left little to the imagination. Intimidated by the
sight of so many heads of state and toffee-nosed first ladies, the second
Mrs Appleton managed to remain reasonably sober until the desserts,
when the appearance of bottles of bubbly meant the lack of inhibition she
had begun to feel after a few cocktails was transformed into out-and-out
euphoria, and she felt the need to share her extravagant excesses with all
the other guests.

The less-than-appropriate comments made by the second Mrs Appleton
on delicate issues of international politics led to Mr Appleton's immediate
dismissal the morning after and he was forced to return to London, where
he had to choose between a small, windowless office in a Whitehall

basement or premature retirement. However, Mr Appleton still had friends in the British capital, and, after knocking on lots of doors and calling in old favours, he managed to get a posting to Barcelona as a replacement for the outgoing consul. Everybody knew that the move from ambassador to consul was to plummet down the diplomatic ladder, but Mr Appleton explained it away by saying it was a personal favour he was doing the Prime Minister who required someone she could trust in the Catalan capital to keep her informed about the manoeuvres of the independence-bound government and the strategies of the opposition.

The second Mrs Appleton was delighted by the idea of going to Barcelona. She'd never been there, but she'd seen the Woody Allen film and been bowled over by the colourful portrait the filmmaker had painted of the city. The prospect of hobnobbing with bohemian artists and toreros and spending the day on the beach quaffing sangria translated into a temporary resurgence of her amatory habits that had recently gone into hibernation. Infected by his wife's youthful ardour, Mr Appleton decided to give their marriage a second chance, trusting that Paige had learned her lesson.

Nonetheless, what promised to be a second honeymoon on the Med was short-lived. From the moment she arrived in Barcelona, the second Mrs Appleton busied herself redecorating the house they'd rented in Sarrià and shopping on the Passeig de Gràcia; however, neglecting to read the memorandum they'd sent her from London, she inadvertently, during the ceremony to accredit the new consul at the Palace of the Generalitat, put her foot in it yet again. She wondered out loud why the hell the Catalans had to speak Catalan if they could already speak Spanish, which didn't go down at all well, and a shamefaced Mr Appleton had to humiliate himself offering all manner of apologies to avoid the autonomous government's protests reaching a formal level and the Foreign Office in London. In the end, there was no such fallout, but Mr Appleton saw that the thread supporting the sword of Damocles hanging over his career was fraying by the second.

The second Mrs Appleton was one big disappointment. And not simply because her lack of brainpower had destroyed his ambition to retire in the most important embassy on the planet, but also because the antidepressants and tranquillizers she'd started taking in order to survive the boredom of diplomatic life had transformed the revitalized fireworks of their sex life into a low-budget backstreet fling. Aware that their sexual jamboree, like his career, was in implacable decline, he started to weigh up the idea of divorcing the second Mrs Appleton and trying to get back together with his ex.

However, Mr Appleton soon discovered that disentangling himself from the second Mrs Appleton was going to be far from easy. His present consort wasn't as docile as his first, and, when he insinuated that perhaps the moment had come to end a relationship that was foundering rather than developing, the second Mrs Appleton reacted by rejecting the option of divorce and threatening to unleash a scandal of epic proportions with a kiss-and-tell interview to the *Sun* if he sent a lawyer her way.

That was the day Mr Appleton sidelined the divorce option and seriously began to contemplate the possibility of becoming a widower.

With the meticulous attention to detail that had been a feature of his life, Mr Appleton began to assess the various alternatives on offer to get rid of the second Mrs Appleton via the convenient method of despatching her to the Other Side. He felt that suicide was the least risky avenue, and, making the most of a note in his possession that could be read as a goodbye message, he wasted no time in activating the plan that had occurred to him.

Mr Appleton had forbidden the second Mrs Appleton, in no uncertain terms, from sending photos or messages by phone (he was afraid she'd hit the wrong key and send her documents to the wrong person's inbox), and as a result she had become accustomed to leaving him short notes on the pillow or bedside table when she felt a need to apologize after she had shown him up yet again. Mr Appleton quickly read these notes and threw them in the wastepaper bin (her spelling mistakes really grated on him), but, luckily, he had kept one she had written to him in Washington, immediately after the reception where she had ruined his career. The handwritten note said, 'I'm so sorry, love', and was signed off with her Christian name. The only drawback was that, under her signature, the second Mrs Appleton had drawn an erect penis and two hairy testicles, which she had enhanced with a sensual kiss from her red lips. It didn't look like your average suicide note, but as everyone in Barcelona was becoming familiar with the second Mrs Appleton's wayward character and aversion to formalities, Mr Appleton thought it would pass muster and decided to go for it.

Mr Appleton chose a Saturday early in September, when their maid was on holiday, to terminate his wife's life. It was a day he had offered to accompany a member of the English parliament to see a performance of *The Twilight of the Gods* at the Liceu opera house. The second Mrs Appleton hated opera, and, knowing his wife's phobias, Mr Appleton assumed she would refuse to swallow four and a half hours of Wagner just for the sake of appearances.

'Don't you worry, it's only a Labour MP. No need for you to suffer,' Mr Appleton told her, laughing it off.

The performance began at seven. At about four, when the second Mrs Appleton was curled up on the sofa channel hopping, Mr Appleton took a bottle of cava from the fridge, opened it, and slipped in a handful of tranquillizers he had previously rendered into powder with the help of a spoon. Then he walked into their dining room and, like a real gentleman, offered his wife a glass of cava knowing she wouldn't be able to resist the temptation of a drop of bubbly. Moved by this gesture, the second Mrs Appleton thanked him for thinking of her and quickly knocked back the whole bottle.

She immediately fell asleep. Mr Appleton helped her to their bedroom on the second floor of their house, but, rather than leaving her on top of the bed, he dragged her into the en-suite bathroom, stripped her and lifted her into the bath. While the bath was filling up with hot water, Mr Appleton fetched a knife from the kitchen, returned to the bathroom and slit her wrists.

While the second Mrs Appleton was knocking on St Peter's gates, Mr Appleton grabbed the bottle of cava, the glass and note he was intending to use as a suicide missive and took the lot into the bathroom. He slowly removed his fingerprints from places where they shouldn't be, checked that everything was in order and, finally, changed his clothes, combed his hair, sprayed scent over himself and went to the garage to get his car.

It was hot and muggy outside. Mr Appleton drove out of his garage but didn't notice the two men following close behind in a grey Ford Focus that had been parked outside his house for a couple of days. He had agreed to meet the Labour MP at 6.30 in the foyer of the Liceu and didn't want to arrive late, but the glass of cava (from a different bottle) that he had been obliged to drink in order not to arouse suspicion was making him feel queasy and headachy. As the opera they were about to see was on the long side, he decided to stop at a chemist's to buy some antacid pills and painkillers. He found one open on the Carrer Escoles Pies, double-parked his car and went inside.

The only people in the shop were an adolescent girl rummaging around on a shelf and the chemist. Mr Appleton strode towards the counter, not noticing the two men who had followed him from his house entering the shop. The second he heard male voices speaking threateningly in a language that sounded like Chinese and saw the expression of panic on the shop assistant's face, he swivelled round and found two Oriental-looking men and one pistol aimed at him.

Two shots rang out.

Mr Appleton fell to the floor, mortally wounded. And, while his life ebbed away, he remembered the fragment of a conversation he'd overheard in the course of one of those diplomatic ceremonies he'd had to attend and how the now-deceased second Mrs Appleton's ears had pricked up when a jaded inspector of the *mossos d'esquadra* had mentioned the new fashion for contracting Chinese hitmen through the pages of *The Times*.

JAVIER CERCAS

Against Optimism

Just as I do every morning, I leap jubilantly out of bed and, once my son has watched an episode of *Doraemon* on the telly ('We are the children of the Earth, / together we're going to build / a city full of marvels and of joy'), I put him in the car to take him to school. For the fifth time in the last two weeks, the car won't start, but, since I am an incurable optimist, instead of collapsing onto the steering wheel and sobbing my heart out, I call a taxi. In the taxi, I hear a Simon and Garfunkel song I haven't heard for twenty years, the one about the loneliness of a half-punch-drunk boxer dragging his failure of a life through the winter of a strange city. I drop my son off at school and go to work. By the time I walk into the classroom, I've already decided that, with Christmas nearly upon us, today's lesson will be about an article by Larra bearing the sardonic title *Happy Christmas 1836*, I say 'sardonic' because it describes a truly ghastly Christmas; it's a terribly sad article written by that father of all Spanish writers only two months before he blew his brains out with a pistol, and in that article he identifies the illness that keeps him permanently high on a mixture of ambition and impotence, namely, optimism, i.e. the absurd and incurable expectation that we are not put on Earth simply in order to be miserable. While I'm telling the class about the article, I notice the room filling with a growing hubbub of noise (a group of boys are

Javier Cercas (b. 1962) was born near Cáceres, but his family moved to Girona when he was four. He taught Spanish literature at the University of Illinois, Urbana, and continues to teach at the University of Girona. He published his first novel in 1987, but it was his fourth novel, *Soldados de Salamina* (2001), that brought him international recognition. He has since published six more novels. His work has brought him many prizes and has been translated into more than twenty languages.

playing cards; an old lady has produced some knitting from her bag; a few girls are debating the charms of Brad Pitt at the tops of their voices); undeterred, I decide to continue my lecture on Larra, mainly because I've just noticed that in the front row I do have one solitary listener – a really beautiful girl, who is sitting there, wide-eyed, drinking in my every word. Finally, the hour is up. In the corridor, I hear someone sigh: 'That was just incredible. The most boring class I've ever been to.' I turn to see who said this, and it's the beautiful, wide-eyed girl from the front row. I go to lunch. In the restaurant I meet the philosopher Josep Maria Ruiz Simón, who has just published a book about the thirteenth-century philosopher Ramon Llull. Being a polite fellow, he asks me how I am; being an equally polite fellow, I lie, but then, halfway through the meal, I break down; however, instead of sobbing my heart out over my macaroni, I tell him about Larra and Brad Pitt and the incurable disease that is optimism. Either out of solidarity or by way of consolation, Ruiz Simón asks if I'm familiar with the theory of the bonus. Surprised to hear that people talked about bonuses in Ramon Llull's time, I say no, I'm not. 'It wasn't Llull who came up with the theory, because he was an optimist,' he explains, 'it was Josep Pla. And, according to his theory, anything in this life that isn't a complete and utter catastrophe is a bonus. We turn the key in the ignition and the engine starts: bonus. We teach a class and someone actually listens: bonus. The optimist believes we were put on this Earth to be happy; the pessimist believes we have come here in order to avoid as many catastrophes as possible and to earn as many bonuses as we can. That's why the pessimist lives in a permanent state of contentment and tranquillity, while the optimist exists in a state of misery and disquiet.'

Chesterton says there are two types of people: those who divide people into two types of people and those who don't. On my way to pick up my son from school, I amuse myself dividing people into optimists and pessimists. Ambrose Bierce, for example, was more optimistic than Larra and Llull, but not as optimistic as Doraemon, which is why he came up with the following definition of the word 'year': 'a period of three-hundred-and-sixty-five disappointments'. On the other hand, Ricardo Reis, who, I suspect, was more pessimistic than Ruiz Simón, but less so than Pla, wrote: 'If you expect nothing, then whatever the day may bring, however little, will be a lot.' I pick my son up from school and, when we arrive home, I announce that he's never going to watch another episode about that insane optimist, Doraemon. To compensate for the ravages of the day, and given that Christmas is nearly upon us, I'm just about to put on the video of *It's a Wonderful Life*, that most optimistic of films made by that most optimistic of Hollywood directors, but I stop myself just in time and instead watch a John Huston film with the sardonic title *Fat City*, sardonic because it's a truly ghastly city, although you could also interpret it as meaning *Wow, What a City!* Or, better still, *City of Marvels and of Joy*, and, while I watch that grim film, I think about Simon and Garfunkel's boxer and about Larra, who lived fast and died young and left a good-looking corpse, and I tell myself that Huston was right: we all live exasperatingly slowly and will probably die old and leave a stinking corpse, and end up like those two boxers, lonely, half-punch-drunk losers adrift in a grim city, peeing blood before we go into the ring, high on a mixture of ambition and impotence, and engaged in a fight to the death with our own shadow in an entirely empty stadium. And everything else is a bonus.

ELOY TIZÓN

About the Wedding

Translated by Kit Maude

She was going to get married, she said.

And then she started to laugh.

She'd decided to drop out of university halfway through her course, we weren't expecting that, were we? Sofia blurted this out all in one go without stopping for breath. She said she was in love with a guy from her home town who wore pebble glasses, they were sending him to work overseas with a foreign research grant, and, rather than letting him escape, she wanted to marry him, the guy from her home town, and go with him so they could live together in Melbourne or wherever, and she was leaving all her books behind, everything else could just go to hell, she wanted to travel.

Sofia was telling us all this, and we were surprised she was telling us anything at all. We barely knew Sofia, we weren't close, we saw her every now and again and said hello and goodbye in the lift or when we passed her in the halls of the Faculty of Education. She was always nervous, agitated, arms full of bundles of notes, blowing her fringe out of her eyes, even though it always flopped back down again. Oh, that rebellious fringe. We instinctively knew we should ignore her when we sat at the same table in the students' canteen or in the language lab reading room.

One day, she brought a basket full of turtles into class.

We neither liked nor disliked her. She was just Sofia Ardiles, with her

Eloy Tizón (b. 1964) was born in Madrid and has written novels and short stories. His novel *Seda salvaje* was shortlisted for the 1995 Premio Herralde, and his 1992 story collection *Velocidad de los jardines* was chosen by the critics of *El País* as one of the hundred most interesting books in Spanish of the last twenty-five years.

academic folders, her notes, her grating nervousness, her green fingernails and her untameable fringe flopping over her eyes, whereas the three of us had been friends since childhood, inseparable, from nursery school to sharing a flat at uni, always together, clones and complete opposites, the three of us like islands united by the very thing that separates them. We shared the same past – Rodrigo, Mario and Samuel – and we'd often exchange long, knowing gazes that declared: we're close friends, we don't need words to understand each other.

But there she was, Sofia, stubbornly insisting on inviting us to her wedding, someone's actually getting married for once, she said to us breathlessly, blowing the fringe off her forehead, even though it fell back immediately, covering her eyes, as though this meant something, and maybe it did. Who knows? She took sheaves of papers out of her bag and solemnly, like a spy, unfolded rustling road maps to explain right there and then how to get to the wedding, along with the phone numbers of youth hostels, campsites, toll roads, bridges and bypasses, handing out thick cards printed with the dates and routes highlighted in fluorescent marker, all to persuade us to accept the invitation, please, please, please, we had to be there, anything to help make the trip to Mudela del Valle, the chosen venue for the event about 600 kilometres north of the city, easier. It's full of mountains, rocks and cows, you can't miss it.

Go to a stranger's wedding? Rodrigo thought. Why not? thought Mario. The weekend of the wedding's still a long way off, and we don't have anything better to do, thought Samuel. We didn't need to think twice, at the time, we'd grab any excuse to get away, a wedding is just another excuse, we said to ourselves, it's no big deal.

Nothing special planned, no girls or exams on the horizon, so one Friday after dinner we pooled our money to buy a wedding gift for Sofia, threw three dark suits, some new shoes, white shirts and black ties into the boot of the car, filled a Thermos flask with coffee, packed the glove compartment with CDs – we didn't want to run out of music – and set off in silence on the long journey north, on that impulsive trip to Sofia's wedding in Mudela del Valle with no real idea as to why we were going or what we would find when we got there.

We travelled expectantly, taking turns to drive the mustard-coloured convertible Mario's father had loaned us, telling us to take good care of it and not do anything crazy, he didn't want to see a scratch or a dent on it, understand? Here are the keys, they glittered for a moment in his hands, Rodrigo, Mario and Samuel, the three of us inseparable friends ever since nursery.

Mustard.

The three of us shared everything, morning, noon and night, secrets and debts, joys and hangovers, books, highs and lows, Sundays sunk in gloom, days spent staring at our hands, the occasional casual girlfriend, everything in triplicate, even that unforgettable afternoon when, high on amphetamine-induced enthusiasm, we discovered the Gran Vía in Madrid with all its signs lit up against the gas-green sky and the row of buildings glinting like quartz in a chromium desert light. The light suddenly went crazy, it turned crude and stupid, it became a bipolar light, and at that very moment, right at that very moment, a Chinese woman's hair burst into flames.

So we left behind us the neon lights and the high plains, the abandoned, graffiti-spattered cement factories, the pine-tree-lined ring roads, the unlikely flower beds tucked between concrete blocks, the fields of sunflowers with centre partings, the blond fire of the maizefields, advancing steadily through the night, going north, inexorably north, towards Sofía and her wedding in the mountains, which, for some mysterious reason, seemed to be reeling us in, hypnotically dragging the three of us along on invisible threads, guiding us through the darkness.

The road was a conveyor belt of bonfires. Someone rolled and lit a joint, and we started to pass it around, taking turns to toke, singing songs together, one of us singing the first few notes and the others joining in, the smoke twisting up in slow spirals and opening aniseed flowers in our lungs, and suddenly it started to get really hot, don't you think it's hot? And we laughed for no reason, the three of us in the car, on the eve of the wedding, the end of the shared joint glowing against the dark glass like a small, motorized torch, while the night swept over the car roof. Mushrooms started to grow in the glove compartment. The motorway unfolded ahead of us, taking on the shape of a cylindrical tube that sucked and sipped at us, and the air smelled of menthol mouthwash.

The final stretch of the journey was quite a lot slower and more tiring than we'd expected; some of the local roads weren't very well signposted or were closed for works, and we got lost a few times, circling pointlessly around, going back on ourselves, thinking we knew where we were heading. Dizzy and exhausted from all those wrong turns, we finally parked for the night to grab a brief nap in the convertible, next to a dimly lit village petrol station, a hamlet of white cubes squeezed awkwardly together at the bottom of a gloomy ravine amid the intermittent barking of dogs, a Romanesque church tower, weary muscles, the odometer spinning more and more slowly, the never-ending ribbon of road that continued to rewind in our dreams, again and again, a broken, saurian line.

Purely by chance we woke up in Mudela. We'd reached our destination precisely when we'd assumed we were irrevocably lost. We just about had time to spruce ourselves up at the petrol station, empty our bladders, change our clothes, shave quickly and run along the cobbled streets to the town hall in the centre of the main square, under the watchful eyes of locals with agricultural faces and rustic hair, to join the crowd hailing the newlyweds with cheers, whistles and confetti.

It was a beautiful May morning, barely a cloud in the sky, just the right day to recover from a tiring journey or, perhaps, for a civil marriage. Maybe the weekend wasn't such a lost cause after all. We were at the wedding, and we were still travelling, eating up the miles, checking road maps, examining signposts and the faces of the other guests as they passed, flashing lights and savoury crackers, hard shoulders and cleavage, an intriguing combination.

Tables. Chairs. Trees with giraffe necks. A finger with surgical tape pointing at something in the distance: over there. The blue puddle of a lake in the mountains. A high, sleepy sky dominated by a huge, operatic cloud. Next to it, a more timid, blurry cloud with shifting colours, like when you look at a 3D photo without the proper glasses.

There are a lot of us, about two hundred. Four large barbecues are roasting an endless array of meat and fish. Since we don't know anyone and no one knows us, we're placed at the table for single people, surrounded by other single men and women, neither too close nor too far from the four-tiered wedding cake.

So the hours passed, and the sky filled with more clouds, gradually changing colour, again and again, day and night, the waters in the lake trembled and rippled and grew smooth, and we were all a little smart and a little stupid, a little handsome and a little ugly, a little quick and a little slow. In the tent lit up with paper lanterns there were jokes and games, the popping of corks, commotion and squeals from the children's table.

Butterflies flitted in and out of the tent, fluttering about among the guests, their wings reflected momentarily in the iridescent sheen of a glass of wine or hypnotized by the glittering flash of a fork.

One of the groom's brothers, who had his arm in a sling, went up to the podium and, in a good strong voice, recited a poem he'd written especially for the occasion. It was greeted with applause. A portly, red-nosed man in a military uniform sang a song, and all the guests joined in the chorus with more enthusiasm than skill. More applause. When night fell and the desserts were served, it was time for the toasts. We drained our glasses, the champagne flowed, the band started to play and the couples got up to dance. We took turns dancing with some very tall girls, not very pretty but very friendly, who we'd just met at the singles' table, and who had come to support the groom, and with them we drank more Martinis than we should have and had to slip out to the portable toilets a few times, dodging the children of all ages who were running around, sprinting, playing, jumping and laughing: a rainbow of children.

The moon rises among the trees. Sparklers are lit. Trails of light and shadow lick at the hands and faces of those present. A professional photographer wanders around taking snapshots on the fly, and a bunch of amateur cameras buzz and store away their digital memories for posterity.

It was after midnight when the tall girls who were friends of the groom came to sit on our laps without asking permission, and then it was us sitting on the laps of the single girls to keep the joke going or because the feast had gone on for so long that we'd forgotten what we were doing there and why and didn't understand when they said, 'That's not fair! That's cheating!'

Finally, not long before the party came to an end, someone came up behind us and covered our eyes with her hands, asking 'Guess who?' and there she was with her shining eyes, blowing her fringe out of the way, she seemed really excited, touching us and mussing our hair, stroking our chins and hands, and we started to tell her how beautiful she looked, but Sofia cut us off, telling us not to talk nonsense, and saying again how much she loved us, yes, she loved us all so much, especially the three of us, no, really. She hated the idea that she'd be losing us, she hated being away from us for a second, never, never, never, she'd rather lose an eye.

And then she started crying, nervously wiping her eyes with the sleeve of her dress. She hugged us all as she said in an amusingly serious tone, 'I'm not crying, I'm not, even if it looks like I am.'

And we squeezed her so tight that we could feel her pounding heart and pulse, and she cupped our faces with her hands and stared at us hard through the dampness of her tears, as if fascinated, frenziedly kissing our foreheads, mouths, teeth and hair, once, twice, thrice, swearing by everything sacred that we were her best friends, her soulmates, that she loved us more than anything in the world, she adored us she said, crying, coughing, hiccuping, then laughing, oh, I'm so happy, quite mad with happiness.

And she made as if to leave us. She took a few steps, then performed a kind of pirouette and came straight back, no, she couldn't leave us, she couldn't separate herself from us, and she kept asking if we wanted more cake, insisting that we have something more to eat and drink, we were too skinny, our hair was too long and, besides, we were her favourite guests, we mustn't be difficult now, come on, wasn't the cake good? We had to have some more for her sake, for Sofia, she'd loved us from the moment she saw us in the halls of the Faculty of Education, it was love at first sight.

'You don't want to make me angry now, do you?'

And, pretending to be offended, she shoved a huge slice of cake in our mouths, so big it barely fit, Sofia was almost choking us, we protested, our mouths full of cake, it was hard to swallow so much cream, we had to wash it down with cava and chew energetically, but we had to admit that the cake was really good, there was no denying it.

She made as if to leave, but then again changed her mind and came back because marriage was, could be, a dark, intimidating place with no simultaneous translation available, like getting dizzy or falling over, incomprehensible, like that chair there, no, like that one, but we, scruffy-haired boys, wouldn't understand it, I'm so thirsty, I'm so hungry, I'm so everything, and there was the grief and courage involved in getting married, taking on another surname, having to live so far away from home, the fear of one day forgetting everything, our faces, and then dying alone. So she asked our permission, as a tribute to this moment, to name her children after us when they came along, Rodrigo, Mario and Samuel, and she said the names all together: rodrigomarioandsamuel.

And, moved by her own show of emotion and by the idea of those three bewildered children (as though their lives were in danger), Sofia hugged us again and kissed us on the lips, on the chin, on our eyebrows, snuffling our necks and saying once again how much she loved us, adored us, truly loved us, the three of us, she wasn't exaggerating, no, really, and as she said this she shed tears of laughter, grief and laughter.

And then her husband with the pebble glasses came up behind her and winked at us. He put his arms around Sofia's waist and started to nibble her ears and kiss her neck, inhaling her newly-wed scent mingled now with a little sweat, and started to dance with her, a funny dance, a silly jig, but then he started to dance for real, dancing and carrying her away little by little outside the tent, a farewell waltz, taking her away from us without her truly realizing it, they had to go, my love, my life, a taxi was waiting for them at the entrance to the venue with its headlights on and all their luggage inside, goodbye, Sofia, goodbye, and she left, still tearful and still blowing her fringe out of her eyes, waving goodbye and blowing air kisses, never tiring of being both happy and sad.

The two of them were in love, and they floated off into their future lives together enveloped in the smell of the fading flowers in the centre-pieces, the bottles of champagne, the smoke from the candles and the marijuana and all the terrible music issuing from the speakers, wedding music, neither good nor bad, just rather hollow and horrible, the kind that if you're not very careful can scratch at your heart and make it bleed.

A pear-shaped little boy, dead tired, fell asleep in his chair, slumped against the backrest, and a wooden old lady, who looked as though she were made entirely of sacking and umbrella frames, pointed her finger at him and said, 'So innocent.'

A few groups were starting to leave, they were going away, hugging each other and slapping backs, endless farewells that lasted hours, the groups began to break up, it was getting late, and the children had to go to bed: it would soon be dawn.

The army man with the red nose applauds the moon. A guest leaves and then comes back to get her shawl. She crosses the empty tent, picks up her shawl, takes a last swig from a randomly selected glass, then goes back the way she came.

The champagne continued to flow happily, the musicians went on playing as if they were engaged in a fight with each other, but something was broken. It was obvious the party was coming to an end. The aftermath of Sofia's wedding was like that of an earthquake, with overturned chairs and tablecloths stained with circles of wine, leftovers from the banquet left steaming among the ruins. When the bride and groom disappeared from view, we sat silently at the singletons' table for a while, drinking without knowing what to say, and then someone suggested going out to greet the new day together, yes, why not?

And together we got up – why not? – and left the tent in the company of those three tall girls who were growing taller and more beautiful by the second, laughing uproariously for no good reason, constantly jumping around on long legs clad in purple silk stockings, their thighs flashing.

We stumbled along the lake shore with the three single goddesses on our arms, laden with glasses and bottles of vodka and whisky and gin and all the experience of the wedding in our eyes, and, outside, the dawn's red glaze started to spread like a kind of gel, tinging our cheekbones a soft, almost alien lilac. It felt like twilight. It was a pleasure to breathe in and out, letting the cool air clear our minds. We dropped down onto the grass. The girls protested, they were so cold in their strappy dresses, and, without a word, all three of us took off our jackets at the same time and like old-fashioned gentlemen draped them over the girls' bare shoulders to keep them warm.

They must have really appreciated that noble gesture because they thanked us by rubbing their perfumed heads against our chests, kissing our lips tenderly and furiously. And, for a while, that's what we did, kissing and exploring each other with our tongues, it was just a naughty, innocent game, meaningless messing around, or so we thought at the time, too blind to guess that there might be a future when a silhouette would emerge from behind the scenes and drag us offstage.

We looked at the tree trunks and the clouds, the beaks of the birds and the fireflies, the mirror of the little lake and the rocks large and small. We were, we suddenly realized, the only people left at the party, ashtrays overflowing with cigarette butts, half-finished glasses, unfinished stories, crumpled cushions, melted ice, the final embers of a human adventure that had begun a long way from there, a long time before.

Why don't we go to Portugal? one of the girls suggested, and this was such a crazy, delightful idea that it had to be considered, yes, it was very tempting, suddenly a fragment of an intricately patterned mosaic wall appeared before us, a glass of *vinho verde*, the murmur of a fountain in the cloister of some luminous convent, the Atlantic sky open to the sea, gravely wounded by seagulls and palm trees, the scribbled lines of electric cables and a tram struggling, panting, up a steep, almost impossibly narrow *rua*, all kinds of things. The syllables of Por-tu-gal knocked around in our heads, Portugal folded into three equal parts like a letter held in the hand of a passer-by (fate?) to be dropped into the nearest postbox, because the important thing wasn't staying or getting to or being anywhere, but prolonging the journey a little longer so that we'd always be anticipating what was to come and never looking back.

A new day was dawning, and before continuing our journey to the mosaics we spent a while lying all together in the wet grass of the meadow under the starry firmament of mid-May with our wine glasses resting on our stomachs and invisible crab claws pinching us all over inside, as we watched the quiet dawn from the shore of a calm lake, feeling pretty drunk and exhausted, with a kind of melancholy dancing around in the pit of the stomach, but a feeling of euphoria too, at how well everything had turned out, flawless, perfect, we all agreed that it had been well worth it. The light was like crinkled muslin. This was how our friend Sofia's wedding in Mudela came to an end, with the six of us lying very still, enjoying the moment, listening to the world breathe, the seamless silence broken only by a distant cricket.

KARMELE JAIO

The Scream

Translated by Kit Maude

I write at night. After my husband and children have gone to bed, I turn on my laptop in a corner of the living room that I've made into a kind of study – our apartment doesn't have a spare room – and that's where I write. But really I've been writing before I actually start writing, because even before my family goes to bed I'm already thinking about what I'm going to write that night. It's during that writing-but-not-writing phase that I've taken many strategic decisions about my works. Two years ago, for instance, I found myself kneeling by the bath washing my boys' hair when the key to my next novel came to me – the protagonist would have a hidden passion, painting, that would change his life – and I've often decided whether or not to kill off a character while I was preparing supper. It's no exaggeration to say that lives often hang in the balance while I'm beating the eggs.

I don't make a living from writing. I work in the library at the Museum of Fine Art. So it's hardly surprising that painting is a major feature in my latest novel, a writer's life slips into her creations like a lizard between rocks. It's not a bad job really, spending your days surrounded by art books is perfectly pleasant, especially if you love painting, but it would be great to be able to spend eight hours a day writing instead of having to do it at night.

Or at least that *was* my routine until recently, but something happened

---

Karmele Jaio (b. 1970) was born in Vitoria and writes in Basque. She has written three collections of short stories, three novels and a book of poetry. Her short stories have appeared in many anthologies, including *Best European Fiction 2017*, and her first novel, *Amaren eskuak* (*Her Mother's Hands*, 2006), was adapted for the screen by Mireia Gabilondo.

this last year that turned my creative process upside down, making it hard for me to spend my nights writing alone in the living room.

My husband is a big football fan. No, wait, he's more devotee than fan. He's a passionate follower of his team, Athletic Bilbao, but that passion isn't limited to a particular club crest or the colours of a jersey; he lives and breathes football. Football with a capital 'F'. He loves football the way someone else might love painting, and whose admiration for, say, Monet doesn't stop him enjoying the work of Cézanne, Zuloaga, Gal, Zumeta or Kahlo.

It's the same with my husband. He's transfixed by games featuring Barcelona or Bayern Munich, but he's just as happy watching Eibar or Lemoa; he enjoys goals, passes and free kicks by star players at Real Madrid, Manchester United and Chelsea, but he can also appreciate a counter-attack by Alavés or a save by his home team Bermeo FC's goal-keeper. And then there are international matches. When the anthems start, and the players are lined up in a row staring into space, his back straightens as though he were standing along with them. Needless to say, during World Cups, I'm a football widow.

But I never imagined football would change the way I write. Although, to be more accurate, it wasn't the sport itself, but whoever decided that matches could be played on weekday nights. Now they've started showing matches at bedtime, I no longer have the living room to myself. Now I have to share my night-time realm with my husband. And it's just not the same.

For a while, I couldn't write a single line, and I even started to long for the next day to come so that I could get back to work. At least there I can nourish my soul with art books. Recently, I've been looking for texts by painters writing about their work, maybe hoping to find a clue as to what I want to achieve with my writing, or some encouragement to keep on going. I remember reading that, according to Edvard Munch, the inspiration for his famous work *The Scream* came to him while he was watching a sunset in which the clouds turned red as blood. *The colours were screaming*, the painter wrote, recalling that moment. *The colours were screaming*, I read in one of those books in the library.

Our living room is quite large, the corner where I write is set slightly apart and I sit with my back to the TV. My husband wears headphones so he won't bother me.

'Just pretend I'm not here,' he says, as he eagerly prepares to watch whatever match is being shown that night.

But he doesn't realize that I can hear his:

'Ooooohhhsss . . .'

His:

'Ahhhhsss . . .'

And his:

'Oh, come off it . . . that was never a foul . . .'

I'm pretty sure he doesn't even know he's making these noises. I know he's trying to keep quiet; he bites his lip when someone scores and never shouts out 'Goal!' But it doesn't make any difference, because I can still tell when someone's scored. Suddenly I hear a kind of hiccup behind me, a stifled scream that makes the paintings on the wall shudder slightly, followed by a long sigh. I look behind me and see my husband with legs stretched out, eyes wide open and fingers spread as if he were reaching out to grab hold of something. He may not open his mouth, but his whole body is screaming 'Goal!' without him even realizing it.

Since my husband started watching football while I write, I've often thought that, if I could make someone feel even half as excited about my writing as my husband does when watching a match, I would be more than satisfied. I don't think anyone has ever felt like that when reading one of my books. Sometimes I wonder why I write and for whom, whether my words are really capable of moving anyone. And, if they're not nearly as effective as a small, round ball, I wonder whether there's any point in continuing to write at all. Maybe that's why I've been consulting the great painters, searching for something that might restore my belief in art and creativity.

My husband's enthusiasm for football far exceeds anything he's ever felt for literature or for my writing; I've known this ever since my first book was published. He reads me, or, rather, starts to read me, but I know he never gets to the end of any of my books. Whenever I publish a new book, he eagerly picks it up, comments on the cover or my author photo, and says:

'Looks good.'

Or he shows the photo to the children, saying:

'OK, boys, who do you think this is?'

Or he'll read the first paragraph and say:

'Hm, it starts well.'

But I know he never gets past page ten. Night after night, the bookmark stays stuck in the same place.

Ever since my husband started watching football while I write, I've become obsessed with a single idea. I look at the computer screen, then at my husband staring at the TV and wonder over and over what it is about the sport that ignites such passion. And, more importantly for me, is it possible to transfer that passion to literature?

So, a year ago, with that idea swirling around in my head, I began to experiment. I started to write while watching my husband watching football with his headphones on, as if I were trying to channel the passion filling the living-room air into my computer, as though trying to suck his blood like a vampire. I write a few lines, then look at my husband, write a paragraph, then look at my husband, like a painter staring at the horizon in search of inspiration. I see him squirming on the sofa at the prospect of a particularly dangerous free kick and I think: what adjectives, what story can I come up with that will make the reader's bottom lip tremble with emotion the way my husband's bottom lip trembles moments before the shot is taken?

In the last few months, something surprising has happened. I've realized that watching my excited husband – I'd never really noticed just how excited he gets – is inspiring my writing. Ever since I started writing while watching my husband watching football I've been writing better, with more passion, the letters seem to grab hold of the blank page, the words have real bite to them. The paragraphs flow, so much so that I've finally managed to finish the novel I've been bogged down in for two years now. Watching my husband's excitement as he watches football has untied a knot I've had inside me for quite some time. I decided that the protagonist had to rebel and drop everything in order to dedicate himself to what he really loves: painting. My protagonist weeps when he finishes a painting, out of emotion and satisfaction. He weeps with pleasure, feeling the blood once again pumping through his veins as it did when he was young.

When my editor finished reading the manuscript, he called me at one o'clock in the morning. He couldn't wait until the next day, he said. Nothing I'd written before had moved or excited him as much, there was something almost compelling about those words and phrases.

The novel was published a month ago. To my surprise, it's turning out to be a real success. The reviews thus far have been excellent, and what they all comment on, more than anything, is the excitement it generates. I'm getting enthusiastic emails from readers, many of them thanking me for encouraging them to unleash their true passion: some found the courage to start writing, others to study something they'd always wanted to, others to admit being attracted to members of the same sex . . . The novel gave them the push they needed to make their hidden dreams a reality.

And it's not just my readers, the novel has also had an unexpected effect on my husband. He got past page ten a while ago and this week he's been walking around the apartment with the novel in his hand. He doesn't seem to regard this as just another book. If I try saying something to him while he's reading, he doesn't answer, just like when he's watching the World Cup.

And, feeling grateful to football in a way I never thought I could, I keep writing while I watch my husband, although to tell the truth I'm watching more and writing less, because it drives me crazy when his eyes well up at a missed penalty, I go nuts when I see his stifled cries of 'Goal!', the way he swallows hard before a free kick is taken.

Today, I came to join him on the sofa. My novel is there with us. To judge from the bookmark, he's almost finished. I told him he could take off the headphones if he liked, that I'm going to take a break from writing and watch the match with him. I saw in the newspaper that it's an important cup game (since I started writing while watching my husband, I've been reading the sports pages). Sitting there next to him, I felt good in a way that I hadn't for years, the two of us actually sitting there, doing something together. I don't think I'd felt like that since we used to go to the cinema when we were just boyfriend and girlfriend.

But, at one point, my husband looked away from the TV, picked up the book and started to read. I couldn't believe it. I didn't look directly at him because I didn't want him to see how surprised I was, so I went on staring at the screen, watching the football. I saw a ball rolling over the green grass with four players chasing after it, dripping with sweat. The one in the red shirt touched the ball with his right foot and the others followed urgently on behind, as though the ball were rolling away with their beating hearts inside it. The commentator said the team in white were pressing very high up the pitch, making them vulnerable to the team in red's counter-attacks. The red player got the ball under control and kicked it hard, another player slipped away, collected the ball, kept possession, running fast, and now there was only the goalkeeper to beat, the commentator started speaking louder, faster, the crowd sprang to its feet, the goalkeeper advanced, arms and legs outstretched, the player in red shot and . . .

'Goal!'

My husband stared at me in amazement.

'Did you just shout "Goal"?'

'Me?'

'Yes, you just screamed out "Goal".'

'Don't be silly, you're imagining things.'

'Would you mind putting on the headphones? Your book's getting interesting.'

I was going to tell him that I don't need the headphones, I don't really care about football, but he seemed so intent on reading my book that I put them on, and now I'm listening to the commentators as though they were inside my head, as though they were whispering in my ear, and my heart is racing.

My husband watches the replay of the goal and goes back to the book. This is just incredible. I could turn off the TV and get back to my writing, but I don't feel like it. Now I'm starting to worry that I'll never be able to write anything again unless I'm watching my husband getting excited over a football match.

There he is, he can't take his eyes off my novel.

The score is one-all with five minutes to go.

I put the headphones back on. I glance at him and see that he's got to the final two pages of the novel and then I think I see an unusual gleam in his eyes, something approaching excitement. He takes a deep breath, holds the air in for a few seconds, then blows it out with a sigh. My novel is about to make my husband cry.

I look back at the TV.

A miracle is happening.

A palette of bright colours is filling the screen: red and white shirts against a green background, the multicoloured crowd, the flashing adverts . . . and across that palette the players' passes are bold brush strokes, their dribbles are scribbled lines, there's a plasticity that somehow lends volume to the screen, the intensity of Impressionistic light, and, above all of this, as the commentators' voices are growing in volume, the goalkeeper of the team in white reaches out one arm like Michelangelo's Adam reaching out to God. But he doesn't make it.

Goal.

Red jerseys jump up and down and hug each other, the crowd waves red flags, a flare lights up the screen. And, in the middle of it all, the forward who scored the goal is kneeling on the grass gazing up at the heavens, mouth open in an exultant scream.

My tears give the scene a *sfumato* effect, blurring everything, melding it all together.

I can't stop crying. The colours are screaming at me from the television, and my eyes just can't take all that beauty.

JESÚS CARRASCO

10/10/10

In the middle of the night on 10 October 2010, I got a call from my wife. At that hour, I was asleep in a five-star hotel in Medellín, Colombia. I was sharing a double room with my then business partner. We'd gone there to oversee the setting up of an exhibition on Spanish architecture as part of the VII Bienal Iberoamericana. I can't remember now if I picked up the phone or if my colleague did. I do remember the room, though, presumably because it was the same as all hotel rooms: a brief corridor leading off from a tiny hallway, with the bathroom on the left and a fitted wardrobe on the right. Beyond that, an open space filled by two ridiculously large beds, very high and very firm.

I remember leaning back against the fake wooden headboard. As well as the darkness in the room, the silence and, at the other end of the phone, my wife's voice, which sounded very faint, as if she didn't want to wake me or our daughter, who would probably be sleeping beside her. Taking into account the different time zones, it must have been six in the morning in Spain when I received her call. She asked me how I was, and I, being still half-asleep, presumably replied in monosyllables. Then she fell silent for a moment before giving me the news. I don't think the silence could have lasted more than two or three seconds, but I remember it as being much longer, because there's only one reason why your wife, who loves you and knows you, would wake you up when you're thousands of miles away, and

Jesús Carrasco (b. 1972) was born in Badajoz. He worked variously as a PE teacher, grape picker and graphic designer before devoting himself to writing. His first novel, *Intemperie* (*Out in the Open*, 2013), became an international sensation, and has been translated into more than twenty languages. There is also a graphic novel version and a film based on the book. His second novel, *La tierra que pisamos* (2016), was awarded the EU Prize for Literature.

that's because she has bad news. Over the years, I've given enormous weight to those two seconds. I've filled them with some of the feelings we humans spend our entire lives avoiding. I've elevated those seconds to the category of myth or foundational moment. I've thought about them so often that I've even adorned them with the crackling sounds that used to accompany telephonic voices, as if her voice were coming to me via thousands of miles of badly insulated copper wire mounted on wooden poles or resting on the bed of an ocean as deep and dark and silent as that two-second pause.

Seven years before, in 2003, the advertising agency I worked for went bankrupt, and all the employees were dismissed. It was a small agency in Madrid with just a few, very select clients, but which was apparently doing very well. In 2003, the Spanish economy was going great guns and money flowed like water. People were buying big cars, big houses and flat-screen TVs. Property developers were making money hand over fist, the banks were giving out canteens of silver-plated cutlery, and advertising agencies like ours were earning obscene amounts of money for doing very little. Just for coming up with some stupid slogan intended to convince people that our car insurance was the cheapest we could earn the equivalent of what my father would have earned in two months as a teacher in a state school. My boss spent his earnings on Ferraris, on taking us out to some of Spain's fanciest restaurants, giving us a pay rise without us even asking, believing we were his friends. When the business finally went under, the head of the accounts department worked out what each of us was owed and, since there wasn't enough ready cash, he allowed us to take away furniture and equipment as a partial payment. So, one spring afternoon, I arrived at the office with my housemate and his van, and we took away the Zanotta desk at which I'm writing now, the Vitra chair I'm sitting on now, a Tolomeo desk lamp and a computer that quickly became obsolete. Plus the enormous Swiss cheese plant that had brought a bit of life to the office meeting room and which was far too big for the small apartment I shared with my friend with the van.

A few weeks later, a tribunal decided that we should receive compensation. We had worked there for several years, earning large salaries, and so we each received quite a tidy sum of money. While that money was still warm, a colleague and I rented a minuscule office in the centre of

Madrid, filled it with our designer furniture and set up our own business. The first thing we did was phone the clients we'd been working with at the now bankrupt agency. After all, just as we'd been left without work, they had been left without a provider, and, almost instantly, we got ourselves a nice little contract to continue creating and producing exactly the same kind of direct marketing material as we had at the agency. It was as if we'd stumbled upon a small treasure chest among the flotsam washed up on the beach by a shipwreck. Initially, the work was thin on the ground and rather dull, but it was enough for us to be up and running. It would be another five years before Lehman Brothers in New York went bust, and six, or perhaps seven, before the tsunami caused by their collapse wiped out the Spanish economy. In the first few years, we worked our socks off and, borne up with almost childish glee by the still buoyant economic wave, we soon acquired new clients who we, in turn, milked for all they were worth. We got used to getting paid simply for smiling, and, for the first time in my life, I woke every morning feeling relaxed and with a sense that my immediate future was assured. The money slipped easily through my colleague's fingers, but, coming as I did from a large, conservative, rural family, I stashed mine away in the bank like a wise ant, thus doing honour to my parents and guaranteeing myself a quiet life when everything eventually fell apart – not that I or anyone else could have foreseen the coming disaster. I looked around me and saw only happy people, crowded bars, beach holidays and other occasional extravagances. It was in that atmosphere of effervescent affluence that I met Ruth on the top of a sand dune, where the sea breeze gilded her firm flesh, and the sun glinted on her white teeth when she laughed. I fell instantly in love, like a teenager, and, a few months later, we were living together. Life seemed to unfurl before me like a very soft carpet along which I was walking towards what I felt was guaranteed success.

On some weekends, Ruth and I would visit my parents in their village about an hour to the south of Madrid. We would arrive on Saturday morning and return to Madrid on Sunday night on the train from Extremadura that passed through the village, and was always full of students and workers who, like us, had spent the weekend with their families. I didn't notice at the time, but it was then that my father first began getting short of breath when going up the stairs. He would reach the landing at the top and be gasping for air as if he had just scaled a Nepalese mountain. Ruth would mention this on the train back, but I didn't really take it in. It was Sunday evening, and my mind was already preparing for another intense Monday at work.

We soon managed to gain the loyalty of the few clients we had and, gradually, almost without us noticing, we built up a relationship of trust with them, especially with one particular client. Indeed, we formed such a strong bond with him that we became almost like another department of his company. A couple of times a week, we would go to his office in Alcobendas, to the north of Madrid, to pick up new commissions or deliver the work we'd been commissioned to do in previous weeks. We usually arranged to meet before lunch and, when the meeting was over, we would invite our client to join us at one of the local restaurants, which were always packed with office workers, executives and others, who, like us, had gone there to cement deals. Doing business over lunch was what we and the rest of the country did. Not that we ever crossed the line into illegality. We never accepted or paid any backhanders, but the prawns and the cool, transparent white wine lubricated or perhaps muddied everything. Would our company's profits have been any different without those lunches and all that expensive seafood and bonhomie? I really don't know. It was in one of those restaurants, a Basque restaurant, that I received a call from my mother. I had to go outside because I couldn't hear what she was saying above the hubbub of voices and laughter. She told me that, during a routine check-up, the doctors had found something on one of my father's lungs and that they were currently doing further tests on him at the hospital in Toledo.

One day, our main client summoned us to a meeting. In the same office where we had so often given our presentations, he told us that, due to internal restructuring, they were going to have to make a substantial reduction in the number of commissions they gave us. We didn't have the manpower to take on the amount of work to be generated by the department that would emerge from that restructuring. Or so at least he told us, but Madrid is a small place, and we soon found out that a much bigger advertising agency had offered to take on all the work currently shared out among smaller companies like ours. We could only assume that, at the lunches organized by that larger agency, they had plied him with even more expensive wine, which had clearly lubricated parts we couldn't reach. It served us right, really. We, too, had made money hand over fist, but this was an end of the era of fat invoices and the modest percentages we regularly slapped on everything we did. And so we were reduced to dusting off our address books and calling old colleagues, clients of other clients, acquaintances and even companies we found in Yellow Pages.

It was then that my daughter was born. We called her Andrea.

The doctors said, straight out, that it was a tumour. The talk was no longer about illness or disease. The word 'tumour' doesn't aim to please or allow for misinterpretations. And what does it mean in medical terms? Perhaps, seen from a cellular level, tumour tissue is no different from healthy tissue. Maybe both are pink and shiny, although, in the layman's imagination, a tumour is always a black mass. It might be even denser than the organ that surrounds and nourishes it. The word 'tumour' conjures up foul odours, as if something like a dead rodent were trapped inside the organism, marinating in the body's juices, rotting away in that inner darkness and infecting all the other tissues with its malignity. A tumour is, then, something that grows from the inside out. A dark implosion which, if not removed promptly, will end up contaminating the whole body. No organism can withstand that searing heat. Sooner or later, the black wave will reach one of the many vital centres, which is why the body must be cut open with a sterilized implement. The surgeon's hands use the delicate steel blade to part the flesh, like Moses parting the Red Sea so that the people of Israel could escape the tyranny of the Pharaohs. However, it wasn't time for that yet. There were various other stages to go through first, stages intended as much to curtail the illness as to set our minds on a different path. The doctors must stay true to their Hippocratic Oath and family members and friends must gradually 'get used to the idea'. Both these things take time. Before accepting that death is a possibility, we have to let go of the various concentric rings protecting us from the horror that the idea of death evokes.

Fortunately, the first stage required no profanation of the flesh. He merely had to undergo sessions of radiotherapy and chemotherapy. Nothing invasive. At least not visibly so. These initial stages proved bearable for everyone, even for my father who was left all alone to throw up in the bathroom of his hospital room in Madrid, where he stayed for a couple of weeks. I went to visit him almost every day. I would meet up there with my mother, have lunch with her in the cafeteria and talk about the village, about my siblings, about my work, about what the doctor had said on his last visit. She would tell me whether my father had had a good or bad night, how the nurses treated him, the changes that would have to be made to the house to accommodate a chronically ill patient. We skirted around the subject as if we were poets, never actually mentioning what lay at the heart of the matter.

The lack of clients was killing our business, and so we considered either moving to an office away from the centre or selling our designer furniture and buying something less expensive. We'd have to sell the furniture off cheap, of course, because any potential buyers of used furniture, however luxurious, would be having as hard a time as we were and might not be in the mood to appreciate the high quality of the materials. My desk, for example, is made up of a heavy six-by-three slab of toughened glass supported on a beech-wood frame assembled with such skill and delicacy that you can't even feel the joins when you run your hand over them. Beech wood had always been my father's favourite. He kept a store of different types of wood in his workshop, where he would busy himself doing all kinds of things, from producing full-size copies of Velázquez's major paintings to helping my brother in his work as a maker of plaster mouldings. He would find pieces of wood in the local tip or perhaps abandoned on one of the many building sites in the village. He used the pine wood from pallets for cruder work: a stool to stand on to reach the top shelves of cupboards; a mount so that the drill could be attached to the work bench and used as a lathe; a coat rack with four nails in it where they could hang their work coats. There was walnut wood from a bookshelf someone had given him, as well as ash, Mediterranean pine, olive, and sapele wood left over from when he had made the internal doors for the house. Some types of wood were better than others, but my father's particular favourite was always beech wood. The beech is a relatively scarce tree and grows very slowly; its wood is dense and smooth and pale. While it has barely any knots, it's full of very fine lines, rather like the lines a child would draw on paper to represent rain. My father would create his finest pieces from that wood: a spindle so that my younger sister could spin wool or silk; a small sculpture of a mother and child; a photo frame inlaid with ebony; kitchen utensils. My father had never visited my office in Madrid, and so had never seen the beech-wood frame of my Zanotta desk. If he had, one of two things could have happened: he would either have been amazed at the impeccable way the frame had been made, or he would have wanted to add it to the other pieces of wood waiting to be dismantled and transformed into tumblers, plates, chess pieces or parts for a spinning wheel.

My partner and I had, *in extremis*, finally abandoned the idea of selling our expensive desks, when a visionary young architect came to our rescue. He had been commissioned to design the exhibition for the Bienal Española de Arquitectura. He wanted us to find and manage teams of carpenters and fitters, and put flesh on the bones of his vision of how best to present to the public the finest examples of Spanish architecture from the last two years. This took months of preparation. We contacted companies who specialized in putting on exhibitions and creating ephemeral architecture, we hired workers, drew up budgets, placed orders and put all the machinery in place so that, when the exhibition space opened its doors to us, we could set the whole thing up in five days.

I hardly saw Ruth during that time. On the few days when I left work early, we would have supper together at home. She would update me on life in the outside world, tell me that she'd spoken to my mother, and, quite rightly, tell me off because she spoke to her more often than I did. She would talk, too, about what she sensed was happening to my father. She had experienced the long-drawn-out death of her own father, during which she had almost lived at the hospital where he spent his last months. It got to the point, she said, where her mother would arrive to visit her husband and immediately put on a white coat and walk the corridors as if she were a nurse or an experienced doctor. She would visit the other patients in the neighbouring rooms, take them magazines and food, console them and keep them company when they were alone. They would even ask her 'medical advice', and since, after all those months of visiting the hospital, her white coat had become almost like a second skin, she would offer her opinion on a facetectomy, would examine an x-ray, holding it up to the light, or would recommend that they try taking clavulanic acid alongside amoxicillin. When Ruth told me this, we laughed, but it was rather hollow laughter, more weary than joyful. A laughter in which fear was already crouching.

The Bienal Española de Arquitectura was a relative success. We had put our very best efforts into it, but the public was so specialized and few in number that we wondered if all our hard work had really been worth it. This was in the days just before my father's first operation. Neither the chemotherapy nor the radiotherapy had succeeded in shrinking the tumour, and it now occupied a large part of his right lung. Even so, the doctors seemed pleased and spoke of having done 'a good job', of having left it all 'nice and clean', referring to the hole they had made in him. They explained that, at this stage of the illness, the important thing was to stop the tumour growing, which is why they needed to eliminate any trace of tumour tissue. The tiniest fragment of that black, stinking mass was like a single spark in a parched pine forest, a spark that might, of course, be too tiny to be detected by even the most advanced diagnostic tools. All that remained was the surgeon's skill and his instinct for where that spark might be hiding. The operation sounded to me like pure butchery, with the surgeon going in with a knife to remove the malignant tissue and, just in case, going in a little deeper, so that nothing would be left behind. Perhaps surgeons take a certain pleasure in those precise movements, cutting into the flesh, separating it from the bones. The kind of pleasure a sushi chef might feel when slicing fish. I really didn't care what motivated the surgeon who opened up my father and penetrated the most hidden corners of his being. Regardless of whether it was professional zeal or a taste for cutting into flesh, what mattered was that he went in as deeply as he could in order to drive out the devil. It had to be that way, because once a body has been sewn up, the surgeons really don't want to open it up again. Bacteria can slip in through the same door as the sterilized steel scalpel. The surgeon who explained what he would be doing certainly didn't stint us on the technical terminology, even though he could see from our faces that we didn't understand. He was doubtless seeking refuge behind all that inflated jargon. Saying 'subclavian artery' and 'mesothelioma' was his way of defending himself against being sucked into our grief and fear. I wondered how many other families he had baffled with his verbiage that same day. But what else could he do? Sit down with us, place a comforting hand on my mother's shoulder, recall his own father, allow his eyes to fill up with tears, join us on our journey? No, thank you. He could keep his tears. I didn't want them dripping into my father's body when he cut it open.

That 'successful' operation left my father prostrate in bed for ten days. My mother was visibly wasting away. Too long spent breathing hospital air drains the colour from the skin. Meanwhile, my siblings and I got on with our lives. We came and went, we visited our father, then went back to our work, to our thriving children who were waiting for us at home like nestlings with their beaks wide open, more beak than face. What saved me were Ruth, Andrea and my work. When you're at the office or in your workshop, you can become as passionately absorbed in what you're doing as children can in the games they play. Or perhaps it isn't passion, just a need to be with someone else, perhaps the colleague with whom you can tell cruel jokes without being judged, whom you trust absolutely, who is loyalty incarnate. Being with him is like being with the brother you yourself have chosen. Essence of brother. Our paths had crossed at just the right moment. We were both bringing up our families and having great fun. We hadn't even had to sell our expensive furniture. What more could we ask?

After the Bienal de Arquitectura, we collaborated on other projects with that same architect. For example: the bridal shower for the daughter of one of Spain's wealthiest entrepreneurs. Our architect was going to transform an old palace just outside Madrid into a kind of dream landscape for her and her distinguished guests. With the money that would be spent that night on subtle lighting and piles of coral sand, you could have bought thousands and thousands of scalpels with which to slice open diseased bodies. We could have decorated a room in that palace with those bloodied scraps of flesh, but we didn't. On the contrary, we spent the family fortune on laying down real turf in all the rooms, in commissioning a twenty-five-foot ice sculpture that would last as long as the party lasted, suspending a real tree upside down from the ceiling, decorating the garden walls with neon verses that I myself had written, installing fountains, chocolate cascades, strings of fairy lights. Food was served in every room, and, in every corner, there were bottles of Veuve Clicquot chilled to a perfect forty-two degrees Fahrenheit. We worked like galley slaves for a whole month just to create that one day. That was what fuelled our relationship: a camaraderie forged in the stinking bilge water of a galley. And, while I was busy stoking the fire of that friendship, my father was back in his village rotting away, taking ever stronger sedatives, silently crying out, burning up inside.

Lehman Brothers collapsed.

The days of exciting projects came to an end, and we were again reduced to producing hastily designed posters and pamphlets to be stuck on car windscreens. We worked longer and longer hours in order to earn the same or less, and one day, in a downtown bar, eating potato croquettes and drinking beer, we reminisced about our boom years. My colleague reminded me of the weekend when we decided to hold an annual general meeting. We rented a luxurious house outside Madrid and spent the whole weekend discussing the future of the company and eating in the best local restaurants. It was just him and me, the agency's only partners, celebrating a congress in the mountains, our own miniature Davos. It seemed an age since that had happened, and, sitting there with our croquettes, it didn't seem that funny any more, and so we finished our beers and went home.

It was time once again to dust off our address books. We phoned every-one and anyone who might have some work for us. We weren't the only ones left idle. The country was in dire straits. Young people were begin-ning to pack their bags to go and try their luck abroad. Every day there were articles in the newspapers about people being evicted from their homes because they couldn't pay the mortgage. Children began living off their parents' pensions. They moved in with them, grandchildren and all. Multiple scandals about corruption and speculation – always rife in Spain – began bubbling to the surface. The people pointed the finger at the government. It was easy to think they were the ones who had made off with what we no longer had. The people roared and seethed.

Every day, my father had to take a bewildering cocktail of medicines: pills of every colour kept in a little box that he, of course, had made out of bits of beech wood. To keep tabs on what he was taking, he amused himself by filling little calendars with his small, neat, schoolmasterly writ-ing. So numerous were the pills and so varied the doses that his whole day was taken up with swallowing those various medicines, all washed down with a glass of water. He had also been prescribed fentanyl patches for when the pain became too acute. Usually, my sister or my mother applied the patches, but, during one of my visits, that job fell to me. The patch had to be applied near the shoulder blade. He lifted his shirt to reveal his bony back, and his skin resembled the patch itself, a delicate film of elastic, semi-transparent plastic. The people who had designed the patch, in Germany, France or the United States, had presumably intended it to match human skin so that the dressing would blend in with the body, becoming part of it. That plastic, which I found hard to stick to his skin without it wrinkling, released analgesic substances that made his life more bearable. He began with just 12 micrograms, the lowest dosage. The patches gave my father a deceptive appearance of normality. He would get out of bed on his own and move around the house fairly easily. He would go over to a shelf to fetch a book or put his favourite video about lions in the video player. What that patch did, though, was disguise reality. If it didn't hurt, then it was as if the pain didn't exist. And I began to consider pharmacology a truly miraculous discipline.

In Madrid, we were getting so few commissions that we ended up closing the office and taking our respective items of furniture home. My spendthrift partner soon had to sell his. I got by on my savings. He, and my other compatriots too, were sliding towards poverty, but as yet, I was unaware that the same thing was happening to me. My savings were my fentanyl patch. The months passed and things became still worse. The government made what cuts it could and made those cuts with a savagery worthy of the most sadistic surgeon. And the bureaucrats did sterling work telling the politicians where they needed to put the knife in. They told us: we're removing tumours, eliminating unproductive tissue. It hurts, but it's for your own good, they said. Once we've finished, things will be better.

Just when everything was falling apart, that same talented young architect got in touch with us again. For some reason even he didn't understand, the same exhibition we had put on earlier had been selected by the school of architecture to be taken to Colombia. We climbed back into the saddle. Since we no longer had an office, we met in bars, in the offices of friends or at home. Wherever we were, we would take out our laptops and set to work. Every now and then, my partner would dig me in the ribs and say: hey, we're off to Colombia, just like a couple of jet-setting executives. Spain might well be in a dreadful state, but we were being paid to spend ten days on the other side of the Atlantic, where we would be staying in a five-star hotel. After weeks of barely bothering to change out of our pyjamas, we would once again be managing teams of workers, ordering materials and being part of Medellín's booming cultural scene. For a few days, I forgot about my father. At one point, my sister mentioned that the doctors had increased the dose of the fentanyl patches to 25 micrograms, but this news barely registered with me; it ran through my fingers like fine sand, because, while I was talking to her on the phone, my partner was on the other side of the desk showing me a colour card with a sample we'd been discussing for the best part of a week. With my mobile phone pressed to my ear, and responding in monosyllables to what my sister was saying, I pointed to a particular dark grey and wagged my finger to indicate my disapproval. My partner returned to his work, and I ended the call, determined to put the case for a grey that tended more to smoke-grey than to graphite.

Two days before flying to Colombia, I went with my mother to the hospital where my father had had his operation. Two weeks before, the hospital had carried out some follow-up tests, and were going to give us the results. It was no longer an illness, a disease, a tumour, or even cancer. Now it was metastasis. Exactly as we feared. Someone had left a live spark inside my father's body. Now his ribs were on fire, and the black fluid was finding concealed doorways into the very centre of the living matter. Into a place so hidden that it was now impossible to dig it out. The doctor told us this, pointing at an x-ray plate showing part of a bone, a solid white shell and, in the centre, a network of fine, calcareous threads. Trabeculae, he called them.

I travelled back to the village with my mother. We stared out of the train window at the barley fields, which seemed drier than usual. When we arrived, my sister was there to welcome us. I summarized what the doctor had told us. She sat down next to my mother and put her arms around her. I went to the bedroom, where my father was resting. The blind was down. The air smelled of pyjamas. I sat him up so as to change his patch, and, while I was doing this, I told him we'd just come back from Madrid and now had the results of the tests. He moaned as he expelled air from his one remaining lung. It wasn't so much a moan as a whistle emerging from his weary airways. When I'd finished, and before he lay down again, I asked if he wanted to know what was in the oncologist's report. He said nothing. His short breaths were almost as fast as the beats of my heart. The dark room, his presence there, his interminable silence. No, he said at last, and lay back down. I stood up to leave the room but, first, I paused in the half-darkness. Papa, I said, I've got to go away for a few days, but we can talk about it all when I return. For a moment, I listened to his breathing, then I opened the door and left.

JAVIER MONTES

The Hotel Life

'What a dreadful night! What a brood of disparate vipers! What an
appalling place! What unhappy lodgings! It is hard enough to
spend a bad night in a bad inn . . . but imagine staying in
such an inn for ever, for all eternity, what do you
suppose will be the feelings of that sad soul?'
St Teresa of Avila, *The Way of Perfection*, ch. 40, 9.

HOTEL IMPERIAL, 17 March

I took only one light suitcase with me, although it was such a short
journey that I could easily have taken more and heavier luggage if I'd
wanted. Ten blocks or one kilometre one hundred and thirty-two metres,
according to the electronic receipt from the taxi. There was so much traffic, though, that it took me twenty minutes. No one said goodbye to me
or closed the apartment door behind me, no one came with me, still less
followed in my tracks. I was, however, expected at my destination, and
the room where I was to spend the night had been reserved in my name.

I live so close to the hotel that it really would have been quicker to
walk, but I decided to hail a taxi so as to get the journey off to a good
start. However short, it was still a journey, and I wanted to show that I
was taking it seriously (but then, I've always taken both my work and my
journeys seriously; they do, after all, come to more or less the same thing).

Or perhaps the opposite was true, perhaps it was a matter of being
capable of a certain playfulness too, when required. I've spent half my life
moving from hotel to hotel, but this was the first time I would sleep in
one in my own city. That's why I finally agreed to do it when the

Javier Montes (b. 1976) is a writer, translator and art critic. In 2007, he received the Premio José
María Pereda for his first novel, *Los penúltimos*, and his novel *La vida de hotel* was translated into
English as *The Hotel Life* in 2013. This story was included in Granta's *The Best of Young Spanish-
language Novelists* (2010).

newspaper called and suggested the Imperial. I think we were all surprised when I did.

'They've finished the refurbishment now and have just sent us their new publicity pack.'

Initially, I refused. They know I never write about new hotels.

'But this isn't a new hotel. It's the same old Imperial. They've just given it a facelift.'

I don't like new hotels: the smell of paint, the piped music. And I distrust the refurbished variety. Any 'facelift' destroys the prestige and character which, in older establishments, are the hotel equivalent of good sense and even sentiment, or, at least, of memory. I don't know that I'm much of a sentimentalist myself, but I do have a good memory. And I've noticed that, after a certain age, sentiment and memory tend to merge, which is probably why I prefer hotels that know how to remember.

I long ago agreed my terms with the newspaper. I choose the hotel of the week, and they pay. Cheap or expensive, near or far, undiscovered or famous, and usually just for one night but sometimes two. No skimping (they skimp quite enough on my fee) and no favours either. I never accept invitations in exchange for a review.

Not even if it's a bad review, as some either very stupid or very astute PR guy once asked me over the phone.

People in the hotel world know my views, but an awful lot of invites still get sent to me at the office (I won't allow them to give anyone my home address). I suppose they send them just in case I do, one day, take the bait, just in case I relent and end up accepting and going to the hotel, where they will treat me like royalty and give me the very best room, so that I will then write a five-star review, which they will frame and hang up in reception or post on their website, and which will bring in money from guests or, even if it doesn't and even if they don't need it, will doubtless bring them other things that are sometimes worth as much or more than money: the approval of fellow hoteliers, the warm glow of vanity confirmed, the certainty that they are, as a hotel, on the right track.

My column, I have to say, continues to be a success. And although the people at the newspaper never say as much, so that I don't get big-headed, I know that hotels, airlines and travel agencies are queuing up to put a half-page advertisement in my section: 'The Hotel Life'.

That success is, of course, relative, as is any success in newspapers and in print. Every now and then, someone suggests I start a blog with my reviews. Even the people at the newspaper do so occasionally. It might be fouling our own nest, they say, but if you started a blog and got some advertising on it, you'd make a mint.

I think they're exaggerating.

'Besides, you only live around the corner. All you'd have to do is spend a couple of hours there one afternoon to check out what they've done.'

Again I refused. They know perfectly well that I don't write about hotels I haven't slept in. It would be like writing a restaurant review having only sniffed the plates as the waiters brought them out (of course, my colleague on the next page sometimes does exactly that in his column 'Dinner is served': he said to me when we met once, I can tell by the smell alone what's cooking. I didn't take to him, and the feeling, I imagine, was mutual.)

'Well, if that's what's bothering you, spend the night there.'

They may have been joking, but I took them at their word. I rather liked the idea of sleeping in a hotel room from which I could almost, you might say, see the windows of my own empty apartment and bedroom. A night of novelty might buck me up a bit. I've grown rather jaded with the years, well, I've been doing the same job for a long time now. My choice, of course. And I do it reasonably well, I think, possibly better than anyone, to judge by the emails I sometimes get from readers and even the occasional letter written the old-fashioned way, with pen and paper, envelope and stamp, and which the newspaper also forwards to me.

The letters always arrive opened. Apparently it's a security thing, but it seems a bit over the top: I might be somewhat harsh in my comments at times, but not enough to merit a letter bomb. Then again, I don't mind if the people at the office read them, always assuming they do, because at least the editors will see that I do still have a public.

On the other hand, there's nothing so very amazing about being better than anyone else at a job for which there's scarcely any competition. There aren't many of us hotel reviewers left, not at least in the newspaper world. The Internet is another matter, there everyone wants to give their opinion and analyse their journey down to the last detail and even write as if they were real reviewers (I think some of them copy my style and my adjectives). There's nothing wrong with that, I suppose. On the other hand, the reviews are never somehow right either: they're nearly always ill-intentioned, ill-considered and ill-written by venomous individuals or by just plain weirdos – I mean, I like my work, but I certainly wouldn't do it for free.

In the end, I gave in, which is presumably what the people at the Imperial were counting on when they tried their luck. The editors were thrilled, so I guess they had some advertising deal going on as well. As usual, they made the reservation in my name. My real name, of course, not the pseudonym I use for my column. The surname on my ID card throws even the sharpest manager or receptionist off the scent and means that I can be just like any other hotel guest. That's also why I won't allow my photograph to appear alongside my name, and why I never go to conventions or meetings with colleagues. That's no great sacrifice, mind: they're doubtless as dull as the reviews they write. Having no face makes my job much easier and, why deny it, more amusing too. That way it has something of the double agent or the undercover spy about it. A double double agent, because, in hotels, no one is ever who they say they are, and who doesn't take advantage of a stay in a hotel to play detective, however unwittingly?

After all these years of only using my real name to check in at hotels, it now seems to me falser than my false name; apart from the people on the newspaper, few people know it, and still fewer – almost no one, in fact – uses it.

At midday on the dot, just as the taxi drew up beside me, it started to rain. I wasn't wearing a coat and had no umbrella. I must have been the only one not expecting rain, because within seconds the street was awash with cars. I didn't mind. In fact, I would have been happy if the journey had taken longer, even though I was paying for it, not the newspaper (I'm very particular about that).

At this stage in my life, taxi journeys are the only ones that mean much to me. I have no qualification in the career or, rather, pursuit I chose for my journey through life, and I've long ceased to think of it in those terms, although I suppose I got off to a pretty good start. In the end, though, I lost sight of my fellow runners, the ones you're so conscious of at first, when you're in your twenties or thirties and keep glancing out of the corner of your eye at those behind, intent (or so you believe) on overtaking you, meanwhile calculating how big a lead the runners ahead have over you and conserving your energies as you imagine the best way of getting past them for the final sprint.

But there are no sprints, and certainly no final sprints. Indeed, I stopped running a long time ago. There's no point. Just walk at the pace that suits your feet and you'll end up arriving at the place you set out for. Or else keep quite still: lately, I've had the feeling that it's the things that do the walking. It's simply a matter of sitting and waiting; things won't fail you, they never do, because nothing ever fails and everything ends up happening anyway.

Certainly, through the taxi windows things continued to happen (and in their proper order too): the familiar streets, the doorways in single file, the treacherous glare of light as we turned a particular corner. Even when we were stuck in a jam, life continued to happen, like in those black-and-white taxis you see in gangster films: the interior of the cars as still and steady as a house you could live in for ever, despite the pretend bumps and jolts created by the brawnier assistants on the set. The actors would sit against the backdrop of a screen on which were projected dripping streetlamps and blurred pavements and the ancient shadows of pedestrians. Fortunately, at night, they always drove with the interior light turned on. It wasn't exactly hard to spot that the landscapes in those films were fake. Perhaps they were so sure of themselves then that they deliberately made it really obvious. The driver would turn the wheel regardless of the fact that there was no bend visible in the perspective to the rear; or else, beyond the silhouetted windows, the backdrop would merely vibrate and shake and be pierced by occasional beams of light. As if the person in charge of special effects had simply given up all attempt at pretence.

It was the same with the cartoons which, when I was a child, always preceded the grown-up feature: the talkative bear or the cat in the hat would run and run. And, behind them, a repeated parade of trees and buildings would speed past. It saved work, because that way they only needed to produce a single backdrop for the one fleeing figure. In fact, nothing and no one moved during those thrilling scenes. As a small boy,

I soon caught on to that use of loops; I became expert at detecting them even before I could come up with a proper explanation.

On the way to the hotel, it occurred to me that *I* was escaping in that unnecessary taxi. Or playing at escaping, like those pretend cops and gangsters. Only a man trying to give someone the slip would get into a taxi carrying virtually no luggage in order to stay at a hotel ten blocks away. And, if anyone did that and someone did actually follow him, it would look most suspicious. He would give the impression that he was trying to cover his tracks, as they did and still do in old films.

But no one was going to follow me or say: 'Follow that cab!' On the way to the hotel, the driver didn't even express surprise at the shortness of the journey, in a car that felt to me like a hotel room where I could find bed and board for a night and imagine I was in hiding from my pursuers. Pure invention, of course. If it wasn't for the articles about the various hotels that I sent to the newspaper, they would long since have lost track of me.

Twelve twenty on a random Tuesday morning in March: the bored porter who failed to open the taxi door for me and pick up my one small case did, however, accompany me to the revolving door beneath a vast umbrella. Given the hotel's large, pretentious canopy, the umbrella was clearly more for decoration than anything else, at most, a baton to set the right note for the rest of the hotel.

The two receptionists in the deserted foyer were bored too; indeed, the whole hotel was bored at that deadest of hours in all hotel foyers, when no one healthy or in a healthy state of mind is still in his room, when it's too late to leave and too early to check in, and when the tide of visitors who have gone or are about to arrive has fallen silent.

From closer to, the receptionists seemed very young, and not exactly thrilled to see me. Perhaps the last thing they expected to have to do in that job was check in a guest. They both became absorbed in the screen showing reservations. At their age, disdain and confusion are hard to distinguish.

I hadn't visited the Imperial since I was a child. I've often passed by its façade, which is as grandiose as its name, and seen its two corner towers from many balconies. The towers still look like new arrivals, even though they've spent the last hundred years helping to locate the city centre and orienting visitors viewing the place from afar (assuming they know where to look). The towers were intended as beacons of the country's cosmopolitanism, but, right from the start, they seemed somehow antiquated, as did the hotel itself, which was home to gatherings of bullfighting aficionados and had the air of a provincial social club, with a lot of people arriving for pre-supper drinks, but rarely, it seemed, any actual guests.

The deadly silence of the foyer was composed of various noises: the distant clink of glasses, the galumphing roar of vacuum cleaners on the other side of the world, and a sinuous, tenuous, techno-stream of piped music. It slithered past the legs of the furniture before coiling around your ankles and up your body in order to go in one ear and out the other. It fitted in well with the new designer décor, so familiar from the publicity packs forwarded to me by the newspaper that I still don't know whether I liked it or not. I probably never will know either, because that's how it is in such cases, knowing or not knowing doesn't much matter.

They say that the previous owners sold the whole place for next to nothing, but renovating it must have cost a pretty penny. The brochures I read were rife with clichés along the lines of: a refuge for the experienced nomad, an operations base for the world traveller. The kind of superhero jargon that comes down to little more than a few flashy but rather dim lamps. Bright enough, though, for you to be able to guess that the armchairs and rugs in the lobby won't feel as good as they look. In the entrance to the hotel, there were no longer the wax flowers beneath glass domes that I seem vaguely to remember; no, not vaguely, but with a nightmare intensity within an otherwise fuzzy recollection. Instead, they had skimped on real flowers and overdone the air freshener – without success, for even in the broad light of day there still hovered in the foyer the ghost of the aficionados' cigars.

The ghosts of the bulls were there too, for on the wall behind the reception desk the new owners, as if in jest, had left the stuffed heads of bulls who had once known fiercer days. A Sobrero, an Embajador and a Ventoso, who gaze upon everything now in stupefaction. For a moment, it seemed to me that I recognized their faces. Or that their small glass eyes glinted when they recognized me. I almost saw myself as a child again, holding someone's hand, surrounded by adults busily talking about their own affairs, while I stared at those same large heads in the old foyer, with their modest tongues poking out from the cheap stuffing. I don't know if I invented the memory or if I really did feel at the time, as I did a while ago, the same twinge of solidarity.

Yet another hotel that acts as a maquette or mascot of the whole country, as a doll's house and scale model of the real house, and which has the bad taste to put it on display in the main living room or to leave it to gather dust in the attic. This renovated Hotel Imperial has watered down its rather tainted quaintness, gone to a lot of trouble to exchange some of its old rough edges for newer ones, and ended up with a precarious kind of 'luxury' held together with pins. Its touch, however, is still uncertain when it comes to creating and providing genuine luxury.

The whisperings and tappings of the two receptionists had been going on for ages. I considered getting out my notebook, which rarely fails as a last resort: taking notes always attracts attention. Then the machine finally spat out the smart card for my room. The receptionist didn't bother to summon anyone to carry my bag, and I could have sworn that they both held out the card to me simultaneously. Or perhaps that was simply the effect created by their disconcertingly double smile.

The corridor on my floor was empty and silent, as if it were five in the morning. Or as if it were precisely the time it was, because hotels are often very noisy at five in the morning. No employees, no guests. The only thing you could almost hear was the gluey smell of new carpets. I reached my room door and it took me a while to work out how to put the card in the slot. Finally, the little red light blinked, then turned green. The door snorted and reluctantly opened a couple of centimetres. Beyond lay a dark area, one of those spaces in hotel rooms that serve as a kind of no-man's-land and provide the luxury of a square metre with no furniture, no name and no other purpose than that of isolating the bedroom, at least in theory, from any noise out in the corridor.

To my right the door of the bedroom stood slightly ajar, letting in just enough light for me to see that the door to the bathroom stood wide open. A gleaming tap dripped in the darkness. Before I had a chance to close the main door to the corridor, I heard a voice inside. Like a thief taken by surprise, I instinctively froze, an instinct I had no idea I possessed and which was, besides, entirely misplaced. To my left, in the full-length mirror in the vestibule, something moved. In the reflection, I could make out the inside of the room that the door was preventing me from seeing. I saw a double bed with a beige counterpane that matched the grey light coming in through a window invisible to me.

A girl was sitting on the edge, towards the head of the bed. She was pretty, despite the ridiculous amount of make-up she was wearing. She looked very young. She had on only a bra and pants. Her hair and skin were the colour of the bedspread. Her hands were resting on her lap, and she was staring down at them with a look of utter boredom on her face. She was blowing out her cheeks a little, drumming lightly on the carpet with her feet and sighing scornfully, exaggerating these signs of tedium, like a child pretending to be bored.

Out of the corner of her eye she was watching something happening on the part of the bed not reflected in the mirror. She wasn't alone. The sprung base creaked without her having moved a muscle and someone – a man, of course – panted once, twice, three times.

I didn't know whether to go back out into the corridor or to walk straight in and demand an explanation. Since they clearly couldn't see me, I took another step forward, my eyes still fixed on the mirror. The girl's reflection disappeared. On the other side of the bed, with his back to the headboard and to her, I saw a naked boy. He was probably slightly younger than the girl and much darker-skinned too. I couldn't see his face because his head was bent contritely over his chest: I could see only a tense forehead, the beginning of a frown. He was still breathing like someone about to make some great physical effort, and was running his hand over his chest with a strangely insentient, robotic gesture. Then the girl spoke.

'Get on with it, will you?'

The boy jumped and looked at her as if he had forgotten she was there.

'All right, all right.'

He again focused on his hand and let it slide slowly down his chest to his navel. He placed it, without much conviction, on his flaccid penis, which he shook a couple of times, like a rattle. Then suddenly a shiver ran through him.

'It's too bloody cold in here.'

'Yeah, yeah.'

The girl's 'yeah, yeah' sounded resigned, as if she had said it a thousand times before, as if she had spent her whole life in that room, sitting there in her underpants, listening to people complaining about the cold. I imagined her arching her eyebrows and nodding in mock solemnity, but, to check that I was right, I would have had to stop seeing the boy's face. She must have liked the woman-of-the-world air that her 'yeah, yeah' gave her, because she repeated it.

'Yeah, yeah.'

The boy started breathing hard again as he went about his business without success. The girl joined in his next out-breath.

'What's wrong?'

'I don't know, can't you help?'

'No, I can't, I've told you already. You have to do it on your own. Then we can fuck.'

'I can't get it up.'

'Well, watch the film then.'

The girl had suddenly adopted the tone of an older sister:

'Wait, I'll turn up the volume.'

I heard her feeling for something next to the bed and heard things falling onto the carpet. I didn't dare change my position in order to be able to see her face again. I was beginning to feel afraid they would discover me there. The idea of marching into the bedroom, pretending to be surprised and asserting my rights had vanished of its own accord. I should have gone down to reception. The truth is, I don't know if I stayed there because I was afraid of making a noise as I left or because I wanted to see and hear more. It seemed to me that I could safely wait a while longer: if the boy or the girl got up, I would still have time to step out into the corridor and close the door before they saw me.

'Where's the remote gone?'

The boy said nothing. He was kneading his penis with both hands now. He did it in a careless, oddly clumsy way, as if he had never touched it before. Suddenly a chorus of moans blared out above the unmistakably inane soundtrack of a porn flick.

'Yes, yes. Just there. Just there. Oh.'

I realized that I was standing in the vestibule, smiling. A solitary smile is never a proper smile. I was probably just trying to quell both my nerves and my unease about the whole situation: given the stimuli available, I wasn't surprised that the boy was finding it hard to get an erection.

'Turn it down.'

'OK, OK.'

The groans and the music abated just as a hoarse, rather unconvincing voice joined the chorus.

'Yes. That's it. Just there. Yes.'

The boy was staring at the screen. He must have been immediately behind the door to the vestibule, and, for a moment, I had the impression that he was looking straight at me through the wood: my pounding heart was in my throat now. But what the boy was looking at through the crack was his own image reflected in the vestibule mirror. This was apparently more arousing than the mechanical heavy breathing on-screen. His apathetic penis began to show signs of life. He turned slightly and looked at his reflection full on. I thought then, this boy is seeing exactly what I'm seeing and is excited by the very thing that I can see without feeling any excitement: the image of himself reflected back at him by the mirror in this small, dark space; the image that would be replaced by my own reflection, the wrinkled back of my jacket, if I were to take one step forwards.

Standing just half a metre from the mirror, in the gloom of that tiny vestibule, which was neither corridor nor bedroom, I felt almost as if I were in the boy's presence. The rectangle of light framing his reflected body blocked my path like a concrete wall: I couldn't go into the bedroom without pushing open the door and interrupting the scene inside, but neither could I retreat into the corridor without coming between the boy and his double. After a few interminable seconds – during which I barely dared to breathe – I again heard the dripping tap in the bath, I became aware of the handle of my bag digging into my shoulder and of how tired I was from standing. Perhaps a still more ridiculous parenthesis of tedium was about to open inside that senseless anxiety. I was aware of the dark space, the terrifying paralysis one experiences in ghostly dreams or during childhood games. I noticed, above all, that the knot in my throat had been growing gradually tighter and would soon resemble a childish black panic.

The boy was masturbating energetically now. For a second or two, I had been watching everything but seeing nothing, and he and I both jumped at the same time when we suddenly heard the voice of another man.

'No, no. That's fine, but don't turn away. Keep looking over here.'

There was someone else in the room. The boy looked round and away from the mirror. I breathed again (and realized that I had been forgetting to do so for some time now).

'That's better. You know, it really is cold in here. I'm going to close the door, but you carry on.'

And I probably really shouldn't have breathed, because the new air made me drop my guard. The panic gathered momentum and went straight to my head: I felt its hands gripping my shoulders hard and brushing my neck and pressing into the corners of my eyes before giving me a silent slap around the face. It had understood before I did what those words meant. The owner of the voice would approach the vestibule door and find me standing there and that would be terrible. I stood with my back against the wall. I could see nothing in the mirror now. Anyone in that room, or, indeed, in the whole hotel, would have been able to hear my heart pounding. On the other side of that half-open door, I heard footsteps walking across the carpet towards the door – I doubtless imagined them or felt them on the soles of my own feet or in the deepest recesses of my ears, because that carpet would have been capable of muffling the noise of a whole army on the march. I saw myself from outside – from above to be exact – and it seemed to me that I had all of eternity in which to calculate what was probably going to happen (and what was probably not going to happen), the various emotions provoked by my collision with the owner of the voice: anger – Where the hell did you spring from?, surprise – What are *you* doing here?, ominous malice and feigned amusement – Well, well, look who's here!, and worse, our absurd shared astonishment – Oh!

Only now, as I'm writing this, do I realize that the one thought in my head at the time was that this room was, after all, mine, and that the law, if you like, was on my side. Of course it was, but, at that moment, the room was outside almost everything, certainly outside the law.

Then the door closed. Someone pushed it shut from inside, that was all. I saw nothing, no hand, not even a shadow. I felt a sense of relief tinged with a feeling of stunned disappointment. On the other side of the door, the footsteps belonging to the owner of the voice moved off. I heard him say:

'There was a bit of a draught coming in.'

I heard nothing more: not the voices of the girl or the boy, nor the soundtrack of the porn movie. I breathed deeply again and that was when the accumulated panic overflowed. For another eternal second, my feet seemed soldered to the floor. I would never escape from that vestibule, which, now that the mirror had been reduced to a blank, black surface, was pitch-dark. Then suddenly, in two miraculous strides, I was out in the corridor and very slowly closing the door to the room. The corridor was still deserted.

Only then did I notice the red 'Do not disturb' sign hanging from the handle, and I even pretended to be angry with myself: honestly, fancy not noticing that, I almost said out loud. My heart was slowing, and I felt the euphoria I always used to feel as a small boy after pulling off one of my rather discreet pranks. I realize now that I was still thinking in childish terms: I was all right, I was safe and well and alive. *They* – the baddies, the grown-ups – hadn't caught me.

Then the adult in me resumed his post, brushed off his sleeves, and relegated to a dark corner the boastful, fearful boy who had taken command for a moment or so. After all, I thought, I hadn't done or, indeed, seen anything very wrong. It had been a curious scene, though. Hard to interpret, odd.

I couldn't face getting in the lift and so I took the emergency stairs. No carpet, no air freshener, no piped music. It was cold and my steps echoed above the dull machine throb coming from the bottom of the bottomless well of the stairs.

'No, not odd, weird.'

This, I believe, I said out loud as I raced down the stairs. I took them two at a time until I reached the basement, only to have to climb them again, one by one.

HARKAITZ CANO

The Keys to the Apartment

It's called a bikini sandwich. And the exotic name is probably the most attractive thing about it.

'When are we going to Burger King?'

'Don't you like your bikini, Izaro?'

'It's nothing special, just an ordinary sandwich.'

At the beach bar, her mother tries to hide the keys underneath a crumpled crisp packet on the table, but Jone immediately sees what she's doing.

'Don't forget the keys, Mum.'

The keys to the apartment are burning the palm of her mother's hand; she weighs them as if her hand was a pair of scales, as if she were valuing a piece of merchandise. When they walk past the hut where the inflatable dinghies are stored, she suddenly hurls the keys as far as she can. Her daughters stare at her in amazement. The keys land at the water's edge, where the waves don't quite reach. Izaro playfully runs to pick them up, like a dog returning a stick to its owner. When she hands back the keys, her mother gives her a reproving look.

'Why are you so obedient when I least want you to be?'

She doesn't say this, she thinks it. And her oldest daughter catches her thought on the wing.

Harkaitz Cano (b. 1975) was born in Lasarte in the Basque Country and writes in Basque, often translating his own work into Spanish. He has published poetry, short stories and novels and worked as a scriptwriter for film and television. His novel *Belarraren ahoa* (2004) brought him the Premio Euskadi, and his 2011 novel *Twist* won the Premio de la Crítica, the Premio Euskadi and the Premio Beterri de los Lectores. This story appears in *Beti oporretan* (translated into Spanish as *El turista perpetuo*, 2017).

As if they weren't perfectly aware that, for a while now, their mother has been trying really hard to lose her keys.

She angrily stuffs the keys into her beach bag so that they're right at the bottom. Does that huge bag have the ability to make metal objects disappear? When they reach the apartment, she rummages around in the bag, trying to convince her daughters:

'You see, they're not there. I've lost them.'

Jone sighs while Izaro empties out the contents of the bag. This isn't the first time this has happened either. Sunscreen, a frisbee, rackets, a towel. And the keys. They're still there.

Izaro picks everything up again and puts it back in the bag. Her mother takes the keys from her and tries to open the door to the apartment with the smallest key. It's quite obvious it isn't the right one.

'It's no use. It doesn't work. The door won't open.'

'Try the other one, Mum. That's the key for the postbox.'

'Do you think so? So you reckon it's the other one?'

Jone nods. Her mother eyes the key suspiciously. She couldn't look more disgusted if she'd found a hair in her soup. She seems perplexed. Finally, she puts the right key in the lock and, for a moment, lets the bundle of keys hang there jingling, unable to bring herself to open the door. Then she carefully removes the key and leads her daughters back down the stairs.

'Let's go.'

Her daughters act as a counterweight: they're the ballast preventing her from taking flight. She should be grateful to them. She's always thought the ability to fly was overrated.

The street cleaners seem to be surreptitiously sweeping the sand from the beach up onto the promenade, as if they were part of a plot to make the city disappear beneath the dust and the mist. Given the choice, she would have preferred the bin lorry, but that won't be coming by until later. Instead, she drops the keys into the nearest litter bin.

No keys, no apartment, she thinks mischievously.

If there's one thing this place has plenty of it's empty hotel rooms. They take one at the Hotel Retamar. 'It's not a double,' the receptionist tells them. 'That's all right,' the woman says.

Hotels haven't used keys for a long time. You open the door with a plastic card.

'Will we have to sleep on the floor again, Mum?'

'You'd like that, wouldn't you? Just like at the campsite.'

She succeeds in sweet-talking Izaro, but not Jone.

The woman is utterly exhausted: she can't remain at her post by the window for a moment longer and, in danger of falling asleep on the spot, she asks her older daughter to take over.

'If you see your Dad's car, wake me up.'

Jone turns on the TV. The night passes quietly. With her back to the screen, curled up on the sofa, but never once taking her eyes off the window, all she has for company are the muted voices on the television, while her mother and her sister sleep, arms about each other, on the narrow bed. When she begins to get bored, she makes a paper aeroplane out of the DO NOT DISTURB sign. Just before daybreak, she sees someone approaching the entrance to the hotel. 'Why are you so obedient when I least want you to be?'

But the person is on foot, not in a car. 'Wake me up if you see your Dad's car.' She hesitates for a moment as to whether she should or shouldn't tell her mother. She decides not to.

Her father pounds on the door to the room. On the television, they're advertising pieces of kitchen equipment very very quietly, as if they were selling them on the black market: knives and electric graters.

'Did you really think I wouldn't find you?'

The mother is so small, and Izaro and Jone even smaller, they just have to crouch down and avoid the trap and the lump of cheese and escape down the little tunnel the mouse has made in the wall. They race down the emergency stairs.

'Where are we going, Mum?'

'You wanted to go to Burger King, didn't you, sweetheart?'

The grass has just been cut or else it grows very slowly. She wishes she could cut her daughters' hair as short as that. A multitude of masts with their respective flags flank the little garden at the entrance to the hotel. When she's older, Izaro thinks, she'll be able to visit all those countries, and then those brightly coloured flags will hold no mystery for her. And that strikes her as rather sad. Gobbling up mysteries and being left with none. Outside, a tap has been left on, and the hosepipe, lying coiled like a snake in the grass, keeps emitting a sempiternal last drop. 'That's the south for you. Then they'll complain when there's a drought.'

'What about Dad?'

'What about him?'

'He taught me to ride a bike.'

'He probably did. That and what else?'

The buzz of insects that aren't insects. It's the hiss of the sprinklers. Not a soul in the street. The shutters on the shops are down, the merchandise quite safe. The padlocks, though, are rather pathetic; they reveal a rank indifference to, a complete lack of respect for, the seasonal junk they're protecting. No one in his right mind would consider stealing that stuff.

The tourist train is still under wraps. It's too early for it to be doing its summer round of the city's marvellous attractions: the second-tallest skyscraper in Spain, a rugby pitch with artificial grass, the tiny bar where Sophia Loren once drank a Campari.

'I'm tired, Mum. Where are we going?'

'To Burger King.'

'But Burger King won't be open yet.'

She knows it isn't the burgers her daughters like best, it's the free cardboard crowns they hand out to kids.

'I'll make each of you a crown if you like, but right now we need to get a move on.'

Along the Paseo Miradero, the deckchairs are piled up one on top of another. So are the tables. They resemble Martians out of Space Invaders waiting for someone to blow their pixels apart. It could happen, always assuming that someone was armed with a laser gun.

'At least tell me you know where we're going.'

'Somewhere.'

'But where?'

If she had been Goliath (or was it David?), she could happily have thrown one of her daughters into the sea – only one, no need to exaggerate – but she has both hands full, and how.

When she walks past the basilica, she feels as if she were back in the Middle Ages. Or the protagonist in a Western. Every building pales into insignificance beside that Romanesque church; she finds the sight of the municipal sports centre particularly depressing. There couldn't be a better reason for converting to Christianity. When did the architects give up making buildings out of stone and start constructing kennels?

She catches a glimpse of a sign warning about 'dangerous dogs', but the dogs are either asleep or pretending to be because they're afraid of this woman dragging her daughters along the deserted avenue. She is clearly not a woman to be messed with. 'Did you see anything, Rufo?' 'No.' 'Neither did I.'

She really is almost dragging the girls along, and they just about manage to keep up with her, taking small poodle steps. No tantrums. They're used to it. The woman wishes the two sisters were the same weight, but Izaro is considerably lighter, thus reducing the woman's traction power.

At this rate, they'll soon need new shoes, like those black kids in blues songs. She's afraid Izaro and Jone might wear their feet down to the ankles with all that walking. The image of a pencil sharpener suddenly pops into her head, and the kind of very fine pencil that wears down really quickly because the point keeps breaking and has to be sharpened again and again.

'Are we nearly there, Mum?'

What can she say? No, they're not. They're never going to be 'there'. The only thing their mother is getting *near* to is losing her patience. They sit down on the seats in a bus shelter to rest a little.

'There aren't any buses at this hour, Mum. Besides, it really stinks here.'
'Yes, you're right.'

The daughters immediately regret having spoken, because they were much better off sitting in the bus shelter.

But there's no alternative. They must keep on walking. Everyone has a mission to fulfil and that is theirs. The woman doesn't dare look behind her, afraid she'll find her daughters up to their knees in a river of mud. They haven't spoken for a while now. She can't even hear them breathing. If you're not very careful, daughters can easily crumble into nothing. Perhaps she's just leading along a couple of weary, disembodied heads each with just a single arm attached to her hands? She does feel a little lighter. Perhaps she's stronger than she thought.

If it were winter, by the time they reached the pine forest, all that would be left between her fingers would be one glove belonging to each of her daughters. If it were winter, the tumescent breeze from the suburbs would seem more bearable.

'What a pong!'

It really does stink. And the smell is getting worse.

Jone resurfaces from the sea of the mute and starts talking again and asking questions, in between intermittent sighs:

'Tell us the truth, Mum. Are we going to the rubbish tip?'

'Yes, sweetheart. We'll see if we can find the keys there.'

EIDER RODRÍGUEZ

And Shortly After That, Now

'Until I did it, I had no idea it was going to be so easy. But I had to do it, then I could forget about it. I was really afraid to take that first step, and I went over it again and again in my mind.'

Floren takes a handkerchief from his pocket and mops his brow. His grandson looks at him, half-concerned, half-respectful, sitting cross-legged on the ground, as his teacher always tells him to. His grandfather turns his back, so as to continue his work in the garden, then he goes on:

'I just had to do it and then leave, that was all, quick and simple.' He looks at his grandson and adds gravely: 'But, first, I had to do it.'

It's a very hot day in Biarritz. It's August.

Manex moves closer to his grandfather so as to hear better. The old man continues talking while he kneels to dig a hole for the shrub he's planting. His grandfather is right, the first step is the hardest. He finds it relaxing watching his grandfather pressing down the damp earth with his bare hands.

'Believe me, Manex, the first step is always the hardest. After that, everything's easy, you'll see. But you've got to be brave and take that first step. The rest is as easy as falling off a log, as they used to say in my village.'

'When will we visit your village, Grandpa?'

'When rabbits ride bicycles.'

Eider Rodríguez (b. 1977) was born in Errenteria in the Basque Country and writes in Basque and self-translates into Spanish. She currently lives in Hendaye on the border between France and Spain. She studied at the Sorbonne and the University of Madrid, and, in 2004, published her first collection of stories, *Eta handik gutxira gaur*, from which this story is taken. Her 2007 novel, *Bihotz handiegia*, won the Premio de Euskadi and the Premio Euskadi de Plata.

Manex smiles and looks down. He's now studying the glossy wings of a ladybird clambering over the grass. His grandfather is right.

The old man mops his brow again and sits down on a plastic chair next to Manex. With a slender twig, he cleans the dirt from under his fingernails. Manex says nothing. He's still studying the ladybird, and, besides, there's nothing more to say, his grandfather is right.

Floren is remembering the spring of 1937. He still can't think of it without feeling a twinge of pain. Or perhaps he doesn't want to think of it *without* feeling pain. The pain is all that's left to him of Manuel. Perhaps that's because he's never told anyone, perhaps because the rain carries away memories, and all that's left are a few small drops of what happened. And it's rained a lot since 1937. But he's never told anyone, not even Geneviève in her final days, when they sat holding hands in the evening, waiting for death.

Silence clung to the walls. The neighbours were silent as stones. People never talked about the dead, not even with family members. With the arrival of the new mayor, the municipal staff underwent some radical restructuring, to use a current term. Any reds, or anyone suspected of being a red, were thrown out of the council offices. Their places were taken by fascists and other unfortunates. They kept Floren on. He was a bit of a loner and didn't seem dangerous. In the village, people thought him rather strange. His mother had died immediately after giving birth to him, and, three years later, his father left for Pamplona to find work. He went to live with an aunt who didn't appear to be a subversive. And so, the mayor with his shiny boots allowed Floren to stay in his post. Floren was a sort of general handyman, but his favourite part of the job was any kind of gardening work. Helping those delicate beings to thrive, feeling their cool stems between his fingers, keeping an eye out for any failing shoots. Theirs was the first town hall in the whole of Ribera Navarra to decorate its balconies with flowers. The previous mayor had allowed Floren to place flowerpots along all the corridors and balconies.

Manex doesn't know what the Civil War was. Or, rather, they were taught it at school, but it's the kind of thing you forget the moment you tuck into your post-exam sandwich. However, he does enjoy hearing his grandfather talking about it, although he finds it hard to imagine him being caught up in an actual war. War means death and enemies, aeroplanes and soot-smeared faces; and he can't honestly connect his grandfather with such things. It's exciting when his grandfather tells him how he escaped the war, then he imagines his laid-back grandpa with his beret on his head as a criminal or a hero out of a film.

'It was really hot that week, and the crickets were screeching all night. It felt as if there might be a storm at any moment. The radio had been reporting the military coup in Morocco all morning. Do you know where Morocco is?'

'In Africa . . . in the desert,' says Manex with a shrug.

'The commander of the Civil Guard called for calm, saying that the police were on the side of the Republic. Do you know what the Republic is?'

'More or less.'

'More more or more less?'

Through the window comes the smell of roasted spare ribs, and, at the same time, a woman in a yellow apron shouts '*À table!*' as only the French know how, '*À manger!*', in a voice that comes from deep in the throat. Manex and his grandfather sit down at the table. The freckle-faced woman is using a huge fork and spoon to serve the salad. Manex doesn't dare look at his mother, preferring to dive back into his grandfather's soothing stories; besides, his mother is always rather sombre. The grandfather prefers to go on talking to Manex, and for him, suddenly, it feels almost like being with Manuel again. The mother, for her part, is quite happy for Manex and his grandfather to continue their chatter; she doesn't feel like going into motherly mode; she is comfortable, as always, in her role as impartial witness.

'What about Serge?' asks the grandfather, seeing that the table is only set for three.

'He had to go to Bordeaux for a meeting. He won't be back until tonight.'

She says this without looking at him, at the same time serving Manex some salad. She isn't in the mood to answer her father's unspoken question. Manex sits there admiring the lettuce leaves, far removed from his mother's words.

Floren has grown tired now of his conversation with his grandson, and has lost his appetite. Nor does he have the strength to confront the wry expression on his daughter's face.

'Serge works too hard, don't you think?' Floren asks.

'*Bof.*'

Bof, which means, will you shut up, I don't want to talk about it, leave me in peace and eat your bloody salad, *cette merde de laitue*, I'm up to here with your double-edged questions, just eat and shut up, you boring old man, and go and plant apple trees and listen to the radio.

All that can be heard is the sound of the neighbour's lawnmower. He's doubtless kitted out in a pair of red swimming trunks and a T-shirt bought at the fiesta in Bayonne, and a pair of espadrilles too small for his feet, which look like snails bursting out of their shells. The leaves on the trees are utterly still, grown flaccid in the heat. There's not a breath of wind.

'I was telling Manex my war stories. Perhaps I'll take him to visit the village before the summer holidays are over. What do you think?'

'Seriously?' and her face lights up, probably because they're talking about something she doesn't care about. 'And why would you want to go there?'

'It's not me, it's Manex who wants to go,' says the grandfather in a slightly guilty tone.

Manex is concealed beneath the peak of his baseball cap. Whenever he smiles, his cheeks dimple. Manex is just two dimples and the peak of a cap. And a few very large teeth. And loads of freckles.

'I'll ask Serge to drive me to San Sebastián and we can catch the bus from there,' says Floren.

'*Ah bon*,' says his daughter.

'We could perhaps go tomorrow.'

'*Ah bon*.' The same words, the same volume, only this time she lifts her eyebrows just half a centimetre higher and forms a tighter circle with her lips.

'I can't tomorrow, because it's the last day of my surfing course, but the day after I can,' says Manex, looking at his mother out of the corner of his eye.

'Fine, I've no problem with that.' And she wearily places a serving of meat on their respective plates.

It was a spring very similar to this one. He'd arranged to meet Manuel behind the town hall for a game of *pelota*. The day before, instead of playing, they'd lain down on the court, shirts off, staring up at the warm blue sky, sweating, talking, looking. Manuel was the only one Floren talked to, well, him and a slightly younger cousin. On the afternoon when Manuel didn't turn up, the heat was suffocating, and Floren was pleased because then, he thought, they could just lie down on the grass again, talking, sweating, looking. Crazy and happy. That was Manuel. And Floren wanted to be the same. With this in mind, he took some wine with him and a bit of cheese, but, that afternoon, Manuel never turned up. And Floren was annoyed, because he thought Manuel must have gone to some secret meeting instead, as he so often had before. And, for the first time in his life, Floren felt alone. Until then, he had never missed anyone, or their presence. And loneliness was an ugly thing, like stealing, like sleeping on a gravestone. On that afternoon spent waiting for Manuel, he finished off nearly all the wine. By the time he got home, he could barely speak, and it was his aunt who told him, in a tiny thread of a voice, that five young men from the village had been shot. Her face remained utterly impassive as she continued scooping milk out of the saucepan and stirring it in with the rice and the cinnamon.

Valentín Sarnago, known as Rabbit. Adolfo Belzunce. Mari Garro: Leonor's son-in-law. Luis: the butcher's son. And Manuel Iroz: Manuel.

Floren felt the salt taste of blood on his tongue along with the taste of wine. And all he could do was keep quietly repeating Manuel's name, until his aunt served supper. It was the clatter of plates on the wooden table that returned Floren to the world of the living or, in this case, the world of the dead.

'*Ma chérie*,' he says to his daughter, ignoring all the rules of French pronunciation. 'I'm going to take a nap. This ghastly heat has upset my stomach. *Mon pot*,' he says, addressing Manex, and, although he seems about to say something more, he doesn't.

Mother and son are sitting side by side, eating watermelon, staring out at the fence surrounding the house, and they both look as if they were wearing big green smiles.

Floren sits down on his bed. He has no intention of sleeping. He feels as if his heart were burning, his throat swollen. When he used to sit with Geneviève on her death bed, he often felt tempted to tell her, to talk about the days he spent with Manuel, but he couldn't. After his wife breathed her last, death took up permanent residence in his mind, and he forgot all about Manuel. Until today. Manuel and Geneviève are both gnawing away at his liver, the smell of blood and fever, his daughter's grey eyes on the other side of the table. And young Manex's fears.

The following day, Floren went to work at the town hall as usual. As he was going up the stairs, he heard the mayor roaring with laughter about something. He was told to go and repair one of the steps down into the cellar, and he used this as an excuse to stay there, giving the occasional blow with his hammer. That day, he was all fire and hatred, with not an ounce of peace in him. Around midday, he saw the mayor and his secretary eating lunch as usual in the local restaurant, and again he felt his stomach turn over.

'How's things?' the mayor said, looking up at him, still chewing, moving his greasy snout like some wild beast.

Floren saw the pig's trotters on the table, a foot covered in yellow sauce and speared by a fork. The secretary had a fried egg and two sausages on his plate, and wore his napkin tied around his neck.

'Cat got your tongue?'

'Oh, sorry, sir, good afternoon.' And, as soon as he said those words, he knew.

There's a knock at the door. Floren rumples the sheets and lies down on the bed. It's his daughter.

'Serge and I have decided to separate. He's rented an apartment in Bidart. He'll move out next month. *Voilà*. Anyway, I don't feel like talking about it now, so no questions, all right?'

She stands in the doorway, not letting go of the door handle, not even entering her father's room. Floren is now sitting on the bed, and he has no idea what would be the right reaction, joy or consternation.

'*Bo*,' he says at last.

'It's a mutual decision. I'll tell Manex one of these days *et voilà*.' She waves her hands about as if she were angry. 'I've left you some fish for supper. I'll eat at Magali's house. You just have to stick it in the oven for twenty minutes, that's all.'

And she went down the stairs, leaving the sound of her heels on the wooden floor in Floren's room.

He realizes that he's really eager now to revisit his village with his grandson; the first time in ages that he's wanted to do anything urgently.

He'd tried to think that Manuel was just a silly story from his youth, but it's not true. Now, like a character in a film, he wishes, sixty-three years on, that he could look at a photo or two, but he doesn't have any. For a while, he kept a few letters his aunt had sent him, and some from his cousin too, along with a *pelota* ball and a Republican insignia Manuel had given him. Now he has nothing. He put them in a tote bag he'd got free from Crédit Agricole. Now all he has in that bag are the letters he sent to Geneviève from Paris, her replies from Ciboure, one of Manex's first drawings, and the photo of his parents' wedding, but nothing evokes any memories, nothing fills him with nostalgia, it's as if he were totally empty-handed. Only the memory of Manuel ties him to his village, that's the only thing that brings back the smell of the earth. And to do that he simply has to trawl through his memories.

Floren knows that it happened shortly after Manuel was murdered, but can't remember exactly when. He asked his cousin to bring him some seeds from Pamplona. The first thing he had to do was plant the seeds in his garden and wait for them to come up. It was a way of savouring his revenge: going to the garden every day to see if the seeds had sprouted, then watering them and watching them sway in the arms of the wind. First, a few colourful buds appeared, delicate and fringed, completely new beings in Floren's eyes. And then they opened out into a bell-like shape. Floren found this an unforgettable sight. On the day the flowers opened, he filled a wheelbarrow with soil and took it to the town hall. He remembers preparing the window boxes on the balcony and filling them with the cool, soft soil.

'What are you up to?' asked the secretary, from the horrific height granted him by his gleaming leather boots.

'I'm going to decorate the balcony in time for the festival of Our Lady.'

The secretary was accompanied by a soldier Floren had never seen before, and the two men moved off, guffawing at something the soldier had said. They kicked up the dust as they went. Floren clenched his fists in rage, until he felt the grit of the soil sticking into the palm of his hand.

Manex has come down to breakfast wearing his baseball cap. On his back is an over-sized backpack, which makes him look skinnier than he really is. Floren takes their two glasses of milk out of the microwave.

'Aren't you going to take your backpack off to have breakfast? You look like a turtle.'

Manex puffs out his cheeks and makes paddling movements with his hands. Grandfather and grandson drink their chocolate milk and eat their toast and blueberry jam. Floren has barely slept because he feels so nervous. It has been longer than he thought since he went back to the village, and he's more excited than he expected to be at the prospect. They hear Serge papping his hooter outside before they have time to do the washing up. Manex waves goodbye to his mother, who is leaning out of her bedroom window, holding a cup and wearing a tracksuit. Floren waves goodbye too, and they get into the car with the engine already running.

'So why are you going back now? Don't get me wrong, I think it's fine, but it's odd, don't you think, after all these years, to suddenly decide to go back?'

Serge drives very fast. He has to shout above the crackle of the badly tuned-in radio. Beside him, Manex is playing with his Game Boy.

'I want to show Manex where I was born. He's curious to see it,' says Floren in the back seat.

'*Ah bon?*' And Serge playfully taps the peak of Manex's baseball cap.

Manex doesn't even look up from his screen. They leave behind them the green fields and the cows with their all-too-human eyes, the white and red houses. When they reach San Sebastián, Serge leaves them at the bus station.

'I'll be back here at eight o'clock on the dot. *Soyez sages,*' he shouts above the crackling radio and again taps Manex on the head.

Once they're alone, Floren and Manex feel liberated. They buy their tickets and get on the bus.

'Have you given any more thought to what we were talking about?'

'A bit.'

'And?'

'Well, yes.' Eyes down, Manex continues pushing the buttons on his Game Boy, even though he's turned it off.

'Yes, what?' asks Floren, pretending to be annoyed.

'Yes, you're right.'

'I'm sure it's no big deal. I mean, you didn't murder your teacher and then bury him in the garden, did you?'

'No,' says Manex laughing.

'Are you planning to kill someone?'

'No!'

'Have you sold your mother's wedding ring to buy drugs?'

'No!'

'That's all right then. Your mother will be fine about it.'

And Manex continued pressing the buttons for a while, before falling asleep on his grandfather's lap with his baseball cap pulled down over his face. Floren is staring intently out of the window, not wanting to miss a single detail. This is like travelling back through his life, returning to the past hand-in-hand with his grandson. As the landscape changes and grows less green, Floren's memory takes wing. They arrive two hours later. If it wasn't for the church he can see from the road, he wouldn't have recognized his village. He thinks he ought to wake Manex up, but keeps putting it off, enjoying his solitude. When he reaches the village, he feels a nervous itching in his balls, just as he used to as a young man. He removes Manex's cap, and the sun lights up his grandson's face. With his eyes half-closed, and the corners of his mouth sticky with saliva, Manex asks:

'Where are we?'

'In my village,' Floren says, and suddenly he feels very alone.

After Manuel, Floren had never loved another man. When he was fourteen or fifteen he'd been with the milkman's son, whose name he can't even remember now. They would have sex lying among the cows in the barn, on the straw that stank of urine. And then they would greedily drink the watery milk from the cows' udders. Another memory he had erased until today. With Manuel, though, it was different. They were friends, or, more importantly, they were going to be friends. Manuel was the last man he had loved. Shortly after that, in the same year that he fled the village, he met Geneviève in Ciboure, and shortly after that, they married. Shortly after that, his daughter was born, and shortly after that, the son who now lives in Dax. And shortly after that, there was now.

Where once there had been countryside there were now petrol stations and supermarkets, geometric houses scarring the horizon. There's an out-patients' department where the hermitage used to stand, and a wide road passes straight through the place where the house he was born in once stood.

'I used to live here, Manex.'

'What, on the road?'

He recognizes the accents, the unique way people here have of pronouncing words. He feels a need to talk to someone, but in Spanish; he hardly speaks Spanish to anyone in Biarritz, or only with one friend from Behobia and a couple of other people, but it's not the Spanish he spoke in his youth. He wants to talk to someone of his own age, to hear again the gentle, touching way they have of speaking. Still looking sleepy, Manex imitates his grandfather's way of walking, hands behind his back, a frown on his face, wearing a baseball cap instead of a Basque beret. They look very alike.

When they reach the town-hall square, they stop.

'This is where I used to work, and it's hardly changed at all. I put up those window boxes, you know. This was the first town hall in the whole of Ribera to have window boxes.'

He fled the village that same night, for ever, and without a backward glance. Until today. Wrapped up in a blanket he had two photos, a piece of stale bread, some chocolate, a slice of cheese, a shirt, a pair of underpants and a pair of socks, and, inside the socks, twenty-five *duros*.

He wept for everything he *wasn't* leaving behind. After a day's walk, he reached Pamplona. It was the second time he'd been there, and it seemed to him that there were far too many people. Floren held his breath when he passed some soldiers, thinking they would somehow know what he had done and would shoot him. However, the soldiers walked on, leaving only the echo of their boots, and for a while Floren stayed where he was, staring down at his dusty alpargatas. Two days later, he crossed the frontier and found shelter in Ciboure. There he met Geneviève, and shortly after that, they married. Shortly after that, his daughter was born, and shortly after that, the son who now lives in Dax. Shortly after that, his daughter married Serge, and Manex was born.

And shortly after that, there was now.

Floren is standing alongside Manex opposite the arcade beneath the town hall, remembering that night. The window boxes are planted now with miniature conifers, and a square banner bearing the word PEACE hangs from the balcony.

'Are you crying?' Manex asks him.

'Why would I be crying?'

'Perhaps it's made you sad coming back to the village.'

'Sad? No, I'm happy!'

'But you *are* crying,' says Manex, playing the detective.

'As we say here, you're more irritating than an itch in the goolies.' But Manex doesn't know what 'goolies' means.

When the flowers were fully open, he dug them up and placed them gently, one by one, in the wheelbarrow, as if they were newborns. He had to make three journeys to transport all the flowers to the town hall, at night, and he was afraid that the squeaking wheelbarrow would wake the people in that silent village of stone, more silent and more like stone than ever. It was a clear, warm night. He prepared the soil in the window boxes and planted the petunias, with the colours that Manuel and the others had loved so much: first, the purples, then the yellows, and then the reds.* Lots of them. That night, the moon looked like a big round cheese, or a very fat woman laughing. There was no one in the streets. Outside the town hall, Floren lit a cigar. He had a beautiful view from there of the flowers overflowing the window boxes and swaying in the breeze beneath a milk-white moon, white the colour of treachery, the colour of a scream. It was the first time he had felt complete since they'd snatched Manuel from him – complete, but alone.

He pinches the back of Manex's neck and says:

'Come on, we've got loads of things to see.'

Hands behind their backs and taking short steps, they head for the small shop next to the town hall.

'Are you Perico?' he says softly to the old man standing among the packets of cigarettes and nuts, his eyes hidden behind a pair of glasses with thick, smeary lenses. 'Do you remember me?'

The man in the glasses shifts the toothpick he's chewing from one side of his mouth to the other, but doesn't answer.

'Do you know who I am? I'm Floren Ainzúa, the nephew of Paca, the woman who used to sell eggs. Do you remember me?'

The man takes off his glasses and cleans them on one of the paper napkins he uses to wrap up any knick-knacks. He finally manages to

---

* Red, yellow and purple were the colours of the flag of the Second Spanish Republic, which was the official flag of Spain between 1931 and 1939, when the Republic was overthrown. It was the flag of the Spanish Republican government in exile until 1977.

dredge up a memory of the woman who used to sell eggs, and of that rather strange, silent nephew of hers who disappeared . . . other memories crowd into his mind too.

'Yes, I do remember.' The man reaches out one hand from behind the window, quickly and fearfully, as if he were committing a forbidden act. 'How's things?'

Floren shakes the proffered hand hard and smiles, revealing a few still healthy teeth.

'This is my grandson,' he says, placing one earth-coloured hand on Manex's head. And, before going on, he glances up at the balcony of the town hall. 'He doesn't speak any Spanish, only French and Basque.'

ELVIRA NAVARRO

Love

She feels fear gripping her chest, as well as the pleasurable shiver that
always runs through her as soon as she's said goodbye to her classmates
and set off along the broad avenue. Instead of going home, she keeps
walking; she pauses for a moment, hesitates, her face red, then walks on,
savouring the enjoyment briefly snatched from her during that moment
of doubt and again a few minutes later by the alarming gaze of a man
who seems about to follow her. A man wearing a black suit. She manages
to give him the slip and plunges into the old quarter of town. Her eagerness to reach the outskirts as quickly as possible makes her walk all the
faster; at times, she even runs. On no account must she let the night catch
up with her, because then she would lose those moments when she feels
freedom and fear in equal intensity: the sense of experiencing something
bordering on the unbearable. In fact, that's what she's feeling as she walks
along, fixing her gaze on the crumbling grey façades of the buildings, and
knowing that she wouldn't dare go down any of the gloomier side streets,
and yet just being so close to them transports her . . . where? She doesn't
know, but it's the same fear, the same fascination – and this is what most
frightens her – the same feeling of certainty that she's close to something
that belongs to her completely. Something dark, unknown, immense. She
still has quite a way to go, and the streets seem endless. Only when she
reaches the new avenues does she calm down, sure now that her walk has

Elvira Navarro (b. 1978) studied philosophy at Madrid University and published her first book of
short stories, *La ciudad en invierno*, in 2007. She has since published three novels. Her novel *La
ciudad feliz* (2009) received the Premio Jaén and the IV Premio Tormento for Best New Writer.
She was included in Granta's *The Best of Young Spanish-language Novelists* (2010).

not been in vain. The passers-by, mostly crowded together at the tram stops on the routes around the periphery of the town, regard her with bored expressions. Clara crosses that desolate area, then suddenly speeds up again, breathing in the many smells from the gardens and vegetable patches: damp earth, stagnant water, the lush green of the ugly lines of trees and shrubs silhouetted against the horizon. Masses of very still, dark clouds stand in marked contrast to the unbroken murmur of the town. By the time she decides to go home, the night is already vast.

The street door to her building is very old, like all the doors in that area. The walls of the high-ceilinged hallway are cold and solid. You can see into the well of the lift through some railings, and, when she was little, Clara liked to wind her fingers around the greasy bars and get them really dirty. Not now though. At most, she peers down the shaft, trying not to put her nose too close. She's in a hurry today, because her mother might be waiting for her, and so she takes the stairs up to the sixth floor, too impatient to endure the slow, clanking climb of the lift. Once there, she pauses for a moment to listen for any noises coming from inside the apartment. If the telly is on, there won't be too many questions about where she's been. Not a sound. She opens the door and finds the place in darkness, although she still can't declare complete victory. First, she has to go down the long corridor to her parents' bedroom, although she's almost certain no one is home. Her suspicions confirmed, she calmly arranges the contents of her rucksack on her desk, as if she had spent the afternoon studying. The light from the lamp falls on her maths exercise book, full of tedious towers of numbers, definitions underlined in green and long mathematical problems. She promptly abandons her homework and looks out of the window at the enormous square block of buildings surrounding the asbestos roof of a workshop, and beyond that a school. Further off she can see the city, with all its lights lit, and what used to be the riverbed.

The sound of the phone ringing reminds her of Jorge, and of how they had agreed that she would call him and arrange to go to the cinema. Clara shrugs. The whole business of her supposedly 'going out' with that boy seems now sad and insignificant. Two days ago, they had sat down on a bench in the playground, he with a witness and she with another, as proof that he had asked her to go out with him. They'd looked at each other for a moment, he'd asked her the relevant question, and then they'd gone their separate ways. At the end of the school day, while she was waiting for the bus, he had come over to her and suggested going to the cinema together. Now she just wanted to forget about him, but was embarrassed to look like a prude in front of her classmates. That same embarrassment made her feel cowardly and incapable of picking up the phone.

Their romance had begun one afternoon that now seems quite unreal to her. She was on her way to a baker's near the centre to order a birthday cake for her father. It was December, it was cold, and the pavements were heaving with people, some of them looking in shop windows and getting in her way. Clara wasn't quite sure where the baker's was, but she liked not being sure because that meant having to walk along several streets and not just one, as well as the possibility of having to ask the way and just generally enjoying herself. She was happily strolling along, looking up at the façades of the buildings. When she looked down again, she was aware of someone following a few metres behind her, and aware, too, that the 'someone' then suddenly turned round and disappeared up a side street. It was a boy about her age. Clara stood in the middle of the pavement, watching. She hesitated for a moment, then went after him. The boy, whose way of walking seemed somehow familiar, went into a building. Clara waited in the doorway for nearly an hour, desperate to know who that slender back belonged to. When she found out, she couldn't believe her luck: three desks in front of her was a boy she'd never noticed before, but who was clearly playing the same game as her. A proffered hand that would lead her to the strange boundary she went looking for each afternoon after school.

Then all the hours in the day became as febrile as her evening walks: she leapt out of bed as soon as the alarm went off, got dressed in front of the mirror and raced off to the bus stop in order to arrive, trembling with joy and excitement, fifteen minutes before class began. She would sit waiting on the ledge of the large window in the corridor, her face beetroot red, fearful that her classmates might guess her intentions, which couldn't have been clearer since she had always been one of those students who is habitually late. If anyone asked, she would say that her father had given her a lift, which would explain her early arrival. As the long, long minutes passed, her embarrassment dwindled and her feelings of expectation grew;

she didn't want to look at the corridor, but she kept turning round; she tried hard to appear to be casually gazing out of the window, but all she saw was her own disproportionately large face.

He walked slowly, his hands in the pockets of his bomber jacket, his gaze fixed on the ground, as if he, too, were aware that something unusual was happening, something that had to do with him, and was trying his hardest to be as unobtrusive as possible while he remained, as he imagined, under observation, although the truth is that, by then, she was already feeling the same intense disappointment she felt every morning: he was rather small and had slicked-down hair, and seemed distinctly absurd given the lengths she had gone to in waiting for him. Filled with regret, she would bite her lip and give him a challenging stare, although without quite knowing why. After exchanging a near-inaudible 'Hi', she would turn back to the window, her mind a blank, empty with disappointment.

The secret was soon out, and one morning, when the rain and the traffic prevented her from arriving fifteen minutes early so that she could sit waiting for Jorge on the window ledge in the corridor, she noticed various groups of boys and girls standing outside her classroom regarding her with exasperating smirks on their faces. She went into the classroom without saying hello to anyone, vainly hoping she might get a little solidarity from the boy, but he appeared to have turned to stone at his desk. Feeling annoyed and upset, Clara sat staring at his rigid back and at the excessively attentive way he listened to their teachers all that morning. He positively oozed the smug, superficial guilt of a complete idiot, she thought. Or was she the guilty one? She didn't honestly care where that confused sense of betrayal was coming from. She hated Jorge with all her heart.

The telephone rings again, and her mother is home now, which means that Clara can no longer postpone the reality of school and boyfriend and will at least have to be polite on the phone, otherwise all Jorge's friends will know he phoned her and that she was rude to him. Inés, her mother, is already calling to her in a meaningful voice, and, when Clara reaches the living room, her mother looks at her even more meaningfully. Then Clara pretends to be very grown up, as if it were the most normal thing in the world for a boy to phone her and ask her out, and she strides rather irritably across the room and takes the phone.

'Hi, it's me. Jorge.'

Silence. Jorge clears his throat, then invites her to go to the cinema tomorrow. He doesn't ask why she didn't phone him.

'OK,' says Clara.

'So, half past six outside the cinema?'

'OK,' she says again. When she hangs up, she chews her lip and again wonders why she has to do something she doesn't want to do, because it really has all been a misunderstanding. Nevertheless, her heart is beating very fast, and, when she recalls the boy's voice, she realizes that she does actually like him. Inés is waiting for news, and Clara decides to go into the kitchen with a brazenness which is no longer a pose, after all, nothing has actually happened. Or rather, nothing worthy of her mother's sympathetic attention. Inés, however, appears to have decided for herself what Jorge's phone call means.

'So who's the nice young man who just phoned you?'

Clara snorts, turns bright red, opens the fridge door so as to conceal her embarrassment, then shuts it again without taking anything out.

'Just a classmate,' she says.

Her mother cannot help giving a triumphant smile. Trembling with rage, Clara storms out of the kitchen and returns to the living room. What would happen if she called Jorge and told him it was all off? That she'd been his girlfriend for just six hours and now it was 'off'. She still feels detached from it all, and tries in vain to ignore Inés, who is laying the table and keeps shooting sideways glances at her. Before she hears the words 'Do something, don't just stand there staring', she gets up and goes over to the kitchen. She is stopped in her tracks by a whistle coming from outside, from the rear of the apartment. Her friend Merchi's beaming face is looking down at her from the seventh floor. A very pink, gummy smile.

'I've finished my homework, have you? Shall we go for a walk?' Merchi says.

'OK, but I can't stay long. I'll wait for you downstairs,' replies Clara.

There's not much traffic in the street, and Clara listens to the sound of their footsteps as they walk along in silence. The cold wind cuts her face, and, by the time they have walked a whole block, she feels like saying to Merchi, why don't we go back and talk in the hallway? But she says nothing. She's too preoccupied to be able to summon up the appropriately casual tone.

Even disguised as a simple wish not to freeze to death, it would probably have sounded like a tetchy: 'Why can't you all just leave me in peace?' Merchi starts talking about unimportant things: art school, the upcoming exams, her plans for the weekend. Slowly, and as if by chance, she begins to approach the subject Clara has been concealing from her, first listing the latest pairings-up in their class and in other schools too, which both she and Clara know all about. Then, seeing that Clara remains silent, Merchi says:

'Rosa phoned me this afternoon and told me about you and that boy. She says it was all a bit strange, and that you didn't say a word to each other for the rest of the day. Why didn't you tell me?'

'Because there's nothing to tell. I don't even like him any more,' Clara says.

'Rosa also told me that everyone in the class has known about it for over a month, everyone except you, that is . . .' Merchi breaks off, searching for the right words.

'What else has Rosa told you?' asks Clara, her heart pounding. She suddenly feels as if she were the focus of some plot, as if she had been spied on not only for the last two weeks, as she thought, but . . . since when? Was Jorge making a fool of her? Did everyone know about the time she'd followed him and waited for a whole hour in the hallway of his apartment block?

'I can't tell you anything more,' answers Merchi. 'All I can say is, well, I wouldn't trust him.'

Clara feels like grabbing Merchi by her coat lapels and shaking her until she's told her everything else that Rosa said. Pride gets the better of her, though, and she says only:

'Don't tell me then. Anyway, I can't stand the guy.' Then she adds: 'But don't say anything, all right?'

'What mustn't I say?'

'That I can't stand him.'

'Fine. So what are you going to do?'

'Nothing. Shall we go down to the river?'

Clara goes ahead and crosses the road, and, when they reach the river, she says: 'Shall we go down?' knowing that Merchi is afraid of walking along by the river at night. Her friend's fear has a petty, but calming effect on Clara, and, for a time, she gazes blankly at the bright paths that now run along what used to be the riverbed, in marked contrast with the dark tree-filled areas. This brings to mind an impossible memory of before the River Turia was divided in two in order to avoid a repeat of the 1957 floods. She hadn't even been born then, but it's an image that quite often comes to her: a dark, heavy, stormy sky, and the bright, torrential river. Perhaps it was a dream. Were there banks you could walk along then?

They walk slowly back, talking about nothing at all. At home, Pepe, her father, having first loosened his tie, is already devouring a steaming bowl of soup. Clara plants a kiss on his bald head, then sits down and nibbles at the asparagus Inés always serves her when there's onion soup on the menu. She doesn't like onion soup. When she finishes eating, she takes her plate to the kitchen, then shuts herself up in her room without bothering to say Goodnight.

In her room, she thinks glumly about her date tomorrow, and wishes some complete stranger really had followed her that evening. A feeling of fear – which isn't really fear, but . . . what? – once again installs itself right in the pit of her stomach, and she wishes she could run and run, but all she can do is lie very still in her bed. At last, she falls asleep. The next day, while she's having breakfast, an idea flits through her mind, but she rejects it as completely mad. And yet, when she approaches the bus stop and spots several of her fellow female classmates waiting there, her feeling of revulsion is so strong that she says to herself: why not?, and turns on her heel, hoping no one will see her, and walks or, rather, runs to the town centre. Once there, she takes refuge in a café, astonished that she had been capable of giving in so easily to an impulse, and to that question hammering away in her head. She passes the time, changing cafés every couple of hours to avoid strange looks from the waiters, who all seem to be scolding her for skipping her classes. She doesn't feel hungry and so, to justify her presence, she orders one Coca-Cola after another, until she's spent all her money and has to resort to sitting on a bench. When her watch says half past four, she walks home.

Winter City

At six o'clock, the sky turns a blue-grey colour that makes the landscape feel strangely dense. The buildings, lit by the bright Mediterranean light, take on a matte quality, and you have to look at them very hard in order to recognize them as the same ones you saw in the morning. The avenues seem to go on for ever and appear to be the only inhabited streets. The adjacent streets, on the other hand, seem still and mysterious, twisting and turning, the street doors closed and the street lamps beginning to come on. As she heads for the cinema, Clara observes the city's slow slide into night. As she gets closer, her attention becomes focused on her own image reflected in the shop windows. It doesn't take her long to spot Jorge, who is waiting for her, sitting on a bench. He makes as if to stand up and say Hello, but Clara turns and sets off in another direction.

For the first few blocks, she's sure he's following her, and is horribly afraid he might catch her up, that he might still not have understood and will think this is just a joke she's taking too far. He *is* following her, and, at first, he does think this is some kind of game, but she seems so determined, putting one foot firmly in front of another, that he doesn't even attempt to catch her up, but keeps a safe distance. They're heading for the old part of the city, where the buildings are ever darker and more decrepit, and the passers-by ever fewer. Clara is now capable of plunging down the gloomiest side streets, and amuses herself by following unknown routes; she even occasionally stops to study the streets, and then he stops too, pretending to be lost, although, for his part, he's starting to think that she really is mad and is growing tired of trailing after a madwoman. And this despite finding a certain fascination in following her as if she really were someone else, because, suddenly, he doesn't recognize her. Clara emerges from the old part of the city, crosses the river and the new boulevards, and heads towards the motorway. When she does finally turn round, he's no longer there.

CRISTINA GARCÍA MORALES

The Generation Gap

Every weekend, in order to feel modern, Señor and Señora Bautista go travelling in their time machine. They normally stay away from Friday to Sunday, but if Señor Bautista's back is playing up, they just go for the day.

At first, when it was all new to them, they would choose really remote destinations. Señora Bautista, who is a bit of a scholar, met Socrates in person, and, feeling that some of his propositions were a little weak, she went back the following Saturday and gave him a copy of Ortega y Gasset's *The Rebellion of the Masses*. Her husband, recently retired from the army, wanted to take a closer look at the military strategy of Hannibal, who, after putting into practice some of the gentleman's revolutionary notions, made him a member of his general staff. Señor Bautista had to tell him regretfully that his old bones would not survive crossing the Alps on an elephant.

On another occasion, they went to a party held at the Palace of Versailles. The whole of Louis XIV's court started gossiping because they were the only ones who danced with their arms about each other. While in France, they also took the opportunity to have lunch with the Curies. Pierre listened open-mouthed to what Señor Bautista had to say about the atomic bomb, and Marie, blushing, asked Señora Bautista to explain one more time how the Wonderbra worked.

That was at the beginning. Now they go no further than their

Cristina García Morales (b. 1985) was born in Granada. She has written short stories and novels, notably *La merienda de las niñas* (2008), from which this story is taken. Her 2018 novel, *Lectura fácil* (*Easy Reading*), won the Premio Herralde and the Premio Nacional de Narrativa and has already been translated into several languages, including English. She is widely considered to be one of Spain's most promising young writers.

childhood or their parents' childhood, because neither Señor nor Señora Bautista knew their grandparents. They recognized the priest, Don Cecilio, who gave them their first communion, but who, at the time of their visit, was a doubt-ridden seminarian. They greeted him as if they were the children of Spanish emigrants to America in search of their roots. Señora Bautista thought him very handsome. They talked about freedom of worship and freedom of expression, about the oppression of women, about Lorca and the coming of a second republic. Don Cecilio, then still just plain Cecilio, sprang to his feet in alarm, called them heretics and fled the café, the only one in the village that served espressos.

The following weekend, they decided to go in search of the friends of their youth. If they remembered rightly, they always used to go down to the river after lunch on Fridays. When Rosita and Antonio saw them appear, they immediately stopped snogging, Teresa hid the cigarette she was smoking, and Juan Carlos dropped the pencil he was writing with. Señora Bautista took a pack of cigarettes and a lighter out of her pocket, rolled up her sleeves, leaned against a tree, lit a cigarette and took a long, slow drag. Señor Bautista took off his clothes, threw them down on the ground and waded into the water. He didn't remember it being so cold.

Then Rafael and Encarni arrived, walking along staring down at the ground as usual, until the laughter of the others alerted them to what was going on. For a moment, Rafael, Encarni and Señor and Señora Bautista stared at each other: Señor Bautista with his sparse hair slicked down on his head, Señora Bautista tapping the ash from her cigarette with one finger, Rafael with his hands in his pockets and Encarni smoothing her one perfect plait. Rafael and Encarni went straight to the Civil Guard and reported the two interlopers for public indecency. Since 21 June 1950, Señor and Señora Bautista have been serving their sentences in separate prisons. Encarni is going to be a teacher and Rafael is going off to Officer Training Academy in Zaragoza. They're thinking of getting married next summer.

AIXA DE LA CRUZ

True Milk

Translated by Thomas Bunstead

1. The children of the 1990s are destined to revive conservatism. The eighteenth century is one of their passions, given that they're the first generation in quite some time who are prudish enough to be shocked by the feats of Lord Byron.

Waking from the anaesthetic, I found myself alone in the hospital ward. Someone had left a picture of the Virgin Mary on the bedside table and, next to it, a red, heart-shaped balloon. I tried sitting up to see if there were any other presents, but this tugged on the stitches in my abdomen – I let out a small cry. I thought a nurse might hear, but a minute passed and no one came. The baby was sleeping opposite the bed; it wasn't making any noise, so I guessed it must have been sleeping. From where I was lying I could only really see the cot, which was made of grey plastic; the same colour plastic as the sick bowl and the bedpan. In public hospitals they're cutting costs anywhere they can – my mother-in-law later explained – so the same plastics company gets the contract for all sorts of things, hence everything being the same colour. Public hospitals here are very monotone and always have one of those cheap Doctor Simi pharmacies nearby. Doctor Simi's that fat, beardy character who stood in the state elections. A few hours later, sitting up in bed and peering out of the window, I saw a Doctor Simi mascot handing out flyers by the traffic lights.

Aixa de la Cruz (b. 1988) was born in Bilbao. She began writing while still at school and has already written five novels, two of which were shortlisted for the Premio Euskadi. Her short stories have appeared in many anthologies, including this story, which appeared in *Best European Fiction 2015*.

True Milk

2. All hippies are dirty and promiscuous; no child of the Facebook generation wants their mother to be seen wearing those flowery skirts. Whereas they find the eighteenth-century poet and necrophiliac José Cadalso a deeply romantic figure.

I thought it strange, the baby not crying. I wanted to get up and check it was all right, but I was worried I'd do myself an injury. I wasn't completely with it – my eyelids felt like lead. I asked myself: what dreams would I have had while I was under? I couldn't remember a thing. Strange, because not only do I always dream, I always remember my dreams. I'd had a recurring nightmare during the previous nine months, over and over: in agony, I'd be giving birth to a baby that miaowed like a cat. It came out covered in all the usual blood and mess, five fingers on each hand, two eyes, mouth – everything as it should be – but miaowing. I still don't understand it; but then I'm not convinced all dreams are meant to be understood.

3. People born in the '90s are into vampires. What they don't know is that this necessarily means they're into Lord Byron as well.

After a while, half an hour or so, I began shouting for the nurse. This woke the baby – the first time I'd heard it cry. The sound grated, it was like the baby had swallowed a rusty spring, but at least it sounded normal; at least it sounded human. I breathed a bit easier and, while I was waiting for the nurse to come, wondered whether Jorge had managed to sort out the cable contract for the TV. He'd promised he would, so I'd have something to do during the days I was going to be spending in bed. In the end he didn't keep his promise – apparently the nappies had been dearer than expected – but I remember finding the thought very comforting. As it happened, the new *True Blood* series was starting that week.

Finally, the nurse showed up: 'How do you feel?' she asked, off-hand, cold even, as she leaned down to look in the cot. I knew the medical staff were being like this with me because I'd had a Caesarean, which is more expensive for them – and you're to blame for having slim hips like a little girl's. 'My stitches are pulling,' I said. She brought me the baby, wrapped in white linen – yellowish linen, in fact, like they'd washed it in too much

371

bleach. The baby's face stood out against the sheets. 'Is it normal for it to be so pale?' She placed it in my arms. It was bald and white and had hardly any eyelashes. It was also really clean, as though it hadn't spent nine months crammed in among my internal organs. Ugly, too, I decided – no way Jorge would ever warm to a child like this. 'The doctor will come by later on,' said the nurse. 'You ought to try feeding.' I felt a shiver run through me.

4. Children from the '90s have no idea who Lord Byron is. It says so in a report by the Programme for International Student Assessment (PISA).

For *that*, I waited for my mother-in-law. She ought to know about it by now, she'd had six children. She finished work mid-afternoon. The baby was hungry, even though they'd given it a bottle at feeding time. Its little snout formed an O as it cried. The effort brought blood to its face, which made it nicer to look at. Its grandmother was also shocked by the whiteness of its skin. 'The doctor says it's thalassaemia,' I said. Before asking what thalassaemia was, before I could reassure her that it wasn't anything serious – *you only have to avoid haemorrhages, miss, and that it doesn't get hit by anything* – she began shouting at the top of her voice that everything would have been all right if only Jorge and I had got married, that she'd warned us. I hated her for this; now that it's in the past, though, I do ask myself if she mightn't have had a point. There are some things you shouldn't meddle with. You can never be too careful, because when God's ire is provoked – how can I put it . . . Anyway.

'Take out your breast,' she said, shutting the door. 'Which one?' I said. I was playing for time. The baby, with that O-shaped mouth, looked so eager to get at me I thought it might be about to suck out my soul. 'Don't be dumb,' said my mother-in-law. I took the left one – like an udder, something strange, something not belonging to me – and offered it up to the pale little monster. It was a bit like a pre-Hispanic sacrifice scene, but, being European, my savage mutilation must have been closer to that of someone like St Agatha. The baby tried to find my nipple; it seemed disoriented. Nothing strange about that: my boobs were enormous, the nipples tiny by comparison, as was the baby's head – ridiculously small. I thought it might suffocate if it got stuck in between my cleavage. My mother-in-law tried to help. The baby kept missing the spot, all gummy nips and saliva, and soon it was crying harder than ever. As was I, in the end – tears of frustration. 'Best leave it,' said my mother-in-law before going off to look for the nurse. She clearly wasn't happy. I lay staring at the baby, which was writhing around, crying hoarsely, its skin all wrinkled, like it was made out of some weird material. We seemed like different species. And where were my maternal instincts? I'd been told it was instantaneous, natural, inevitable – a chemical change that would just happen during birth. But I'd heard other things too: that I shouldn't be a mother; that I was too young; that in Mexico City, where the Democratic Revolution Party are in power, abortion, like homosexual marriage, was legal.

5. On 17 June 1816, a meeting took place that was vitally important to both that century and our current one; for Mary Shelley, for John Polidori, as well as for the likes of Stephanie Meyer, the HBO network, author of The Vampire Chronicles *Anne Rice, and extreme metallers Cradle of Filth.*

6. Lord Byron's summer residence was called Villa Diodati. Accused of having dishonoured his sister, he had fled England and was squandering his inheritance entertaining a number of quarrelsome exiles, including Mary Wollstonecraft Godwin and her husband-to-be, long-winded Shelley. On the evening of 17 June 1816, also in attendance was John Polidori – Byron's shadow, his doctor as well as his personal Salieri – a copycat, but not a very good one.

7. The Romantics – impervious to cliché, again exactly like the children of the 1990s – read horror stories by the fire in gothic houses at nightfall. On that symbolic evening, Villa Diodati's retinue of adulterous literary types read to one another from a German collection of fantasy stories. Byron used the stories to challenge the others.

A number of days later, I tried feeding again. I was back home by now. Jorge had just left and wasn't going to be back all weekend. I'd hugged him as hard as I could and pleaded with him not to go. The thought of being alone in the house with the baby frightened me. But a recruitment agency had called and offered him a job driving the truck down to Tamaulipas overnight; and the money was decent, so he couldn't turn it down. Plus, I'd begun walking without any help, the stitches had started to heal, and Jorge's mum was going to come in the evening to help around the house. 'We'll pick a name when you get back, shall we?' The baby was six days old already and it not having a name was starting to feel weird. It reminded me of our dog Xena, which we bought as a puppy at the market. Since my Mum said they always come sick, she wouldn't let me christen it until it had survived two weeks. I couldn't get the idea out of my head that the same thing was happening now with my baby. It clearly wasn't healthy, it hardly ate. But children, even if they seem likely to die, ought to be baptized, so at least there's a name to place in the death announcements.

8. If Byron had been Spanish, he would have challenged them with blunderbusses, but, being British, he proposed they write a novel. Only Mary Shelley and Polidori took up the challenge. Polidori was a second-rate talent, meaning no one paid much attention to what he came up with. Frankenstein, *on the other hand – even 1990s' kids know about that.*

I felt less uncomfortable – no one was watching this time. People can say it's all natural, but if you don't go topless on the beach, why would you breastfeed in full view of the world – with random families watching on, saying, well done, well done? I took the little thing in my arms, with its deathly white, tuberculosis-looking face, and began humming a song I'd learned when I arrived in Mexico about the Wailing Woman, a ghost that appears at night in search of her dead children. Jorge said that when he and his sister were living out on the plains, they used to hear her, particularly in winter. The baby let out a burp, twisting its face into something resembling a smile. 'You have to eat, tiny,' I said, putting my nipple to its lips, 'otherwise you're going to die without a name.' It took a while ferreting around and then, suddenly, I felt pressure and an excruciating pain. I let out a scream and pulled it off me. And screamed again: it had blood dripping from its mouth. It licked its lips. There were two tiny punctures right next to my nipple. Face contorted, the baby was trying to get close to the food source again, writhing around, but as far as I could see, not a single drop of milk had come out. Putting it back in its cot, I began to cry uncontrollably. I put the TV on full volume and shut myself in the kitchen. Trembling, I took some powdered milk out of the cupboard and started making up a bottle. The sound of the TV drowned out the baby's cries, but I knew they were ongoing, masked by the presenter's voice on *Lose to Win*, that weight-loss programme. I couldn't get the picture out of my mind: the ghostly image of my thalassaemic child with blood around its mouth.

9. Polidori's fate was a tragic one. He lived in Byron's shadow, and Byron mocked him, his love of medicine, and his love of poetry – and it so happened that these were his only loves. He took revenge on Byron by writing a story called The Vampire.

That week the doctor came to the house. He said the baby was weak and that if we didn't get it to eat, it would have to go into hospital. It was the four of us in the kitchen: the doctor, my mother-in-law, Jorge and me. Every one of them looking at me like it was my fault. *You couldn't give birth to it on your own, and now you can't even feed it,* their looks seemed to say. I waited until they'd all left, and then I cut my hand. I never thought I'd have it in me to self-harm, but when it came to it, I didn't hesitate. After all, I was the worst mother in the world; I had to do something to atone. The blood flowed freely. I let it drip from my hand and collect in a bowl. I drained myself almost to the point of passing out. Then I mixed it in with the milk powder – stirring it, it turned a perfect pink, like a strawberry smoothie. My heart was pounding, I didn't know if it was right what I was doing: I knew that God condemned vampirism, I knew I was infringing certain laws, though I couldn't have said which, or exactly why. But there was no doubting the fact it was disgusting, and there's a direct link between that which we find disgusting and that which God condemns, like bestiality, cannibalism, incest and homosexuality. But the fact is – God forgive me – this bottle full of pink milk was the first thing my baby drank down with any sort of appetite since the day it had been born.

10. In The Vampire, *Polidori revives the legend, this one taking the shape of an eccentric British aristocrat who goes around Europe corrupting upper-class women. It's basically a thinly veiled Byron. This was the only thing Polidori wrote that garnered any attention; it had an impact at the time because everyone thought Byron must have had something to do with penning it.*

The baby perked up straight away; its new diet was invigorating for it, and we even started to see some colour in its cheeks. Obviously, I was the only one who knew its particular likes. Each day I'd cut myself somewhere new, trying to do it in places where no one would see. Not that Jorge was going to notice; he found the scars over my womb disgusting, and always turned out the lights before I got undressed. But his mum, she could definitely have been suspicious, so I focused particularly on my upper thighs. I'd numb the area with an ice cube, and the bleeding, in that part of the body, wouldn't last long. I used ferns to stop it – a home remedy.

Everything was under control, but after a few days I began to feel incredibly weak. One morning I woke up even more tired than usual, started making scrambled eggs and immediately passed out, falling backwards into the china cabinet. When I opened my eyes I found myself on the floor, broken plates all around me. The glass had cut me on the shoulder and I was bleeding hard. The baby was crying more fiercely than ever. I thought something must have been attacking it; I felt its crying deep in my ears, like the pressure swimmers feel underwater. Then it hit me: it was the smell of my blood; it was driving it crazy. I got up and followed my impulse to lock the door to the baby's room. I felt terrified. There had been a moment where I'd *known* that the baby was coming for me, its mouth open in that O, ready to suck me dry through the wound. Then I heard it scratching at the door, and my fear intensified. How could it have got out of its cot on its own? I grabbed my jacket and some money, locked up and hurried away from the house.

11. The vampire in The Vampire *is Byron, and the vampire in* The Vampire *is also the vampire from* Dracula *and* Twilight; *which means that at least they dress like British gentlemen and not medieval Romanian zombies.*

Pregnant women are prone to being frightened. They worry that their children will come out albino, or with an extra finger, or colour-blind, or that they'll have Down's Syndrome, be haemophiliacs, freaks of nature, hermaphrodites, have no arms, have no legs, be of a different race from the father, have a heart that's too big, have bones made of glass. But they don't generally contemplate the possibility of the child coming out a vampire. But that's what had happened to me. After I'd been to the Emergency Room, where they gave me two stitches to my shoulder, I went to a bar and ordered tequilas with *sangrita*. I thought about how strange my destiny was. I tried to get straight what I knew about legends of bloodsucking creatures: *Dracula*, *Twilight*, *Diary of a Vampire* . . . In the stories, they never try it with children, it's taboo – which is because we like to think that children come into the world pure, blameless in the eyes of God. I thought about my literature professor back in Spain, who said that books help us to understand life, which at that moment seemed like a big lie, because there was nothing in Anne Rice that was going to guide me through this.

The tequilas went straight to my head, which is what happens when you've been losing blood day after day – cheap date. I took out my mobile to check the time and saw I had more than ten missed calls from Jorge and his mum. My heart started pounding. What might they have found in the house? During the bus ride home I tried to think about nothing. Nothing, nothing, nothing; I repeated it to myself. The first thing I saw was an ambulance outside the front door. If there had been any fatality, if the shape they were carrying out to the ambulance *was* a corpse, I only wished it would be that of the child. Eternity would preserve it, after all, the same as any member of its species.

12. Nowadays, there are around a hundred vampire sects in the United States alone. On Yahoo Answers Mexico, there's a thread with dozens of people asking if drinking human blood will make them more beautiful, or stronger, or immortal. Anyone interested in pursuing the matter is advised to Google 'drink human blood?'

Copyright Information

My Fellow Translators

Thomas Bunstead is the translator of some of the leading Spanish-language writers working today, including Agustín Fernández Mallo, Maria Gainza and Enrique Vila-Matas. His own writing has appeared in publications such as *The Brixton Review of Books*, *LitHub* and *The White Review*.

Peter Bush is a former Director of the British Centre for Literary Translation and Professor of Literary Translation at the University of East Anglia, where he founded the BCLT Summer School. Recent translations include *Why? Why? Why?* by Quim Monzó and *Barcelona Tales*. He is currently translating Balzac's *Le Lys dans la vallée* and Najat El Hachmi's *Mare de mel i llet*.

Kit Maude is a translator based in Buenos Aires. He has translated dozens of Latin American and Spanish writers for a wide array of publications and writes reviews for *Ñ*, *Otra Parte* and the *Times Literary Supplement*. His translation of Armonía Somers' *The Naked Woman* was published by The Feminist Press in 2018.

Kathryn Phillips-Miles and Simon Deefholts have jointly translated literary works from Spanish into English across several genres. Their translation of *Nona's Room*, a collection of stories by Cristina Fernández Cubas which includes 'A Fresh Start', was published by Peter Owen in 2017, together with *Wolf Moon* by Julio Llamazares and *Inventing Love* by José Ovejero, which was shortlisted by the Society of Authors for the Premio Valle Inclán.

Translator's Acknowledgements

I would like to thank Chloe Currens of Penguin for inviting me to compile this anthology, my fellow translators for being willing to share their work, and my dear friend Annella McDermott for her continuing support and advice.

THE PENGUIN BOOK OF
DUTCH SHORT STORIES

'We were kids – but good kids. If I may say so myself.
We're much smarter now, so smart it's pathetic. Except for Bavink,
who went crazy'

A husband forms gruesome plans for his new fridge; a government employee has a haunting experience on his commute home; prisoners serve as entertainment for wealthy party guests; an army officer suffers a monstrous tropical illness. These short stories contain some of the most groundbreaking and innovative writing in Dutch literature from 1915 to the present day, with most pieces appearing here in English for the first time. Blending unforgettable snapshots of the realities of everyday life with surrealism, fantasy and subversion, this collection shows Dutch writing to be an integral part of world literary history.

ISBN: 978 0 141 39572 2

THE PENGUIN BOOK OF THE
CONTEMPORARY SHORT STORY

'Like its predecessors, this volume is a feast, and every morsel
worth savouring' Edmund Gordon, *Literary Review*

We are living in a particularly rich period for British short stories.
Despite the relative lack of places in which they can be published,
the challenge the medium represents has attracted a host of remarkable, subversive, entertaining and innovative writers. Philip
Hensher, following the success of his definitive *Penguin Book of
British Short Stories*, has scoured a vast trove of material and
chosen thirty great stories for this new volume of works written
between 1997 and the present day.

Edited with an Introduction by Philip Hensher

ISBN: 978 0 141 98621 0

THE PENGUIN BOOK OF
JAPANESE SHORT STORIES

'Filling up with sugar – what a lovely way to die!'

This is a celebration of the Japanese short story from its modern origins in the nineteenth century to remarkable contemporary works. It includes the most well-known Japanese writers – Akutagawa, Murakami, Mishima, Kawabata - but also many surprising new pieces, from Yuko Tsushima's 'Flames' to Banana Yoshimoto's 'Bee Honey'. Ranging over myth, horror, love, nature, modern life, a diabolical painting, a cow with a human face and a woman who turns into sugar, *The Penguin Book of Japanese Short Stories* is filled with fear, charm, beauty and comedy.

Edited by Jay Rubin with an introduction by Haruki Murakami

ISBN: 978 0 241 31190 5

THE PENGUIN BOOK OF
ITALIAN SHORT STORIES

'An enticing collection . . . the tales are by turns startling, moving, intriguing and provocative' *Times Literary Supplement*

Jhumpa Lahiri's landmark collection brings together forty writers that reflect over a hundred years of Italy's vibrant and diverse short story tradition, including well known authors such as Italo Calvino, Elsa Morante and Luigi Pirandello, alongside many captivating rediscoveries. Poets, journalists, visual artists, musicians, editors, critics, teachers, scientists, politicians, translators: the writers that inhabit these pages represent a dynamic cross section of Italian society.

Edited with an introduction and selected translations
by Jhumpa Lahiri

ISBN: 978 0 241 29985 2

THE PENGUIN BOOK OF
CHRISTMAS STORIES

'Bring out the tall tales now that we told by the fire as the
gaslight bubbled...'

This is a collection of the most magical, moving, chilling and
surprising Christmas stories from around the world, taking us
from frozen Nordic woods to glittering Paris, a New York speak-
easy to an English country house, bustling Lagos to midnight mass
in Rio, and even outer space. Here are classic tales from writers
including Truman Capote, Shirley Jackson, Dylan Thomas, Saki
and Chekhov, as well as little-known treasures such as Italo
Calvino's wry sideways look at Christmas consumerism, Selma
Lagerlof's enchanted forest in Sweden, and Irène Nemerovsky's
dark family portrait. Featuring santas, ghosts, trolls, unexpected
guests, curmudgeons and miracles, here is Christmas as imagined
by some of the greatest short story writers of all time.

ISBN: 978 0 241 39670 4

THE GARDEN PARTY

Katherine Mansfield

'Kisses, voices, tinkling spoons, laughter, the smell of crushed grass'

Innovative, startlingly perceptive and aglow with colour, these fifteen stories were written towards the end of Katherine Mansfield's tragically short life. Many are set in the author's native New Zealand, others in England and the French Riviera. All are revelations of the unspoken, half-understood emotions that make up everyday experience – from the blackly comic 'The Daughters of the Late Colonel', and the short, sharp sketch 'Miss Brill', in which a lonely woman's precarious sense of self is brutally destroyed, to the vivid, impressionistic evocation of family life in 'At the Bay' and the poignant, haunting miniature masterpiece 'The Garden Party'.

Edited with an Introduction and Notes by Lorna Sage

ISBN: 978 0 14 144 180 1

METAMORPHOSIS AND OTHER STORIES

Franz Kafka

'Gentlemen, esteemed academicians! You do me the honour of inviting me to submit a report to the academy on my previous life as an ape'

Kafka's masterpiece of unease and black humour, *Metamorphosis*, the story of an ordinary man transformed into an insect, is brought together in this collection with the rest of his works that he thought worthy of publication. It includes *Contemplation*, a collection of his earlier short studies; *The Judgement*, written in a single night of frenzied creativity; *The Stoker*, the first chapter of a novel set in America; and an eye witness account of an air display. Together, these stories, fragments and miniature gems reveal the breadth of his vision, his sense of the absurd, and above all his acute, uncanny wit.

Translated with an Introduction by Michael Hofmann

ISBN: 978 0 24 137 255 5

A ROOM OF ONE'S OWN /
THREE GUINEAS

Virginia Woolf

'A woman must have money and a room of her own if she is to write fiction'

Ranging from the silent fate of Shakespeare's gifted (imaginary) sister to Jane Austen, Charlotte Brontë and the effects of poverty and sexual constraint on female creativity, *A Room of One's Own*, based on a lecture given at Girton College, Cambridge, is one of the great feminist polemics. Published almost a decade later, *Three Guineas* breaks new ground in its discussion of men, militarism and women's attitudes towards war. These two pieces reveal Virginia Woolf's fiery spirit, sophisticated wit and genius as an essayist.

Edited with an Introduction and Notes by Michèle Barrett

ISBN: 978 0 24 137 197 8